IMPERIUM VOLUME 2 | BOOK 1

THE

WINGS

OF

MERCURY

TRAVIS STARNES

Maps available at

https://tstarnes.com/book-series/imperium/

Signup to get free previews of upcoming books before they're released at

http://tstarnes.com/preview-notification-newsletter/

Contents

Chapter 1

Port Amicitiae, Africa

The port commander sat hunched over his desk, poring over the day's shipping manifests and schedules. The scratching of his pen, one of the Consul's many inventions and much superior to the writing sticks they had previously used, had become almost hypnotic over the hours. When they'd sent him down to command one of the farthest outposts of the Empire, Arn had imagined it would be the peak of his career since joining the Britannian legions and becoming a citizen. He had pictured dealing with strange and interesting people and the chances for glory that would come his way.

Yes, there had been strange and interesting people, and it had sometimes been a chore to ensure that they paid the tariffs and that the conflicts with the locals didn't get too out of hand. Mostly though, there had been paperwork. So much paperwork.

He'd just finished the latest stack and was contemplating a stroll out to the docks, just to clear his head, when there was a series of aggressive knocks on his door.

He hadn't even bid the person enter before the door thrust was open and a flush-faced legionnaire, his breath coming in short gasps, rushed in and said, "Tribune! Strange ships have been sighted on the horizon!"

It wasn't clear what this man was so excited about. They got ships in, while not all the time this far out on the edge of the known world, on the far southern coast of Africa, regularly. They were, in fact, expecting a supply fleet anytime now and had word that ships out of the Sea of Reeds should be stopping here on their way around the cape.

"What do you mean, strange? We were expecting the …"

"No, sir. Not one of our ships. They're huge, larger even than a caravel, with strange sails. It's like nothing I've seen before."

Grabbing a spyglass from his desk, he went to the window and looked out. The ships were still a bit far away, but he could see them closing. It wasn't a few ships either. There were maybe fifteen that he could see, but bunched as they were, it was hard to tell if there were more behind those.

The newest spyglasses were good, better even than those used during the war with Carthage that ended five years ago, but the ships were still a little hard to make out. They may be large. Actually, they were very large by his estimation, which had become a lot more expert since becoming the commander of a major port. The ocean, however, had a way of making everything appear smaller.

He squinted, staring at the ships as they grew larger and larger in his eyepiece. There was something familiar about them. Something stirred in the back of his brain. And then it hit him.

He'd seen reports about ships with some of the same features, including a reminder earlier this year about their design, along with the instruction that ships with those odd, folded sails that seemed to go the wrong direction should be considered hostile.

Ships with similar sails, although described with many differences, had fought against Admiral Valdar in the famous Battle of the Sea of Reeds, which helped close out the war.

"Sound the alarm. I want every available man armed and ready to defend the port. Dispatch message boats for Port Vikhavn telling them what we've seen and request the message be relayed to Britannia. Man the fort cannons. Now."

The legionnaire didn't even bother to salute. He just turned and dashed out of the office.

Arn was about to call out for another messenger to order the only warship in port at the moment, the schooner BNS Lugh, put to see but he saw its Ulaid captain had already begun to push away from the dock. Good. At least some of the men had their wits about them.

2

Grabbing his gladius, that had been leaning against the wall, and thankful they no longer had to don armor for battle, Arn ran after his legionnaire, toward the small fort on the far left of the port.

He'd only made it halfway to the fort when alarm bells began to sound, the urgent clanging sending people and merchants running for cover. At least, some of them.

There hadn't been an attack since the war, when the port had been just a few damaged ships cannibalized for parts, but Arn and his predecessors had been warned this day might come, and the bell had never been rung more than three times in a row. Insistent ringing was saved for true emergencies. For war.

The newest arrivals to the port and some of the locals from out in the grasslands to the west, who come to trade cattle for wares, stood around looking confused, but they'd figure it out once the cannon started firing.

"Man the battlements," he commanded as he arrived at the fort. "Roll out the cannon."

"Already done," the centurion on watch at the fort said. "Additional powder is being brought up from the stores now."

"Good man. Order all civilian ships to flee. Tell them not to wait for any crew not aboard or any merchandise. If they don't get out now, they won't be leaving."

The order gave away any pretense that the port would survive this. Not that any seasoned officer would believe otherwise. He just hoped the Lugh, which had already made its way out of the port and was picking up speed as it headed toward the enemy fleet, would buy them enough time to get people out. It was a suicide mission and anyone on board had to know that. But, they were buying time for the civilian ships to flee.

Besides, what else could they do?

He saw the Lugh cut north, bringing its broadside to bear smartly, and the flashes of fire before the booming sound of the cannon made its way to them. The battle had begun. The first salvo had been deadly accurate, and the lead ship coming toward them began to drift south, as the top half of its main mast was severed and sent over the side.

3

The enemy wasn't sitting still and was turning its broadside in turn, but much slower. It was clear whoever had designed these massive ships had done so without a care for handling. The smaller Lugh was already turning around to sail back toward the port, probably in order to swing south and try to get out of the line of their broadside.

Breccan, its captain, almost succeeded, managing to make a small circle and begin traveling south as he brought his other broadside to bear. But only almost.

The enemy fleet, which was indeed more than fifteen ships, Arn could now see, had turned as well, and salvo after massive salvo thundered from the front six ships.

The poor little schooner never stood a chance. Their aim also didn't seem quite as good as the Lugh's, but it didn't need to be with the weight of fire as dozens of cannonballs smashed into the smaller ship. Its speed dropped dangerously as hole after hole appeared in the sails. The mast didn't go, but enough spars had been sheared off to cause half the sails to droop and sag, no longer able to catch significant wind.

Breccan managed another salvo of his own, shot low into a single ship, with most of his shells landing. They must have hulled it low because it started to drift lower and lower as its front dipped and the belly filled with water.

And then a second salvo sounded from the enemy. Arn could see whole sections of the Lugh disappear as it began to roll over. Men were jumping into the water, some looking like they intended to swim back to the port.

Not that it would do them any good. With that many ships, Arn was under no illusion that his port would survive much longer than the schooner did.

Devnum, Britannia

Ky hunched over his desk, studying a map of the rail lines in eastern Germania. Hortensius's work, or at least the surveyors he'd sent out on this mission the previous summer, had done excellent work and Ky could see very few changes that needed to be made. They'd already made great progress connecting most of Europe, especially the more heavily occupied western half, but the east still only had two lines going past what had once been, or would be, it was still hard to determine how to phrase that, the borders of Germany.

Those areas had been fairly depopulated during the war as Carthage stripped men from every meter of their former empire for conscripts, but they were repopulating as more and more people arrived from further east. So far, the arrivals had just been looking for a new land to settle, and there was plenty of land available, so there hadn't been any problems. If that was going to continue, they needed to integrate the newcomers into what Ky had started to think of as The Western Alliance, which was essentially all of the regions that had allied with Britannia during the war and had consolidated into regional powers since.

They were also still deep in negotiations with the Greeks, who were not willing to see the benefits of modernization, or at least the benefits of doing it under Britannia's direction. Ky was confident Lucilla would untangle that knot eventually and wanted to have the support infrastructure in place when she did.

"Up early and back at it, I see," Lucilla said from behind him, drawing his attention from the map.

He turned, smiling as he saw her standing in the doorway, their three-year-old son Titus balanced on her hip.

"I am. Hortensius has made good progress so far, but there is still a lot of work to do, and I want to make sure Sophus runs his numbers before we start. It's a large investment and correcting it will be even more expensive.

She walked over, handing him Titus. "I don't doubt it, and the Empire will always be grateful for you, but you don't need to push yourself like this. We're not at war anymore. You can take things more reasonably … like you're doing the work equal to that of ten men, instead of twenty."

"I'll try," he promised, lifting Titus and making a face at him, eliciting a giggle. "How are my two favorite people this morning?"

"We're doing well, although I think your son is more interested in playing than being held at the moment."

Ky set Titus down, watching as he immediately started exploring the room, picking up and examining everything he could reach.

"He's curious."

"Like his father."

Lucilla moved to her dressing table, picked up her brush and started to work it through her long hair. Ky watched her, marveling at her beauty. Motherhood had done her wonders, and she was a little more radiant every day.

"So, what's on your agenda for the day?" she asked, glancing at him in the mirror. "Aside from rail lines."

"I need to speak with Faenius about the peacekeeping forces we still have in Carthage. It doesn't look like that situation will be resolved anytime soon. If anything, things have started to degrade. We need to discuss what kind of additional forces he can commit to the region. After that, I'm meeting with delegates from the Gallic states and the Germanic alliance to discuss trade agreements and border security."

"Roti's reports don't indicate any serious problems."

"No, but the steady trickle of injuries does. Well, maybe not serious, but they indicate something's going on. I at least want to put a word in his ear about it, have someone look into it."

"I see," she said, frowning.

Ky knew her. She was already working through the possibilities of what that could mean, how it would affect other parts of the Empire and their network of overlapping alliances, and what she could do with it. She was always an excellent politician and administrator, but during the war, necessity held her entire focus on the needs of the moment. The last five years, however, she had really honed her skills.

It was also why, other than building out capabilities and some minor work with Sorantius, the chemist, the technology level of the Empire had held relatively static since the end of the war. Part of Ky had wanted to continue to push ahead, moving them beyond the industrial age and into early twentieth-century levels of technology, but Lucilla and Sophus had argued against it.

They had believed that industry needed to shift to supporting their allies reaching the same level of technology that Britannia had reached during the war, and ensuring that their living standards reached all parts of both their allies and their own Empire, instead of just the major settlements. She had received serious pushback on that, from elements inside of the Empire who wanted to hoard the technology for themselves, and supply every other nation, making them beholden to Britannia.

Lucilla had argued that they were building more than their own wealth. They were building toward true stability. Not just militarily, but politically and socially. They weren't giving everything away, of course. Military technology was still hoarded and limits put on what they could sell, keeping rifled artillery and muskets for only their forces. Everything else, though, they'd begun to give out. It had been a slow process. Most of their allies were now able to produce much higher quality steel, had better medicine and sanitation, but were still catching up on everything else.

Even five years later, a lot of rebuilding had to be done to make up for the toll of Carthage's long reign, and the war that ended it.

"It's under control," Ky said. "Faenius knows his job. If there is anything wrong, he'll tell us."

"Fine. I'll leave it alone," she said, faux-sullenly. "Besides, I have enough to deal with. I have a host of meetings today."

"Still the Ptolemies?"

"Yes. I'm not comfortable with their demands for restricted military supplies, or just how many of our senators are supporting those demands. They say the right words, claiming they're looking to build an alliance and foster goodwill, but ..."

"It doesn't feel right," Ky finished.

"No. Not right at all. Besides, even if I give in to them, it's a dangerous precedent to set. If we give in to these demands, what's to stop them from asking for more? My first meeting is with Medb and Ramirus. I want them to look at our own senators first. If any have sold their allegiances, I want to know it."

"Just … be patient. Even if they come up with evidence of something, think it through. Talk to Ramirus."

"I'm not that bad," she said.

"Do I need to remind you about Fiacha?"

The Ulaid senator, who had been slapped down by Medb during the war, felt after the war that he could profit using some of the things he knew, and some of the people he had access to. Medb had given the man a chance, and he'd been foolish enough to try again. A furious Lucilla had him and his brother-in-law, who'd joined him in the endeavors, executed, his family stripped of titles and lands, and his wife exiled. Even among Lucilla's supporters, it had been seen as harsh.

"He deserved his fate. But I get your point," she said. "I'll play nice."

"Good," Ky said, glancing over to where Titus was attempting to pull a large tome off a low shelf. "I should start getting ready, too."

He crossed the room, scooping up their son and tossing him over his shoulder, much to the child's delight. "Why don't we send for the …"

Ky handed Titus to Lucilla and crossed to the door to answer a knock, finding a young Praetorian at their door. He was wearing one of the new uniforms Ky, Lucilla, and Sophus had designed to replace the heavier segmented armor the Romans had been wearing during the war. A simple tunic that was similar to that most Romans wore, although they had a heavy, full-length wool jacket that could be worn in rain or cold weather combined with wool trousers and closed-toed boots; it was lightweight but offered good protection from the elements on long marches.

One of the nice additions, beyond the weight reduction, was the cap that held rank insignia and unit insignia just above the brim, making it easy to know where the soldier you were addressing came from.

"Your Majesty, Consul, forgive the intrusion, but I bring urgent news," the man said, panting and visibly sweating in spite of the snow still on the ground outside.

"Catch your breath, Decanus," Ky said. "Then speak."

The man nodded, gulping air.

"Port Amicitiae has fallen," he said after a moment, steadier.

"What? How?" Lucilla asked from behind Ky.

"We received a telegraph from Londinium. Four ships from the port arrived an hour ago. They said there were ships, strange ships with odd sails, that came out of nowhere, attacking with cannon. They said that one of our schooners had sailed out to meet them, but there were dozens of the attackers."

"Did they give any specifics as to what they meant by strange ships?"

"They described them as huge, far larger than our own, and said the sails were very different. They were square, but with ridges going down, like they folded that direction, segmenting the largest sails."

It was vaguely familiar to Ky. He remembered that Valdar had faced ships like that during the war, ships that belonged to the foreign power from the east that had been supplying the Carthaginians with rudimentary cannon.

"Thank you. Go back to your command, but go slowly," Ky said to the messenger, who gave a thankful smile, and then Ky turned to the Lictore standing at his door. "Send word for any commanders in the city to gather here in an hour, along with Ramirus."

The man saluted and ran off in the same direction as the messenger.

"The Easterners?" Lucilla asked as Ky closed the door.

"Probably."

"But why now? It's been five years without a word from them."

"I don't know, but I imagine they feel ready to deal with us. We may have lost one ship we sent to open relationships with them to nature, but four means they were sinking anything we sent, and had no plans toward diplomacy."

"I know, I just … it's been so long, I'd hoped they'd given up, or something had happened and they'd collapsed."

"Apparently not. This is just the beginning. Port Amicitiae was the closest port we had to them and would be one of the first targets they might choose if they were coming for us. We won't know for sure until they make their next move, but I think we should begin preparing for war."

Chapter 2

Three hours later, Ky sat at the head of a long table, Lucilla at the opposite end, with a collection of whatever leaders they could get together on such short notice between them. Bomilcar, Aelius, Ursinus, Ramirus, Medb, and Cormac were seated along the sides, along with representatives from Scandi, Gaul, and Germania, all of whom happened to be in the city at the moment, working with Lucilla on a new trade deal that would have the Scandi give up their insistence on dominance of the trade lands bordering Mere Suebicum.

"Thank you all for coming on such short notice," Ky began. "I'm afraid I have grave news. We've received reports that Port Amicitiae has been destroyed by a fleet of strange ships that we believe to be the same Easterners who supplied Carthage during the war. The same ones Valdar faced in the Sea of Reeds five years ago."

A murmur of disbelief and concern rippled through the room. Ky held up a hand for silence.

"This is clearly an act of war, Consul. One we cannot ignore," Bomilcar said.

"I agree," Ky said with a nod. "But we need more information before we act. We don't even know who these people are, let alone what their capabilities are or what they want. It leaves us very blind, which is a bad place to find yourself at the start of a war."

"Perhaps we should send a large, armed fleet to the east to investigate," Ramirus said. "I know we have had other, unsuccessful attempts to open communication with these people, but we haven't sent a significant force yet, for fear of provoking a reaction by accident. That is, clearly, not an issue anymore, so we could ensure our men are able to return while finding out why they attacked us."

"No," Medb said. "If this was their opening move, with a fleet nearly as large as our own, then they knew exactly what they were doing. They prepared for this. Blundering into their seas with the bulk of our fleet would be a mistake. It doesn't matter why they attacked us, just that they did."

"She's right," Ky said. "We can't risk our fleet on a blind mission into their territory. Not only do we not know how large a force they have, but we have no way of knowing how advanced their military knowledge is. They demonstrated at least an ability to make gunpowder and cannons, which probably started before we gained that ability. From Valdar's report of the battle, and based on the weapons we found with the Carthaginian army after their final defeat, the quality of the cannon was inferior to ours, but that doesn't mean it has stayed that way. From the descriptions given to us by Valdar and now by the captains of the ships that escaped from Port Amicitiae, they have made significant advances in their shipbuilding capabilities, possibly drawn from what they learned from our own ships. There is no reason to believe those advancements are limited solely to their ships. If we sail our entire navy into a larger fleet with comparable weapons to our own, we will lose most of our navy before the war, if it comes, ever truly starts."

"Which might be why they attacked us the way they did," Medb said. "To draw us out."

"Possibly. Either way, we can't risk it. Besides, seaborne attacks aren't our only concern. We also have to prepare for a possible landward invasion as well. If this is the first move of war."

"You think they'll attack through Persia?" Aelius asked.

"Maybe, but they could also come through Anatolia or even Sarmatia. We know they used caravans from Asia all the way through to Persia and into Egypt during the war, so the route is known to them. Look back at the maps I made for you after the war that show the rough outlines of Asia. It is possible to go south, along the Hindu Kush and into Persia, across the middle through Anatolia, or up and around the Inhospitable Sea, as the Greeks call it, although my people always knew it as the Black Sea. It's

11

also very possible they could come up over the Caucasus Mountains and through Scythia. This is our biggest problem. There are literally hundreds of ways they can come at us, and until we know which way they plan to come, we won't be able to prepare for it.

"We need each of you to talk to your people and at least begin probing your eastern fringes, especially you," Lucilla said from the other end of the table, directing the last at the representative of Germania. "If they come by the northern route, that would bring them directly into your territory. I will send word to the Greeks and the Ptolemies to have them begin scouting their eastern fringes as well. The sooner we get an indication of where they are coming from, the better."

The Scandi representative still looked doubtful, but the Germanic's attitude shifted noticeably when it became clear his lands were a likely point of attack, if war was coming. Reality had a way of sobering up even the harshest critics, after all.

"Good. Aside from that, we also need to pull back on all civilian works projects. I know there are still a lot of projects in the planning stages, many being counted on by all your governments to help continue the growth and expansion in your lands, but if the enemy has matched our technology, then we need to begin focusing on our military tech again. We slowed down most of our military production to accommodate civilian production or the production of muskets. While our gunpowder production stayed the same, everything else has fallen behind. It's time to refit our factories for war."

"And if we're wrong?" Ramirus said. "We will have a lot of unhappy allies out there who were relying on us if war doesn't emerge."

"I know, but it's a risk we have to take. I don't think we're wrong, though."

Ramirus just ducked his head in response. Ky knew the old spy didn't think he was wrong but was playing devil's advocate, as the saying went. Ky appreciated it, but it wasn't needed this time.

"I will begin to work on new plans for Hortensius. I know he was excited about the new textile works we just started, but that isn't critical and can wait. In the meantime, have the legions start on training regimens with the equipment they have currently. Even if we start now, it will take months, maybe longer for any new weapons to be available, and I strongly suspect we don't have that kind of time."

"Probably not," Bomilcar agreed.

At least, in the interim, they'd finished the reorganization of the legions from the old Roman way, which worked when legions were essentially their own operation, run independently from the rest, but didn't work in a world where command was a telegraph away. Now, each legion was essentially a corps of an overall army, still broken into ten-by-ten cohorts and centuries. The main change was above that, with four legions being an army with an overall commander, allowing for more centralized control and coordination between the legions.

After seeing the weapons that emerged at the end of the war, Ky knew the next fight would be larger and bloodier and had at least gotten the military structure in place for it. That had taken longer than he had wanted, more than two years to get the Senate to agree to the change, promote officers up to their new positions, and replace all the cohort and century commanders who'd fallen in the war. Another year to train them all.

It was a good start, but Ky was almost certain it wasn't going to be enough.

"I want the existing legions brought up to strength as much as possible. Any scattered units on public works details are to be brought back immediately. We can't afford to have our forces dispersed right now. I also want you to call up the veteran reserve, all those still in shape to fight. We're going to need every able-bodied soldier we can muster."

Bomilcar glanced at Aelius, who gave him the same look in return and said, "You're still in charge, Legate."

"I know you were looking forward to retiring, old friend," Ky said. "But I need to ask you to hold off, at least until we know what we're facing here."

"I suppose a quiet retirement was too much to hope for. You can count on me, Consul."

Thank you. I'll talk to Valdar as soon as the admiral gets back from Carthage. The navy will have to begin looking at its situation, as well."

"We should send an expedition to the Port Amicitiae and see what, if anything, is left," Medb said. "It might also give us some further idea of the enemy's strength.

"Agreed," Ky said. "I'll bring that up with him as well.

"I'll send word to Conchobar and Talogren, let them know what's coming, so they aren't surprised by it," Lucilla said.

"I know this is frightening," Ky said to the table as a whole. "And we'd all hoped this conflict, if it had to come, wouldn't come so soon. The important thing is to not let it overwhelm you. Stay focused, and remember that we survived the very edge of destruction. We can survive this as well. I'll have more for you in the coming days. Till then, may the gods smile upon us all."

"Would you two please follow me," Lucilla said to Ramirus and Medb as the council meeting wrapped up.

The two looked at each other but said nothing, just following in Lucilla's wake as the Empress led them to her private study. As soon as she closed the door behind them, she rounded on the pair.

"How did we let ourselves get blindsided like this?" she demanded. "I rely on you two to be the eyes and ears of the Empire. To learn we are blind is troubling, to say the least. Was there any kind of warning, even an inkling, that an attack like this might be coming?"

Medb returned Lucilla's angry expression with one lacking in affectation. Ramirus, on the other hand, looked away when she turned her eyes to him, looking to the floor.

"No, Your Majesty," he said. "You were right to say we were caught completely off guard. All I can do is apologize for my failure."

"Your Majesty, I have been pushing for more aggressive intelligence gathering to the east for months now, but I haven't had much success in gaining approval to proceed. If you recall, I've sent you several reports to this effect. Hopefully, now someone will listen to me. The Easterners are an existential threat that demands our full attention. We cannot afford to prioritize anything else."

Lucilla studied the former queen. It was clear that Medb was attempting to cover herself by shifting the blame to Ramirus, but she had, in fact, sent reports arguing against Ramirus's choice of strategies. At the time, Lucilla had sided with Ramirus. There hadn't been any word of the Easterners in more than four years, when the argument happened, and Ramirus made good points that unrest in Italia and Carthage and keeping a closer eye on Persia, which was in chaos nominally under the control of the Ptolemies, took precedence.

So, in reality, the fault was as much hers as theirs.

She was also right that Ramirus had always been cautious, at least when compared with Medb's much more aggressive approach. His approach had made sense in a time of peace, but now … maybe something else was required.

"Enough," Lucilla said, cutting off further protests from Medb. "We cannot change what has already happened. All we can do now is learn from our mistakes. Ramirus, you have been a loyal and trusted advisor to both my father and myself for many years and I will always cherish your counsel and friendship."

"What are you saying, Your Majesty?"

"We're facing new threats, and must find new ways of dealing with them," Lucilla said, and then paused for a long moment, having trouble saying what she needed to say. "More aggressive ways. Which is why I am appointing you, Medb, as the head of our intelligence gathering moving forward."

To Medb's credit, she maintained her stoic front, refraining from showing any pleasure at Ramirus's replacement and her own elevation. That alone gained the former queen some respect in Lucilla's eyes.

Ramirus nodded firmly. She could see the hurt in her old friend's eyes, but he understood. Or at least she hoped he did.

"You've earned this," she said to Medb. "You proved yourself in the war with Carthage and in the years since then. I am putting my faith in you to see that this is done."

"Thank you, Your Majesty," Medb said, bowing.

"If you will please leave us, although don't go far as I'm sure Ramirus will have things to discuss with you. While you may be taking responsibility for this duty, I do suggest you use Ramirus to the best of your ability. Aggression is good, and a needed trait, but it should not come at the expense of experience."

"I will, Your Majesty," she said, bowing a second time.

Medb gave Ramirus an odd look before she turned and left, a look not of pity but something closer to apology. It was an expression Lucilla hadn't thought the former queen capable of.

After Medb left, closing the doors behind her, Lucilla took Ramirus's hands and said, "Please do not take this as judgment against you or your abilities. You know I respect and love you as one of my oldest friends, and if there was another way to handle this, I would have."

"You don't need to apologize to me, Lucilla," he said, using her name for the first time since she ascended to the throne. "Medb has a lot of ... let's say, less than desirable qualities, but a lack of intelligence isn't one of them. She was right, and I was wrong. I fear I've grown too old. You probably made the right decision. If this new enemy is as well prepared as they seem to be, this will be a harder war than the one we faced against Carthage. It's best to have younger people fight it."

"Don't get maudlin on me," Lucilla said in a faux-chastising tone. "I still need you. You will remain one of my most valued advisers, and I will require your attending me just as regularly as before, if not more, now that you do not have to travel to meet with your little spies. I may not have my father to guide me anymore, but I have you, which is as close as anyone short of the gods themselves can get me."

"Thank you, my dear," Ramirus said, patting her hand. "I'd best catch up with Medb. If she is to do this, she needs access to my full network, to have as many options as possible. Although I might keep a few, just in case her old tricks resurface."

He smiled at his own cleverness, patted her hands again, and left. Lucilla's heart ached, watching him step out the door. He seemed to have aged ten years since walking through the door just a few minutes before. He had, in his own mind, become lesser, and it was her fault.

The realization almost made her cry. Sometimes, she hated what responsibility asked of her.

Ky stood on the docks, watching the Bellona as it made its way into port. It was a beautiful ship, one of the first caravels they'd put into the water. It was also now a relic of the past.

While everything was conjecture at this point, Ky could feel a change coming. While they'd made great advancements in military technology in their war against Carthage, each of those had been designed to widen their lead against their enemy to overcome the manpower advantage that nation had.

This was going to be a very different war, if it came. The enemy ship designs had Ky very worried. They showed that the Easterners were able to, at least to some degree, copy Britannian technology. If they could, that would mean a whole new kind of war. An arms race where new weapons would have to continually be developed if they wanted to stay on top.

The Easterners also had some significant production capability, if they produced as large of a fleet as it sounded like they had.

Ky could make out Valdar standing on the deck of his ship, leaning on the railing, his blond hair whipping in the breeze. The admiral, recognizing Ky, probably thanks to the small gaggle of guards around him, waved, standing up straighter as the ship pulled into the dock.

"Consul," Valdar greeted him, hurrying down the gangplank. "I didn't expect to see you here."

"I know, but I didn't want to wait until you were settled. I have some unfortunate news that you need to hear as soon as possible."

"What's happened?"

"Port Amicitiae has fallen."

"Fallen? To whom?"

"That's still not completely known. There were strange ships, unlike any we've seen before. Massive vessels with odd sail configurations, with a chain of horizontal ribs down a large square central sail."

"How many?"

"Reports indicate a fleet of at least a dozen, probably more. We only have word of it because the port commander got several civilian ships out, sacrificing the one schooner that was in port at the time to do it. They were armed with cannons, for sure."

"That sounds something like the ships we encountered in the Sea of Reeds, during the closing days of the war with Carthage. They had cannons, although inferior to ours, and a similar sail plan."

"Yes, that's what I thought. We've already started responses based on that assumption."

"Are you sure they were the size of our caravels?"

"From what the witnesses who escaped the port's destruction said, they are larger. Maybe a third bigger."

"But otherwise looked similar to our own?"

"Again, based on the survivors' descriptions, yes. You're right to be worried," Ky said. "I think they've managed to modify some of our technology. It seems unlikely they would come up with a similar design on their own, or that they would have been able to design cannons, but didn't work up a larger, more efficient boat design until after they met us."

"In five years, that's pretty fast. If they're able to incorporate our designs so quickly, it suggests they have significant shipbuilding capabilities and resources at their disposal. Especially if they were able to put out dozens of them."

"Agreed. I believe our only real course of action is to again focus on pushing our naval technology forward. We've allowed it, and much of our other military technology, to go stagnant for too long."

"You sound like you have something specific in mind."

"I do, although it will take time. There is a way to, instead of using wind, use steam power like we use for the trains to move the ships. It allows for larger ships capable of much larger payloads, which would include armoring the ships, to allow them to withstand cannonballs. It's not one hundred percent, and some will get through, but the armor could both deflect and slow any cannonballs that get through."

"I can't see how you would use something like a train to move a ship, but you've shown many times over we shouldn't doubt you, so I will wait to see what wonders you create. If I do have to face ships armed with cannons again, I do like the sound of armored sides."

"There are other changes I want to make. For instance, instead of cannons like we have now, cannons that fire shells much like a rifle bullet but filled with explosives, so that they burst when they hit the target. It will be deadly in land combat, but at sea it will be devastating."

"That sounds great, right up until the enemy copies it."

"I was just thinking that," Ky said. "If they were able to copy our ship designs, this will be a new kind of war. We'll be constantly trying to move to new weapons, to stay ahead of an enemy that can copy them."

"Considering how long it takes to make a ship, that will be difficult."

"Yes. It will," Ky said.

"Which means, we will have to move fast on these developments. If they have dozens of ships, I would have to clear out most of our warships just to match them one-for-one. I would not be surprised if they sail around and come for our remaining port in Africa. Especially if they believe their technological advantage is temporary."

"I know, but you should temper your expectations. We will not be able to do this quickly. In fact, we will almost certainly first do a smaller version for rivers, probably for use in Germania, as an in-between test platform."

"Damn," Valdar said, and looked off to the south, clearly working through ship deployments. "I'd like to assemble as many warships as I can, while not weakening our security elements, and sail south. If they are coming, I want to face them far away from our home waters, to give myself room to retreat."

"You don't want to wait until we can gather more ships?"

"No. Most of our ships that aren't here already are needed elsewhere, so what we have here is all we have for this. Besides, waiting just gives them more time to reinforce themselves and take out more of our assets. I'm hoping they wouldn't expect us to come at them, and we'll have some element of surprise. Although I would do it even if they knew we were coming."

"I see. Yes, that makes sense. Request whatever supplies you need, and make sure you stay in contact. I need reports of whatever you find, even if it's nothing. The more we can find out about these people, the better."

"I will, Consul," Valdar said, saluting in the new fashion.

Chapter 3

Factorium

After the busy first day following the news of the attack on their port, Ky spent most of the time locked away in their rooms, writing out instructions all day and night.

He'd made the right decision at the time, by not continuing to push military technology forward, considering the devastation left by the war and the state of all their allies, but as with all decisions it had come at a cost. Now, he was scrambling to make up for that cost.

Lucilla was equally busy, sending messages to their allies across Europe, trying to set up some kind of meeting with all of them to begin putting together the kind of combined force they would need if things went the way Ky feared they would. Britannia had lost a lot of men over the years it had been fighting, losses that would take a generation to replace. If this was going to be a war of almost equals, the legions couldn't be almost entirely Britannians. They would need to field larger armies, and the casualties would be greater against a firearm-wielding opponent.

Getting a combined force, however, might be harder than designing and producing new weapons. Which is why Ky was glad to leave it to Lucilla while he focused on the weapons.

He'd made enough progress on the designs to finally make a trip out to Factorium and get them started on the setup and production. He made a brief stop to see Hortensius, mostly to look at what had to be done to retool some of the factories producing civilian goods to produce more rifles and artillery, and what supplies were needed to support those weapons, like bagging for cannon charges and primer caps.

While Hortensius was getting that going, Sorantius would start working on some foundational steps for their next weapons.

Ky found the chemist in his workshop, going over figures for ammonia production, which was possibly the thing in highest demand from their allies. They had been skeptical at first, but after the second year, when the harvest started to show the effects of more modern fertilizers, they began banging down his door, demanding more.

"Consul," Sorantius said, waving off the assistant he'd been talking to. "We're on track to meet the Ptolemy's request. It is a fairly large order, but the Empress emphasized the need to do a favor for them, to help with some diplomacy or another, so I shifted some things around, and I think we're going to get it done."

"I never had any doubt," Ky said. "Unfortunately, I'm about to make your life a lot more complicated than it is already."

"Of course you are," the famously prickly chemist said. "And what can I do for the Empire today?"

"It looks like we're on the verge of a new war and they have access to some level of gunpowder, which means it's time to elevate your work again. There are a series of new weapons I want to implement, but many of them rely on some basic components I need from you. In addition, I expect that the wounds received in this war will be significantly harsher than those of the last one, which means we also need to look at some of our battlefield medicine, which again, must start with you."

"I have for years attempted to explain to Hortensius that the chemical sciences are the most important of our fields, so in this, at least, you've done me a favor by proving that to be true."

Ky didn't respond to that. Hortensius and Sorantius got along and made a fine team, but Sorantius always saw them as being in some sort of competition that the more genial Hortensius never played into. Which didn't stop Sorantius, for some reason.

"Well," Ky said, not engaging him. "Here are the plans for the first two things I need from you, which are connected. You'll be processing coal into coal gas and coal tar, each of which will have its own uses and is critical for our next stage of development."

Sorantius flipped through the pages, reading thoroughly, as he always did. Ky sat patiently, watching him read.

"The process seems straightforward enough," he finally said. "We're already heating some products in an airless environment, so it's really just an extension of that process. Capturing the gas, however, will be harder."

"Yes, which is what this is for," Ky said, handing over another set of instructions. "We'll have a lot of uses for this, which is essentially a system for capturing and containing gas for use elsewhere. Another thing that will have long-ranging uses. The key here is that the coal gas is very flammable and can be dangerous to work with, so it's important to follow the safety procedures I've laid out. Once you start producing coal tar, we can move to your next step, which will ultimately be a replacement for the priming caps and is what we're actually after. The coal gas has fewer direct military uses, but will be useful for civilians and if we're already producing one, it makes sense to do both."

"I see. The quantities you're listing are pretty significant."

"I know, and we'll have to start expanding again. We won't be making this forever, as there are more advanced and better replacements, but we are nowhere near ready for them. Until then, you're probably going to have to start up a new line. I, however, have faith in your ability to handle it, as long as you understand it is urgent."

"I always assume as much."

Ky handed Sorantius another set of papers. "These are for some medical improvements we're going to need. Neither will be difficult, although storage will be a problem, at least for this first one. It is saline solution, which is essentially slightly salty water that is close to the level of salt in, say, your sweat or tears. The key part here is that it has to remain pure after production, free from contamination, such as rust, and capable of being completely sterilized. I believe we'll need to step up glass production pretty significantly."

"That would be Hortensius's area."

"I know, and I already informed him about the need for increased production. What I want to emphasize is the extreme necessity of a sterile production environment."

"We have the same for some of the acid production."

"To a degree, although you still rely on the acids themselves to remove biological contamination, which is what I'm worried about here."

"But you included it in your notes? Correct?" Sorantius asked.

"Yes. I wanted to draw your attention to it."

"Consider my attention drawn."

"Yes, this and the burning of seaweed, which, confusingly, seem very straightforward. Both should be easy to produce," Ky said. "I know it's more a question of volume than anything else, although the iodine solution needs to remain sterile as well."

"Yes, I saw that."

"Good, then I'll leave you to it. I'll have more for you soon, although, as before, a lot of it will come through Lucilla, as I am not confident I will make it back to Britannia anytime soon. If our forces do engage east of Germania, as I think they will, I do not want to be all the way back here, waiting on messages through the telegraph."

"That's fine. I work well with the Empress."

"I know. Thank you as always, Sorantius."

The chemist gave a small bow and left, assuming he was excused to begin planning these new productions with his assistants. Ky couldn't help but smile at the man's back. Sorantius might be brusque, but he was a good man. Besides, Ky would prefer prickly over unpredictable any day.

Devnum

Medb barged past the guard standing outside of Ramirus's office, holding up a hand when the young man tried to say something to her. It was strange that even though she was no longer a queen, her position as first in command of the Empire's intelligence apparatus had caused people to shy away and even fear her more than they had when she had absolute power.

Stranger still was the fact that Ramirus, who looked more like a grandfather than a spymaster, never received the same reaction. Admittedly, over the last five years she had taken a direct hand in the more difficult assignments they'd been given, mostly dealing with routing out the last Carthaginian holdouts and squashing unrest in Carthage and Italy. While she had been firm and there had been people executed on her orders, the stories she'd heard about herself had been wildly fantastical. And particularly gruesome.

It also didn't help that instead of squashing these rumors, she'd instructed her agents to bolster them, even adding some flourishes she suggested, to make sure her reputation was secure. She didn't do it just to feel power again, although she would be lying if she said it didn't do her ego good. It was useful. She found that level of reputation often led to mistakes and outright retreat of dissident elements without the need to expend blood.

So she didn't take it personally when the guard flinched away at her warning gesture, as if she was a heavily armed raider.

"We need to talk," she said as she burst through the door.

Ramirus was completely unflustered, as was his way. He simply took off the small glasses he'd started to use to read, one of the many advancements given to them by the Consul. They were impressive, in spite of the Consul's repeated apologies for how imprecise and rudimentary the design of them was.

The spymaster set them aside and folded his hands, one on top of the other, and said, "I would assume as much based on your rather dramatic entrance. What can I do for you?"

"I just got yet another lecture from Her Majesty about how little we've found out about the easterners' intentions. I'm sick of being caught empty-handed every time she asks. We have to do something."

"I agree, but our options are very limited. I have explained that to the Empress, but I can understand her frustration."

"I can't. If she knows our options are limited, then why do I keep getting called to task for not achieving anything?"

"Because she is as frustrated as we are," Ramirus said, annoyingly calm and unbothered. "A port was destroyed and we still know nothing other than a threat looms on the horizon. You should know, as well as anyone, the pressure that can put on a leader. Would you have been more patient with your subordinates?"

"We still need to do something," Medb said, circling back to the topic again.

He wasn't wrong, but she wouldn't give him the satisfaction of saying so.

"I agree something needs to be done, but I'm not sure we can do anything. At least, not proactively."

"What do you mean?"

"I mean that, given our capabilities at the moment, just sending resources to try and get intelligence from the east will, at best, use up those resources with little return. At worst, anyone we send could end up being used against us. You've read the same reports I have. The descriptions of these easterners we've been able to get all said the same thing, they looked very different than anyone here. As different to Carthaginians and Italians and Egyptians as those people are to the Nubians to the south. The specifics were a little vague, but it was very clear that no one in our employ would pass for one of them, and would easily stand out as a foreigner. Their features, their coloring, it is all very distinctive from ours. Due to these differences, it's clear our people cannot pass for one of theirs, which explains why we've been so completely unsuccessful with any of our attempts to date."

"There are places in between where I have heard the people have a different look. East of Persia, but still close enough to be in contact with us. Places Alexander conquered. Surely someone recruited from those regions would pass?"

"We have no significant relations with those people. While it is something we can explore, I'm not sure how much we want to rely on people whose loyalty to us would be, at best, paid for. There are those who believe intelligence gathering is a nail that, if hammered enough, can produce results. I am not of that belief. The more you attempt and fail to infiltrate a foreign people, the more suspicious they become, and the more they are on the lookout for further attempts. It is better to wait for the right opportunity and be prepared to take it, to use that to gain a foothold. We would make more headway by putting assets in places along the periphery where we know we can operate, such as Persia or Sarmatia, to act as an early warning system, on the lookout for opportunities."

"That will only tell us of an attack as it's happening. It's not good enough."

"It is what there is. We could place people along the trade routes previously used by the easterners. They shut those down as we moved into the Mediterranean, and no caravans have come from that direction since the Carthaginians' fall, but they could begin to use them again. Having people along that route might give us some warning."

"As I understand it, most of the time that route was used by intermediaries, goods passing from one set of hands to others, and not direct trade shipments. How would that help us?"

"True, although near the end, they were bringing shipments themselves. It's possible they would do that again."

Ramirus spread his hands as if to once again say, 'what can you do?'

Medb crossed her arms and began to pace. "Patience is all well and good in peacetime, but this is war. We need information, and we need it now."

"I understand your concern. I do. But you must remember, I've been doing this for a long time. Most of my career has been spent under the threat of war or during actual conflict. Trying to push too fast, too hard, can often backfire, putting the enemy on alert and making our job even harder."

"And when the Empress demands answers, demands action?"

"We tell her the truth. That we are doing everything in our power to gather the intelligence she needs, but that it takes time. That rushing in blindly could jeopardize our entire operation and put the Empire at risk."

Medb stopped pacing, turning to face Ramirus fully. "She won't like that."

"No, she won't. But she is a wise ruler. She will understand, even if she doesn't like it."

Medb didn't like it, that much she knew. She wouldn't tell Ramirus, but she'd come to him partially hoping that he would be able to create a solution out of thin air. She had turned the problem over and over, and she'd always come to the same solution he had just offered. One she did not want to accept.

While his agreeing with her initial, if unspoken, assessment should make her feel good, a confirmation of her abilities in this area, it only frustrated her.

Patience was not one of her virtues. The lack of it was one of her weaknesses, in fact. Knowing that, however, didn't allow her to accept the fact. Instead of admitting defeat, or at least a draw, she turned and stormed back out as she had come in.

It was moments like this that she wished she could still terrorize guards and servants, at least to relieve her frustration. People parted for her as she marched through the palace halls back to her own office.

She didn't even notice them.

After four days in Factorium, getting Sorantius started on his stage of the new developments, Ky returned to Devnum with Hortensius in tow. Ky wanted to spend the time walking the manufacturer through what needed to be done before they got there, so at least he understood what was needed, but he had so much to do that he spent most of the trip writing furiously, trying to finish transcribing the actual plans and instructions he'd need to hand over to them.

Hortensius, genial as ever, seemed to understand and waited patiently while Ky focused on his work. This had always been their biggest bottleneck, getting ideas and designs out of Ky's head, or more appropriately Sophus's memory banks, and onto paper where people without a connection to the Artificial Intelligence could access it. Even with Lucilla's help, there was a limit to how fast either of them could write, or the time they could allot to sitting in one place, writing for hours at a time.

By the time the train arrived in Devnum, he was still not quite done, but he had enough to get them started. They were also running late, as he'd sent a message by telegraph to Lucan and Valdar requesting their presence, but the train had some kind of issue shortly after pulling out of Factorium that delayed them for fifteen minutes. Hortensius had been apoplectic for that whole time, as naturally, most of the people on board looked to the man who'd 'invented' it to get it running. It had been a simple issue and easily fixed with Hortensius and Ky there, but it showed that no matter how much foreknowledge they had to design equipment, maintenance always won out.

Ky was eager to get started and set a little too brisk a pace, leaving the older manufacturer out of breath by the time they arrived at the docks and Lucan's office.

"Sorry we're late, gentlemen. Our train had some unexpected difficulties," Ky said as they walked into Lucan's office, the shipwright and Admiral Valdar already there, waiting for them.

"At which point our illustrious Hortensius lifted the beast on his shoulders and carried it to its destination on his own," Valdar said, giving Hortensius a teasing smile.

"Laugh all you want, but this is the fourth such occurrence that I know of. I'm about one day from having the praetorians stand behind the maintenance crews to ensure they do a proper job. I can abide a lot of things, but sloppy workmanship is not one of them."

"I have no doubt you'll solve the problem of workers cutting corners, but for today, we have new problems to deal with. I already spoke to Valdar about some of this, and I assume you and he have spoken, but given what happened at Port Amicitiae, we need to overhaul our entire fleet with ships of an entirely new design. Unfortunately, that is much easier said than done. I've designed a plan to get us to the end goal I have in mind, but it's not going to be fast enough for anyone's liking. Unfortunately, we're looking at a very significant increase in complexity and essentially an entirely new way of sailing, which we can't jump straight to. That means the sooner we can start this project, the better."

"You mentioned starting with smaller, river-borne ships first," Valdar said.

"That's the plan," Ky said, handing over a thick stack of papers filled with instructions and diagrams. "While part of this is because I think our biggest fight is going to be somewhere on the continent, since even with the fleet they used at Port Amicitiae, I don't think they'll have enough ships to sail an invasion fleet around Africa and to us. Smaller ships are going to be easier to build and test, and rivers will offer a more controlled environment, which we'll need because this is going to be a significant departure from how ships have been designed in the past. But, once we have this down, a lot of the basic principles should scale up without a lot of difficulty, allowing us to directly apply what we learn to ocean-going vessels."

He paused a moment as Lucan, Hortensius, and Valdar gathered around the schematics, poring over them. "At the heart of the new design is a steam engine, although somewhat different from the ones we use for trains. These will be more advanced, using high-pressure steam and a more efficient reciprocating design, for starters."

"These boilers, they're massive," Hortensius said. "And centrally located in the lowest decks?"

"Yes," Ky confirmed. "Placing them there provides the most protection from potential damage. Besides the downside of having one of these boilers rupture, these ships will be without sail, so losing steam would leave the ship to be dead in the water. The steam they generate will be piped throughout the ship via a series of high-pressure lines to wherever it's needed, and being at the bottom will allow the bulk of the power to be put into these devices here, which are called screws because of the way they turn, or the side wheel, depending on the design we're talking about. They'll be turned by a drive shaft connected to the steam engine, similar to the setups in some of our factories. The steam engine's power is transferred through a gearbox to the propeller shaft, which then turns the screw, propelling the ship forward. That's in the screw-driven design, of course. The other set of plans you see is for a paddle-wheel design. That design can't be applied easily to seaborne ships, which will all use screw-driven propulsion, but it allows for a much more shallow draft, which we'll need on some rivers. They're more vulnerable to damage than the screws, since they're above water, of course."

"This is … I'm not sure I even know where to begin. Your previous plans were at least close to what we've done before, but this … I just don't know.

"It's an advancement certainly, but not as far out as you might think, Lucan," Hortensius said. "As the Consul said, the steam engines, the boilers, and the drive shafts are already being used with similar principles in our factories. I'm confident we will be able to get all that installed. The only real new thing is the paddle-wheel, but it's not that much different than a water wheel, at least. It's just a matter of adapting it for use on a ship. It'll take some work, but I think we can manage it."

"Good. I'd hoped you'd be able to connect these ideas to what we'd been doing at the factory and apply it here. Now, once we have the power to propel the ship, the next step is the application of iron sides. Initially, we'll be putting iron plating over a wood frame, but eventually, we'll make the ship entirely out of iron."

"Entirely out of iron? Won't that make the ship too heavy to float?"

"Not if we design it correctly," Ky said. "The key is to distribute the weight evenly and to make sure the hull is watertight. We're not there yet, but once we are, I'll have designs for you that I promise will work, although there will probably be a learning curve to implement them. For now, let's focus on plating our ships. The metal composition for the plates and the thickness should be enough to stop a shell from any of the cannons we have now, with a little wiggle room. A lot of it depends on how the shell hits, but this will work even if it isn't perfect. When this technology was first developed, where I come from, they started by just wrapping chains around wooden ships, because the techniques I have described here for attaching iron plates to the ships and dealing with rust and wear hadn't been developed yet."

"Interesting," Valdar said.

Giving Valdar a nod of agreement, Ky said to Lucan, "I need you to be prepared to start experimenting right away. I can see a need for these river-born ships quickly, and for the ships that come after this. If I'm right, the faster we can make this happen, the better."

"We'll start right away."

"I understand this will take some time to get right. I know I'm pushing you hard, but I also know you're up to the challenge," Ky said. "In the meantime, we need to start turning out more caravels. It'll probably be two years before we have the first ocean-going, ironclad ship ready, and we'll need more naval forces well before then."

"We'll get started on the caravels right away. We've been filling orders for schooners from merchants for years now, and I'm sure those still waiting will howl, but I'll handle it. I'll have my men working double shifts to get as many built as possible."

"Good. And Hortensius, I know it seems too early, but you should probably start working on the iron plating and the parts for the steam engines. It will take time to get the first test bed made, but let's not do this linearly. The sooner we have everything ready, the faster we can start building them. We need to get this done as soon as we can."

"I have faith in all of you. Now, let's get started."

Chapter 4

Devnum

Ky was again in his quarters, writing out endless stacks of instructions. It had been years since he'd done this, since well before the end of the war with Carthage, and he had forgotten how tedious the process of transferring all the knowledge Sophus could give him onto paper could be. It was also a stark realization of how much they had slowed innovation over the last five years, that he hadn't written this many technical documents in all that time.

He'd done some, as they hadn't stopped advancing altogether, but they'd definitely slowed. He kept reasoning with himself as to why that had been necessary and the right call, but part of him couldn't help but feel that he'd become complacent in the time of peace.

He was pulled from his thoughts when the door to their quarters opened and a very tired Lucilla walked in.

"You look exhausted," Ky said, setting the pen down.

"I am," she said, flopping onto one of the short and narrow couches that were still all the rage in Rome. "I've been in meetings nonstop for what feels like a month. I swear to the gods, everyone is so concerned with tiny perceived slights and petty squabbles that they'd rather be swallowed whole than put it aside and look to a real threat."

"For many of them I'm not sure this is real yet. Port Amicitiae is far away, something easily put out of mind. That goes doubly for our allies, who had no investment there and didn't see the value of having a position so far from the continent."

"And yet, it seems obvious that this is just the beginning."

"Which is all the more reason for people not to put their heads in the sand and to stop pretending everything's fine. I assume you just finished a meeting with someone like that?"

"I did. The Greeks are maddening. They are on the very edge of Asia, and will be the first to feel the effects, and yet they push back at all but the most basic treaties. And that's with each of them, since none of the fools want to come together and form any kind of single whole, despite what they have in common. Still, I do have some good news."

"About the Greeks?"

"No, but I've managed to arrange the summit we discussed in Eastern Gaul, two weeks from now, with most of our allies. I think I'm going to propose the western alliance, like we talked about, and a unified military."

"Do you think they'll go for it, though?" Ky asked.

"I think so. I don't know, I hope so. Some are on the fence, but Germania and Gaul's representatives said they think their leaders would agree. The representative from Hispania seemed receptive too."

"But not the Greeks or the Egyptians," Ky said, as a statement and not a question.

"They are resistant."

"But they're the ones who need this the most. They're closest to the Easterners. If they come, the first contact will be with the Greeks or the Egyptians."

"I agree," Lucilla said. "I've made that argument to them, and I'll continue trying, but both are stubborn and fiercely independent. Same with the Scandi, although I think they're softening. It helps that we're the bulk of their supply trade and if the alliance forms, everyone they trade with will be in the alliance. Once I get the Germanics and Gauls on board, I can enlist their help in exerting pressure on the Scandi."

"Good. I can feel things starting to pick up out there. I know it won't be long until the Easterners stop picking at the edges and come at us directly. But we're going to need more than just manpower. What won the war with Carthage was our technological advantage, and we need to have that again, and the only way that happens is if I'm here with Hortensius and the rest. This meeting, summit thing you have set up in Gaul, is more your area, diplomacy and hand holding people, guiding them to obvious decisions, which was never my area of specialty. I think I would be better served staying here than going with you, to ensure we get the new weapons off the ground."

"No. It's critical that you go. If we're going to build this alliance, and especially if we're going to create a combined army, it needs to be done closer to where the conflict will happen. And it's critical that you're there. Everyone, even our allies, know that you're the center of our technological advantage, and they need to hear that we aren't going to fall behind. Besides, the Gauls and Germanics love you, more than they love me. If we're going to get them to agree to put all of their warriors under arms and under our leadership, we need to reassure them that they're not going to be used as ... what was the word you used? Cannon fodder? They need to feel like they're part of the overall strategy, not just pieces we're moving around on a game board. And they'll only believe it if you tell them it's so."

"They hold you in pretty high regard too."

"Maybe, but comparing the two of us, it's not even close. You also have to look at how these new weapons will change how we operate. You, yourself, said that it might end up creating yet another new way to go to war. We can't train the armies here. We're too far from where the fight would happen and I'm not sure our islands can support the kind of numbers this war is going to take. We're going to need room to really do that kind of training, which means Gaul or Germania. Probably Germania, considering it's close enough to Sarmatia and Greece to allow you to respond when the Easterners do appear. I'll be here, because we're going to be asking a lot of our own people once this starts, and there's still some fatigue from the last war. We'll have the telegraph and you and I can communicate. I'm confident Sophus and I will muddle through and get the weapons you two decided on produced."

"Lucilla is correct. I believe we will be effective without your guidance," Sophus added.

"I'm not doubting you. Either of you. Fine, I'll go."

"Isn't it easier when you just agree with me up front?" Lucilla said.

"Apparently. If we're going to train in Germania, I'll talk to Bomilcar and have him prepare the bulk of the legions to be ready to travel once we've identified and set up the training grounds. Assuming everyone goes for the alliance, of course."

"They will. They have to."

A coo from the crib in the corner drew Ky's attention as their child woke up from his nap. "I will miss Titus, though. I've never been away from him for more than a day since he was born."

"I know. It will be hard, but he's strong, like his father. Besides, I was raised much of my life by tutors and nannies, while my father tried to hold the Empire together. He will adjust, I promise. Besides, I will be here with him."

"Which doesn't help me missing him."

"I know, but you'll adjust. Maybe we'll see if I can put the earpiece in his little ear, let him talk to his father. Besides, maybe there won't be war, maybe we're overreacting and this will all be short-lived."

"Maybe," Ky said, but his tone lacked conviction.

He knew better. War was coming, and no matter how much he wished it, he couldn't protect his son from everything. Which meant he needed to go and fight all the more, to make sure Titus had a future to grow up in.

"Get this to the telegraph office immediately," Valdar said, handing a slip of paper to the messenger, who saluted and ran off the ship and toward the dock telegraph office.

The message was an order to send messenger ships to half the combat vessels in the Middle Sea, ordering them to gather at Port Kalb and lay in supplies for a long voyage. After reading the full report from the ships that escaped Port Amicitiae, he wanted to bring every ship in the Britannian fleet. The report claimed that the Easterners had dozens of ships, which put them at a third of Valdar's entire Navy … and they had cannons.

He wanted … needed, numbers to make sure he did the job, but he had to leave some on patrol. The Middle Sea might have been small in comparison to Oceanus, but it was still huge. Aside from pirates, which would always be a problem, it was possible the Easterners might make their way overland, get ahold of some ships, and start making trouble in the Middle Sea. Depending on how far they chased their ships, and if it was a diversion or not, he might not be able to get back in time to respond to requests for help there. Which meant leaving ships behind.

"Start loading supplies, as much as we and every ship in harbor or coming in now can carry. Including any cannons unassigned to active ships, as much gunpowder and shot as you can load, food, and the rest. Pack us to the gills."

"Sir, we headed somewhere?" his first mate asked as dock workers began carrying supplies aboard the ship.

"Port Vikhavn, on the west coast of Africa. We need to reinforce their defenses, especially their cannons. It's the most logical place for the enemy fleet to go next, and I want it to break across our teeth."

"Do we have enough ships? I read the report …" his first mate trailed off, his conclusion obvious.

"We don't have a choice. We'll take as many as we can. Let's get going. I want to sail before dark."

The man saluted and ran off to begin his task as Valdar paced the deck, giving out orders and sending signals to ships still coming in, instructing them on loading and their responsibilities for the long voyage south.

Two hours passed as goods were loaded onto the ships, Valdar was pleased with how diligently his people worked, knowing the task ahead of them. As it looked like he was getting close to leaving, a commotion on the dock drew his attention.

Turning and leaning over the railing, Valdar saw the Consul, and the small retinue that followed him everywhere, coming down from the main thoroughfare toward his ship.

"Admiral," Ky called out, raising a hand in greeting.

"Consul," Valdar replied, moving to the gangplank and descending to meet him. "Come to see us off?"

"I have. This mission is crucial and I wanted you to know the level of support you have. We need to know what we're up against and the whole Empire stands behind you."

"The men appreciate it, Consul. They will do the Empire proud."

"Your first priority is to protect the fleet. Gather intelligence on their capabilities but avoid direct engagement unless absolutely necessary. We're still in the dark about their true strength. Don't take *any* unnecessary risks."

"Understood," Valdar said.

"Good," Ky said, reaching out a hand. "I'm counting on you, Admiral."

"I'll do my best to not let you down," Valdar said, shaking the offered hand.

"I know. Safe journey, my friend. May the winds be at your back."

With a final nod, Ky turned and walked back down the dock, his lictores falling into step behind him. Valdar watched him go, the weight of his mission settling on his shoulders.

"Double-time on those supplies!" he shouted to his crew. "I want to cast off within the hour!"

As the last supplies were loaded, Valdar sent for all the soldiers not on their ships to join him in front of the Bellona.

"All right, you lot! Listen up!" Valdar shouted as they milled about on the dock, waiting for their next orders. "I'm sure you all heard the news by now, about the attack on Port Amicitiae. Today, we go to avenge our fallen brothers. This isn't a fleet of war and our orders are to avoid loss if at all possible, but I won't lie to you, this will be a dangerous journey. Our biggest goal is to ensure Port Vikhavn doesn't suffer the same fate, and then to find out everything we can about the enemy. I've promised the Consul that we will complete this mission. I made this promise, sure in the knowledge that you would not let me down. That together we can accomplish our mission, learn what we need to know about the enemy, and prepare our people to defend themselves. This is our duty. It's our duty to protect Britannia; it's our duty to protect our families. And, it's our duty to defend our way of life. And we will do our duty. I'm counting on you, every single one of you. Now, get to your ships. I want to sail out of harbor while the light is still with us. May the gods bless you and long live Britannia."

"Britannia," the soldiers cheered.

He waved them off, the men starting to move to their various ships, finding their stations.

"Now let's hope that wasn't just wishful thinking," Valdar said to himself as he watched them.

Factorium

Ky and Lucilla stepped out of the train car and onto the platform, back in Factorium. It seemed to Ky that the air here was a little darker and smokier than the last time, and he knew it was only going to get worse.

For now, there was no choice but to make progress towards real electricity and away from the mounds of coal being used to operate hundreds of smaller steam engines. Even if they could get to one large coal-fired turbine and a rudimentary electricity grid, it would be better than this since fission power plants were off the table. Maybe hydro-electric, although it would have to be something simpler than even the large ocean-based generators used before the first fission plant came around.

That, however, was a problem for the future. For now, they needed all their resources focused on what he was positive was going to be war, maybe a larger war than the one with Carthage.

Hortensius was waiting for them on the platform when they arrived, bowing deeply, as was proper, as Lucilla exited the train first.

"Your Majesty! Consul! Thank you for coming."

"I'm always happy to see you, my friend," Lucilla said, taking his hand. "Besides, we wanted to see you before we left for Gaul."

"Of course. Of course. Although the Consul should think about renting permanent lodgings, with how frequently he's been here."

"It feels that way sometimes. Thankfully, with the train, we don't have to spend half a day on horseback. So it's not that big of a burden. Let's head to your offices. I have a lot to show you, and they're holding this train for us to make the journey to Londinium," Ky said, pointing at the messenger bag being carried by one of his lictores.

"Certainly," Hortensius said, waving for them to follow after him.

Hortensius led them to the largest of the factories, navigating between workers heading in every direction. In spite of how many times Ky had come to this factory, his lictore were on edge with how many men were close to their charge, between them and him.

Not that they could protect Ky better than he could himself, but they took their job very seriously.

Hortensius called out greetings and instructions as they walked, unable to stop himself from making corrections to everything he saw being done wrong, in spite of Ky's reminder that they were in a hurry. At the far end of the factory, Hortensius opened a sturdy door leading into his cluttered office, with stacks of papers and even a few books, which had started being bound and printed now that paper and printing presses were less scarce.

Ky and Lucilla's guards closed the door behind them, after handing Ky the satchel full of papers, forming a wall between the office and their leaders, leaving Ky, Lucilla, and Hortensius to confer in peace.

Ky pulled out a stack of papers from the pack and handed it to the manufacturer. "I know I've given you a bunch of priorities, but this one needs to move up to the top of your list."

"A spindle?"

"Fuse, not fusis, but they are similar words, if not meaning. Turn to the next set of pages and you'll see what they're for."

"Explosive shells? Clever ... very clever," he said, pausing as he sifted back and forth through the documents. "And the body of the shells themselves become a form of canister shot as they rupture."

"Exactly. The explosion and attendant shockwave will kill those closest to the shell when it goes off, but the shell fragments are equally as dangerous. Especially to infantry."

"So the fuse itself is a small explosive charge?"

"Yes. Right now, it's essentially the same charge as in the shell as a whole, especially for the timed shot. It's pretty straightforward. The impact fuse will be much trickier, although you can see from the drawings of the new projectile, which is designed to land point down to ensure the impact is in the right place."

"It looks very similar to a rifle bullet, but how reliable will this striker on impact be?"

"Not very, which is why the percussion cap is in there. It won't be reliable either, since it has to be very small to keep from being dangerous in transit, but the two together should give us enough reliability for maybe four out of five. I hope. We can replace that with fused shells if possible, which will work somewhat against armies, but less well for fast-moving targets like cavalry or ships."

"Yes. I can see that. You say there's something more reliable than that though?"

"Yes, but we're not there yet. I actually have something here for that, but it's one step in a long process and we won't see that for at least a year. Maybe two. But we'll get to that in a moment."

"Sure."

"For testing, use the howitzers. It's really what they were designed for, since they lob the shell in an arc, which the shell design helps with, so that the shell plunges down into the ground. Out of a standard cannon, they might bury themselves as they impact and not go off. I got the design of that going during the end of the war, but then our priorities changed, so I didn't give you this part of the overall design."

"Still, it means we already have that designed, so we're one step closer."

"An excellent point. I want these to be your top priority, but it's going to need thorough testing. The last thing we want is these going off in the tubes. That means testing the shell to make sure they are thin enough to burst on impact, but not so thin that they burst in the tubes. I have some notes on page twelve about shell design that should move you in the right direction."

"I'll make a note," Hortensius said, doing literally that on page twelve.

"Speaking of the more stable explosives, I know Sorantius is busy at the moment, and this is low priority, so I'm just going to pass it along to you. We do need to work on it, but he has things that are higher on his list at the moment."

"Can you give me a hint as to what it is?"

"It's a sub-component of a much more advanced form of gunpowder that will have good advantages, but there are many steps between where we are and there. It's called nitrocellulose. Make sure Sorantius knows to only work on it when he has time."

"Will do."

"Lastly, there's this for you. Again, this is not a top priority because it is going to be used for an updated firearm platform. It won't be needed until we get there, but once we do, we're going to need millions of them, so the sooner we can get it in production, the better."

"This is going to take a lot of metal."

"It is, but look at the new press design. The metal is a lot thinner than we use for other things, which is what this press does, creating an even, thin casing. The important part is the built-in primer on the bottom, which allows us to save a step of generating a separate primer cap. But right now, this won't help us, as I said, address this only as you have the manpower and time to work on it."

"This is very interesting, especially this press, but I understand where the priorities are. Unless I run into issues, I think I might be able to have some working prototypes of the fuses ready for testing within a few months."

"Excellent," Ky said. "Lucilla and I will be staying in a village with a telegraph line while we're in Gaul. If you need anything, we'll be reachable, and Lucilla should be back in a few weeks to see how things are coming along and to provide any assistance you might need."

"Your help is always appreciated, Your Majesty," Hortensius said with a slight bow.

Lucilla shook her head as Ky smothered a laugh. It had become something of a running joke between the three of them, that Hortensius knew, but never directly said, that the technical information provided by Lucilla came from Ky. Of course, he didn't know that it actually came from the AI in Ky's head. For someone living in a time before electricity, let alone computers and artificial intelligences, it was a close enough guess.

"Let us know if you have any problems. Now, we should be going. The train won't wait forever, and we still need to get to Londinium."

"Certainly," Hortensius said, standing and leading them back out of the office and through the factory floor.

Workers paused in their tasks, bowing their heads respectfully as the Empress and Consul passed. Ky and Lucilla acknowledged them, as they always did. Besides good and dutiful citizens, the men and women working in the factories were every bit as responsible for the victories the Empire won as the legions were.

Hortensius paused at the factory entrance, clearly wanting to get started on the new designs rather than accompanying the group back to the train. "Safe travels to you both. I hope the summit is productive."

"Thank you, my friend," Lucilla said, clasping his hand.

With final farewells completed, Ky and Lucilla departed the factory, their guards falling into step around them, the train whistle sounding in the distance.

Next stop Gaul.

Chapter 5

Gaul

Gaul had changed a lot since the end of the war. From big changes like rail and telegraph lines leading from the coast all the way to Italia, Hispania, and eastern Germania, to smaller ones like the buildings in the villages, which were more like towns than the smaller settlements they had been five years before.

They still showed signs of how rapidly they'd advanced, with older longhouses made of logs with thatched roofs next to larger, Roman-style buildings with stone walls and tile roofs. In another ten years, most of the log buildings would be gone, modernized to Roman standards.

Assuming Ky didn't change those standards by then, of course.

The building they were using was large, a replacement for their central hut, capable of holding several hundred people at a time and a rival in size, if not opulence, of the forum in Devnum. Most of those spots were already filled and tightly packed, with the rows of seating looking down at the center speaking area.

Lucilla could feel the eyes on her as she made her way to the center of the room. Representatives from every other collective government that had formed, like in Germania, Hispania, and Gaul, as well as tribal leaders and city representatives from the more fragmented areas such as Greece and Scandi, had all come. The messages she had sent out made it clear that Britannia had a major announcement that could affect every person on the continent and Africa, but had not been specific as to what it was.

Some would have already figured it out, as Lucilla had begun backchannel conversations with the more friendly representatives well before the summit was called, but she was glad to see so many had taken the invitation seriously. Part of that was because so much of the known world was now not only using but becoming dependent on Britannian technology, especially the harder to produce but consumable things like gunpowder and fertilizers, both of which they had kept the formula as secret as possible. But she hoped part of it had to do with the cost Britannia had paid, and the respect they had earned by finally ridding the west of the Carthaginian menace.

The realist in her knew it was almost certainly the former that was motivating most of those in attendance, however.

"Thank you all for being here," Lucilla said, her voice carrying throughout the hall. "I know some of you have traveled a great distance to attend this meeting, and I am grateful for your commitment. Your presence here today is a testament to the importance of the matter at hand."

She paused, looking around the room at those in attendance, making sure she had their attention.

"By now, many of you have heard about the attack on our port in Africa. For some of you it may seem like a distant event, far removed from your daily lives and concerns. But I assure you, that is not the case. What happened at Port Amicitiae is not an isolated incident. It is an early warning. A warning of a danger threatening every one of you."

She paused again. There were some murmurs and a few scattered conversations, but she had the attention of most of them.

"At the end of the war we disseminated reports from sources inside Carthage and prisoners captured after the city fell. Reports of an eastern power that supplied them with advanced weaponry greater than anything seen in the west, aside from those weapons designed in Britannia. Weapons not copied from our own but developed in the east. I know for many of you, that seems like a long time ago, and perhaps many of you have forgotten about this threat, but the destruction of Port Amicitiae shows that the Easterners have *not* forgotten about us. What's more, every one of you should be concerned about a people who had no problem supporting a power like Carthage. It shows what these Easterners value, and what we should expect from them. For five years, we have lived as if the threat of annihilation and subjection was defeated alongside Carthage. It was a naive hope, one born of exhaustion from war and strife. A hope that's time has drawn to an end. These Easterners have set their eyes on the west, looking to take up the mantle Carthage once held."

"What does that have to do with us? Who cares what they value or crave?" a representative from Athens asked. "The East is far away. No one has ever even seen one of these people, let alone had any dealings with them."

"We have seen their ships," Lucilla answered. "We fought them in the battle of the Sea of Reeds, their ships standing alongside the Carthaginian ships, at the end of the last war. We know the ships that attacked our port are the same ones that assisted the Carthaginians. Their designs are too unique and recognizable to be anything else. And we are nearly positive that this is just the beginning."

"What do you want us to do about it?" a Scandi chief asked.

"It is time for the west to come together. Just as many of us came together during the last war, now is the time for us to unite. Britannia cannot afford to face this threat alone. The Easterners have shown that they are not another Carthage. For one, they've shown a technological ability much greater than that shown by Carthage. Britannia will continue to work to keep our armies ahead in that regard, giving them an advantage in the field, but we do not know how far the Easterners have come in five years, while Britannia worked to rebuild the west. We cannot do this alone. If we stand divided, we will fall one by one."

She turned, slowly, looking to each of the groups seated around her. "Which is why we asked for this gathering. Britannia is ready to take a stand, and we ask you to stand with us. We are proposing a unified response, an alliance of the West. A pooling of resources and manpower to withstand the coming storm."

"So you want to use our people while you sell us weapons?" a representative from Hispania said.

"No. Britannia will provide the majority of the technical and material support. We have the most advanced weapons and the means to produce them, and we will put our people on the line as well. Britannia has already begun new recruitment efforts and will make up a significant portion of the armies that need to be fielded. But our war with Carthage bled our people deeply and there are not enough of us to do this alone. We want partners who are willing to join us in the defense of our lands. I should say that Britannia could sit back while those of you on the continent are rolled over, crushed by these new invaders. You stand between us and danger and our island offers us protection. But we understand that we, as a people, are not an island. We exist in cooperation with you, our neighbors. Which is why we want to stand with you."

"As you said, some of us are not in the way of this storm, as you call it. Why should we worry about what happens on the continent?" a Scandi asked.

"For the same reason you joined the fight against Carthage. Because it's in your best interest. These are your neighbors, the people you trade with. Your prosperity is tied to theirs."

One of the Gallic representatives called out, addressing the Scandi chief. "You might have been able to sit out the last war, selling to both sides while my people died for their freedom. But if what Britannia says is true, you won't have that same luxury this time."

The Scandi chief bristled. "We didn't …"

Lucilla held up a hand, silencing them both. "I appreciate your concerns. I in no way downplay the part you played in defeating Carthage, but our friend from Gaul is right. This fight is going to be larger and more consequential than the war with Carthage. When the Easterners come, and they will come, everyone here will be in their way. We will all be in danger if we don't band together."

The Scandi chief looked away from her. Lucilla turned again, sweeping her eyes over the crowd.

"Britannia is ready, once again, to defend itself and anyone who would join her from this new Carthage in the east. We have faced great challenges before, and we have emerged stronger. Now is the time for us to stand together, to safeguard our future. I ask you now, who among you will stand with us in this Alliance of the West?"

A representative from Germania stood and said, "Britannia has proven themselves true friends to all freed people. You have fought alongside us, bled with us, and helped us rebuild. We will gladly stand with our friends, now and forever."

Lucilla nodded, a smile of gratitude on her face.

The Gaul representative rose next. "Our people have seen the horrors of subjugation, and we will not let it happen again. We are with you."

They looked to the collection of Scandi chieftains. Oen, the one who had spoken before, and was clearly the one designated to negotiate with others, shook his head, "We came to listen only. We cannot commit Scandi to war. We will take your words back to our people."

"Hispania doesn't need time. We've had our differences, but you helped us when one of our tribes tried to replace our Carthaginian overlords and showed you can be trusted. We're with you."

"You're all fools," the Athenian said. "Can't you see they're playing you, trying to get you all to continue bowing and scraping? Their influence and power was waning, and so they invented a new enemy, a new fear for you all to cower against. We will have no part of it."

The rest of the Greek representatives stood. Bickering, petty people who hardly ever came to agreement had managed to find a common ground. And it was going to doom them.

"You're making a mistake. When the Easterners get here, you will be first in line, the first to fall to their cannon."

"Greece will stand forever, against both fictional threats to the east or against the very real threat to our west. Should you try to come to our lands in the name of protection, we will fight you. We see through you, Empress," the last word was almost spit, the man's contempt on full display.

With that proclamation, the Greeks as a group left the building, making their promise of not wanting to be a part of the alliance a fact.

"While we are not reacting as aggressively as our Greek counterparts, Egypt needs time to consider this. We lived under Carthaginian rule longer than most of you, and know the pain of that occupation, but we are also closer to the west, and see no sign of these Easterners, in spite of those caravans that supposedly went through our lands during the war. We will have to think on this."

The representative of the Ptolemy stood and left, followed by the Scandi. Lucilla watched them go. The Greeks were no surprise. She invited them because their position on the continent would be important, but she knew they would never agree. No one is as difficult as a Greek.

The Ptolemy were a surprise. While they had been hesitant at every interaction since the end of the war, they were pragmatic to a fault, and tended to make the right decision when it counted. She'd actually listed them in the likely-to-agree category in her head.

Those were problems for later. For now, they had allies willing to stand with them, which was the purpose of this whole exercise.

"I thank you, all of you, for your commitment and your courage. We have a long road ahead of us, but together, I believe we can survive what's coming."

Central Germania

As with Gaul, Germania had changed significantly since he had been there during the war. He'd been back since, of course, and seen the stages of progression, but it still shocked him a little each time he came. The large village where he'd spent part of the war, fighting with guerrilla bands through the winter, was almost all permanent buildings now, and had become a rail hub, connecting lines further south and to the edges of Greece, and to the Far East through the ports to the west.

That was one of the reasons this spot had been chosen for the new training camps. It allowed the armies training here to be easily transported to other places on the continent as well as have supplies brought in to support a large collection of men.

That, and Ky had friends here that he'd made during the war. Some had not made it, of course, which created bittersweet memories, but those that had helped ease what was sure to be another long separation from Lucilla.

With the summit only a week behind them, the camp itself was little more than an outline in the dirt, laying out what would be a sprawling camp in the future. Ky watched as the backbreaking work to tear into the still mostly frozen ground commenced. He felt for the men given the task and ensured they were paid fairly for it, but Ky was almost certain they were on the verge of war, which left little time for delay until the weather was more favorable.

The facilities were also needed now. Recruits had begun to arrive from other areas of Germania, with more expected from Gaul, Hispania, and even Italia any day now. In addition, Bomilcar would arrive soon with the first two legions, who would serve as a training cadre while the remaining five made their way to the camp.

"Consul," Sellic said, approaching him from behind. "A large contingent of recruits from Gaul just arrived by train."

Any day could be today, Ky thought. He turned to Sellic, seeing the man's displeasure and feeling for him. His lictores hated when he used them as messengers and aides, instead of letting them stand by his side, protecting him, where they thought their rightful place should be. Unfortunately, the needs were many and the manpower few. Ky had brought a handful of aides with him, but not enough to take up all of the slack to accomplish the task of preparing the training camps. And they could not wait until Bomilcar and additional hands showed up.

"Good. Get them settled, and we'll start training in the morning. I know the temporary accommodations are cramped. Make sure they know this is only until we get more permanent facilities built."

"Yes, sir. Also, Legate Primus Bomilcar sent word he's ahead of schedule and should be here late tomorrow with the 1st and 2nd."

For once, Ky wished everyone was just a little less efficient.

"Talk to the chief and see if we can find somewhere to house them. We might just have to throw up some canvas and let them sleep outside. It won't be pleasant, but at least they won't freeze. Make sure they know that, regardless of where they sleep, I want training to start immediately. We already have recruits waiting, and every day of training is another soldier ready when the ball drops."

"Of course, Consul," Sellic said, giving him a look before saluting and heading off to carry out his orders.

The men, his lictores especially, had grown used to his colloquialisms that would never make sense in this new world, but that didn't stop them from giving him looks every time he used one.

As Sellic walked away, several of the Germanic chieftains, who had gathered in the village to take part in the start-up of the armies, were making their way over to Ky. While Ky appreciated them being here, to show support for the new alliance, at this point, he had a lot to do and limited time to do it, and putting on a dog and pony show, as the old saying went, wasn't all that welcome.

"Consul," Aliverko greeted him with a nod. "The work progresses well."

"It does," Ky agreed. "But we have much to do before the rest of the legions arrive, which will be sooner than expected."

"Yes. We saw the Gauls unloading on our way here," Givellan said. "We've sent word on your telegraph to some of the Anarti requesting additional manpower for the construction. Aside from the Gauls, your shipments of weapons and food have started coming in from the coast, and we are going to try to get you the supplies for the storehouses as well. We know how much of a priority this is."

"I'm glad to hear it, but I'm not sure that helps us now. I sent one of my men to talk to you about additional temporary structures."

"Yes, we saw him. We'll check to make sure it's done."

"Good. So, let me walk you through what's been done so far."

Ky led them through the encampment, showing them the progress they'd made since the day before, with the foundations being poured for the first few buildings and the latrines, possibly more critical than the barracks, which were being dug.

They nodded and made the right noises, but to Ky it felt like a waste of time. Important men wanting to seem important. Lucilla had reminded him, before he'd come out, of the importance of massaging relationships, that this combined effort would get a lot of attention, which would bring out people wanting to see, and be seen. And that he should be nice to them.

So nice he was. As they neared the makeshift command tent, a young man came running up wearing messenger insignia.

"Consul, this is marked urgent."

Ky took it, scanning the message quickly, his expression darkening with each sentence.

"Problem?" Aliverko asked.

"News from the east. The attack we warned everyone about has begun."

That set all the men on edge, each looking alarmed. They supported the alliance and Britannia, but it had been clear to Ky that they had not taken the warning as seriously as Ky wanted. They had treated this as more of an exercise in cooperation than a true preparation.

"The scouts we sent after the attack on our port have reported attacks on Greek colonies in Anatolia and a line of villages in Sarmatia."

"Are we sure it's the same people? Did they see these attacks? Perhaps it's neighbors. Or bandits."

"They did not see them, just the aftermath, but it seems certain. The survivors are describing firearms being used, including cannons, which rules out muskets sold by third parties."

The Britannians had been selling firearms in large numbers for the last five years, but they had all been muskets, keeping cannons and rifles for Britannia itself, just in case someone tried to use their weapons against them. The use of cannons all but confirmed who it was. That, however, wasn't the news that was upsetting Ky.

"It gets worse. They found spent rifle bullets in the sites, not just musket balls, which suggests they have indeed copied some of our technology, which is a bad sign."

"Sarmatia is close to our borders," Bernia said, concerned.

"I know, which means we have even less time than we thought." Ky handed the telegram back to the messenger. "Send a reply. Tell them to keep scouting and try to catch sight of their formations. I want descriptions of weapons, number of men, any organizational details they can get, but do not engage. Repeat to them, do not engage."

The messenger nodded and hurried off, leaving Ky with the uneasy chieftains.

"We need to accelerate our timeline."

Aliverko and Givellan exchanged a look before Aliverko spoke. "Of course, Consul. We'll do whatever is necessary. Germania stands with Britannia."

"What about the training? The additional men?"

"We still need them, and the training will still happen. Actually, we need them more than ever. I'll send for additional praetorians from Britannia and leave the last of the legions that arrives to train the recruits. Not an ideal number of trainers for the number of men we hope will come through here, but it will have to do. I'll need to march as soon as the first legions arrive. I want to block them before they move into Germania."

Ky just hoped it would be enough.

Chapter 6

Gaul

Lucilla tried not to let her annoyance and exhaustion show as she listened to the representatives from Italia.

It had been a busy few weeks, even busier once Ky, whom she missed desperately, had left the week before. Worse, she knew this was just the beginning, and she was not likely to see him again for a long time. The last war had been mostly fought at, or at least near, home. Compared to this new one, even Carthage would be considered close. Ky had sent along the reports of clashes in Greece and Sarmatia, which they hoped would be the edge of the incursion into Europe, as Ky sometimes called the continent.

If the war went well, they would likely have to fight even further away, to the Far East, that is, by Sophus's estimate, putting Anatolia as the halfway point, very far away indeed.

Which meant Ky would be a world away from her for years to come. At least she had Titus, whom she longed to get back to. Thankfully, that separation would not be nearly as long. While she would have wanted to return home as soon as the summit ended and Ky headed for Germania, it was her duty to stay. At least for a time. With this many representatives and leaders from nearly every major polity in the known world, it would be foolish of her not to take the opportunity to meet with each, both individually and in groups, to strengthen relationships that were strong and hopefully build on the weaker ones, hoping to turn them around and gain their support for the alliance.

It looked like it might be working with Greece, who was still frustratingly segmented and stubborn but who had to take reports of attacks on their Anatolian colonies seriously. None had committed yet, but they had begun to ask about the possibility of alliance support in their defense, which was a step forward.

The Ptolemies, however, were maddening. A dozen meetings, all ending exactly as they'd begun with no progress. They seemed to be born with the ability, or inability, to commit to anything. They demurred, obfuscated, hedged, and delayed every time. They were unfailingly polite about it, always thanking Britannia for helping free them from Carthaginian rule, but words of thanks were about as far as their gratitude seemed to carry.

"I'm not sure I understand what you mean when you say close," Lucilla said, keeping her face neutral.

"I apologize for my lack of specificity, your Majesty. Unfortunately, this is an area that is hard to quantify," the lead negotiator said, a man from Rome whom Ramirus and Medb said was one of the wealthiest men on the peninsula.

"Try."

"All of the major tribes on the peninsula and northern Italia are in agreement with the unification your government has set up."

"I hear a 'but' coming," Lucilla said.

"Sadly, you do. But the tribes in Sardinia are proving to be a challenge. They are resistant to the idea of unification and want Italia to distance itself from Britannia specifically and the Western Alliance as a whole."

"Did they give reasoning for their disagreement? Surely, they stand to benefit from your unification. Considering their island status and that the alliance controls most of the shipping in the Middle Sea, they stand to gain more than the tribes on the peninsula itself."

"Some, but none that were believable."

"Do what you can, but if they refuse to join, Italia can still function and prosper without them. What's important now is that we move quickly. The peace we've enjoyed is ending, and war is on the horizon once more."

"I heard your speech, but it sounded as if we still did not know how that would end."

"Things are moving fast. The easterners have attacked Greek colonies in Anatolia and villages in Sarmatia. The war we warned of is here."

The representatives looked at each other, worried. "Your Majesty, in the event of an eastern attack on Italia, can we expect military support from Britannia?"

They could read a map. If the easterners attacked through Greece, then Italia would be their next target should the Greeks fall. And the Italians saw the Greeks turning down help from the alliance.

"Britannia will do what it can to help its allies, but our primary focus must be on the members of the western alliance. Once Italia is unified and joins the alliance, you will be able to participate in that defense and gain the protections it offers."

"But what if we are attacked before unification is complete?"

"Then you must rally your people and defend yourselves as best you can. Britannia will provide what assistance we can spare, but our resources will be stretched thin. The sooner you unify and join the alliance, the sooner you will have access to the full might of our combined forces."

"We understand the urgency, Your Majesty," the lead negotiator said. "We will do our best to address the Sardinian issue and send envoys as soon as possible."

"See that you do. With the war starting, Britannia will be pulling most of our security forces out of Italia in the coming weeks."

"But, given our proximity to Greece ..."

"I am aware of how concerning that is, but you must also understand our position. We are spread thin, and our forces are needed elsewhere. The war is here, and we must respond to defend the alliance we have built."

"But if Greece falls, we will be next. Surely you can spare some troops to secure our eastern border?"

"I cannot make any promises. Our commanders are still assessing the situation and determining where our forces are most needed. But I will discuss it with them and see what can be done."

The representatives looked at each other, clearly unsatisfied with her response.

"Your Majesty, we are grateful for all Britannia has done for us, but we need more assurances."

"Then you have work in front of you. I know this is difficult to accept, and I promise you it is also difficult for me to say. I have pushed for Italian independence and unification since the end of the war and have tried to give your people every opportunity to reach those goals, but my obligations must come first. I will be returning to Britannia shortly. In the meantime, I urge you to resolve the issue with Sardinia and send envoys to join the alliance. Time is running out."

None of the men were happy with her answers, but at least they finally seemed to understand the urgency of the situation.

Devnum

"I don't care what you have to do; get it done," Medb said to the man dressed in riding clothes, wearing no identifying marks or rank.

Before the man could respond, there was a knock on the door and one of the praetorians stuck his head in the door.

"I said we were not to be disturbed," Medb snapped.

"I understand, my lady," the guard said. "But the Praetorian Daelith is here. He says he needs to see you as soon as possible, and that it's a personal matter between the two of you."

Medb ran through dozens of names in her head, and Daelith, which sounded Caledonian to her ear, was not one she knew.

"Go out the side," Medb told the man in riding clothes, pointing to a small door in the side of her office. "And don't come back until you have something for me."

The man grimaced but nodded and left. Medb then waved to the guard, who opened the door and let the stranger in.

"I don't know you," Medb said pointedly once the door was closed.

"No, my lady. I am sorry for the deception. I was sent by Tribune Claudius, who asked me to stop and see you, and to keep my meeting with you quiet. It seemed like the best way to explain my meeting with you."

Claudius she did know, at least by name. He'd been a low-level praetorian who had exemplified himself several times during and after the war, and rose through the ranks rapidly following the war. She'd never met him, but knew he was one of the Empress's favorites.

"I see. I assume he sent you with a message then."

"No, my lady. He thought it best that I not write it down, as … if it became known, it could cause problems in some parts of the Empire."

"I see. And what is this urgent message?"

"The centurion is concerned. He's seeing a significant growth in unrest in Carthage itself and the region as a whole, as well as a growth of criminal organizations, who seem to have an uncanny ability to always avoid his patrols or raids."

"We knew it would be a problem, and security is a praetorian concern. What does he want me to do about it?"

"It's not the security problems themselves, my lady, but what seems to be driving them. Claudius is concerned about the decisions being made by Governor Eoghan, who seems to be making not only the wrong decisions, but decisions that are making the situation progressively worse."

Medb frowned. She knew Eoghan, a former Ulaid senator, and one who was uncomfortably close with Senator Fiacha, the exiled traitor. She'd never found anything that suggested Eoghan had been involved with Fiacha, but their closeness had always made Medb uncomfortable.

"In what way?"

"He's favoring some factions over others, and is too friendly, turning a blind eye to elements that we believe are fronts for criminal organizations in the city, while taking harsh measures against others with similar connections. It is the favored groups that we have had trouble catching in their actions, always managing to avoid us. We don't want to blame the governor or his agents directly, or at least not openly, but the coincidence has not gone unnoticed. Beyond that, the favoritism he has shown has caused the factions getting harsher treatment to scale up violence to counter their opponents. The city has become a powder barrel."

Medb leaned back, crossing her arms, thinking. Daelith began to shift from foot to foot, uncomfortable with her focus on him as she processed the information.

"Anything else?" she finally asked.

"No, my lady. That's all I was told to relay. Tribune Claudius wanted you to be aware of the situation, given your ... history."

She crooked an eyebrow at him but did not comment. The statement could be considered either an insult or just an acknowledgment of her history with her countrymen.

"Thank you for bringing this to my attention. You're dismissed."

The man bowed and hurried out. For several minutes, Medb didn't move. She stared at the closed door, thinking. By all accounts, Claudius was a good soldier, not easily spooked and calm under pressure, which meant that it was less likely he was overestimating the problem. Medb, however, wasn't a fan of trusting the judgment of others, no matter how unflappable they might be.

While there had always been concerns about Eoghan's friends, he himself had never been much involved in any scandals. This was, in fact, the first. She'd seen the reports the governor had been sending back, and they told a very different story than what Claudius reported. By Eoghan's telling, Carthage was progressing well and would be able to make a smooth transition toward self-governance in the next year or two.

What spoke to her more than the message itself was the fact that Claudius had seen a need to send it through unofficial channels; through a friend.

Wrapping her knuckles on the desk, she stood up and headed for the door, ignoring the guards who snapped to attention and fell in behind her as she left her office.

Lucilla had just returned from her trip, and Medb found her in her private study, writing out documents, probably for Hortensius or one of the other inventors. The Empress was intelligent, no doubt, but the level of detail and advanced knowledge needed for those instructions, from what Medb had seen, was well beyond what she had ever shown. At least in Medb's presence.

For a moment, Medb's eyes went over the technical specifications. Ky was something she couldn't understand. He was otherworldly, and she'd witnessed him perform feats no mortal could. Lucilla, on the other hand, was very much mortal. She'd heard the explanation, that Ky had explained it to her and she was simply writing down what she was told, but Medb wasn't convinced of that. Medb stayed silent for a beat too long, and Lucilla raised an eyebrow.

Medb pushed her thoughts away. It was a mystery she'd love to solve, but not one she needed to deal with today.

"Yes?" Lucilla said.

"We have a problem," Medb said. "Claudius, the man you put in charge of the praetorians in Carthage, sent a message to me through back channels, describing concerns he has with the security of the region. Concerns that directly contradict a wide number of the governor's reports."

"Can I see his message?"

"He chose to send it with a close friend, apparently not wanting to commit it to paper."

Lucilla frowned, and Medb could see the Empress mirroring her own thoughts. As much as she'd hated the idea of bowing to another ruler, after the loss of her kingdom, she appreciated that if she had to that it was ultimately to someone like Lucilla. She'd met few people quick enough to pick up on the intricacies like the Empress did.

If Medb had to serve another, at least it was one worthy of that service.

"That is troubling," Lucilla said. "If Claudius says it is so, I'm inclined to believe it. Which do you think it is, then? Incompetence or treason?"

"It's hard to know, this far removed. It could easily be either, but that isn't the issue. He has connections with factions inside the Empire that you will need as the war heats up. We can't just take action based on the suspicions of a praetorian, no matter how trusted."

"I agree. I also get the sense you came here with more than just concerns. You don't need to prime me, as Ky says. Just tell me what you have to say."

"Send Cormac. He outranks Eoghan in Ulaid society. He can apply pressure without removing Eoghan outright, and any evidence he provides will be enough to cow the factions in Ulaid that support Eoghan."

"An excellent suggestion, since it provides a reason to send you with him," Lucilla said.

"Your Majesty, I have many things here ..."

"I have no doubt," Lucilla said, cutting her off. "This isn't a punishment, Medb, but an appreciation of your abilities. I know you're having difficulty getting information on the easterners, leaving you and Ramirus at something of a standstill. Carthage, on the other hand, could cause us issues. Cormac is a good man and he's become a fine diplomat with an active military mind, but subtlety is not one of his attributes. If there is a problem, it will have to be handled carefully. Also, if Claudius had been able to secure any solid evidence, he would have made the report to me. He sent it to you because he knew how weak his position was. This needs the touch of someone like you. I also want you in the region, as there are concerns with Italian unification, which I might need you to look into. It would give me peace of mind if you were nearby."

"I see," Medb said, inclining her head in tacit surrender to the Empress's position.

"I'll send orders to Cormac today and inform Eoghan that the prince is coming to inspect the good work he's been doing, and as part of a reevaluation of our force dispersion in preparation for the coming war. As always, I trust your judgment to do what is needed, but contact me should you need any additional support."

Medb didn't answer, simply bowed at the waist before turning and leaving the Empress behind.

Far Eastern Germania

Ky crouched behind a fallen tree, his eyes fixed on the small Germanic town below. The early morning mist still clung to the ground, providing additional cover for the Fifth Legion as they advanced silently through the forest. He watched it both through the drone flying high above and using his advanced vision, focusing on the foreign soldiers moving through the town, herding villagers into a central building.

They were armed with long guns of some kind, longer than the muskets the Britannians had been selling to their allies through the inter-war years. The design was different, although that was more of an impression at this range than anything he knew for sure. He'd have to open them up to see just how different they were.

The fact that they had firearms at all was concerning, and confirmed his worry that the enemy, with their access to gunpowder during the last war, even lower quality gunpowder, meant his men would be facing an enemy armed with firearms for the first time.

Which changed a lot of their strategies.

"They're armed with muskets," Ursinus said beside him, peering through a looking glass.

"Or firearms of some type, that's for sure."

"We saw their cannon. While it was rudimentary next to our own, it still caused you a lot of problems in that last battle. These are, I think, going to be worse. I'd like to keep them at long range, so we can hammer them from outside of their own, and only have to worry about the cannon."

"They also outnumber us," Ky pointed out. "If we're going to hit them, we need to do it by surprise and take out as many as we can before they can form up."

It was hard to tell, with the enemy spread out as they were, with a large group close to them, an equal size group much further out on the eastern side of the town, probably outside of Ursinus's position, and a whole lot of men scattered in the town itself.

"We're about as close as we can get without moving beyond the tree line, Consul," Ursinus pointed out.

"I know. Here's what I want. The assault will begin on the group closest to us. It's nearly as large as our own force and looks to be the bulk of their men. Hit them with artillery and have the infantry double-time until halfway across and then charge. As soon as the infantry charges, the artillery is to shift their aim to target the far group. I want to hit them before they can form up and push them into the town itself. We can use its streets to funnel them and counter their manpower advantage."

"It will be done, Consul," Ursinus said, sneaking back from the edge of the tree line to begin passing the orders.

While he waited, Ky studied the enemy themselves. Definitely Asian in physique, and their banners had what looked to Ky like a kind of early Chinese, although the depictions of that early writing did not survive into his own century. It felt right, though.

It took almost thirty minutes to get all of the men in position, far too long for Ky's taste, but he understood Ursinus was trying to be quiet about it, to keep the element of surprise.

More of the enemy had gathered on the outskirts of the town, perhaps preparing to continue their march west. Ky gave the signal and the earth itself exploded as both of the legions' attached batteries opened fire, raining solid shot down onto the unexpecting easterners. Spots of dirt and bodies shot up into the air as the shells ripped holes through the enemy's flanks.

Ky could hear the enemy's cries of pain and surprise from where he was.

Those voices became a crescendo as Ky's men burst from the tree line, shrieking like banshees as they marched double time, quickly crossing the opening to get into range, all the while the artillery continued to batter the opposing forces.

While the carnage outside of town was creating chaos through the enemy forces, Ky could see that the easterners in town were hurrying to form up and that their forces outside of the town were already moving to support their men under attack. These people had seen a lot of combat and weren't just conscripted labor. These were much closer to soldiers than anything the Carthaginians had possessed.

"Keep them moving," he yelled at Ursinus. "Don't let the enemy regroup before we can get into the town."

Ursinus nodded and began to call out orders to the buglers, but there was just too much ground to be made up. Halfway across the field, just as his men entered their effective range, a wave of small arms fire rippled out from the edge of town, from the men that had been coming to their comrades' defense and from men who were forming up into firing lines much like those of the Britannians, even under the artillery barrage.

The first volley from the enemy confirmed the fear Ky had since hearing about the attack on Port Amicitiae. They had rifles.

As the first volley crashed into his men, sending waves of them to the ground, the advance slowed. Some, never having tasted gun fire, started to run while others held their formations and continued marching. The lead cohorts were in danger of breaking entirely.

Then, it got worse as a much larger boom sounded from inside the city itself. They'd rolled out cannons, similar to his but different, more slender and thinner. The differences didn't seem to affect their effectiveness, however, as cannonballs now began to tear into his line.

His men had pulled up their own rifles, cohorts beginning to return fire into the town on their own.

The positioning was terrible. Half the enemy's force was in the town, firing from cover, while his men were standing in an open field, being torn down by weapons every bit as good as their own.

"Get them moving," Ky bellowed at Asiaticus, the tribune of the rear cohort. "Close up. Close up! Ursinus!"

Ky turned his horse, looking for the legate, who came riding up at his call.

"You need to get them moving. They're exposed out there. Push through the fire and get into the town. Their shots are hitting brick as much as men. Just get them to move."

Ursinus saluted and rode into the field, shouting at his men. It was a dangerous move, but it was what was needed in this kind of fight. They started moving, but still too slowly. The men just didn't know how to deal with this kind of fight.

Ky looked at the officers around him, searching for something they could do. His eyes fell on Cynan, tribune of the Ninth Cohort, which was being held in reserve along with one other cohort.

"Tribune," Ky called out, waving the Ulaid officer over. "Take your cohort and the seventh and circle wide to the right. I want you to fire on that artillery and keep pouring it on until they're silenced, then push into the outskirts of town. Do not enter the town proper."

He needed something to pull the easterners' focus away from his men on the field, but he did not want a separated unit pushing in too deep without support, which would put it in danger of being surrounded.

Cynan saluted and rode off. The Ulaid was smart, moving them through the woods until they were far to the other side, and swinging in hard. Ursinus was getting the rest of the cohorts slowly moving, which had the added benefit of keeping the easterners' attention focused forward, missing Cynan's group until they were nearly at the northern edge of the city. Men from the town started to swing in, but not before the two cohorts opened fire down a straight lane, looking directly into the artillery setup.

Easterners fell as the artillery silenced.

It was like a wall lifted in front of Ursinus's other forces, which surged forward as the deadly artillery barrage lifted. Small arms fire continued coming in, but the reduction in death and carnage was what his men needed to continue their assault.

Ursinus pushed them on, and the front cohorts pushed into the edges of the village, forcing the easterners back deeper into the village. It wasn't easy, however. The forces gathered on the east side of town had already begun to rush in to provide support. His men had a good position, but they were outnumbered, and concentrated fire in the streets could thin his men out.

He needed to get the advantage, hold the town square to allow him to mass fire on their more compact formations. Ky spurred his horse forward, drawing his gladius.

"Forward! Push them back!" Ky shouted.

He rode just behind the front line, ignoring the crack of bullets. His men responded, pressing forward, using their bayonets to great effect in the tight quarters. The easterners' rifles, so deadly at range, were muted.

"Drive! Drive through the opening. Push to the town square."

A small group of easterners gathered down the street, preparing to line up to fire. As Ky began to shout a warning, Ursinus came riding up, shouting orders.

"Front rank, rapid fire. Fire! Fire!"

His men pulled up their rifles, the firing was sporadic but fast enough to beat the enemy to the shot, as they fell in twos and threes. It didn't stop their volley, but when it came, it was thinned out enough to keep from being devastating. Deadly, but not enough to break his lines.

Ky dismounted, handing his horse to an aide. To his left, a Britannian soldier went down, struck by an eastern bullet. Ky grabbed the soldier's rifle as he fell and snapped off a shot, dropping one of the men still left firing.

"Forward," Ky shouted as he reloaded the rifle.

He pushed deeper into the town, firing as they pushed forward. The streets were thick with smoke and bodies, but the enemy was giving way. Just as they got to the town square, a large body of enemy soldiers, who had not been in the fighting, pushed in from the other side, in better order and with loaded weapons.

Ky's men were caught flat-footed, without time to prepare. A wall of smoke exploded across from them, lead slamming into his men, bullets ripping through Ky's clothing, coming close enough that it would have created burns on someone without genetically toughened skin.

"Form up," Ursinus shouted.

Ky loaded and fired. This wasn't going to work. They'd lost too many men, and more of the enemy were coming up, creating multiple rows of fire.

"Ursinus!" Ky called out. "Send a runner to the 5th Battery and order them to shell the town center hard. I want a fire break between us and them. As soon as it starts, fall back to the starting positions."

Ursinus nodded and began passing orders to a runner while Ky returned to firing, moving much faster than the men around him, getting off almost seven shots a minute thanks to his lictore continually reloading for him, knowing he would have an accuracy they could not match.

Each of his shots connected, dropping a man. But none of it mattered. The legionnaires did him proud, holding their position in spite of the withering losses, but there were too many of the enemy soldiers and too few of them, and the odds were getting longer with every minute.

It felt like forever since the runner had left, but only a few minutes had passed when the first shells rained down. They were close, starting in the center of the square not far from his own men and then creeping out toward the enemy. It was a dangerous move and shrapnel hit a few of his own people, but it was preferable to being back in their line and pushing forward. This way, the ground-shaking impacts would push the enemy away from them, giving his men a break.

As soon as the first shells began to fall, the bugler began playing the retreat. His men held their discipline, continuing to fire while falling back, even through the rain of shells to keep the enemy from advancing. Through the drone Ky could see the flanking units, who were also under heavy fire, beginning to pull back also.

Worse, the enemy's artillery, which had been forced to relocate earlier, began again, with a shell landing among his men to the left, sending men flying in all directions.

"Hold formation! Back up and fire! Keep the pressure on!" Ky shouted.

With both sides' artillery shots landing in and across the square from each other, it was doubtful that the enemy would try to push forward, but Ky wanted to ensure that didn't happen. His men were near the breaking point, and one push was all it would take to cause a full rout.

They'd faced longer odds, much longer than this, many times and won. With a parity in weaponry and, apparently, training, that would no longer be possible. Until he could get the new weapons to his forces, some of which were going to take time, he'd have to be much more careful about how to deploy his men, which meant they were going to start losing a lot more ground before he was going to be able to stop them.

Ky turned to order Ursinus to pick up the pace of the retreat when another enemy volley slammed into his line. Ky felt something slam into his side with tremendous force, knocking him off his feet.

He hit the ground hard, pain exploding through his body.

For a moment, the world spun around him. Ky blinked, trying to clear his vision. He tasted blood in his mouth and felt a burning sensation in his side. Looking down, he saw a bloody hole torn through his uniform.

"Commander, you have suffered a critical injury."

Warnings flashed across his vision, showing the damage done to his side. Nanites returned information to Sophus, who displayed the damaged liver and intestines, punctured by the bullet.

Deadly to any un-augmented human, but all soft tissue, thank God. His nanites were able to repair both, and they'd already begun isolating the bullet lodged not far from his spine, removing damaged tissue and breaking the metal down for excretion. Had it been bone, the repair time would be significantly longer.

As it was, the injury was serious even for him.

"I know," Ky said out loud, the pain blurring his thinking.

"Nanites are at insufficient capacity to affect the necessary level of repairs. You need to be sedated to allow all resources to be diverted to healing you."

"Not yet," he growled.

"Consul?" one of his panicked legates said as they began checking his injury.

"Bring a stretcher. Get Ursinus," Ky managed to get out, pushing down the pain.

"Consul!" Ursinus yelled, rushing to him as if on cue, looking at the wound in horror.

It hadn't taken long for the Britannians and anyone else who'd experienced combat to learn just how deadly a bullet could be, or the likely outcome of a gut shot.

"It's alright. I'll live," Ky said, pulling up his shirt to show that the bleeding was already slowing. "Keep the men falling back in order. Don't let them break."

"But sir ..."

"That's an order, Legate. You're in overall command now. Get the legion out of here and retreat as far as you can if they give chase. Get as many of the wounded out as you can, but the legion as a whole is your priority now."

Ursinus hesitated for a moment, then nodded. "As you command, Consul."

He turned, shouting commands to nearby officers, spurring the men on with renewed haste, as a stretcher came up and Ky was placed on it, his lictore insisting that they be the ones to carry him out.

"Commander, you must be sedated for effective repairs," Sophus repeated, somehow with greater urgency.

"Sellic," Ky said, grabbing the lictore's arm. "Transport me with the troops, but do not let ..."

His voice trailed off as pain lanced through him. Sophus had moved even the nanites that dealt with pain control off, probably to help with repairing his injuries. Which meant the wound was worse than the readouts indicated.

"We know, Consul. We will keep you safe and won't let anyone touch you."

Ky squeezed the man's arm lightly and then said, "Okay, do it."

He'd just realized he said that out loud when oblivion descended.

Chapter 7

Devnum

Lucilla paced the length of her private chambers, wearing a deep line in the carpet. She loved the ability to hear Ky's voice from so far away, but on days like this, it was a curse as much as a gift. She'd known about the loss in Eastern Germania for hours and couldn't say anything or even let on that she'd heard such devastating news.

Worse, she knew that Ky had been seriously wounded and had to swallow down the fear and anger that news caused. Sophus had sworn to her that Ky was alright and would fully recover, but that did not keep her from spending the day dwelling on it. Which just made her more and more furious each time someone brought her a very valid request, going about their lives not knowing how bleak the world was at that moment. Or at least her world.

So she paced and fumed and snapped at everyone who came into her presence. It wasn't fair to them, but she wasn't feeling fair.

Especially after hearing that the enemy was now armed with the same rifles they used. Sophus said that the rifles they were using looked remarkably similar to the model the Britannians had been using during the war with Carthage. They had made some very minor changes, mostly with the aiming mount, which they noticed was missing from the version the easterners had wielded that morning. Sophus hypothesized that they had, in fact, received weapons lost to Carthage during the war and had managed to reverse engineer them.

Apparently, their cannons had some notable differences, but Sophus had been less sure if that was because they had not gotten an intact cannon, if they had some way of coming up with an alternate, ahistorical design, or if they'd just been forced to work within their existing production chain and alter their previous lower quality smoothbore cannon to match the cannon Ky had introduced.

She wasn't sure what Sophus had meant by ahistorical, or much else of what he'd said, but she got the gist of it. The enemy had weapons that rivaled those used by the Britannians, and that was bad. At least this first clash indicated that they did not have the inexhaustible supply of men that Carthage had on its side. The enemy force they faced was larger, but Ky had also gone out with only one legion. If he had brought two, the odds would have shifted in the Britannians' favor and suggested they might not have overwhelming numbers like Ky had feared.

Or perhaps that was just Lucilla's wishful thinking.

Even if the manpower difference wasn't as great as that of the war with Carthage, the parity in firepower meant their losses would be significantly higher, so the challenges of this war would be the same as the last.

How to get enough men to wage it.

A knock at her door interrupted her pacing.

"Come."

A messenger with the stripes of the signal service came into her office holding a slip of paper out to her. She snatched it from him and waved him away as she read the first few lines to ensure it was the message she'd been waiting on.

"Gaius!" she shouted before the door closed behind the messenger, crumpling the message in her fist.

Her assistant came dashing in, looking around the room, probably concerned by the tone of her voice. As assistants went, he was tall, fit, and not bookish at all, but then he'd been placed in the position by Faenius, head of the Praetorian Guard, as an extension of her personal protection. Luckily, he was also a fair assistant.

"Faenius and Ramirus. I want them in my office in the next five minutes. Not a second later," she said, making sure he did not mistake her tone.

He did not, his eyes widened slightly as he spun on his heels and hurried out of the office. She resumed her pacing as he left, thinking through what she wanted.

Not that she needed to. She'd run the possibilities through her head again and again, all day. Not that she was confident in her decision. It came with risks. Serious risks.

The two men hurried in, Ramirus looking a little red in the face and puffing hard. Lucilla relented slightly at seeing her old friend. He'd always seemed old, even when she was a child, but the last five years of building alliances and dealing with recovering the remnants of the Carthaginian empire had taken a toll on him.

But this was important.

She handed the message to Ramirus, who glanced at it only briefly before handing it over to Faenius. Lucilla eyed him for a moment. If she didn't know better, she would suspect he knew the contents of the message before he walked into her office.

Faenius's reaction was closer to what she was expecting.

"This is very bad. Nearly four hundred dead or missing, and another seven hundred wounded. That's a fifth of the entire legion, gone in a single engagement. Not to mention the Consul."

"Is there any word on his condition?" Ramirus asked.

"You've seen the same message I have," she said, trying to keep her face neutral and not show what she was really feeling. "But I believe he will recover. He's resilient."

Ramirus saw through her and seemed to know what she was really saying, nodding slightly. He'd hinted before that he'd figured out that Ky and Lucilla could speak over distance, but she'd never confirmed it or even addressed it directly.

"The legion is now in retreat, and I am concerned about how far they will be forced to fall back," Lucilla said. "Even with the other legions en route, we can no longer rely on our technological advantage. Which means we cannot afford to let our forces be outnumbered. The legions need men, and they need them now. It also means we cannot wait for our allies to train their troops."

Faenius looked to Ramirus, silently asking where this was going. Ramirus shrugged but had a concerned look on his face.

"Which is why," Lucilla continued. "I'm ordering that we pull half of the praetorians currently in service across the Empire and prepare to send them to the legions on temporary assignment as replacements, until such time as we get enough reinforcements to keep our forces at combat effectiveness, as Ky likes to say."

"Your Majesty, with the increased unrest in Carthage, and parts of Italia that remain unstable, I am concerned what that will do to the Empire's safety."

"I'm aware. Cormac will have to manage with what he has when he arrives. I have faith that he will find a way to make it work. I need you to begin making arrangements now. I want them to begin marching toward the staging point of the other legions preparing to head east within the week to join those forces. I will send notification to Bomilcar that they are on their way."

"But …"

"This is not open for debate," she said, stopping the argument before it started.

Faenius frowned, clearly not happy with that answer, but Lucilla wasn't here to make him happy. She met his frown with a stern expression. He understood that this wasn't a suggestion or a debate and nodded once.

"I'll take care of it at once, Your Majesty," Faenius said, bowing and glancing at Ramirus, the two exchanging looks before he turned and left the office nearly as quickly as he entered it.

Ramirus waited until the door closed behind Faenius before saying, "This decision will come back to haunt us, Your Majesty."

"I know it's a gamble," she said, dropping into a chair and sagging a bit. "But what choice do I have? The legion is in retreat. We need to limit how far the easterners push into Germania and buy time for the new legions to mobilize. And I can't wait for Ky to recover and request help."

"Your Majesty," he said, sitting next to her, concern in his eyes. "You have to ask yourself, are you doing this for the Empire, or for Ky?"

"The Empire. I'm not some lovesick girl, Ramirus. I am, of course, worried about him, but my concern is for the Empire and the alliance. We have to hold them before they get a strong foothold in Germania. It's going to be our largest source of manpower. If it becomes compromised, we will be left in a bad position."

"And if unrest spreads in Carthage or Italia while our forces are depleted there?"

"Then we'll deal with it. I think Italia will not be that much of a problem. Only Sardinia remains an issue, and they are more contained. If it was just Cormac alone, I might be concerned, but Medb is with him. She's shown she is quite capable, if ... what's the phrase Ky likes to use? If she's given runway?"

"Yes, although I still don't understand that one."

"Me either, but either way, I'm just going to have to rely on her to make the best decision she can."

"I hope so," he said.

It was clear he did not think her plan was the right decision. She could only hope he was wrong and that Medb was up to the task.

Carthage

Medb stepped off the gangplank of the small schooner they had chartered to make passage to Carthage and paused, taking in the city. She had been here several times since its fall on various missions for the Empress, but the city never failed to impress. It was huge, sprawling. Maybe not larger than Devnum was now, with the massive expansion it seemed to constantly be under, but it was impressive, nonetheless.

It had been spared damage in the war, so its classical buildings still stood, untouched and nearly pristine, with the massive palace in the heart of the city looming above everything else.

She felt a hand on the small of her back as Cormac came up behind her, pointing subtly down to the docks, where a praetorian waited for them. She pulled the hood hiding her trademark red curls a little lower and made her way off the ship.

"Welcome to Carthage, my lady. Prince," Claudius said, greeting them both.

To an outside observer, it might seem odd that a man who was heir to the Ulaid throne and in line for the imperial throne itself wasn't the first one greeted in this situation, and his wife a distant second in precedence. Those who'd worked in the palace in Devnum would have known the truth.

Not that there was anyone around to witness the interaction. The fishmongers and sailors were the only people on the docks and paid little notice to the lone praetorian speaking with two new arrivals to the city. They had traveled there with none of the ceremony that usually followed Cormac, and Medb was glad for it. She'd found it strange that, as much as she loved the pomp her formal title gave her, she'd come to value the much more real respect she was shown now. It wasn't just courtiers and nobles kissing up to her any longer. It was men like Claudius showing subtle indications of her standing, not for an audience but because it was what she was due.

She liked that very much. But her getting due deference was not why she was here.

"It was fine, Centurion. But we didn't come on a pleasure cruise. Your message was alarming, to say the very least."

"It's worse than I conveyed in my message, my lady. I'm relieved you've come to witness it firsthand."

He led them away from the docks and into the city proper. As soon as they got off the main road from the docks to the palace and onto some of the side streets that would be more frequented by commoners and not by official processions, what Claudius had been talking about became readily apparent.

A few streets in, they saw the first of several scrawled graffiti with messages like 'Britannians Go Home!' and 'Death to Invaders.' There were slapdash sections of paint on other walls suggesting there had been more that had since been covered up.

"We've been getting a lot of this. Not on the main thoroughfare, which is heavily patrolled, but in the city proper, they keep appearing faster than we can cover them up."

Medb only nodded, looking over the graffiti. Devnum had its fair amount of similar public artwork, and it was a common thing in most cities she'd seen. The messages were, however, concerning. This is what happened when the population was frustrated and felt they didn't have an outlet with the people that governed them. It was also a warning sign that the government in power should heed, since it often led to much more direct and bloody expressions of that frustration.

Entering a market area, they came across something different, but equally troubling. Rows of shops in what looked like a well-built-up area were boarded up and closed, with only a few out of several dozen left open. Several had notices on them, torn and fading but still readable, announcing that the shop was closed by order of the governor.

"On what grounds?" Medb asked, pointing to the notice.

"The official reason varies. Harboring criminals, health and safety, lack of a permit, which is something that's recently being introduced to 'better control public services.' In reality, they upset someone with the power to shut them down or didn't pay off the right person."

"The praetorians are demanding bribes?" Medb demanded angrily.

"No. My people would never do that, at least not if they wanted to remain in their position. No, the governor has a series of tax collectors that are outside of my chain of command, although we have orders to support them as needed. Which they take advantage of often, using my people as muscle for their little schemes."

There it is, Medb thought. She'd wondered what motivated Claudius to act. He was loyal to the Empire, but it seemed to her that there was more to it that she hadn't been able to put her finger on. The governor using his men in ways he disapproved of and leaving him no recourse but to go outside of the ranks to report it, made sense.

The praetorian's domain was being encroached on, and he was unhappy about it.

"I see," she said, not letting those thoughts show on her face. "Do you have evidence of these bribes?"

"A very little. I turned some of it over to the governor when it first came to my attention and it was swept under the rug. Suddenly, the tax collectors were much more careful about what they said in front of my men, so evidence is harder to come by now."

Which suggested, to Medb, that the governor was involved in the graft, to at least some degree. Medb made note of it and continued on. Claudius took them back toward the main thoroughfare. As they neared it, the stink that any large city had was suddenly replaced by a wet acrid smell.

"There was a fire?" Cormac asked, identifying the smell.

Before Claudius could answer, they turned a corner where Medb recognized what had been a small guard shack. The praetorians used them in larger cities for patrols to be based out of without having to return all the way back to the full barracks during a shift. This one, however, was half burned to the ground, blackened and charred.

"When did this happen?" Cormac asked.

"Last night. Someone dropped a flask of oil and then a torch from the rooftop above. By the time the praetorians inside got the fire under control, the person was long gone, and no one knew, or would say they knew, who it was. All of our men made it out, thankfully, but no arrests are likely to be made."

This was the kind of step up in aggression that Medb was worried about. If they were doing this, it wouldn't be long until someone outright attacked a praetorian or some other civil servant. Claudius was right to worry. They were on the verge of the city exploding in anger.

"Take us to the palace," Medb commanded.

Claudius gave a slight bow and led the way toward the central palace. Now, back on the thoroughfare, there were a few stray stares, probably wondering who the hooded strangers were following a praetorian. They quickly looked away though, Medb noticed, not wanting Claudius or any of the other praetorians patrolling the road to notice them staring.

They crossed a plaza to the left, where a small commotion was starting. A patrol of four praetorians and a man in expensive clothing surrounded a middle-aged woman, her cart of fruits and vegetables overturned. The praetorians looked displeased, but Medb thought, perhaps not at the woman.

"Please," the woman pleaded, "I have a permit. I'm allowed to sell here."

The finely dressed man sneered, kicking one of the fallen vegetables. "New regulations. Your permit is no good anymore."

Claudius took a step toward the guards but was intercepted by Medb's hand grabbing his arm.

"Not yet," she said.

"I can't just ..." he began.

"You can and you will. I'm sure what he's doing is condoned by the governor, or your men wouldn't be backing him. A confrontation now could just as easily cause a riot or embolden rebellious sentiment. Let's get to the palace and deal with the source of the problem."

Claudius frowned but nodded and continued them on their way.

"This happens daily," Claudius complained. "We are given new regulations and rules, written almost as if on a whim, and ordered to enforce them strictly and aggressively."

"We didn't see much of this at the docks," Medb pointed out.

"Some districts get less attention than others. The more affluent areas, near the palace and down at the docks get the least. For the rest, it varies which district is targeted, but it's always heavy-handed and oppressive."

"Has the governor seen what's happening down here?"

"I doubt it. He rarely leaves the palace these days, and when he does, it is rare that he ventures down here. When he does travel, he makes us clear the streets, claiming fear of 'dissident elements,' so there is no one *for* him to see."

"How has he let it come to this," Cormac said. "I should have him sent back home and tell my father how he has been mismanaging things. This is the most prestigious post any of our people have been given in the Empire and was a sign of Ulaid's importance to the Empire. He's blackening not only his name, but my people's name as well."

"We will play it carefully. Yes, there is enough here to have him recalled home, but he didn't get to this point by accident. He has friends who have to be at least soothed. We need a big enough single incident to show his ineptness, before we have him marched home in chains."

Cormac didn't seem pleased, but gave a slight nod to his wife, in deference. She reached out and gently squeezed his arm, a rare sign of public affection, even one as tame as that. Unlike many men, he never doubted her abilities or looked down on her. In addition, he'd matured significantly since they'd been wed, becoming an effective partner. She'd worked hard to train him properly, and she was pleased with the results.

This wasn't going to be the last time they dealt with something like this, however, and he needed to learn patience for this type of work. She'd come to realize, over the past five years, that in an Empire, spread out like they were, graft was impossible to stop. It was more about plugging the largest holes than eliminating it altogether.

"It's gotten very bad, my lady. The people are restless, angry. But it's hard to tell how much of it is genuine sentiment to push us out and restore Carthage to independence, and how much is just blowback from Governor Eoghan's policies."

"Is there any sign of outside influence?" Medb asked.

"I don't know. It seems sporadic and unorganized, but a smart planner could use that to their advantage. Without evidence of a central group or agitating figure, it's hard to tell."

He wasn't wrong. This was the exact situation a foreign agent could use to their advantage. More so if there were legitimate grievances they could play on. A volatile public didn't take much to push it into acts of rebellion.

"I see," she said, thinking. "We will have to start dealing with this and find out."

"It's been made worse by the drawdown of my praetorians. I have half the number I had a month ago and the governor's men still draw the same number as before, leaving me very few to actually patrol the city. We've had to reduce the size of patrols to sometimes only two or three men. Making them small enough that, if the unrest gets worse, they would be vulnerable."

"Yes, we only just heard about the redeployment when we stopped in Kalb. I'm certain the Empress has good reason for it. This war she and the Consul saw coming in the east ... it will mean difficulties for us all."

Claudius bowed his head slightly in acceptance, but clearly was not happy about it. She didn't blame him, but this was the burden of command. Sometimes, you did not have the luxury of the choice you would prefer.

When they arrived at the palace, they left Claudius behind, sending the praetorian off to his duties. If Eoghan wasn't a complete idiot, maybe he would figure out that Claudius was the one who summoned them, but she thought it best not to tie him so specifically to their arrival.

They climbed the steps of the palace, stopping as the two praetorians guarding the front entry stiffened, preparing to bar their way. Another concerning move, Medb thought. If the very seat of government itself was closed to those seeking admittance, where were the people who needed redress of their grievances supposed to go? Was there any mistake this fool wasn't willing to commit?

Medb slowed, falling in step behind Cormac, who straightened and moved in front of her as she did so, understanding what she wanted him to do. Another sign that she had made the right decision in keeping him. Except for rare cases, such as Claudius, men tended to respond better to other men, and Medb wasn't beyond using Cormac as her messenger, if needed. He knew what questions to ask, and the more she was overlooked, the more room she had to maneuver.

Stopping in front of the guards, Cormac pulled off his hood, with Medb following suit. One of the guard's expression didn't change, but the other one certainly did, standing more erect in a posture of attention.

"Prince Cormac," the guard stammered in a distinctly Ulaid accent. "We were not expecting you."

"Because I did not want our arrival announced," Cormac replied. "I need to see the governor. Now."

The man looked at his fellow guard before saying, "Of course, my prince. Please, follow me."

The guard led them into the palace, through the halls toward the audience chamber. Medb hadn't been in the palace for several years, but she couldn't help but notice some of the damage done at the end of the war, with legionnaires and civilians looking for valuables or souvenirs before the area was fully occupied and secured.

They were swiftly ushered inside the former emperor's palace, now serving as the regional center of governance. As they traversed the opulent halls, Medb observed the surroundings with a critical eye. The palace appeared to have been restored to its former glory, with even the most intricate details meticulously replaced. It was evident that Eoghan had spared no expense for his lavish lifestyle, and had used either forced labor or Empire funds to do it.

The throne and the dais were gone; even Eoghan wasn't foolish enough to use those, but the room was otherwise as extravagant as it had been before the fall of Carthage, with a not-quite-throne set up in the large audience area at the far end of the room, backed by tapestries and finery. A stark contrast to the near simplicity of Lucilla's own audience chamber.

Which had been one of the things Medb had actually liked early on about the Empress.

The other guard must have set off at a run to inform the governor of their arrival, because Eoghan burst in from the door near the 'throne' a moment after they entered.

"Prince Cormac, Lady Medb!" he said, a little short of breath. "I had no idea you were coming. Why was I not informed?"

"The Empire does not answer to you, Eoghan," Cormac said, his voice commanding in a way that forced Medb to repress a smile. "In fact, it works the other way around. You serve at the pleasure of the Empress. She does not serve you."

Eoghan's face reddened slightly, but he quickly composed himself. "Of course, my prince. I simply meant that had I known of your arrival, I would have arranged a proper welcome befitting your status."

"The welcome I want to see is a properly run territory, *Governor*. Something I have yet to see after touring Carthage."

"I'm sorry, I stated my question wrongly. I am simply surprised to see you and was wondering what I can do to help you and your ... wife."

Medb almost reached out to grab Cormac, who heard the slight pause and started to tense up, but he pulled himself under control. Another sign of his maturation. She was used to being referred to in that way. It's why she preferred to stay in Rome, where everyone treated all Ulaid the same, unlike those from her homeland, who very often treated her with contempt.

"We've received troubling reports about the city that contradict the official accounts you've been sending, and have come to investigate those discrepancies and correct the management issues plaguing Carthage."

"Who told you my reports were lies? I assure you, my prince, I have been nothing but faithful in my duties. Whoever you've spoken to must have a grievance against me, besmirching my name. I have been nothing but faithful in my duties."

"It doesn't matter who told us of the situation, only that it exists. We toured the city before coming here, and from what I've seen, the only lies spoken have been by you, Eoghan," Cormac said, not raising his voice, but taking a calculated step toward the governor with each point, his hand going to his belt near the sword, but not actually gripping its hilt. "Guard shacks burned to the ground; threats painted on public walls? I don't remember these in any of your reports. I also saw a number of decrees about permits and businesses closed by order of the governor. I familiarized myself with your mandate thoroughly before we sailed here, and I do not remember that being part of it. Nor do I remember reading about guards barring the way to the government center. So, I am the one asking the questions here. Questions about your decisions and what the hell you were thinking."

By the time Cormac stopped listing off Eoghan's failures, he was practically standing over him, the governor slowly backing up to avoid Cormac's rage.

Good. Very good. She'd taught him that, how to use his body to intimidate more subtly, instead of just beating his chest and screaming like so many men did. Intimidation was about presence and the threat of violence, not just going straight to violence itself. You wanted your target to think about what might happen, not react out of instinct.

"Minor problems, my prince, and none that should trouble you. The fires are a temporary problem that I am already dealing with, which is why there is increased security in the city. We were unsure if these people would damage more government facilities, which is why we put it under guard and why I've enacted the decrees. If we can just stamp out their support, the handful of dissidents will wither and die."

"You've closed down strings of businesses! I saw an entire street of shops all but deserted, each with a notice that they were shut down by your order. This seems like quite a lot of effort to catch a few dissidents, don't you think? And what place do these new tax collection officials, who are reporting to you directly instead of the interim city council, have in your mandate? Or these permits that they continually change again and again, requiring people to pay taxes not levied by the city council."

"I assure you, my prince, these measures were necessary to maintain order and stability in the city. Anyone being assessed fines are likely troublemakers, or at least their sympathizers."

"From what we saw, it is fairly widespread. We saw a lot of signs of these crackdowns. Are you trying to tell me that the unrest is so widespread that this is what's needed to suppress it? That does not sound minor or limited."

"I ... that's not ..." Eoghan stammered.

"It's not what?" Cormac said, interrupting him. "Limited? Because I understand your cells are crowded with just average people, who get no trial and are allowed to waste away, while the wealthier sections of the city remain untouched. Is restricting the movement around the city to certain sections of the city part of it being limited? A restriction I will note is again, only for the poorer sections of the city."

"I'm just trying to keep peace in the city," Eoghan said, agitated, clearly trying to find a way out of the sudden, unexpected attack he found himself under.

"Peace?" Cormac scoffed. "You're not keeping peace; you're creating a powder keg waiting to explode. Your actions are making the situation worse, not better."

Eoghan's face flushed red. "With all due respect, my prince, I have been governing this city for years. I know what it takes to maintain order."

"Do you? Because from what I've seen, you're doing the exact opposite. You're suppressing the people, not addressing their concerns. You're creating resentment, not loyalty."

"I'm doing what needs to be done to keep the Empire's interests secure."

"By alienating the very people we're supposed to be protecting and governing? It is clear what we heard in Devnum was accurate, and we are here in the Empress's name, as well as my father's, to set things right."

The governor opened his mouth to protest, but Cormac cut him off with a sharp gesture.

"Lady Medb and I will be staying in Carthage for the foreseeable future. We will be sitting in on your meetings, your audiences, and correcting the mistakes you've made. It's time to start undoing the damage you've caused."

Eoghan's face paled. "But my prince, I assure you that's not necessary. I have everything under control."

"Clearly, you don't. If you did, we wouldn't be here, would we?"

Cormac turned his back on Eoghan, who was opening and closing his mouth like a fish, stuck in a loop, trying to figure some way out of his predicament.

Cormac turned to a nearby attendant, who had been hovering uncertainly at the edge of the room. "Prepare rooms for Lady Medb and myself. We'll be staying in the palace."

The attendant bowed deeply. "Of course, my prince. Right away."

As the attendant scurried off, Cormac turned back to Eoghan, who looked like he had swallowed something sour.

"I expect your full cooperation, Governor. We have a lot of work to do."

With that, Cormac turned on his heel and strode out of the audience chamber, leaving a nervous Eoghan behind. Medb fell into step beside him.

"Well done, husband," she said. "I think you made quite an impression."

Cormac glanced at her, a hint of a smile tugging at his lips. "I learned from the best."

Yes, he had. And he'd been an excellent student.

Chapter 8

Factorium

Lucilla was back in Factorium. Once again she was happy that the train line had been installed, making this a quick morning visit and back home by mid-afternoon.

Hortensius was away, dealing with an ore supplier that had significantly slowed its output, but Lucilla's main goal was to talk to Sorantius. The chemist had a habit of getting overly focused in his workshop, failing to report on his progress, which was very much needed as the war started to heat up.

The city, always busy, had been kicked into high gear, as Hortensius had started saying lately. People were everywhere, carts and wagons delivering supplies and finished products, and workers going in every direction. Lucilla was happy the city was taking the war seriously.

It was so busy that her arrival didn't disrupt the crowd, drawing attention as she normally did. Her guards had to actually clear the way for her to keep people at a safe distance, more concerned about her being run over by the crowd than by someone attacking her.

Reaching the primary chemical plant, she and her guards had taken only a handful of steps inside when a young assistant, wearing one of the ubiquitous leather aprons and arm coverings found in the chemical plant, came running up to her, bowing deeply.

"Your Majesty, this is unexpected."

Lucilla frowned. She had sent a telegraph message communicating that she was coming, and this lack of preparedness spoke to the disorganization in Sorantius's domain. Workers tended to reflect their leader, exemplified by this miscommunication and sloppiness that would not have happened in one of Hortensius's factories.

"I need to speak to Sorantius."

"Certainly, Your Majesty. Please follow me," he said, bowing again.

The assistant escorted her through the crowded factory full of large vats and cauldrons and packed with employees. Passing through one of the several barriers that separated sections, mostly for protection in case of an accident rather than organization, they found Sorantius near a large drying table of some kind.

Even with the entourage following her, the chief chemist didn't seem to notice her right away.

"Master Sorantius," the assistant said, prodding his boss and pointing to Lucilla. "Her Majesty, the Empress, is here to see you."

Sorantius looked up from his workbench, at first annoyed, the information clearly not registering right away, before his eyes widened in surprise. He quickly set down what he'd been working on and wiped his hands on his apron.

"Your Majesty, I'm surprised to see you here."

"Really?" she asked, a little annoyed. "I telegraphed ahead to let you know I was coming. I am surprised the message did not reach you."

"You did?" he asked, looking around as if he might find the message right next to him somewhere.

"I did. Sorantius, I appreciate your brilliance in this area, but you have been lacking in reporting and communication for some time. I know how you get absorbed in your work, but you need a factory manager of some type to help run your domain and keep things on schedule."

"Your Majesty, I'm not sure ..."

"I'm sure I didn't word that as a suggestion, Sorantius."

"Yes ... of course. Of course, Your Majesty. I will ... umm ..."

"Talk to Hortensius and get his assistance in finding the right fit for you. I will mention to him that you will be coming for advice once he returns."

"Certainly," Sorantius said, clearly none too pleased.

While the two were certainly not adversaries, both defended their domains rabidly and did not like the other intruding. She didn't have time to address their feelings in this regard. The train may have made visiting faster, but many of her visits could be eliminated by properly sent reports.

"Good. Since we have not been informed of your progress so far, I came to check on it myself. Specifically, on the nitrocellulose production Ky gave you instructions for before we left for Gaul."

"We did encounter some difficulties initially, Your Majesty, but I assure you, we've made significant progress in resolving them."

"What kind of difficulties?"

"Heat. The Consul's directions were very detailed and, while it was complicated in some places, we were able to follow them and replicate the process laid out in the blueprints. However, we have had significant problems with temperature regulation, as this process seems much more sensitive to heat than the other formulations we worked on in the past. Once the reaction starts, it generates a significant amount of heat, which then causes the nitrocellulose to break down, making it all but worthless."

"Wasn't this mentioned in the instructions, the need to control the temperature?"

"It was, but once the reaction started, it wasn't clear how we could lower the heat and it was hard to determine how bad the problem was until it was out of control."

"*This is an error I have been concerned about for some time,*" Sophus said in Lucilla's ear. "*As we begin to push further into more complex, reactive formulations, heat was always going to be an issue and we have yet to devise a properly functional thermometer capable of measuring those reactions. I will speak to the commander about options for dealing with this issue, as it will only get worse as we increase the complexity of formulations.*"

Lucilla listened to him but gave no reaction, keeping her focus on Sorantius.

"However, I believe I have come up with a solution to this problem that seems, at the moment, to be working."

"Ohh?" Lucilla asked.

Sophus had already started listing off possible solutions they could give him. The chemist was very good at his job, but he tended to be more workmanlike than Hortensius, following instructions more than experimenting with variations. So his offering a solution was a surprise.

Sorantius waved for her to follow, leading her and her retinue to a new section of the factory. He stopped in front of what looked to be a complicated setup. A large vat was crisscrossed with copper tubing, in a loop, one side toward a cistern and the other toward a trough coming through the wall and filled with water, which then returned to the tube-covered vat.

"He's created a water-cooling system," Sophus said.

"You've implemented a water-cooling system," Lucilla said, repeating Sophus's words.

"Yes!" Sorantius said excitedly. "You see it right off. We run these pipes over the mixing vat with cooled water, which allows it to exchange some of the heat from the vat itself with the water in the cooling pipes, which we then shunt off to a holding cistern. From there, it slowly runs through our water intake, which is generally very cold, and then back to the vat to start the process over again. We have these valves, here and here, that allow us to control the flow of water or, of course, shut it off when we are not processing the sulfuric and nitric acids together."

"Why not just run it from the vat to the water intake and back?"

"It was picking up enough heat to not be cooled off sufficiently by the time it made the round trip. We needed it to drop some of the heat first, to allow the stream water to bring it below room temperature, which is why we add to the top and pull from the bottom. The water pressure created by the cistern filling pushes the water up and creates pressure through the process, although we have a steam pump connected to help it get started."

"That's very clever," Lucilla said.

"Thank you, although it's still very difficult. If we cool it off too much, the reaction can be stopped, ruining the batch, and obviously, it's hard to tell how hot it is. We're still in the trial-and-error phase, I'm afraid. Small-degree changes are causing the nitrocellulose to either break down or become volatile. It will take time to find the precise temperature for maximum potency."

"Of course. I'm still very impressed with what you came up with. I will message the Consul and discuss the problems you're having with him to see if he has any thoughts for you."

"If that were possible, Your Majesty, it would be excellent."

"What other projects have you been working on?" Lucilla asked.

"They are all either on or ahead of schedule. We've had successful batches of saline, which was relatively straightforward to achieve, only leaving us to work out the process of scaling up production. The chemical the Consul called 'ether,' however, has proven far more challenging, especially when it comes to storage."

"How so?"

"It's highly volatile, evaporates quickly at room temperature and is extremely flammable. We've repurposed some of the containers the Consul designed for acids to prevent it from escaping or igniting. That seems to be working, but we are currently limiting the production to small batches, leaving the ether to sit for a time to test its long-term effectiveness."

"It sounds like you are handling your assignments well and everything is on task. I will send over what notes the Consul has for how to better control temperature and talk to him about your storage issues as well. Until then, keep up the good work. And please see to getting that manager. I would hate to have to come see you to get another update."

"Certainly, Your Majesty. I'll take care of it."

"Good man," she said.

Eastern Germania

Ky lay on his cot, staring at the canvas ceiling of his tent. The pain in his side had dulled to a persistent ache. His frustration, however, had only gotten worse. Sophus had only woken him a few hours ago, pulling him out of the medical coma he'd been in to allow his system to repair the massive damage done by the bullet more quickly.

That should have been good news. It meant he was out of any serious danger and would be up and moving in a week or two. Unfortunately, there was not a lot of cause for celebration. As soon as he'd woken, Sophus had told him he had to remain prostrate and still; Ky had sent his drone out of the tent to get a look at what was going on.

The first thing he'd noticed was that their position had changed from the more rugged ground near the Urals to the thicker forests further west. Another legion had joined them, but they'd continued to retreat, with the Easterners close on their heels. He'd watched a short skirmish that morning as his army's rear guard pushed back their pursuers to allow the wounded and supplies to put more distance between them.

His men had done well, fighting exactly as they had been taught and had given the enemy a bloody nose when they'd gotten too close, but it had been costly all the same.

While it had been the right call when faced with cavalry and massed infantry attacks, Napoleonic-era tactics with tightly packed men firing in volleys weren't going to work here. Not when the enemy was using the same tactics against him with the same weapons. That would only result in the larger force winning.

Ky had issued orders changing their standard fighting style, and Ursinus was already putting the men through whatever training they could provide as the retreat continued. They would, for now, try to fight on the defensive, in looser sections. They still had to be somewhat tightly packed, due to the slow-firing nature of rifled muskets, but they could at least do it from cover, instead of marching in the open. They also could stop using volley fire and switch to isolated, targeted fire from cover, if they weren't worried about infantry charges. It would make them more vulnerable to cavalry, but so far, it appeared to him that the enemy was more infantry-focused.

For now, the enemy had pulled back for the night, creating a mile gap between their forces. Ursinus was still being cautious, running heavy patrols to ensure he knew where the enemy was, but even through heavy forest, Sophus was able to read the heat signatures and pick out most of the men, and they were in the clear for the time being.

More than anything, though, he was frustrated. Frustrated that he'd misjudged the enemy so badly. Frustrated that he was stuck in the tent. Frustrated that there seemed to be little choice but to continue retreating.

Ky was pulled out of his thoughts when he received a ping in his head. One he'd been waiting for. Ky had wanted to talk to Lucilla since he woke, but she'd been pressed for time all day and hadn't been able to get away to talk to him.

"Ky?" her voice came through the communicator, echoing in his head.

"Yes, my love. I'm here."

"How are you?"

"Alive. Stuck in this damn tent."

"I received a report from Ursinus this morning. It's from a few days ago, but it sounds like things are bad."

"Bad is an understatement. We're bleeding men every day, on a non-stop retreat. It's a disaster."

"I thought Marcus's legion had joined you?"

"He has, but the enemy has also been reinforced and each clash is leaving a mounting death toll. And there's not a damn thing I can do about it yet."

"Bomilcar should have the last mobile legions to you in a day or two. That should let you at least stop the retreat for now. And recruits are starting to pour into the training camps in Germania. I think now that the war has started, they're realizing how serious this is."

"Too late, as always."

"You know how these things go, Ky. But we're making progress on getting more men into the field and the weapons programs here are starting to pick up steam. We'll make it through this."

"Maybe," Ky said.

He wasn't trying to be so negative, but it was hard not to be, stuck here watching his men die.

"Not maybe, Ky. *We will.* If you have to figure out a new way to fight this war, to change our tactics to match this new way of fighting, then that's what you'll do."

"Yeah," Ky said, knowing he was being stubborn hanging on to his negativity, but unable to push past it. "How are things at home?"

She didn't answer right away and he knew she was considering if she was going to let him distract her by changing subjects, instead of continuing to press him.

"Progressing. Recruitment has been slow here, but Gaul and Germania have both exceeded their targets, so we're still on track. Sorantius is on track and Hortensius tells me he should be ready for his first fuse trials next week. If successful, we should be able to start production of shells in a few weeks. He's also stepped-up production of the howitzer-style cannon significantly, to ensure you have enough once the new shells are ready."

"Good. I don't know how long it will take them to copy us, but we really need to start getting a technological advantage over the enemy. Victorian era tactics may have worked against the Carthaginians, but they lead us into meat grinders against an equally armed enemy."

"I'm not sure what that means, but I know you'll figure out how to change it to something that will work," she said.

"Yeah. Any word on Italia?"

"Nothing so far about what the problem is. I'm starting to think the Italians can't get this done themselves."

"Send Llassar to work it out," Ky suggested. "He's got the experience at diplomacy, is forceful enough to make something happen, and if there are outside influences at work he'll find them."

"He's planning on retiring soon," Lucilla said. "He's been spending much of his time at home in Caledonia."

"I know, and I wouldn't suggest this if it wasn't important, but we need Italia's manpower and supplies. They are going to be on the front line of this soon, because there is no way Greece survives the enemy invasion. Not with the small number of muskets they've been allowed to purchase. We need Italia to be ready to defend itself, and that means unification."

"I'll talk to him," Lucilla said. "I also heard from Medb. Carthage is worse than she was told. She thinks the city is ready to fall into outright revolt, although she can't say if it's pure mismanagement or something worse."

"Are you sure it's a good idea to trust her on this?" Ky asked.

Although Ky had made the suggestion of marrying her into the Ulaid family, he'd never grown to trust her. Even over the five years of peace, he'd remained skeptical of the former queen. He knew Lucilla did and trusted her judgment, but it still concerned him every time she talked about handing Medb power.

"I am. She's proved herself, Ky. Again and again. Or do you not remember the assassination attempt."

He did. Three years prior there had been a fairly concerted attempt on Lucilla's life by a group of mostly Roman businessmen, who were unhappy with the continued pressing of shipping and production taxes, and wanted more punitive measures against allies on the continent who were competing with them financially. Medb had uncovered the plot and had her agents dig out every one of the conspirators before tearing their group apart.

"This is different, but I'll trust your judgment."

"Good. Don't worry, we'll have more men to you soon."

"Now I just have to figure out what to do with them, other than just wasting their lives needlessly," Ky said.

Devnum

"Find Llassar, and if he's awake," Lucilla said, opening the doors to her quarters, "bring him here."

The guard frowned but nodded and hurried away to carry out her orders. She knew tongues might wag as she shut the door. She found proper clothes to wear, preparing to greet Llassar without making it seem too scandalous. Although tongues would wag nonetheless, an older unmarried man being called to the chambers of a married woman at this time of night, but she didn't care. Those who knew her, and more importantly, knew Llassar, wouldn't believe any of it, and those who didn't would believe anything about her, and it didn't matter what she did.

There had been dozens of well-traveled rumors about her being some kind of temptress, luring ex-gladiators and legionnaires to satisfy her insatiable whims while destroying the Consul's manhood. There were always those who tried to diminish her. She could stand the gossip.

It took a little while, long enough she feared he'd left the city, but eventually there was a knock at the door, which opened a moment later admitting a tired-looking Llassar. His hair and beard had gone mostly gray over the last few years, and he'd lost some of his impressive muscle as he aged, but he was as energetic as ever.

"You summoned me, Empress?"

Lucilla noticed Modius left her door standing open, perhaps trying to protect her reputation. Normally, she chafed at his doting, but she'd let it pass this time. They weren't talking about anything sensitive, so the door could remain open.

Not that it would stop the gossip.

"I did. I'm sorry for the late summons, but we have an issue in Italia, and it has reached the point where we need to intervene and push things forward. I received a telegram from Ky not long ago suggesting that perhaps you were the right person for the job. And I agree."

"Problems with unification?"

"Yes. Specifically, problems with Sardinia. Several merchant factions on the island are vehemently opposed to joining the mainland tribes and are shutting down any talks about it almost as soon as they start up."

"Why not simply let Sardinia stand on its own then? If they don't consider themselves part of Italia, perhaps it's best to respect that."

"Normally, I might agree. The mainland and Sicilia have all but agreed to unification, and mostly along our recommended lines, but Sardinia is holding out, and the rest of Italia is holding off to see if they can't convince the islanders that it's in their best interest to join. Time is not a luxury we have. The eastern threat grows by the day. We need Italia unified and committed to the

Western Alliance as soon as possible, giving us access to their manpower and supplies in time to do us some good."

"And you think it's possible to get the Sardinians to change their minds?" Llassar asked.

"The Italians think so, at least. I hope that if we give them a push, it might get things moving. Or at least tell us more specifically what the issue is. There seems to be a lot of deep-seated tension between the mainlanders and the Sardinians that I hope is all that is making this difficult."

"But you think it could be something else?"

"I always think there could be a conspiracy, but the fact that we are having issues with unrest in Carthage and now Sardinia, it feels like more than just a coincidence. Either way, it's why I want someone there. You specifically."

"I'm flattered by your confidence, Empress, but surely there's someone better suited for this task. I'm just an old warrior, after all."

"Nonsense. You've been handling diplomacy for the Empire ever since our first major contacts with the Ulaid. You guided Cormac in Hispania and helped arrange our final alliance there, and you ended a potential war between Gaul and Hispania two years ago without any bloodshed or losing either as an ally. You have been incredibly valuable to the Empire and shown that you have a true ability for this type of assignment."

"Those were different situations, Your Majesty. We were at war for two of them and the third nearly became a war, putting it much closer to my ability. This is straight tribal politics."

"First off, you might not have noticed, but we are at war again. And this is no different than you helping Talogren negotiate the original Caledonia League or getting the tribes of Hispania together. Yes, Cormac was there, but we both know your advice played a big part in that."

"The original Caledonian League was not so much diplomacy as conquest."

"Which is another reason I want you to go. We don't know what is happening and if someone is behind the scenes causing problems, that might be an eventuality. No, you are absolutely the best person for this assignment. Ky thinks so, and so do I."

"I appreciate that, Your Majesty, but I must confess, I'm tired. I served Talogren for nearly my entire life, and the Empire for the last seven years. I'm an old man, something most warriors never achieve. I was hoping to retire soon, to live out my final days at home in peace. A reward for my years of service."

"You're not nearly as old as you like to put on, my friend. I've seen you training and you are nearly as strong as you always were. People are living much longer these days, with our advancements in medical science, and you've got plenty of good years left in you."

"Perhaps, but the desire for a quiet life remains."

"I understand, truly I do, and I wouldn't ask this of you if it wasn't absolutely crucial. We need Italia and its people, Llassar. And for the Italians to join us, they need Sardinia. The enemy is already in Greece, and they have yet to request our help. We can stop them at the borders of Germania, but to truly hold them, we need Italia's border secure as well. We need them in this alliance, and to make that happen, we need you. It's that simple."

Llassar dropped his head with a heavy sigh. Lucilla knew she was pouring it on thick, putting an unfair amount of pressure on him, but regardless of what she wanted to do, it was absolutely what she needed to do.

"Very well," he said, finally lifting his head. "I'll do as you ask."

"Thank you, Llassar. I knew we could count on you, even when you wish I couldn't."

He gave a wry laugh at that, as she escorted him to the open door.

"Please get what supplies and staff you need. I will arrange for a ship to take you in two days' time. I know that's fast, but it's how things *must* be."

"I'll be ready," he said with a nod, before turning and walking briskly out the way he came in, again belying his claims of being too old for the position.

Now, she just hoped there was actually something he could do to move the situation along.

Chapter 9

Outside Factorium

Hortensius scrutinized the percussion cap and fuse assembly inside the cone of the shell. His calloused hands, stained with grease and gunpowder, made minute adjustments as he muttered under his breath. Around him, his team of assistants peered over his shoulder as he finished examining their work.

"The wire seems to be under a lot of tension," Hortensius said, pointing at the device inside the nose of the shell.

The setup was actually quite simple. A percussion cap with a wire above it holding a striker. The theory, according to the Consul's notes, was that on impact, the wire would bend enough to allow the striker to hit the percussion cap, which would, in turn, detonate the gunpowder in the body of the shell. A wooden dowel extended from the side to a grooved, circular piece of the shell body. When turned in one direction, it held the striker in place, so it didn't get jostled and hit the percussion cap while in transport.

To Hortensius's eye, however, it looked as if the wire was too taut and did not have a lot of give to it.

"The ranges in the Consul's notes were imprecise, or at least were very wide," one of his aides said. "There were notes that said we would have to make adjustments based on testing, as the quality of the gunpowder made it impossible to estimate the exact tension needed. We were concerned that the initial kick of the round being fired would be enough to cause it to strike prematurely, so we opted for the high end of his range."

"But it should be enough to go off upon impact, yes?"

"We believe so," the aide said.

Hortensius did not find his tone convincing, but that was what this test was for, after all.

"Well, I guess there's one way to find out," he said, stepping back.

His men quickly reassembled the shell and carried it to the waiting howitzer, which had been designed to fire remotely using a pull cord and fuse assembly of its own, with the men in a trench quite a distance away for safety. Carrying the round to the weapon, they turned the safety wedge at the front, which would allow the striker to hang free, and slid the shell into the artillery tube before running back to join him and the rest of the observers in the observation trench.

"Now's the moment of truth," he said as another assistant gathered up the pull cord and looked to him for approval.

There was a brief moment of silence after the assistant tugged the rope; then the cannon boomed and the round sailed downrange. Hortensius viewed the landing area through one of the newest spyglasses, watching as the shell smashed into the ground, sending up a geyser of dirt and debris.

And then nothing.

They all waited, watching the round sit there, half-buried in the dirt, doing nothing. Hortensius lowered his spyglass and turned to his assistants, a rare frown on his face.

"I don't know what happened," the aide said, looking past him nervously at where the test shell sat, unexploded.

"Someone's got to go retrieve it so we can examine it to determine what happened," Hortensius said.

The men all looked at each other. They knew he was right, but none of them wanted to be the one to actually go out and retrieve the weapon. The safety was removed and it had impacted. There was no telling how unstable the round was.

After a long stretch of everyone trying to avoid his gaze, Hortensius said, "Fine, I'll do it myself."

Instantly, his team erupted in protest.

"No, you can't. It's too risky and you're too important," one of his assistants said.

"I appreciate that, but someone has to check on the round, and if no one else will do it, it's my project, so I am responsible," he said, turning to walk up the ramp out of the trench.

"I'll do it," one of the younger men on the team said, pushing past him.

Hortensius couldn't help but feel a twinge of guilt. They were all good men and he knew he was pushing them so that one of them would put himself in danger.

But it had to be done.

The lad made his way through the testing field, past craters and divots from past tests, cautious as he approached the unexploded shell. The men around Hortensius all seemed to hold their breath, waiting to see if their young friend would be ripped to pieces if the shell finally exploded.

But it didn't. He reached the shell and knelt beside it. Hortensius hadn't been specific, but he was a smart lad and began disassembling it there, instead of trying to haul the entire shell, and the danger it represented, back with him. They watched as his hands moved over the shell, removing its cap carefully before finally standing up and lugging the heavy metal nose of the projectile back with him.

The boy was covered in sweat when he made his way back, and Hortensius was sure it wasn't just from the exertion.

"Let's have a look," he said as they sat the artillery cap in front of him.

The wire had bowed slightly, but not enough for the striker to hit, dangling just above the primer cap.

"Well, that doesn't work, does it? It looks like we went a little too far on the amount of tension we put on the wire."

"No, Master Hortensius, it doesn't," an aide said. "We can adjust it now and try again."

"You don't have any of the precision tools with us to do that," Hortensius pointed out.

"I think I can get it to the correct balance," the man said.

Hortensius considered it. There was a risk there, for sure, but the setup was specifically the way it was because testing any new shells was dangerous. And taking it back to the shop and retooling the test shells and trying to test them internally would add more days. If they could get it right now, they could move it to production faster, and get the new shells out to the Consul in time to be useful.

"Fine. Go ahead."

The young man pulled out tools and began working on the shell cap, removing the striker and wire, putting in a new wire and carefully adjusting the tension, testing it with his finger and adjusting it several times. It was slow, careful work, and the man stayed amazingly focused, considering his boss plus many of his peers were watching him closely.

"Done," he said, stepping back.

"Good. Attach it to a new shell and let's test it."

The men all sprang into action, reattaching the shell cap and securing it, making sure the safety screw was in place and set. Hortensius stayed where he was, letting his men work, carrying the shell back over to the howitzer, unlocking the safety, and sliding it into place.

The Consul had said that there were better methods for both detonation and more stable gunpowder that would make something like the safety mechanism unnecessary, but as it was, there was real worry about a strong jostle bending the wire and setting off the primer. Which could be catastrophic if it was stored with other rounds.

So, for now, they would have to work with this safety mechanism and look forward to days of more reliable munitions.

His men reattached the firing cord and scurried back to the trench, jumping into it and getting into position. Seeing that everyone was ready, his assistant pulled the cord.

It was as if the world exploded as the howitzer literally ripped itself to pieces, the concussive wave knocking some of them back, even though they were standing in the trench. Thankfully, everyone had ducked down, looking downrange, and no one was injured aside from a few bumps and bruises, but Hortensius was sure his ears would be ringing for several days as the sound around him was muted somewhat following the terrific explosion.

"Is everyone alright?" the manufacturer asked, helping some of his men to their feet.

When it was clear that everyone was alright, they hurried out of the trench to examine the gun. The barrel was ripped open like a peeled fruit. It didn't require much to figure out what had happened, all eyes turning to the aide who'd wired the fuse assembly.

"I'm sorry, the tension must have been too light," he said, almost sheepishly.

"It's fine, son," Hortensius said, placing his hand on the man's shoulder. "It might not have been possible to get it exact. I hate to say it, but we are not going to be able to wing our way to a solution, as the Consul likes to say. Let's gather all of this up and take it back to the factory to examine. I believe we're going to have to do a lot more small-scale studies before we attempt to take it to the test phase again."

The men didn't have to be told twice, hopping to their jobs as they began to collect debris so they could, hopefully, reassemble everything and determine at what point the explosion happened, and if the shell had traveled down the tube at all or blown on the instant of contact. They knew how much powder was in the weapon, which meant they should be able to determine how close they had been to getting the projectile out before it exploded, which might give them an idea of the baseline of how far off they were.

What was certain, though, was that the Consul wasn't getting his projectiles anytime soon.

Carthage

It was dark but not really late, and yet the streets of Carthage were almost completely deserted, a sign of the chilling effect of Eoghan's curfews. No one dared stop her, although that was most likely due more to Claudius's presence than her own. While she liked the mystique that her position gave her, and the extra fear it put behind her name, it did make cowing the average praetorian harder.

She didn't bring Claudius along to ease her passage, however. She'd sent him on an errand the day after they arrived in Carthage, and he'd finally come through. Or so she hoped.

"Are you certain this contact of yours is reliable?" Medb asked.

Claudius didn't look at her directly, instead keeping an eye on the patrols marching past. While she suspected part of that was just his professionalism, wanting to make sure his men were living up to the standards he set for them, she was also sure that part of it was concern about what was happening around them.

Since arriving in Carthage, it had become clear just how upset Claudius was about the whole thing, and how little Eoghan valued the praetorian. The governor seemed to think of himself as not only a bureaucratic genius, but as some kind of petty despot, where every aspect of the domain he'd been given to manage was in fact just a plaything of his to do with as he wished.

"As certain as one can be in these times, my lady," he said as he watched his men. "He has reasons to hate the old regime, reasons that align with our interests."

She made a small skeptical noise, but otherwise didn't say anything. She knew Claudius to be a competent soldier and guardsman, but he wasn't used to the kind of work she needed, or the traits required to do it. Until he proved to her that he understood something more than marching and stabbing, she would remain doubtful of his judgment related to cloak-and-dagger activities.

They stopped in front of one of the many shuttered storefronts, Claudius looking up and down the streets before he pushed open the door that should have otherwise been locked. Inside the shop, which looked to have belonged to some sort of tailor before its owner fell under Eoghan's bad graces, the air was stale and heavy.

A small noise came from the darkened back room and Claudius's hand dropped to his sword hilt, only to relax when a thin young man emerged from the shadows. While it was obvious this was who Claudius was looking for, he was not what Medb had been expecting.

For one, the boy was much younger than she anticipated, maybe in his late teens and, at the very least, several years younger than

Cormac. His eyes, however, were those of a much older man. Even in the dim light, she could see how haunted they were, weighed down by a life she could probably never imagine. Although the massive scar down the left side of his face, traveling from chin to temple, did give some ideas as to what he had suffered.

"This is Geral. He's well known with a lot of people in this section of the city and is sympathetic to our goals," Claudius said.

She knew he was being diplomatic. By saying 'this section of the city,' he meant the poor section of the city furthest from the center of government and the wealthy sections that bordered it. Parts of this area didn't even have homes, just open areas filled with tents and hovels. The homes that were here housed five or even six families, each of which included multiple generations of family members. Making the area cramped, noisy, and dirty.

And exactly where a lot of the unrest seemed to be originating from.

"I would rather hear about his sympathies from him," Medb said, keeping her entire focus on the boy.

She needed to find someone soon, but it was critical they met the standards she was looking for. What she needed required not only motivation, but brains and ruthlessness.

Not an easy combination to find.

"What Claudius means is that I hate the former emperor and anyone who ever worked for him. They killed my parents. They killed my brothers and sisters. All because of some imagined slight against the emperor in one of their many purges of the city."

"If they were so ruthless in killing everyone in your family, how is it that you still live?" Medb asked.

"Luck. I'd been sent on an errand by my mother before they came for them and was away from the house. When I came back home, a neighbor stopped me and hid me. I spent the next several years running and hiding, living like a rat, one step ahead of the emperor's thugs."

"Which explains why you hate the former ruler, but not why you are interested in helping us."

"My hatred for them is why I'm here. There are people who'd like nothing more than to see the old empire return, bring it back from the ash heap where it belongs. You people may have gotten rid of most of the regime's leaders, but there were many people who benefited from it and want to see it return. They lived in luxury and have no idea who I am, but I know who they are. Or were. I've met some of them and heard the whispers. Whispers about bringing it all back. I will never let that happen," he said, spitting onto the dusty floorboards. "Not while I still draw breath."

Medb didn't say anything for a moment, just stared at him, her eyes tracing the scar down his face. He'd been through a lot, no doubt.

"You understand what I'm asking will put you in a significant amount of danger."

Geral's lips curled into a bitter smile.

"Danger? I've been living on borrowed time since I was a child. How do you think I got this?" he said, gesturing to the scar.

Other men would have blustered and preened, continuing to try and defend their manhood. Surprisingly, Geral didn't. He glared at her, his annoyance clear, but saying nothing else.

A rare quality in a man, especially a young man.

"Very well. I'm interested in the groups you mentioned. The ones with remnants of the old regime and their sympathizers. I want you to join them and gain their trust."

"You want me to join the very people I despise?"

"That's exactly what I want you to do. I need eyes and ears in their ranks, telling me who they are and what they are doing."

"So I'm just supposed to pretend to be one of them?"

"Yes. In fact, that's all I want you to do. You are to strictly observe and do nothing else to expose yourself. If you're discovered, they'll become more paranoid and getting a second agent in their ranks will become impossible, so I don't want you attempting to disrupt their activities in any way or doing anything else that would reveal yourself. Your sole purpose is to gather information."

"What kind of information?"

"Everything you can find. Who their leaders are, what their plans are, who their members are, what their structure is. Most importantly, though, is that I need to know if there is any indication of connection to the provincial government now in place or any kind of outside influences working with the leaders. Those two are critical."

"What if they ask me to do something ... extreme? Hurt someone, maybe even a praetorian?"

Claudius opened his mouth to respond, but Medb cut him off with a sharp gesture.

"You do it," she said, her voice firm, and eyes locked on his.

Claudius made an almost strangling sound. Medb turned and glared at him, daring the praetorian to speak, before turning back to the boy.

"I want you to listen carefully. I don't care what you have to do to maintain your cover. Hurting or even killing a praetorian would be terrible, make no mistake. But if this rebellion is allowed to grow unchecked, many more will die. Not just praetorians but your neighbors, your friends, everybody in this city."

Geral looked to Claudius, who reluctantly nodded after a moment's hesitation.

"Good. Claudius will arrange a secure location for you to leave messages for us and will tell you how to use ciphers so that your communications can't be read. He'll show you how to signal that there's a message to be picked up or if you need an urgent meeting, although that needs to be used extremely rarely. Every time you meet with us you could be seen, and we can't risk that."

She'd have to explain that to Claudius, but there was time for that. Ramirus had taught her the tradecraft, and she knew it well enough now to teach it to him. Besides, she had things at the government buildings to deal with; she didn't need to be watching for dead drops in the outskirts of the city as well.

The boy was quiet for a minute, seemingly weighing if he was ready for what she was asking. She didn't push him. In situations like this, she needed him to buy in, or he'd fail.

"I understand," he said, finally coming to his decision.

"Good. Don't be too overeager. You know these people, but they clearly know of your history, too. Slowly ingratiate into their midst. Listen to them and their complaints. They'll be biased to believe everybody believes like they do, so just accept it, reluctantly, piece by piece, and they will not question your conversion. If you do it slowly enough, they will even convince themselves that they converted you to the cause, earning your loyalty. Which you can use. Now go. Claudius will meet you here in two days to give you instructions on how to pass information. I don't expect regular updates, but I do expect updates at least once a week. Sooner if you discover something. Until then, just move closer to the group, listening to them. Don't say or offer anything yet."

"I will."

"Good," Medb said. "Now, go."

The boy looked to Claudius once more and then went into the back-room area, presumably which had an exit he'd used to get into the building.

"My lady, perhaps we should discuss ..." Claudius started to say.

"There's nothing to discuss, Claudius," she said, predicting what he was going to say. "This isn't war, where everything is noble and right. This is about results, and you can't fight your way out of this problem. Or would you prefer to see Carthage descend into chaos?"

The praetorian didn't say anything.

"Good. Now, let's get back. I have a lot to teach you if you're going to manage Geral."

Chapter 10

Factorium

"... appreciate it, but I really came to find out how the steamship project is coming along." Lucilla said.

It had been a week since she'd received notice that the fuse test failed, and she hadn't heard from the manufacturer since. She'd sent requests for updates, which had been met not with silence, but with demurs. Which was unusual for Hortensius and enough to prompt Lucilla to visit to see what was happening.

"We are working as fast as we can, Your Majesty. These things take time."

"I understand that, but the Easterners are advancing into Germania at an alarming rate. We need something to stop them, and soon. They will be out of the mountains and onto the plains, where the rivers will give us a chance to block them, but only if we have the ships in place to make it work."

"I appreciate that, Your Majesty, and we really are trying, but it is much more difficult than we'd originally thought it would be. The main issue we're facing is creating a compact, high-pressure boiler that's efficient enough to power a ship. The Consul's plans were thorough, but we've yet to have a successful test."

"Is it really so different from the scaled-down engines we use for trains?"

"Yes and no. The principles are similar, but the scale and application present unique challenges. A ship's engine needs to be much more powerful and more reliable than a locomotive's. Primarily, our issue has been with pressure regulation and fuel efficiency. We've managed to create a boiler that can generate the necessary steam pressure, but maintaining it consistently is proving to be difficult, especially over the distance needed. With trains, we have the luxury of space and proximity. The engine sits close to the boiler, and the power transfer is relatively straightforward. On ships, it's not so simple."

"Why not?"

"On ships, the boiler must be situated deep within the vessel's core to protect it, and we need to transmit that power to the propulsion systems at the ship's extremities. It's a matter of distance and efficiency."

"Couldn't we simply scale up the engine?"

"No, in fact, we need to scale it down, as much as possible. It's a problem of size and weight, especially for river vessels. A larger engine might solve our power transmission issues, but it would render the ships too heavy for shallow waters. It wouldn't be an issue in larger screw-driven ships intended for ocean use, or even in the larger rivers, but for the paddle wheel design needed for the smaller rivers, it just doesn't work. If I had my preference, I'd concentrate on the screw design. It has broader applications, including ocean-going vessels. However ... that's not possible."

"That's fine. But we need to accelerate the progress you're making. I know that's asking a lot, and you're already pushing as hard as you can, but we need to begin building a technological advantage over these people, and we cannot wait until the end of summer to do it."

"I understand, Your Majesty, and I will push my people to go faster, but I am not willing to compromise on the quality of the work. Sending faulty equipment to the Consul is no better than sending nothing at all."

"That's fine, but please go as quickly as possible," Lucilla said. "What about your other projects? Any progress?"

"I messaged you about the fuse failure."

"You did. Have you come to any conclusions since your report?"

"Only that it continues to be a challenge. We're struggling to find the right balance of sensitivity. Too sensitive, and they're unsafe to transport. Too stable, and they won't detonate on impact. We're aiming for that sweet spot in the middle, but it's proving elusive. We continue to work on it and understand that it, too, is a priority."

"Very well. So I guess I will just wait patiently to hear of your success," Lucilla said, a little more bitingly than she intended.

She knew that Hortensius was doing his best and understood how important these advances were, but she needed something. Aside from promises, both here and from the allies, little forward momentum had been achieved, which left Ky dangling dangerously unsupported in the east. She needed to do something to help him, and she needed to do it soon.

"Not everything has been a failure. We do have one success to report."

"Really?" Lucilla asked, perking up. "What?"

"Come with me."

He led her across the compound to the cluster of buildings dedicated to chemical research, finding Sorantius inside, bent over a workbench as always, oblivious to their approach.

"Sorantius," Hortensius called out. "I brought Her Majesty to see the hydrogen tanks."

The chemist looked up, blinking as if emerging from a trance, his expression becoming excited as the words finally registered. "Of course. Of course. This way, Your Majesty."

He guided them to a series of large, cylindrical containers connected by an intricate network of pipes.

"These tanks," Sorantius explained, "are designed to capture and store the gas the Consul called hydrogen. Actually, we were already creating it as a byproduct of other processes, but it is odorless and colorless, and light enough that it floats away instantly, so we had no idea of its existence until the Consul explained it to us. With these tanks, we can now redirect the hydrogen as needed, although aside from adding it to a few other chemicals, I'm not sure what the Consul needs it for."

Lucilla wasn't sure either, but Ky had said it would be important, so she didn't question it.

"I remember there being something in the instructions about portable containers."

"We've made progress there as well," Hortensius interjected. "We've developed prototypes that can be filled from these larger tanks. However, we're still in the testing phase, checking for potential leaks or corrosion issues."

"I'm pleased you two have made progress on this," Lucilla said. "I would have liked something more immediately useful, but that does not mean I don't recognize the work you've both put in."

"We understand, Your Majesty, and we will continue to push as hard as we can to get you the results you need."

Sorantius looked a little perplexed at how the conversation had turned, but nodded along nonetheless.

"Good. I have faith in both of you to come through for us."

Now, she just had to hope it didn't take too long for her faith to be proven out.

West of the Horn of Africa

Valdar had made the trip around the horn of Africa a dozen times, and had learned to both appreciate and, to some degree, mitigate its dangers. And yet now, as they neared the bottom of the continent once again, he was as nervous as he had been the first time, when he had sailed into uncharted waters.

He and all of his men had been on edge ever since leaving Port Kalb and starting the trip south. Weeks of anxious, nervous sailing wasn't good for a man, and yet there was nothing he could do to stop it. There was a fleet out there somewhere. Supposedly a large one, and he was hoping to stumble across it.

Worse than his concern of what would happen when he did find the enemy was the more catastrophic outcome ... if he did not. That their fleets, and Valdar had no doubt they were out here, might sail past each other, putting an enemy fleet in his home waters and him, and more than half the Britannia fleet, an ocean away from them.

So he was waiting for those two little words that ...

"Sail Ho," came the cry from the crow's nest.

Valdar shook off everything he'd been thinking and focused on the moment, raising his spyglass and staring into the distance. It took him a minute to find what the lookout had spotted. But he found them.

How could he not?

"Thirty-one … no, thirty-two ships," he muttered.

"That many?" his first mate asked.

He could be off, of course. Counting sails at this distance wasn't an easy task, but even if he had missed badly, he was still going to be outnumbered. He'd brought fourteen caravels and nine schooners. A formidable force, but if these ships were anywhere close to what had been described to him, they would be undermatched for the mass of sails even now turning toward him.

"Bring us about. Signal the fleet to form up. We're intercepting."

His men snapped to faster than he'd ever remembered them moving. Of course, they'd been waiting for this moment as long as he had.

As the Britannian ships maneuvered into position, Valdar studied the approaching vessels. They were the same people he'd fought on the Sea of Reeds five years ago; he had no doubt. The horizontal design of their sails was unmistakable, and not used by anyone else he'd ever met.

And Valdar was pretty sure he'd met or encountered every captain who'd ever sailed beyond sight of land.

The ships weren't exactly the same, however. The sail design was the same, but they had smaller sails, too, much like his own sail plans. The bodies of the ships, though, were completely different. Closer to his own caravels, actually. Not exact, but very close. He was also starting to make out the square openings of exposed gunports. Which meant cannon.

"Signal the fleet. Line of battle formation. We'll engage them broadside."

The first mate nodded and relayed the orders. Flags unfurled as the signalmen waved the message across, sending it rippling down the line of ships. His men responded well, each vessel maneuvering into position.

Valdar left the details to his men, keeping his attention focused on the enemy, watching the distance close, envisioning the battle in his mind. Seeing the whole field, as the Consul liked to say.

"Bring us to windward," Valdar ordered as the enemy crossed an invisible line.

The helmsman complied, adjusting their course with the rest of the fleet changing course in accordance. The enemy followed suit, taking a similar line formation, the two fleets angling toward each other to close the distance while keeping their guns more or less pointed in the right direction.

Who would shoot first? There was a benefit to being the first to fire. If your rounds hit the target, you might cripple some of the enemy's tubes and lessen the damage they could do in return. Fire too soon, though, and your shots would invariably miss, leaving your men to reload as the enemy got a clean, and closer, shot in return.

They answered that question for him as puffs of smoke erupted across the line of enemy ships. Valdar didn't call out a warning. His men saw them.

Besides, it was going to happen quickly.

Moments later, his prediction held true as dozens of rounds splashed well short of his boat. How fast could they reload?

Valdar let the range close a little more before calling out, "Let's return the favor. Fire one salvo. Let's get their range."

The order was carried down to the gun deck, where the men were waiting. His guns, and those of the rest of his fleet, roared to life in a wave of smoke and fire. They were at long range for his men, but they'd practiced these distances.

Valdar watched through his spyglass as their shots landed. Most fell short, but not all did. Rounds found their mark, tearing into ships here or there, ripping through wood and flesh. Not all of the rounds resulted in damage. At this range, thick timber could bounce the iron balls off, and some did just that.

Still, he'd drawn first blood.

"Good shooting," he said. "But we can do better. Adjust elevation and reload."

The exchange of fire continued, with both fleets finding their range. Valdar's ships proved more accurate, landing more hits on the enemy vessels. But the Eastern fleet's guns were significantly more numerous, and his ships began taking damage.

"Report!"

"Minor damage to the Seadreki and the Hrafn, but both are still seaworthy."

That wouldn't last. The range between the fleets was closing.

"Signal the fleet to loosen the formation but stay in line. Bring us northeast, tight into the wind."

He could feel his men looking at him, but no one questioned his orders, as the command traveled to the other ships, followed by them opening the gaps between the ships. The line of ships turned wide, almost completely reversing course as they headed away from the enemy.

They were sailing straight, not exactly into the wind, but close to it, while the enemy adjusted almost twenty degrees more shallow to the east than they had been, able to use more of their sail. The distances closed and the enemy had their guns still more or less pointing at his ships. The angle was oblique and most of the shots missed, but not all of them, and his rear two ships began to take a beating.

Valdar waited and watched as the enemy line pulled closer and closer, opening more of his ships to their fire.

"Sir. We're losing ground and have no angle of fire on them," his first mate said, unable to contain himself any longer.

"I know," Valdar said, as the man looked almost beside himself at the answer. "Just a little bit longer. I want them to think we're panicking and for their captains to rush to be the ones to get to us."

And they did. The enemy ships were mostly in line, but they'd started to bunch, putting scant distance between themselves, causing a few to pull next to each other, partially blocking their comrades' broadsides.

Which is what he had been waiting for.

"Hard to starboard, swing us across their line. All ships, ready broadsides and fire as they bear. Mind their spacing."

The line turned like a cracked whip, heading southeast, now sailing almost completely with the wind. The enemy didn't try to change their trajectory. They'd been caught off guard and were too bunched up to react quickly. He had the wind and was going to cross their T, as the Consul had trained him. They were in the perfect position for an attacking force using cannons, allowing him to shoot down the length of their line.

If his ships shot high, they were likely to hit the ships behind their targets and their cannonballs wouldn't just punch through and out to the sea, but rip long lines through the enemy ships and out their bottoms. It would be a deadly result.

"Fire!" Valdar shouted.

The thunderous boom of cannon fire echoed across the waves as Valdar's fleet let loose their devastating broadsides. Iron shot whistled through the air, smashing into the hulls of the enemy vessels with brutal force.

"Reload, damn you!" Valdar shouted toward the gun deck. "I want another volley before we clear. Roll out the guns!"

His men were doing well, working quickly and efficiently, and if he was being honest, they were making him proud. The long hours of training for exactly this moment were paying off, but he wanted more. Two volleys per ship before his ships passed and the following ships got into position. He might not get another opportunity like this, and he wanted to cause as much havoc among the enemy as he could.

He'd caught them off guard, and through his glass he could see men scrambling as cannonballs tore into several of the lead ships. A particularly well-aimed shot from the caravel behind his found its perfect mark, plunging down through the deck and tearing straight through to the sea. The way the ship suddenly started veering hard to the east told Valdar that the cannonball might have taken the ship's rudder with it. The ship's rapid listing to starboard meant it had been a crippling blow. He could see the terror on the faces of the men trying to patch the hole that was allowing a flood of seawater into the ship.

And then another ball slammed into it. And another, sending the main mast over its side, dragging the ship down even faster. It would be on the bottom in a matter of minutes.

He didn't have to order his men to change their target as they switched to the next ship in line, pouring on the fire.

"That's how it's done, lads!" he shouted. "That's how it's done."

They were taking a beating and, even as he watched, the next ship in line began to follow its comrade to the bottom, but the enemy wasn't beaten and they started to react. Instead of straightening their line out, the enemy began following his line as it continued to bend, both fleets twisting more and more to the south.

"They're trying to turn with us and punch through our line," Valdar said.

He hadn't spent the last five years idle. After the battle of the Sea of Reeds, he'd known a moment like this would happen, with his ships forced to face an enemy equipped with cannons in properly made seafaring ships, and not just a bunch of caravels.

And he'd practiced for it. If the enemy wanted to break through his line, he was happy to let them. They were too close to get clear broadsides from their entire fleet and tightly packed enough that his own could cause devastation if they could get them in a crossfire.

"Order the fleet to break after the Caer and take them on either side. They are to reform in position after we clear the enemy."

Flags flew, passing the order.

The fleet responded well, splitting into two groups, each sailing almost directly south, the wind at their backs, flanking the enemy. The eastern ships, caught off guard by the maneuver, found themselves sandwiched between the two lines of Britannian vessels.

"Now!" Valdar bellowed. "Fire at will!"

Canon belched smoke up and down his line as they cleared the line of ships. From both sides, Valdar's ships unleashed a punishing barrage. Iron shot ripped into the enemy and wood splintered and cracked as the projectiles tore through decks and gun ports.

One of their shots smashed into the base of the mainmast of a large enemy ship, sending splinters flying in all directions. Sailors tumbled from the rigging as the mast swayed precariously.

"Keep it up!" Valdar shouted to his gun crews. "Aim low! Aim low!"

The last thing he wanted was for his fire to go over the enemy and into his own line opposite them. It was going to happen, but he wanted to avoid it as much as possible. The ship's hull buckled under the impact, water rushing in through the newly formed breaches. Another of the enemy vessel's foremast toppled, crashing onto the deck and crushing several of the gun crews beneath it.

"Well done!" Valdar exclaimed, allowing himself a grim smile.

The crossfire was taking its toll on the enemy ships, with many finding themselves taking hits from multiple directions. They were not, however, helpless. Some of their broadsides might have been blocked by their fellows, but not all of them, and the enemy cannon roared to life, free to fire their own broadsides.

The Bellona shuddered as multiple solid hits struck home. Valdar stumbled but kept his footing.

"Damage report!" he barked.

"A breach below the waterline, sir!" came the reply. "Carpenters are on it!"

They were also focusing their fire. Two of the schooners on his end of the line took punishing fire, maybe because the enemy thought they would fall faster. Round after round slammed into them, ripping their hulls apart. He could see his men desperately trying to man pumps to push the water out and plug the holes, but it was a losing battle.

The first schooner's bow dipped beneath the waves, its stern rising skyward. Sailors leaped from the railings, plunging into the churning sea. By the time the ships behind it maneuvered to sail around it, the vessel was already half underwater.

Its sister ship lasted a minute longer. A direct hit to its powder magazine resulted in a thunderous explosion that tore the ship in two. The bow and stern sections briefly stood vertical before plummeting into the depths.

His men kept up their fire. An Eastern ship, taking rounds from both sides, exposed to twice as much fire as it could put out, began to come apart, literally splitting in half like a cracked egg before disappearing under the waves.

Another enemy vessel erupted into flames, with thick dark smoke pouring through its gunports. The fire didn't stay contained and with the rigging blazing shortly after, the fire spread with terrifying speed. The ship listed heavily to port as the crew abandoned their posts to fight the blaze. But it was too late. The flames reached the powder stores, and another massive explosion sounded.

Two more enemy ships went down in short succession.

The enemy line, however, started to get its act together, spreading out, opening clear firing lanes for more of their ships. He lost two of his newer caravels, one sent wheeling out of line the other going down as it bore onwards, plowing lower and lower in the water.

And then a death personal to him came as the Tyrfing went down. Valdar had known Alfhildr since they were boys first learning to handle a sail. He'd been the first to sign up when Valdar put out the call for Scandi captains to join the fledgling Britannian navy.

And there was nothing he could do about it as his ships sailed on, leaving the sinking ship in their wake.

As his line cleared, Valdar watched two more of the enemy ships succumb to the fire of his rearmost ships, their crews diving into the churning, and now somewhat crowded, sea as their vessels began to slip beneath the water.

It came with a heavy cost, however, as the enemy began to turn their own line, allowing them to concentrate fire on the rear ships in his westerly column, sinking another schooner and a caravel.

"Signal the fleet to reform the line and prepare to turn west."

He had positioned himself to set the enemy up to travel against the wind to the east, while he was on the western side of it. He hadn't been thinking of escape directly, but part of his positioning for the entire battle area was with an eye to keeping routes open. By pushing the enemy to the east and into the wind, they wouldn't be able to just swing west and give chase. They would have to reverse their line to the east, putting distance between their fleets before they could come at him, while he could turn and run straight west, toward open ocean, perpendicular to the wind.

They might have copied their cannons, ship design, and sail plan, but it seemed less likely they had gotten ahold of the smaller, but still incredibly brilliant inventions given to them by the Consul. The maps and charts he had drawn for them, the astrolabe and compass, and all of the other tools that Valdar could use to sail away from the coast. The fact that they had stayed close in to the shoreline suggested that, even if they had gotten those tools, they were not confident using them.

So if it came time to run, he had always wanted to escape west, away from Africa. And the time had clearly come. He had inflicted real damage on the enemy, but the exchange was too even in the number of ships sunk. The enemy had a large enough fleet that Valdar would run out of ships first.

His heart ached looking back at the shattered hulls of his own ships, those that had not yet slipped below the waves, and his men struggling in the waters. This had been the most costly day in the Britannian navy's short history, and Valdar feared it would not stay that way. Not without something major happening to push the odds back in their favor.

Chapter 11

Carthage

Medb slipped through the narrow alleyways of Carthage, her cloak pulled tight against the cool spring air. The streets were quiet, partially because of the early hour and partially because of the continued pervasive unease that had settled over the city, everyone feeling how close it was to boiling over. She approached a small, abandoned house, its once-white walls now stained and crumbling, the door hanging slightly ajar, broken by sword and club.

She was aware that being alone in this area of town, as a woman, was dangerous. She had battled with Cormac for an hour after she told him what she was planning to do, that her informant had left a mark indicating he needed a meet and that she had responded for it to be tonight. Claudius had been even worse, demanding to be allowed to come with her.

She had to put her foot down. They couldn't both be meeting up with Geral every time. They needed to be able to switch off, to keep people from noticing who he was meeting with, or seeing a pattern of the two of them leaving together traveling to this area of town and paying more attention to their movements as a result.

She paused at the door, listening for any sign of life within. Silence greeted her. She pushed the door open, wincing as it creaked loudly. The house was small; a single room with a hearth at one end and a dark stain in the center of the room, suggesting that whoever had lived here had met an unfortunate fate.

She didn't question the places Claudius picked for meeting spots, trusting his judgment, but she did wonder sometimes. She stepped outside again and pulled a small piece of chalk from her pocket and drew a symbol on the wall next to the door before moving back inside. Then she waited. Patience was a key to her work. Sometimes doing nothing was better than doing something for the sake of doing it.

She didn't stir out of her meditative waiting when she heard a rustling outside the door. Her hand dropped to her knife, only to relax as Geral emerged through the doorway.

"Sorry to keep you waiting," he said. "I had to wait until the meeting broke up and until I was sure I wasn't being followed."

"It's fine. What was this meeting about?"

"It was a gathering of low-level operatives, like myself, along with our group leader, to hand out new instructions. They do it somewhat regularly."

"And? What were these instructions?"

"Mostly to continue the small disruptions and demonstrations against the Britannian occupiers."

"So, nothing about their bigger plans? Their endgame?"

"If there is an endgame, they're not sharing it with us. It's all vague talk about 'restoring Carthage's greatness' and 'dislodging the Britannians.' Nothing concrete. That and they're pushing us to recruit more people, especially youths. They've talked to us about targeting the poorer quarters, looking for those with little to lose and plenty of anger to spare."

"We knew this was happening, though. This seems like things are remaining the same and you've gained no new information, so why the request for a meeting? You understand each time we meet, it puts you in danger and opens a chance for this to all fall apart?"

"No, there is something new to report. You asked that I keep an eye out for any outside agitators behind the movement, or at least involved with it. And I think there are."

"You've seen them?"

"No. They've never admitted it to us, but they can't keep people from gossiping, and there is a lot of talk of benefactors supporting us, a powerful group willing to come in and help us when the time is right."

"If they're not telling you about what's happening outside your group, how would they know?"

"The gossip is pervasive, and our leaders have told us it isn't true and that to talk about such things is tantamount to hurting the cause. For a rumor that only energizes the true believers, who think we need outside help and have been asking when someone would come to our aid, it doesn't make sense for them to so aggressively deny it. Unless it's true, and whoever this benefactor is doesn't want us to know about their involvement."

"Maybe," Medb said, although she wasn't sure she agreed with his reasoning. "Do you think it's the Easterners? The people who helped Carthage during the war?" Medb asked.

"I don't think so."

"But you just said they're not telling you anything."

"I know, but part of the talk is coming from a few of our people who were lent to one of the groups on the other side of town for some kind of big operation, the one I messaged Claudius about. They said the leader of that group was much more talkative, mentioning that there were friends visiting, and that they had been observing some of the meetings of the various cells, including ours. They must have blended in well, since I don't remember anyone standing out. New people, sure, that happens all the time, but no one notable. From the stories I heard near the end of the war about the Easterners, people who saw them delivering weapons, we would notice them. They stood out."

The big operation Geral had mentioned was an attempt to break into one of the praetorian armories and steal rifles and ammunition. They'd bribed one of the tax collectors, who'd used his position to demand a key to the armory, which he had planned to give to the insurgents. Eoghan had denounced the man at once, but it was another sign of the deep corruption that ran throughout the governor's administration. The praetorians and even bureaucrats assigned from home were well vetted and watched for this kind of thing, but the system he put in place, independent of the checks, was clearly rotten to its core.

"Yes, that is how I understand it to be. If there is someone else in play, other than the Easterners , I need to know about it."

"That won't be easy to confirm. Other than the one leader who seems to be more willing to talk, they're all very tight-lipped."

"I know. See if you can get moved to his group, or try to move up the ranks. Push for a leadership position. Get yourself in a position where you'll be allowed to know more."

"I'll try. But it won't be easy. They're careful."

"Just do what you can. Finding this out could be crucial."

She knew pushing him to expose himself more, bring notice to himself from whoever was behind this manufactured uprising, would put him in more danger, but that's what assets like him were there for. He said the danger was worth it to keep the Carthaginians from returning.

Now, it was time for him to prove he meant it.

Devnum

Lucilla made her way down the main street that led from the palace through to the Colosseum. As with every time she set foot outside the palace, a small procession followed behind her. Guards, courtiers, aides were added to by throngs of citizens curious about what was happening and joining in until they filled the street and stretched out far behind her.

While she knew her people appreciated, and even loved, spectacles, she also knew impromptu parades such as those created in her wake disrupted the city that she needed running as smoothly as possible to continue transitioning the Empire back onto a war footing.

Today's parade led her to what had once been a traditional hospital but had been slowly converted into something that would have felt more in place in Factorium.

She had, under Ky's urging, replaced every physician and natural philosopher supported by the Empire with men less stuck in their ways and more willing to learn the new techniques Ky had to teach them. The men who'd served as his father's chief physician and advisors on all matters medical had shown an inability, or at least an unwillingness to adapt to Ky's methods and directions.

She understood it, in a way. She'd always paid strict devotion to the gods and understood their teachings to be paramount, and Ky's explanations for what caused sickness and diseases went in the face of everything the priests had ever told them. It had been a struggle for her, if she was being honest. She'd fought it in the beginning, stuck in her belief in Ky's supernatural existence, but he, and mostly Sophus, had finally convinced her that it wasn't that at all.

She wasn't sure she grasped the idea of him coming from the future where this magic was an everyday occurrence, but he'd never given her a reason to doubt him. And it meant that, no matter what tradition and the physicians said, the old way of treating the sick and injured had to change.

And he'd been proven right. People survived illness at a rate nearly unheard of before, and children were living to become young adults more than twice as often as they once had. Ky was still appalled by the rates of death during pregnancy and from illness, but from what Lucilla saw, what he'd managed was nothing short of a miracle.

And part of that miracle was what brought her here today. Four years ago, she'd finally had enough of her father's physicians stalling and procrastinating in adopting Ky's new techniques and removed them all from their positions, and found new people with some background in more traditional methods but who were willing to learn the new ways.

Surprisingly, there had been few Romans who'd fit that description. She'd never thought of her people as particularly hardheaded, especially not with how much they'd taken to Ky's other innovations, or how advanced they'd been before Ky. Well, advanced for the pre-Ky world, anyway.

Thankfully, her people weren't just Romans anymore, and there were plenty of Ulaid and Caledonians who'd been more adaptable. Which included the Caledonian who'd adapted the fastest, and who, two years ago, she'd named as the Imperial Physician and put in charge of training new physicians and setting imperial standards. She'd also placed him in charge of the legion's medicos, but that was more to set standards for legion physicians and appoint deputies that would travel with the legions themselves.

He was waiting in front of the Imperial Medical Center when Lucilla arrived, along with what looked like most of the building's staff. The man was almost as busy as Hortensius with how busy he kept himself, so Lucilla had sent a warning that she would be visiting to make sure he was available to talk to her, since she had limited time in the day and too much to deal with herself.

It was always a surprise to see the man in person. Had she not known he was Caledonian, Lucilla might not have guessed it. Most of the Caledonians she'd known were large men with thick mats of hair. Hywel was almost frail-looking, his arms thin and his back slightly hunched, which explained why he also walked so slowly.

There was nothing, however, slow about his mind.

"Empress, it's good to see you again," he said, bowing. "Your message did not say to what I owed the pleasure of your visit."

"The Consul has sent instructions for you. Now that we've met the enemy, it is clear we will be facing a new type of war which will create new types of wounded, and we need to be ready to adapt to that."

"Certainly, certainly. Please, follow me inside."

Lucilla waved to her protective detail to wait outside along with most of the courtiers, taking only her private guards inside, walking past rows of beds, which were only about a third full at the moment. That was to be expected. This was not the only, or even the largest, of the hospitals in the city, and it only took the worst cases, and was otherwise used for teaching and medical study.

She passed through into a series of smaller rooms and hallways, eventually ending at a nearly pristine office, full of papers, but all organized neatly, everything in its place.

Lucilla settled into the chair across from Hywel's desk, waving her hand at Gaius, who pulled a stack of papers out of his bag and set them on the physician's desk.

"The Consul has sent instructions regarding new medical techniques," she began. "Before you say anything, I know this is going to be challenging and a lot to ask. But it's imperative we manage to reach the goals he's set. Facing firearms now, we are expecting, and already seeing, new types of wounds that will require new medical procedures to deal with them. The death rate among our wounded is much higher than what the Consul feels is appropriate. So this is now your top priority."

"Surgery?" he said, shocked, looking over the pages and then back up to her. "Does the Consul understand how high the mortality rates are with surgery?"

"He does, but that is what these instructions are addressing. You've already learned so much about diseases, which was important for healing people, but was also to prepare you for what we are facing now. It's not that much different from how you lowered mortality from cuts and puncture wounds. Any opening into the body allows infection, as you've learned. Surgery is just a larger opening into the body, so infection control becomes even more important. Which is what a lot of these instructions cover."

He continued to flip through pages, nodding as he looked through them.

"Yes, I can see that," he said.

"Ky said the key to handling the kinds of wounds we will see, if the bone is not broken, is cutting away the infected or damaged flesh, and then stitching the wound closed to allow it to heal. The damaged flesh will decay in the body and allow new infection to grow, which is why surgery so often results in death. There will be a point where enough flesh is dead, or bones are broken badly enough, where the limb might have to be removed. This is dangerous, and it is harder to control the spread of infection, but is often the only way to save a patient. This is more likely with the large-sized bullets, which will shatter bone easily."

"This seems very difficult," the physician said, looking at the diagrams. "I only understand part of it myself, which will make teaching it difficult, to say the least."

"I know, which is why the sooner we can start, the better. We're also ramping up production of antibiotics and other medicines to help, as well as additional distilled disinfectants. In addition, you'll see that the instructions on some of the surgeries and amputations include putting the patient to sleep. There will be a new medicine coming that, when used, will render the patient unconscious and unable to be woken, allowing them to withstand the extreme pain of the procedures. However, it is incredibly dangerous and must be used extremely carefully. Used inappropriately, it could render the physician unconscious or kill the patient and it is extremely volatile and easily set afire. However, without it, most of these procedures would be impossible on a practical level. Until you get it, it's important we focus on the basics. Sanitation, debriding the wounds, closing the wounds properly, and maintaining post-surgery care."

"This is all fascinating, Empress. Truly groundbreaking work. But I must confess, theory can only take us so far. The only way to truly master these techniques is through practical application; real surgeries on actual patients."

"You're right, of course," Lucilla said. "Which is why I've made arrangements to ensure you receive the necessary experience."

The physician's eyebrows rose in curiosity.

"I'll be instructing the praetorians, and expect you to instruct your people, to bring the persons with serious injuries directly here. We will, of course, be looking for specific types of injuries for you to work on. Injuries that would typically require amputation or complex surgery for the patient to survive."

"That's ... quite a responsibility, Empress. The odds are against many, or even most, of the people that are brought here for quite some time."

"Again, we know that. To be fair, many of these people would not live regardless, and of course, if you think you can heal them otherwise, then by all means, do your best to save them. But if not, then you can attempt these methods and ... pray to the gods."

"And what should I be doing until you find my first patients ... although I should probably call them victims?"

"Study the techniques provided thoroughly," Lucilla said. "Practice on animals where possible. Do everything in your power to prepare yourself and your staff for what's to come."

He didn't like the instructions, but after a moment, he nodded. "I will, of course, do my best, Your Majesty."

"I have every confidence in you. Keep me informed of your progress," Lucilla said.

She just hoped he could prove her right in the time they had.

Eastern Germania

The early morning sun cast long shadows across the sprawling military encampment as Ky, Ursinus, and Bomilcar stood outside of the command tent, watching the men assemble for the march. Their mobile camp had grown during the month of retreating, adding more legions to the one that had retreated out of Sardinia.

Unfortunately, the enemy's ranks had also swelled, growing at a faster rate than the Britannians had. They didn't outnumber the Britannians the way the Carthaginians had, but firearms made any difference more impactful. The style of war had changed, and Sophus and Ky had been working on identifying new tactics for the legions. Simple line tactics worked when facing off against more ancient-style weapons, but there needed to be a change.

They had gone over as many options as possible, with Sophus going over the deadly styles of combat seen in Victorian-era combat, particularly after the invention of the rifled musket. Ky had Sophus go through its records and give him an idea of later combat techniques, but most of those only worked if the units had a higher rate of fire or were mechanized, neither of which were likely in the near future.

The lower rate of fire meant that the best use of firepower was still massed volleys unless his men could attack from a prepared position. Rifled muskets weren't as accurate as he would have liked, not compared to later weapon systems, which made loose skirmish formations safer in terms of loss of life, but less effective for breaking enemy units.

Beyond the rate of fire, black powder just had too much drop over range to be accurate in real practice, when the smoke was thick and adrenaline high. Ky doubted having his men spread out and firing independently would be accurate enough to cause sufficient damage to enemy formations.

The other big issue that limited changes to their tactics was that they had to stand up to reload their weapons at all effectively. It was possible to do it lying down, but it was much slower, which was saying something considering the already slow reload times.

There were, of course, changes that could be made to increase the effectiveness of the tactics they had at hand. Sophus's records showed, again and again, that defense gave a significant force multiple advantages to offense, especially when used in a prepared position.

That wouldn't always be possible, but he and his officers had discussed for several weeks now how to best achieve that result, and why that was so important. Ky could only hope that his knowledge of real-world tactics in these kinds of engagements would give his men an advantage.

"It's good to see you on your feet, Consul," Bomilcar said to Ky.

Although he had been out of his coma for several weeks, Sophus had insisted he stay more or less immobile and bedridden to allow the nanites to do their job, which meant bringing commanders into his tent to go over strategy while he recuperated.

"Indeed, Consul. The injury you sustained would have felled any other man," Ursinus said. "The men have already started to talk about it."

Carus had already reported to him some of the gossip going around the camp since his first steps out of his tent yesterday, when Sophus gave him the go-ahead to get up and move around again. The gossip was getting back to the levels it had been at when he first arrived in Britain almost ten years ago. Ky had hoped he had put that kind of talk behind him, but apparently, it took just one preternatural feat to bring them back.

"I've heard," Ky said. "I appreciate their concern, but please tell your commanders to keep a lid on that kind of gossip."

"It does the men good and makes them feel confident to have an agent of the gods with them," Bomilcar said. "Morale was very low after our defeat and the constant retreating did not make it better. Your recovery is the one thing they've had to cling to. Don't take it from the men now."

Ky made a non-committal noise. He didn't enjoy the talk, but Bomilcar had a point. Carus had said something similar about the men's morale finally starting to turn around.

He just didn't love the way it was happening.

"That's all fine and good until I don't pull through a miracle and let them down. Then morale will plummet further than ever."

"Except that hasn't ever happened," Ursinus added.

Ky shot him a look, but it was clear from both of their attitudes that they had no plans to shut down the gossip any time soon. It had been the same reaction he had gotten from Carus.

"Well, let's focus on the matter at hand," Ky said. "What's the latest from our scouts?"

"The easterners are advancing again. They've been pushing hard since dawn."

"I'm not sure how much longer we can run," Ursinus said. "We've run out of ground to give. We're only a few days' march from our only rail line out this far, and if that should fall, we will have trouble supplying our army."

"Which is why we're done running. Now that Marcus has fully joined us and with that last batch of replacements, I think it's time to take the fight to them again."

"His men do build us to four legions, Consul," Bomilcar said. "But the Easterners have not been idle. They've continued to get reinforcements as well."

"True, but slower, since most of their men are marching quite a distance to reach us without, it seems, supporting railroad."

"That we know of," Bomilcar countered. "Our scouts haven't been able to get that far behind their lines as of yet. At least not and return with usable information."

"True. Which is why we have to make the men we have count, because until we get better intel of what is happening in the Far East and what we're actually facing, we have to assume they won't stop coming. It's why we need to stay mobile and ensure that the battle, when it comes, will force them to make tactical mistakes ... attacking us where we are strongest, and hitting them where they are weakest."

Ky had already discussed this at length with Bomilcar, the need to split their forces at times, to withdraw to pre-planned points, to make themselves appear weak to steer the enemy. Bomilcar had been leery about it since Ky had first brought the idea up.

"A risky strategy," Bomilcar commented. "If miscalculated, we could end up with the opposite result."

"Perhaps," Ky agreed. "But necessary. We can't afford another head-on engagement like before. Which is where you come in, Ursinus."

"Me?"

"Yes. We need to take the fight to the Easterners, but I don't want to just march right toward them, so I have a job for you. I want you to take your legion and Marcus's 2nd and split from the main body. I know you're going to be mobile and we'll be out of contact, which is why I need you to hit the timetables I set for you as precisely as you can while Bomilcar takes his and Aelius's legion and marches toward the enemy."

"Consul ..." Bomilcar started to say.

"I know what you're going to say, but I think this is necessary," Ky said, interrupting him and keeping his attention to Ursinus. "Do you think you can handle it?"

"Yes, Consul. We won't let you down."

"Good. Start to break camp. I want the legions on the march within the next three hours."

Both men saluted and started for their men. Bomilcar wasn't wrong, it was a risk, but the Carthaginian tended to play it safe in battle, especially when firearms were in use. Now they had a need for aggression and decisive action.

Ky just hoped he didn't let his men down.

Chapter 12

Carthage

Claudius ran as fast as his legs could carry him, which was at least easier now that the guard had gotten rid of the heavy armor, which would have severely weighed him down. What he really wished for, however, was more men.

He just happened to be at the guard post, checking on the rotation, when the messenger arrived with a warning of a disturbance nearby. Claudius had grabbed every man he could there, stripping the guard post to just one man, and every man he came across as he ran through the winding streets, his men drafting behind him.

As they rounded the final corner, they found the market in chaos. A seething mass of bodies surged around two of his men who stood above one of Eoghan's tax collectors who was slumped on the ground.

"Form around them. Move!"

His men responded well, creating a circle around the fallen bureaucrat, using their bayonet-tipped rifles to keep the crowd back as the incited people yelled curses.

"Run to the main garrison," Claudius said to one of the two guards who had been standing over the tax collector. "We need reinforcements, now!"

The man darted away, pushing through the crowd, which thankfully didn't try too hard to stop him, more focused on getting to the tax collector.

"Pick him up," he said to the other guard. "At the group, step back toward those shops. Keep together."

With the number of men he had, he needed a thicker line, which meant he had to limit the size of his front. They walked back several steps until his men were able to shift into a semicircle. The tax collector leaned against a guard. He had a serious cut on one leg and his clothing was soaked through with blood. Claudius looked to the entrance of the market, trying to gauge if they could march out, back toward the barracks, but the crowd had continued to grow and was pressing them hard. It was impossible for them to move out of the market at all.

Suddenly, a rock flew out of the crowd, whacking into the shoulder of one of his men. The man stumbled but held his position.

"Citizens!" Claudius yelled, making his voice project. "This riot ends now. Disperse and return to your homes, or we will be forced to take action!"

"What about the actions taken against us every day?" a woman yelled.

"These vultures bleed us dry while our children starve!" a man shouted.

The allegations were all true. Claudius knew that. But he also needed to keep the peace, and crowds like this tended to get out of control very easily, which he hoped to prevent.

"I hear your grievances, and the empress has sent her personal representative, who is even now looking into what is happening to you. Please, be patient and we will give you justice. This will achieve nothing but more pain and loss."

"Britannian promises are worth less than donkey shit!"

The crowd responded to the statement, surging forward, pushing against his men, who shoved back, keeping their rifles parallel to the ground and using them more as clubs than firearms, as they had been trained to do. Here or there a butt was turned, striking out when someone became too aggressive, thudding into chest or shoulder, but avoiding smashing any skulls.

"You can't protect that leech forever!" a man with a scraggly beard shouted, spittle flying from his mouth.

More rocks sailed through the air, pelting the guards. One struck Claudius in the chest, eliciting a grunt of pain. He gritted his teeth, maintaining his composure.

Suddenly, a bottle arced over the heads of the crowd. It took Claudius a moment to realize what it was. A bottle of pressed oil with a rag stuffed into the spout, the tip of which was burning.

It sailed past the guards and shattered against a nearby market stall. Flames erupted instantly, as the splashed oil caught on fire.

"Fire!" someone screamed, and panic spread through the crowd like wildfire.

"Put that out," Claudius yelled.

Two of his men broke from the line, which shrunk as the rest of his men moved to closed the space they had once occupied. Using their waterskins and digging up dirt, they managed to get the flames under control before they spread beyond the burning oil.

Thankfully, no one else followed that person's example. The pushing and shoving continued, but the firebomb seemed to have shocked even the crowd, which lessened their resolve slightly. There was still no way out of the square, but at least his men didn't seem to be in danger of being overrun at that moment.

The standstill wouldn't last, however. Tensions built again as the crowd riled themselves up once more.

"Last warning!" Claudius bellowed. "Disperse now, or we will be forced to take harsher measures!"

Claudius's warning fell on deaf ears. The crowd's fervor intensified, their shouts growing more hostile with each passing moment as the number of objects being thrown from the crowd began to increase with stones, rotten fruit, and makeshift projectiles raining down on them.

Several men from the crowd surged forward, attempting to breach the guards' formation. They grappled with the soldiers, trying to wrest their weapons away.

"Decanus, warning shot!" Claudius ordered.

A sharp crack split the air as one of his men fired skyward. For a heartbeat, the crowd hesitated, but their fury quickly overcame their fear. They were too angry. Beyond reason. The mob pressed harder and Claudius felt his men's resolve wavering under the relentless assault.

"Sir, we can't hold much longer," one of his men said, struggling against the tide of bodies.

Claudius scowled. He'd tried so hard to keep this situation from getting out of hand. And he'd failed. He'd exhausted every option, every plea for reason.

"Weapons front!" Claudius commanded.

Rifles swung around, from butts pushing against people to sharpened bayonets. People tried to push back, away from the sharpened blades, but the people behind them pushed them forward, shoving them into the weapons.

People screamed and blood spilled, and it still wasn't enough. The crowd continued to push and shout, oblivious to what was happening ahead of them. Claudius cursed silently to himself. He'd hoped he wouldn't have to resort to worse measures.

"Fire at will! Aim low!"

The guards hesitated for a split second before rifles cracked, sending a wave of acrid smoke over the crowd. That did what the bayonets had not as screams of pain and terror replaced the angry shouts. The crowd's momentum shattered as those in front fell or scrambled backward. Panic spread like wildfire. The mob that had seemed so unified moments ago dissolved into a chaotic mass of individuals, each scrambling for safety.

Just as they began to run, his reinforcements finally arrived, forming up along the outskirts of the market.

"Let them go," Claudius yelled. "Form a double line here."

He didn't want to box the people in. It might net him the ring leaders of the riot, but it might not. There was a chance this had been a spontaneous event ignited by the tax collector and not some kind of plotting by whoever was inciting the unrest in the city, since Eoghan had been doing as much as possible to inflame tensions as whoever the mystery party was.

Many had already made it out of the market, so the leaders could already be gone. Trying to box the remaining crowd in would just lead to more panic and death. Besides, he still had the real problem to deal with.

"Push forward!" Claudius ordered, seizing the initiative. "Clear the square! Rifle butts only."

The combined forces of the guards advanced, driving the remaining rioters out of the square. The riot had broken and was over.

As the square emptied, Claudius turned to the tax collector. "Secure him. He's got questions to answer. Take him to the palace and hold him, only I or Prince Cormac, or his representatives, are allowed to release him. That doesn't include any of the governor's men."

He knew word would reach the governor, who'd want to see one of his lackeys released. Claudius knew taking this kind of forward stand would put him in jeopardy, especially if the prince or his wife were to depart leaving Eoghan still in place. However, Claudius thought that the longer this went on, it became more unlikely that would happen.

And he wasn't willing to let this one go. Dozens of bodies littered the ground and dozens more were wounded, including minor injuries among his own men. Among some parts of Carthage, this was going to be known as a massacre, and would make tensions even higher. The only solution, he could see, was to have someone to blame. Since he wasn't planning on volunteering, it meant the real instigator needed to be publicly tried and dealt with.

Or at least, he hoped Medb saw it that way. Because he knew there would be calls for his head as well.

Factorium

Hortensius could never understand how Sorantius stood being inside his workspaces. The heat and noise were, of course, familiar, but the smell was something he'd never adjust to. Acrid, almost burning his nostrils, and thick, the feel of it made his skin crawl.

If he had his choice, he'd stick with the smell of metal and oil that permeated his spaces instead.

He could, however, admire the chemist's work ethic. The man made Hortensius feel slow, since he never seemed to slow or stop.

"How goes the work?" Hortensius said, coming up behind the chemist, who stood up and turned around, confused.

"What are you doing here?" he asked. "Did we have a meeting?"

"Can't one inventor simply pay a visit to another?"

"Not unless he wants something," Sorantius replied.

"Fair enough. I did want something, that is, if you have a few minutes to spare."

"I don't, but I assume this is important if you walked all the way from your factories to here. You three try that out and see what happens. And by the gods, go slow. Any sign of reaction, dunk it."

The last part was directed at the three men he'd been talking to, who nodded nervously and hurried off. Hortensius was happy to see the man finally delegating. He'd always had a bad habit of trying to do everything himself, and it really slowed down the work.

He followed Sorantius back to his office and settled into the seat opposite him.

"So what can I do for you?"

"Well, I'm sure you heard about the disaster with the fuses and our exploding cannon."

"I did. I'm glad no one was hurt."

Hortensius could see the slightly haunted look in the chemist's eye. During the war, there'd been an accident with some of his acid production, which had created a toxic gas that had killed over a dozen of his workers. While he hadn't been at fault, and this kind of experimental work was dangerous, Sorantius had taken it personally, seeing each of the dead men as his fault.

"Yes, the gods were certainly watching over us that day. Since then, we've taken the entire platform back to the design stage and have reworked it completely. Instead of a simple system of a primer cap at the front, which had a habit of going off when fired and had to be stabilized in transit, we opted for an inertia block system. Basically, we have a large block that is held in place with a wire, suspended over a primer cap, all in a self-contained, stabilized system, meaning if I dropped the round or even hit it as hard as possible with a hammer on the end, it won't go off. When fired, the block is forced backward by the speed of the acceleration, snapping the safety wire. When it hits the ground, however, the sudden change in speed slams the block forward, into the primer cap like the hammer of a musket, setting it off. So in effect, firing the round out of a cannon is what activates the fuse system."

"That's ... an interesting concept, Hortensius. But I'm not entirely sure how it relates to my work here."

"I'm getting to that, I promise," Hortensius said. "My biggest problem with the new system is the ignition of the payload itself. The design puts a whole series of elements between the powder in the body of the shell and the exploding primer cap in the tip, and it is unreliable in setting off the powder, even if the primer goes off nearly every single time. Sometimes they explode, sometimes they don't. I've tried putting a trail of black powder in the small gap, but it shifts in flight and isn't always close enough to the primer to ignite."

"That is a problem," Sorantius said, clearly still waiting to find out how he fit in.

"While working on this, I've been reading some of the reports you've sent to the empress. Based on how the tests on your stabilized nitrocellulose are going, I think it might be the answer."

"Except, it isn't stabilized yet. We've gotten the nitrocellulose production working and started, but it's been our main focus so far, so we haven't gotten to working on the distillation of the hydrochloride to make a chemical we can mix with the nitrocellulose to stabilize it."

"Damn. How bad is it without that?"

"Let's just say we are very careful with every tiny bit we produce."

"How soon until you can start to stabilize it, because using it in between the primer and the main charge would solve my problem, but not if it's too volatile."

"I honestly can't say. Maybe a few weeks, maybe a few months. I won't know until we start working on it and find out what kind of complications we run into."

"Is it at all possible to expedite the project? Because I can't find anything else that will work as effectively. Anything that might be poured inside the chamber with the impact fuse has the possibility of softening it, and keeping it from hitting the primer, but sealing it away or putting only a small amount near the primer won't set it off."

"I can only say we'll start working on it and see what we can accomplish. It was already lined up to be my next priority anyway, since the consul is eager for this new type of gunpowder he keeps mentioning, and says this is the first step to that."

"Good. If there's anything I can do to help you along, please let me know."

"I will."

"Good. While I'm here," Hortensius said, "there's something else I've been thinking over that I wanted to talk to you about."

"Okay?"

"It's about the balloon project," Hortensius explained. "While we meant our original balloons for the observational balloon, the consul said that was just the beginning and that the end goal was a larger balloon capable of carrying messages and even equipment, as well as being used for tactical purposes. He also told me that while we're using hot air to lift the balloons now, there was a gas that could be used that is lighter than air and capable of carrying larger weights than simple heated air. At the time, I hadn't heard of hydrogen, but now that we're building the tanks for them, I realize that's probably what he meant."

"I seem to remember that, and I think you're probably right."

"I am. Putting it all together, and knowing that he only introduces things as steps toward a larger plan, I deduced that he'd eventually ask us to build this higher efficiency balloon and decided to beat him to the punch."

"Shouldn't we wait for his instructions?"

"No. I mean, if we run into trouble, we can send questions through the empress, but I believe we have enough knowledge with what we know about both the hydrogen and the previous balloon project to work out how this is done. At least for a prototype. I'm sure once he sees it, he will have corrections, but we were never men who waited on others to tell us what to design and build. We've been spoiled by the consul and his endless wealth of knowledge, but we shouldn't use that as a crutch."

He could see in Sorantius's eyes that he had him. The man wasn't a narcissist, but he had the vanity that all men who dream of creating something new have.

"I assume you've given thought to how much trouble we had sealing those damn tanks to keep the gas from escaping?"

"I have. Clearly we'll have to change our methods, as the metal tanks we have now will be too heavy, but the basic principles we used, with the double envelopment and pressure-expanding seals, should work here using the viscose rayon we created for the current balloons."

"Until there's a breach, which if it enters combat, there will be."

"That is a concern," Hortensius said. "I would counter that anyone who goes into combat is in danger, so this is no different, but I think there are steps we can take to help mitigate the danger. For one, I'm experimenting with a compartmentalization system, basically smaller bags inside a larger container bag, so that if one is punctured, it doesn't affect the next and doesn't release the entire hydrogen supply. Secondly, we'll need to look at additional fire-retardant steps. Which is where you come in. While the rayon is mostly fire-resistant now, I'd like some kind of chemical coating that would reduce the chance of flame or spark from the built-up lightning the consul told us about."

Sorantius was quiet for a long moment, clearly thinking it all through. Finally, he said, "I've never discussed anything like that with the consul, but I have no doubt something like that is possible, just looking at the building blocks we have now. I'll send word to the empress and see what she has to say about it. It's an interesting problem."

"Thank you, Sorantius. I appreciate it. To be clear, this is a side project. The stabilized nitrocellulose is still our priority."

"That I understand, if from nothing else from the weekly messages the empress sends me over the telegraph."

"Good," Hortensius said, standing. "Then I look forward to your success in making it happen."

Port Vikhavn

The proud fleet that stopped for supplies just a few weeks previously limped into the West African port, much different than when it had left. Battered and missing several of the ships that had sailed out with it.

Valdar was aware of how low the morale of his men was, and felt it acutely himself every time he looked for the Tyrfing, its absence pushing home the loss of his friends once again. It was a comfort to see the two stone forts, built and reinforced over the last several years, that sat at the mouth of the estuary. While not indestructible, they had large, rifled cannons, bigger than those available on most ships, with stable mounts to fire from, making them more accurate and longer ranged than what the enemy could deploy.

Should they come after them here, they would take a beating doing so. It brought him at least a measure of comfort, and he hoped his people felt a little of the same.

The fleet sailed deep into the inlet to the small port built in its center, land granted to them by the locals and used as a bustling trading port both for Britannian trade and between the local tribes themselves. The small garrison worked almost as mediators between several of the tribes in the area.

They'd had some issues with local unrest, but for the most part, they'd managed to get along well with the natives, keeping to their small coastal enclave and even assisting their allies in several small skirmishes with outside tribes that tried to push their way in.

It made for a safe port with a steady supply of fresh food sold by the locals and even contract labor as it was needed.

As happened every time they sailed into port, the small fishing boats that worked the harbor and coastal waters began to coalesce around the larger vessels, looking for trade.

Valdar signaled his first mate.

"Tell those fishermen we have no trade today, and warn them to be careful leaving the estuary. Try and let them know of the hostiles that are on their way. Then signal the fleet. All captains are to repair aboard the Bellona for a captain's conference in an hour, along with the commander of the port garrison."

They had managed to break down some of the language barrier in the last five years, with some locals learning Latin, the base language of Britannia, and some of his people learning the local dialect. Most, however, communicated using hand signals and gestures, which limited the amount of information that could easily pass between them.

"Aye, sir," the first mate replied, moving toward the railing to flag down one of the ships.

It took some time, as nearly every ship had sustained damage from the battle and they hadn't been able to drop anchor until now, forcing everyone to repair under full sail, in hopes of beating the enemy to Port Vikhavn. It had been a struggle, with several ships nearly sinking on the return voyage. Truthfully, Valdar was surprised he'd managed to not lose any more ships.

Now that they were here, they could at least anchor and access fresh supplies, but this was one of their most far-flung ports and it had no drydock facilities. For some repairs, that was fine, but many of the shots had impacted very near the waterline, and the ships had to pump out their holds almost constantly to keep afloat.

Over an hour later, the last captain finished getting his men working on necessary repairs and made his way over to the Bellona.

"Gentlemen," Valdar began as they all crammed into the captain's quarters. "We've suffered heavy losses and I know you all have a lot of work to do to get your ships back in fighting condition. For most of you, that is going to be the priority. Word from the Ghaoth Álainn is that the enemy is still two days south, which doesn't give us much time to prepare for their arrival. Tribune, we will need to borrow as many of your craftsmen as you have available, to speed things along."

The last part was directed to the praetorian who had been assigned to command of the small garrison at the port.

"My men are, of course, at your disposal."

"While repairs are going on, I want all of the remaining schooners to unload their cannon. Once that's done, I want the Marinus to set sail for Port Kalb, and I would like you to leave before nightfall. You are to tell them of the battle, the enemy's capabilities, including the similarities with our caravel design and the near comparable cannon they seem to possess. Give them the known position and course of the enemy fleet and that they are clearly headed north, toward the homeland. I want the fleet elements currently in the Middle Sea and the Sea of Serpents to collect at Port Kalb and begin patrolling the approaches north aggressively. The assembled fleet is to remain in combat readiness and is authorized to pull in every naval asset to contest their approach, should the enemy fleet get past us. They will also send word to the capital of our intention to use Port Vikhavn as our base to block the enemy fleet's passage north. Go now. Get your cannon unloaded and your ship underway. I want you sailing north before nightfall."

The man looked like he wanted to ask questions, but it took one look at Valdar's face to realize the admiral did not plan on answering any. Valdar had chosen the Marinus because it didn't need much in the way of repairs, suffering the least damage of any of the smaller schooners.

"Why are we giving up our cannon?" one of the other schooner captains asked after their compatriot had left.

"For our current plan, speed and maneuverability are not an issue, and I want to use your cannon and powder stores to reinforce the forts at the mouth of the estuary. At the same time, I would like you to scour the port for as much thick chain as you can find. I want it strung across the mouth of the estuary using the forts as anchor points, so that it sits just below the waterline. Secure it well enough to tear out their rudders and damage the hulls of any ships that try to force their way in. If possible, if we can find the supplies, I'd like hooks attached to the chains to better grab the ships.

"Why wouldn't the enemy just push past and avoid us entirely?" Nectan, the Caledonian captain of the Aventinus asked, correctly understanding the precautions Valdar laid out were to prevent the enemy fleet from sailing into the estuary directly.

"Based on our escape, I'm fairly certain now that the easterners lack the navigational tools to venture far from the coasts, at least not without scattering their fleets," Valdar explained. "Considering the wide arc we took to the west and back to shake off pursuit, they should have been well past us by now, not slowly crawling up the coastline two days south of here. Best guess, they have to slow or even stop for supplies, which have to be coming from the other side of the continent, since they can't sail clear of the mainland. If they were to pass us by, they'd leave a fleet at their back and astride their supply line. The enemy may have bloodied our nose, but we still have enough ships to cause them major problems should they try to bypass us."

Several of the captains nodded, following his train of thought.

"No, I believe they will try to dig us out, which is precisely what we want," Valdar continued. "We have forts and supplies here, and time to devise a plan. However, if the enemy does attempt to bypass us, we'll make them pay dearly for that mistake."

Valdar waited for other questions. When none came, he said, "Gentlemen, you have your orders. Get to work and prepare for the attack we know is coming. I want damage assessments and repair estimates by nightfall. Tribune, I'd like all of the cannon installed in the forts by the end of day tomorrow."

As they all filed out, Valdar spent a moment looking out the large rear window of his cabin, toward the mouth of the harbor. It was a good position to fight from, with supplies, solid defensive fortifications, and even a trained, land-fighting force. All of that combined, however, was still significantly smaller than the force the enemy had at their disposal.

It was going to be a close thing, even if he made all of the right decisions.

Chapter 13

Devnum

Hywel was leaning over a patient, looking at the bandage. It hadn't been an overly serious wound, but one he'd offered to treat in order to test out some methods the Consul had given them for different wound types. This one had been a man who'd gotten a bad burn while working in one of the local factories. The issue with burns was that they could fester and sickness would set in, and the larger the burn, the more chances of sickness.

The Consul had explained that this was, again, an infection caused by bacteria. Hywel had spent his life treating illnesses in the villages of Caledonia, learning the trade from his grandfather, who had been a healer in his own village. Back then, sickness was just a way of life. Sometimes the gods allowed you to recover and sometimes they didn't. The fevers that came, if you survived them, were a test by the gods to show your strength.

And then the Romans came, or at least their Consul, as he'd later learned that was who all the Roman innovations originated from and showed him that much of what he'd learned was not true. Some was, of course. Bones should still be set, rest for sickness was best, but those were in the minority.

The Romans had taught him much, but by far the biggest was learning that so much of their ills were caused by a variety of these tiny creatures, which the Consul called bacteria and viruses. It seemed unbelievable that all of these problems were related, but everything he'd seen since he was told about it said the Consul was right.

"Sir!" called one of his assistants, bursting through the door. "We've got an urgent case coming in. Wagon accident, crushed arm. It … it's bad."

Hywel knew why that was important. That was one of the injuries they'd discussed for testing amputations. It had been weeks and none of the injuries on their list had showed up. The more Hywel had studied for the procedure, the more nervous he'd gotten. He'd seen men get cut before, trying to remove foreign objects or cut off mostly severed limbs, and in most cases, the patient had died. Those who hadn't had been blessed by the gods, and it had been a close thing.

Even understanding the errors they made that ended with those results didn't remove his nerves. But this was what he'd been waiting for.

"You two," he said to two of his assistants who'd been reviewing patients with him. "Prepare the operations room. Boil more water and ready the instruments."

His team hurried away to carry out his orders. They had yet to use the room the Consul had given them designs for and had called an operations room. Completely marble, with a drain in the floor at the center of the floor, to let out the water. In the center of the room was a solid steel table, polished and smooth with no channels or divots where blood and other biological material could settle and fester.

The Consul had been insistent that the room be cleaned down with caustic acid and boiling water prior to use, after use, and daily to keep the surfaces clean and free of germs … as he called them.

His assistants had left to do exactly that, in fact.

Hywel's thoughts were interrupted as the patient was brought in on a stretcher. The man's arm was a mangled mess, crushed beyond recognition and partially hanging loose. Thankfully, one of the stretcher bearers was one of the praetorians who'd undergone some of the rudimentary first aid training they'd started providing, which included how and when to apply tourniquets. One had been applied here, and early enough that the man was pale, but not bled out, which could happen with wounds like this.

"Take him to the operating room," Hywel ordered. "Prepare a saline drip and time it for four hours, remove his soiled clothing, and clean him."

Besides the sterilization methods, another universal practice the Consul had given them was the use of infusions to help keep patients from bleeding out. The easiest was a saltwater solution that Sorantius's chemists had begun producing that matched the salt levels found in human sweat and tears. According to the Consul, the increased fluids helped the body produce blood on its own and was a major help for both injuries and situations where a patient had lost a lot of fluids, and just drinking them would not add it to the body fast enough.

It wasn't something easily done without direct medical supervision, since the Consul had been very specific that too much would cause a kind of flooding in the body that could strangle the patient's organs. Although, as with all of his explanations, he'd then said that was an adequate but wholly inaccurate description, which Hywel found somewhat disconcerting.

There was, apparently, an additional step that could be taken where a family member could be used to transfer their own blood into the patient's body, although the steps required to do this were complicated. Apparently, not all blood was the same, and different people had different blood. Worse, it wasn't even evident what made one person have one kind and another a different kind. People in the same family could be different and there could be a match with complete strangers.

That, however, was important and the Consul had given them a test that included a foot-pedal powered spinning machine that would separate out the donor blood into a clear liquid and a thick, more solid one. They could then test a sample against similarly prepared blood from the patient. The Consul had said that if coagulation was seen, it meant the blood was incompatible, and if you put incompatible blood into a patient, it could cause them infection and often death.

There were apparently other issues. Some people could have conditions where their blood would be damaged and others would have infections in their blood, both of which could pass those problems on to the patient.

So far he hadn't dared attempt that that process, as the strength and sheer variety of the Consul's warnings about the blood transfusions caused Hywel some hesitation.

Thankfully, with the tourniquet in place, it wasn't needed by this patient.

By the time Hywel had changed into clean clothes that had gone through the sterilization procedure, and a clean and sterilized leather apron, the patient had been stripped bare, washed, and cleaned.

An assistant was standing near the man's head, which had a cloth over his mouth and nose, holding a small container with a bag attached to it.

"Start the administration. Remember to control the flow rate," Hywel said to the man before looking to a woman who was holding onto the man's uninjured wrist, thumb pressed against it. "Make sure you let us know if his heart rate slows."

They had attempted this on a few test subjects, and even Hywel had asked to be put under to see what it was like. Thankfully, none of their test subjects had died from it, thanks mostly to the Consul's extensive notes.

The man's moans of pain subsided and then ceased, his body relaxing as the chemical knocked him out. The woman holding his wrist looked up and nodded. He was alive, at least.

With the patient now unconscious, Hywel approached the operating table. He took a deep breath, steadying his nerves. This was it.

"Iodine," he called out, and an assistant quickly handed him a sterilized cloth and a small bottle of the inky substance.

Hywel liberally applied the iodine to the crushed arm and surrounding area, staining the skin brown.

"Scalpel," Hywel said, holding out his hand and taking one of the instruments designed by the Consul.

The cool metal of the instrument felt reassuring in his grip. With practiced precision, he made the initial incision. Blood welled up immediately, but an assistant was ready with more sterilized cloth to wipe it away. He worked his way through muscle and sinew, cut away the flesh above the crushed area of bone, exposing it while leaving the rest cut evenly. He also cut away as much dead tissue as he could find, since they now knew that was the source of many postoperative infections.

However, he saved as much skin as possible, knowing he'd need that at the end.

"Saw," he called out.

The bone saw was heavier than he expected. As he cut through the bone, the vibrations traveled up his arm. The sound was unsettling, a grating noise that turned his stomach. The bone was left jagged after he finished. He took another tool and began to file down the edges, smoothing it and rounding it to keep the sharp sides from cutting into the patient or causing cuts in the tissue.

He also tied off all the major blood vessels he could find. The Consul had said there were smaller ones, but that the 'suture' would only work on the larger ones. The Consul had developed two kinds of material for sutures. For internal work, they used a sinew from cat gut that had been trimmed into a thin line and sterilized. Apparently, it would dissolve over time, once the wound itself had scarred over and closed. The goal of closing off the larger blood vessels was to keep the patient from bleeding internally until the cuts healed over.

Without the large lens the Consul had devised, Hywel wasn't sure this step would have been possible. Even with it, seeing what he was doing was difficult and it was a slow, painstaking process.

Finally, however, he finished, closing up all the ones he could see. As he began to fold the skin flaps over the exposed wound, closing it up to allow it to heal and protect the muscle and tissue from infection, the patient jerked suddenly.

"Put him under," Hywel hissed at the assistant standing by his head, who had been more focused watching him work than on the patient.

Thankfully, he hadn't woken up all the way, which would have been a terrible memory for him. The ether soon took effect and the man slipped back into sleep. The last steps were to use horsehair sutures, which were stronger than the cat gut but would have to be removed later, to tie up the flaps of skin so they covered the wound completely. He left it slightly baggy, not tight, to lessen the chance of ripping and tearing, and to allow some room for swelling without tearing the sutures.

Hywel stepped back from the table, his brow damp with sweat. The amputation was complete, although that was only the first step. Now the man just had to survive the recovery, which was going to be the hard part.

"Remove the tourniquet and let's get him cleaned up, the wound dressed, and I want someone with him at all times, monitoring his condition."

There was going to be seepage, even with most of the large arteries sewn up, and standing biological matter would be a problem. The stump itself was neat, but there would probably have to be skin trimmed over time, based on the instructions he'd read.

Until then, all they could do was watch for infection, administer penicillin and hope it worked, and manage the man's pain. If he made it through the initial recovery period, the next step would be to train a few more healers to go to the legions and train their people on how to do the technique.

One step at a time, though.

Eastern Germania

Ky stood on the crest of a low hill, a patchwork of thin forest and field stretching out before him, smelling of pine and damp earth. He had ten thousand men dug in along the forest edge in a long line stretching in both directions. That number was, however, a far cry from that of the slowly advancing tide of men and steel coming toward him.

The enemy had almost three times his number. They were being cautious; something he'd never had to deal with when fighting the Carthaginians. Ky's advanced vision could pick out skirmishers pushing forward, taking shots at his line, trying to expose the trap they expected from him.

"They're being careful," Ky said.

"We know they worked with the enemy in the last war," Bomil-car said, still not comfortable directly naming his own people after all these years. "Enough that they know you have a flair for the dramatic."

Ky gave a small smile but didn't look at the general directly. He would argue he had a tactical mind that knew how to turn a weakness into an advantage, but he could see the general's point.

"Then let's show them what we have. Tell the artillery to open fire. Target their skirmishers first, then shift to their advancing infantry. I want to disrupt their formation as much as we can before they start in on their main assault."

Bomilcar signaled an aide and relayed the orders. Moments later, the distinctive boom of Britannian cannons echoed across the battlefield. Plumes of earth erupted among the eastern skirmishers, sending men flying. The enemy's line paused ever so briefly, but the respite was brief, and it continued its roll forward.

It also had an answer for the Britannian artillery as its own cannons replied. Shells screamed overhead, crashing into the Britannian lines with devastating effect.

His men had only been under artillery fire in one battle, and this was much more intense. It was focused at the center of his line, which started to waver slightly.

"Shift the sixty-third cohort to cover their left," Ky ordered.

His most veteran units were shifted toward the center, in hopes of keeping it together, since it looked like that was where the enemy was going to hit the hardest.

They entered rifle range, and the battle commenced in full. His men were able to stand and fire away while the easterners continued to march forward. It was a terrible sight, seeing waves of easterners fall as they tried to close the gap to reach his men, who'd had a chance to dig in, while the enemy had an open field to march through.

They took it and continued on.

Not that it was one-sided. A unit here or there would stop and take shots, and the enemy artillery continued its barrage on his center. Men fell. Much more on the eastern side than on his, but not enough more.

"They're going to reach our line," Bomilcar said, watching through a spyglass.

"I know. We need to hold on a little longer. Send in the reserves."

"Consul, sending them in now will …"

"I know. I know. But the line can't break. They have to hold."

Bomilcar saluted and went down to the men to relay the orders himself. It was still a close thing. The enemy had closed, bayonets fixed, and charged, slamming into the center of his line. It seemed to Ky as if the whole thing was on the verge of breaking until the reserve cohort smashed into the melee.

It was still chaos, but the line stiffened and held. The flanks continued to fire, putting pressure on the easterners still coming across the field, almost funneling them. That was good in that it kept his flanks solid, but it was still putting too much pressure on the center.

"Consul …" Aelius warned, taking up Bomilcar's position.

Ky, however, no longer looked worried. He'd had his drone out, scouring the battlefield, and saw what he'd been hoping for.

Out of the far tree line on the left flank, more cannon erupted, their shots crashing right into the middle of the enemy line, as ten thousand more Britannians marched out, toward the enemy line.

"Right on time."

The enemy seemed torn, unsure if they should handle this new attack on their flank, or if they should continue to focus on the line in front of them. And then Ursinus's lines stopped advancing, and with a ripple brought their rifles up.

A wall of smoke appeared as the first volley was fired, crashing into the enemy forces. And then a second. And then a third. For a moment, half of the enemy army looked as if they were going to turn and charge this new threat, but the fire from both the front and the side was too much. They started to waver, a unit here or there breaking and running for the rear.

It was not yet, however, a rout.

"Order the cavalry to swing in and hit their left flank. Hard. They're on the verge of breaking," Ky said, turning his horse toward the right flank and heading down the side of the mountain.

"Consul," Aelius said, reaching out and firmly grabbing Ky's arm. "You cannot go down there. We can't afford a repeat of last time."

"The men need someone to lead them and they will be riding into unbroken lines," Ky said.

"The men need their leader alive," Aelius countered. "You're too valuable to risk. Let the officers handle this."

For a moment, Ky considered arguing, but he knew Aelius was right. He nodded reluctantly.

"Fine. Go."

Aelius saluted and rode toward the front rank, his aides falling in behind him. Ursinus's line held strong and continued to fire into the enemy's flank, so much so that the pressure began to ease off the center. New enemy soldiers weren't being thrown into the melee, while his continued to fight, with the reserves still pressing into the fight.

And then Aelius and the cavalry struck. Some of the enemy saw them coming, but engaged as they were, they couldn't form a cohesive defense against the wall of men and horses.

The impact was devastating. The cavalry slammed into the enemy lines, cutting deep into them before curving back out. Sabers slashed through men, and hooves crushed them into the ground. It was too much for the battered enemy lines, which collapsed almost as soon as the cavalry hit, with wave after wave of the enemy running for the rear.

"Signal the infantry to press forward. We need to capitalize on this moment. Ursinus is to angle and maintain fire until pursuers reach his lines, and then join the advance."

Trumpets blared and flags raised as the word was passed. The Britannian lines surged forward. The enemy's break intensified, men throwing their weapons to the ground trying to avoid being caught in the three-sided press of death.

It had turned into a full-on rout, with the exception of the rear guard. This section of Germania was a series of slow-rolling hills, and his men had set up to fight in the valley created by two of those hills, giving them a clear, open lane of fire and room for Ursinus's men to do what they did.

Unfortunately, he was not the only one who could take advantage of the landscape, and the enemy had set up their reserves on top of the slope on the opposite hill. Worse, after Ursinus's arrival, when it had become clear they were unlikely to break the Britannian line, the enemy commander had pulled all of his artillery onto the top of that hill and had a commanding view of the area. The artillery now opened up with devastating effect, meaning if his men tried to pass, they would be bleeding casualties and put a not insignificant number of enemy soldiers in their rear.

"They are not as broken as we thought," Ky said to one of the messengers near him as those cannons now opened up on his men. "Send word to Bomilcar to assault that position and silence those guns."

The young man nodded and sprinted off. It was going to be costly all the same. They had plenty of rifles on the hill and they would be shooting down into his men. True, he'd be able to surround them, which is why he hadn't set up a similar position himself, but with their small force, this is what they wanted. Their goal was to keep the rest of the enemy army from annihilating them, and it was going to work.

Bomilcar sent them in scattered waves, with enough distance between each to keep the canister-loaded cannon at the top from wiping out swaths of his men with each pass. He didn't need the massed men for volley fire because shooting uphill as they were, a lot of those bullets would sail into the sky, hitting nothing. What he needed was for them to get into bayonet range long enough to occupy the enemy for more waves to catch up and reinforce them.

"Commander, there are multiple battles from the era of rifled muskets where this type of attack became deadly to the attacker, leading to large casualties.

"Did they have the same variance in the number of men?" Ky asked.

He hated this plan, but he couldn't see another way out. He was happy to hear of one that worked, but so far Sophus had little to supply once their initial plan was executed.

"While the attacker had a larger force in most instances, no, the odds were not as large," Sophus said.

"Do you have a better suggestion to keep those cannons from tearing us apart?" Ky asked.

"We could pull back and concentrate our fire on the hilltop," Sophus said after a beat.

"I don't remember saturation bombing being effective when we did it short of the kiloton range," Ky said. "I find it hard to believe that it would be successful with just cannon. Would we be able to shell them into silence or would we just be waiting for their ammo to run out?"

"It is impossible to predict without knowing more of their capabilities."

"Which means you have no idea. And if they have enough ammunition, we could take significant damage before that moment is reached."

And so they watched as waves of men went up the hill, only to be torn apart by cannon and rifle fire. A few times his men got close, finding a little cover and firing at close enough range, gaining some accuracy. They didn't last long, but they created enemy casualties even without getting into bayonet range.

When they faltered or ran, another wave was sent in, screaming and charging uphill. Taking a shot when they got close enough and then continuing the charge until the return fire became too great.

Bomilcar did direct some cannon fire onto the ridge, and even managed to hit some of the enemy artillery, sending the cannon tubes sailing into the sky. But not enough of them hit to greatly accelerate the course of the battle.

And then a wave finally reached bayonet range. The enemy fire had slackened, probably through lack of ammunition, but it was enough. Ky could see the fight from his position, and it was brutal. Had they been all he had, the enemy might have pushed them back, but Bomilcar had seen it too, as the men got close, and pushed the next line up early.

Just as the men in contact began to run, the next line hit. This time the enemy was less prepared. More off guard.

And then the line after that arrived. And then the next.

The pendulum swung fast, from the enemy holding off a hundred times their number, to collapsing quickly. His men swarmed the hilltop, wiping out artillerymen and soldiers alike.

Ky knew there was no use trying to stop the slaughter. His men had been at their mercy for too long, trying to make it up the hill, and they wanted revenge.

They'd won their first victory. The bulk of the enemy might have gotten away, but they'd lost several thousand men in the process.

Now to find out what the cost to his own people was for this 'victory.'

Chapter 14

Carthage

It was startling to Medb every time she had been in this audience chamber just how ornate it was. She had always loved finery and the symbols that befitted her status when she was queen, but even she would have blanched at the gaudiness of these surroundings.

And yet, the governor had done everything he could to increase that lavishness. Nowhere was that more evident than the throne Cormac currently sat on. Golden with arms that resembled intricately carved fern leaves and a high back, the top of which resembled a crown, it was more of a throne than even the one used by the Empress, and definitely not the kind of thing a governor should be using.

Especially since, after looking into the province's finances, Medb had found that it wasn't a leftover from the excesses of the Carthaginian emperor, but something designed specifically for the governor at his request.

Just one in a long list of reasons she and Cormac were here today.

The governor usually started his day very late, a side effect of his late-night entertaining, which is why she and Cormac had come here so early. She wanted to start this off this meeting in the right way, putting the governor back on his heels. She knew she was successful as soon as the man showed up, responding to the summons Cormac had sent, requesting the governor's presence.

Eoghan's first steps into the room had his normal arrogant confidence, but they faltered as soon as he saw Cormac seated on 'his' throne, Medb at his side. Eoghan was a lot of things, but an idiot wasn't one of them, and he got the message that Medb was sending loud and clear.

"My prince," Eoghan said, stopping in front of the throne, clearly unbalanced by the reversal in position. "I'm ... this is a surprise."

"Should it be, though? Considering the sheer scope of incompetence and avarice we have seen in this city, and the recent riot in one of its markets, I would have thought you might have predicted our needing to have a conversation."

"I will admit, the riot was unfortunate and I am working hard to deal with its root causes. And of course, I am happy to entertain any questions you might have."

"The time for questions is over, governor. We have completed our investigation into the governance of the province and have found you wanting. This is not an audience, governor. This is an accountancy for your failure."

"I ... I don't understand what you mean. I know there have been some problems, but ..."

"To be clear, you have failed in every aspect of your duty," Cormac said. "I'd like to just believe you are incompetent and unable to carry out your duties, because at least then you wouldn't blacken the name of all our people, but it is clear to me that this goes beyond mere inability to do your job. Graft is rampant. For example, huge sums of tax revenue are disappearing after being collected, a problem we'll get to in a minute, but the provisional treasury is still strained. Do you care to explain where this money has gone?"

"I assure you, there is no graft, my prince. The tax money has been used for city improvements and additional security measures."

"I'm happy to hear how diligently you've been working to improve your domain. I think it should then be easy for you to provide proof of these improvements. Or even evidence of the additional security forces you've supposedly funded. I've looked at the treasury's ledgers, but they show nothing but shortfalls and unexplained expenses."

Eoghan shifted uncomfortably. "These projects are in progress, my prince. It takes time for such things to show results, and ..."

157

"According to the records, you've been siphoning funds for these so-called projects for over a year," Medb said. "Yet, there's no sign of any improvement, and the only additional security has been for your personal estate. Are you telling me that you have other ledgers, perhaps, that reflect this work ... ledgers outside the official records?"

"My prince," Eoghan said, looking at Medb but addressing Cormac. "That would be a violation of my duty. All my dealings are above board, I assure you."

"And yet you can provide nothing to show the work you've done? That is confusing, governor. As is the fact that the taxes you've been collecting are higher than what was authorized by the Senate. What's more, is where the taxes are going. You've been withholding a portion of the collected taxes for 'special projects' that have no clear documentation."

"My prince, if there has been any oversight, it was not intentional. Perhaps my subordinates have misappropriated funds without my knowledge. I can only say that any additional taxes beyond what the Empire approved for me to collect were necessary and approved by local officials to ensure the city's stability."

"It's interesting you should bring up the officials who helped approve these increased taxes," Cormac said. "Our interviews have brought up a surprisingly large number of stories about some very lavish sounding parties where you happened to invite most of the city's elite, including the very same individuals who approved these increased taxes. An interesting coincidence."

"My prince, those gatherings were merely to foster good relations within the city. It's essential for smooth governance. If anyone is telling you they were unnecessary or excessive, they are simply lying."

"And I suppose the timing of these approvals and your extravagant soirées is purely coincidental?" Medb interjected.

"Absolutely. There's no connection between the two."

"Really? Because we've noticed several of these local officials have suddenly begun living far beyond their means. Their estates have expanded, their wardrobes have become more luxurious, and their influence has grown considerably. All since you began implementing these new taxes."

That's ..." Eoghan started, but Medb cut him off.

"A coincidence as well? How convenient for you, Governor."

"What isn't a coincidence is that your attempts to retain control of this region have made it worse!" Cormac said. "The streets are filthy, crime is rampant, and the people are on the verge of revolt. Meanwhile, you and your cronies grow fat off the suffering of others."

"My prince, you don't understand the complexities ..."

"I understand perfectly," Cormac snapped. "You've failed in your duties, plain and simple."

"We've spoken to the people, Governor," Medb said. "They're angry, desperate, and losing faith in Britannia's rule. Your mismanagement threatens everything we've built here."

"The situation is under control," Eoghan protested weakly.

"Under control is not what we've seen. And amazingly, you have been foolish enough to take the same approach you have taken with the city itself with the praetorians entrusted to you for management of the province. The payments to the praetorians have been consistently short, so much so that they have lodged a formal complaint. And at the same time, you have been using them for activities outside of their, and your, mandate, such as intimidating local merchants, shutting down businesses that do not pay your new taxes, or don't give enough kickbacks to your tax collectors."

"The Praetorian Guard serves to maintain order, which is all I have asked of them. As to their payments..."

"We have spoken to some of your tax collectors and managed to convince them to give us an honest accounting of their activities. Besides confirming to us that a portion of the money that ends up back in your pocket comes from them, as part of the requirement for being allowed to shake down the populace, we have also confirmed that the tactics of punishing those that aren't quick to pay, under the cover of law, is part of that directive to your tax collectors."

Apparently, there was nothing the governor could say to that, or excuse he could invent to justify it, because he opted for a much more aggressive response instead. "You have no right to come here and make these accusations! This is my province to govern as I see fit!"

"No, Governor. This is the Empire's province and one entrusted to you to govern as the Empress sees fit. Something I believe you have forgotten."

"This ... this is all a misunderstanding. I simply ..."

"I am done with your excuses. Praetorians!"

Claudius, who had been standing along the back wall of the room, along with more than the normal complement of men needed for a ceremonial post, stepped forward.

"Eoghan mac Ailill, you stand accused of graft, abuse of power, dereliction of duty, and high treason against the Britannic Empire," Claudius said as two praetorians flanked him on either side.

The color drained from the governor's face as the realization that he wasn't going to be able to talk his way out of this sank in.

"This is preposterous!" Eoghan sputtered, backing away from Claudius. "You cannot do this to me! I am the governor!"

"You were the governor," Cormac corrected. "Praetorians ..."

Before Cormac could give the order, Eoghan made a sudden lunge toward the nearest exit. His attempt at flight was pathetically brief as Claudius's men grabbed him, pulled him back, and restrained him.

"You will regret this! Both of you!" he shrieked, all pretense of dignity abandoned. "You do not know who you are dealing with!"

"Take him away," Cormac ordered in disgust.

As the praetorians dragged Eoghan towards the door, he continued to rant. "You have made powerful enemies today! Mark my words, you will pay for this! Both of you!"

The heavy doors slammed shut behind them, cutting off Eoghan's ranting. A weighty silence settled over the audience chamber.

Medb turned to Cormac, giving her husband a small smile. "Well, that was certainly dramatic."

Caralis, Sardinia

Llassar had never seen himself as a diplomat, having grown up as a warrior fighting for his tribe and then Caledonia, and yet ever since becoming a Britannian, it was all he had done. If anything, it had become more so post-war, with him traveling across the continent along with a few others, negotiating treaties and partnerships with the newly formed nations, as the Consul called them.

In that time, he'd been in tiny meeting halls, open squares and massive marble structures covering the breadth of architectural styles found in those places. The most common, though, was an amphitheater. They were able to hold a lot of people and, thanks to the Carthaginians, by way of the Greeks, this structure had spread widely over most of the western world. So it was not a surprise that he was once again in one of the bowl-shaped, open-air venues to talk to the assembled leaders. In most towns, this was the largest space available, and Llassar preferred to be in a place where he had more room to move, should things turn hostile.

Which seemed likely to happen here. The Sardinians that he had met so far in setting up this meeting had been nothing short of bristly, and it turned out that those were the ones predisposed to listen to him. As important men came from the surrounding area and even distant towns, it became clear there was a hard bias against unification, and anyone who advocated for it.

He could feel the tension coming off of the assembled men in waves as he made his way down toward the center of the amphitheater.

"I thank you for convening on such short notice," he began. "You do not know me, but I know your situation well. Not long ago, my people were like yours, scattered towns and villages that fought and argued among ourselves and our neighbors, blind to the greater threats just over the horizon. Thankfully, we listened to wiser voices in time to prevent those threats from overwhelming and destroying our people as they did so many others. Italia now stands at that crossroads, and Sardinia stands with them. Your people, Sicilia, and the mainland have been connected for generations. You share blood and coin, and each of you is stronger with the others, and weaker alone. That couldn't be more important than it is now."

He paused, giving that a moment to sink in. Over the years, he'd grown more comfortable doing this type of thing, and had learned, both from watching people like the Empress, who were true masters of the art, and through his own trial and error, that there was a rhythm to this type of thing that had to be followed.

"A new threat has come out of the east, and has already begun to cut deep into the continent. In Germania, where its people are unified, we have managed to stop the incursion and stand against it together. Unfortunately, not everyone in the easterners' path has been prepared to do what they needed to do to protect themselves. Greece stood fragmented, as you are now, and the easterners have cut far into their lands, burning their cities and enslaving their people. They are on a path leading to Italia, and you along with it. Now is the time to stand up and do what you need to for your people, to ensure their future. I know you have concerns and need assurances, and I have been entrusted by Italia and the Britannic people to give those I can and to listen to what you need to make this happen."

A portly man with a well-trimmed beard that Llassar had met briefly when he'd arrived and knew as one of the leaders of Caralis stood up from his seat near the front.

"You speak of unity, but what of our autonomy? Sardinia's needs are not those of the mainland. Our ports, our trade routes, our very way of life - they're unique. Why should we bind ourselves to them?"

"You raise a fair point, but are you as autonomous as you think you are? Do you truly have the breadth of natural resources to fend for yourselves? Your ports are valuable, yes, but they rely on trade. And trade relies on the stability of your neighbors and your biggest trading partners. And when you do trade with the mainland, do you want to be taxed as a fellow citizen or a foreigner? I

162

don't think your profit lies as closely with your autonomy as you might think."

Llassar had never been a trader himself, but he'd come to realize over the last five years that money, more than manpower, decided the fate of nations. It wasn't a coincidence that much more time was spent discussing economic policy and trade relations than military arrangements when drafting agreements between foreign powers.

"We've managed well enough since the fall of Carthage, haven't we?"

"You have," Llassar conceded. "But only because you've benefited from the protection of other powers. Italia has been subsidized by Britannia for the last five years, and we have made their policy with an eye toward stability in the region and not profit. If Italia unifies without you, do you think your relationship with the mainland will not change?"

"And what of our culture?" someone else, a planter by the look of him, asked. "I've worked this land for decades. Our traditions, our very identity, will be swallowed up by the mainland!"

"Unification doesn't mean erasure. You only have to look toward Britannia. I am Britannian but I am not Roman nor am I Ulaid. I am Caledonian. The two are not incompatible. You can be part of a whole without becoming the whole. Besides, I've seen what happens to those who cling too tightly to the past at the expense of the future. The world doesn't stop changing just because you wish it would."

Llassar paused again. Money wasn't the only thing that would convince them, or at least it shouldn't be.

"You should also take the threat from the east seriously. They have rivaled us in weapons and technology and have a seemingly huge source of manpower to pull from. We are working to regain the technological advantage, but they adapt as fast as our own people do, which means we cannot rely on advanced weaponry this time. The only thing we can rely on is each other. Standing together, we can present a force they have to take seriously."

"We're an island, far from the path of these invaders. Why should we concern ourselves with mainland affairs? Why should Sardinian men die for them?" someone else asked.

163

"You were an island when Carthage conquered you, were you not? How many of your men died when Carthage first came to your shores? The sea is no barrier to a determined enemy with superior naval power, and we have seen their navy. It is large and formidable."

The man sat back down, looking to the portly man who'd spoken earlier.

"What specific protections or autonomy might Sardinia retain under unification?" the man of Caralis asked.

That was the first non-confrontational question asked, and one that suggested he was willing to listen. "That's certainly open for discussion. As I said, unification doesn't mean subjugation. The rest of the tribes of Italia are willing to guarantee some level of autonomy in exchange for your participation."

"We've seen their promises before," one of the wealthy landowners said, giving the man from Caralis a pointed look. "They offer the world and then provide nothing when it's done. We thank you for your words, but it is the same as we've heard before. I suggest we postpone making any decision. We need more time to consider all the implications."

The landowner stood up, which seemed to be the signal for the rest to follow suit. Llassar stayed silent. Chasing them or demanding they stay wasn't the way to go. This result had been pre-ordained, and until he found out why, further discussion was futile.

Llassar could see the man from Caralis holding the landowners' gaze, and then looking away, almost defeated. It wasn't hard to figure out what was happening. The landowners were blocking Sardinia from joining Sicilia and the mainland, but why was the question. The port he could see. It would allow them to make their own trade deals and decide what fees to charge. Llassar was almost certain that was what he meant by having their autonomy.

Farmers, though, want more markets for their goods. If anything, their stance should be the opposite.

He needed to find out what was behind this dismissal before he tried again.

Factorium

Hortensius knelt next to the small hydrogen balloon, making some final adjustments. Small was subjective and he couldn't hide a smile at the reaction he would get from someone outside the project for calling the massive metal and fabric contraption "small."

Roughly the size of a large wagon, horses included, it took up a large space on the testing field and looked massively impressive. It was, however, a fraction of the size of the final balloon. It would be massive, larger than many buildings. They'd been forced to build a huge production facility to assemble and finish the balloons with massive doors to get them in and out. Transport had actually been a problem as well.

It wasn't until he'd started working on this process that he'd realized how many of the small, and even large, projects over the last five years had been building blocks to projects like this one. From the massive steam-powered propeller with its blade shaft covered in a rolling circle of wide metal that prevented it from digging into the ground from the weight it carried, to the new metal that the Consul had taught them to make.

The metal itself, which the Consul called aluminum, had been an interesting process, and one Hortensius had not been convinced was needed when it had first been proposed to him. The process of even getting the metal separated from rock and into a workable state was involved, needing an electrolysis process very similar to the one they'd created for the batteries to make the telegraphs work. After all of that, what he got was a metal that was indeed lightweight but did not have the durability of even lower quality steel, let alone the most recent type of steel they'd begun working with.

It was all but useless for barrel linings, or gun parts, or even swords. Now, however, he could see a use. One of the biggest concerns in the early designs for the airship, as he'd been calling it, was weight. To make it anything more than a hanging basket off a balloon, he needed a semi-rigid frame with enough room to carry men or a payload, along with a minimal crew.

Steel was his first thought, but the weight created a real problem, which was amplified by a scaling problem. Each time the balloons got bigger to account for the weight, the frame would have to get bigger, and so on and so on, with the balance point between the two creating a massive structure much too large to be feasible.

The aluminum fixed this problem. There were still some steel parts, of course, where there could be no acceptance of lower strength thresholds, but the majority of the parts were made of this new metal, which meant the Consul had been working towards this all along.

It made Hortensius wonder how much else he had been given was just preparation for something more in the future.

The sound of wheels grinding against gravel caught his attention. Turning, he saw Sorantius approaching with several assistants, pushing a wagon filled with large barrels.

"Right on time," Hortensius called out, waving his colleague over. "Did you finish testing it?"

"As best we could. It's impossible to know what's going to happen to it up in the sky. As the Consul describes it, the air is much more wet and we've seen firsthand with our current balloons how much the temperature drops. I have tested it on those balloons and it did not seem to have a noticeable effect, but if these airships of yours do go as high as you say they will, it seems likely it will be even colder."

"I appreciate the warning, but we'll have to take our chances with that. As long as it works on the ground, I am willing to test it in the air. I've finished my checks and I believe we are good to begin," Hortensius said, waving at the men standing far off to one side next to another large wagon holding two large, cylindrical tanks.

"Let's begin the fill," Hortensius said, gesturing to his lead assistant.

The men pulled a thick, leather hose with large, copper attachments on either end out of the cart, attaching one side to one of the tanks and the other end to one of the numerous small balloons attached to a honeycomb of aluminum brackets that made up the hydrogen 'bay' of the balloon.

"Is it safe having that much hydrogen in one location?" Sorantius said, jutting his chin toward the tanks sitting on the wagon.

"It should be. We have not had a leak since the last set of protections we put in place, and we have thoroughly tested the hoses as well."

"You're not worried about sparks when connecting the metal ends?"

"Until that leather is pulled, a rubber and leather seal keeps any hydrogen from coming out. It also helps prevent any of the hydrogen leaking out after they're disconnected. The rubber does degrade over time, so we have to replace them often, but that is worth the extra safety."

Sorantius nodded, and they fell silent as the assistants filled each leather sack, causing the metal superstructure to lift slightly off the ground after each one was filled. It was a time-consuming process, but Hortensius felt it was superior to a single hydrogen-filled bag that, if punctured would suddenly release all of the hydrogen in one go, both creating additional fire hazards and causing the airship to fall out of the sky.

When the final hydrogen bag was filled, the entire thing was floating, held down by dozens of ropes tying the vessel to the ground.

As his assistants pulled the hose back and disconnected it entirely from the tanks, Hortensius said, "Now I believe it is your turn."

Sorantius nodded and followed Hortensius's lead, waving his men forward. The assistants wheeled the wagon over and offloaded drums, bringing them closer to the frame. When the lids of the barrels were removed, the smell of the substance inside hit Hortensius. It was strong, almost overwhelming. The men then took out brushes on long poles, dipped the brush ends into the buckets, and then proceeded to 'paint' the hydrogen bags with the dark substance.

Hortensius had proposed to dip or even soak the bags in the liquid prior to installing them onto the frame, but Sorantius had vetoed that idea. Aside from the fact that the substance would have to be reapplied often, which meant that the procedures they developed needed to also work with the bags that were still filled with gas, there was also apparently an issue with the dried substance. The liquid hardened the bag's viscous nylon slightly, as if it formed almost a lacquer around it. This did help add another layer of protection, but if allowed to dry and then the bag was filled, it would cause severe cracking.

It was one of the reasons it had to be reapplied. The fireproofing would crack, chip, and fall off in patches just from normal use. The last thing they needed to do was to speed up that process.

He'd seen the tests, though, and had been impressed that even when fire was applied directly to the treated cloth, it didn't burn and the lacquer didn't melt. Sorantius said prolonged flame would eventually melt the lacquer and cause it to run off enough to stop protecting the material, but Hortensius had a solution for keeping prolonged flame away from the hydrogen bags.

As with filling the bags, painting them took time, even with a dozen men involved in the painting. They would have to time this and determine just how many men they could get to work on preparing a balloon for flight before the efficiency dropped. Even at their most efficient, though, this would never be a rapid process.

Once they were out of the way, Hortensius shouted, "Close the outer shell."

His men scrambled forward again, securing a large outer shell of fabric over and around the hydrogen-inflated balloons and the superstructure to which it was attached. Once that was done, another cart with another hose was brought forward.

Seeing the wide range of supply wagons needed for this, they would have to find a permanent launching area for these vessels, so that they had better storage facilities for preparing them for flight. In the field, of course, it would be back to a range of wagons loaded with equipment and supplies, but he needed to look toward creating something more permanent, at least in major cities where these ships would dock regularly.

Instead of hooking this hose to a tank, it was hooked to a small motor of some kind, which itself was hooked to a large, but portable, steam engine.

"You'd mentioned the outer shell, but not this."

"After seeing our design, the Empress contacted the Consul, who had new ideas for design to improve upon my shell idea."

The two shared a look, both of them doubting the public story that all of the ideas came from the Consul to the Empress across the telegraph lines. Messages were almost certainly sent and received, but Hortensius was convinced that an easier, and more fantastical, option was in use. Not that he planned on speaking the words out loud. Even if Sorantius had guessed what he had, it did not do to make accusations, even if he knew them to be true.

Whatever the source of the instructions, the Empress had not yet failed to supply him with what he needed for a given project, and he was not one to look a gift horse in the mouth.

"We'd talked about filling the outer bag with air, but I was concerned about it pressing against the hydrogen bags, which would defeat the purpose. The Empress had a suggestion of a pump that essentially compresses air, creating pressure inside the void between the outer shell and hydrogen bags. We've attached another valve on one end of the ship that, as the pressure reaches a certain level, will automatically open and let some of the compressed air out. More ingeniously is the scoop at the front. As the airship moves forward, pushed by the steam propellers, it uses the force of the air itself to push in new air, expelling already compressed air out the back. This allows for, if there is a rupture, air to continue to be added, keeping it from deflating and the moving air will allow any escaping hydrogen to be diluted by the air around it and it will be expelled. Which is useful, as there will be times we will be forced to manually reduce the amount of hydrogen available to reduce the altitude. We have the ropes to pull us down without expending hydrogen, but there will be times descent is needed away from prepared positions, and just filling the shell with hydrogen is not exactly a good idea."

"That is clever, but I'm still not convinced of this propeller idea. I know you like calling it an airship, but water and air are very different, and I cannot see how moving blades will force the ship forward."

"I will not lie, I have similar concerns," Hortensius said. "But, the Consul's instructions do say that it will work, so we have to assume it will."

A cheer broke their concentration. The outer shell had filled, giving the top of the balloon almost an egg shape, flat at the bottom where it attached to the frame. The frame would, later, be attached to the carriage that would hold payloads or people, but that was a secondary concern to getting the balloon section working correctly.

"Let out the ropes by fifty hands!" Hortensius called out, and the assistants hurried to each of the moorings, releasing the ropes holding it in place slightly.

It was a jerky process as the ropes were released not all at the same time or evenly across the frame and would need to be perfected before anything sat underneath the balloon, but for now it worked. Slowly, the balloon ascended into the sky, until it hovered well above them, the ropes pulled taut.

"I'll never not be amazed by that sight," Sorantius said.

"And just imagine what it will look like full-sized, capable of carrying hundreds of talents of product. We are entering a new age, my friend."

"We are at that," Sorantius agreed.

Chapter 15

Devnum

"Do you have a minute?" Lucilla asked, standing in the doorway of Ramirus's small, cluttered office.

"Empress!" Ramirus said, standing up quickly, knocking several papers to the floor.

She should have warned him she was coming, to keep from giving him a shock. Even though his office was situated very close to her own private study, so that he was on hand in case she needed him, she could count on one hand the number of times she'd visited him here, instead of him visiting her. And all of those times had been before she'd become Empress.

For this, though, she wanted to be the one to come to him, since she was planning on asking him for something she knew he would not want to give.

"I was reading over your reports from Anatolia," she said as a prelude.

"Yes. Unfortunate their colonies fell so quickly. I know I predicted this outcome, what with how little support their city-states have to give them militarily, but I'd hoped they would last a little longer. The easterners' southern army should be across the Dardanelles and marching into Greece proper by week's end. I do not hold out a lot of hope for the actual city-states themselves to hold out against the enemy when they reach them either. Even if we started selling simple cannon to them, they won't be able to survive the attack."

"I know, and it worries me. I know you said you think they will march into Italia in an effort to cut us off from the Middle Sea, but I think their plan is to turn north once they break through Greece and attack Ky's forces from behind, putting him in a vice between their two forces and isolating him. Should they do that, we will be finished."

"Possibly, although if they get close, the Consul could always retreat and prepare to face the combined armies head-on, at least to keep from being surrounded."

"Which is almost as bad."

"We should, hopefully, have the Italians with us by then. They won't be able to go through much training, but they did not give up a lot of manpower during the war with Carthage, at least, not compared to Hispania and Germania, and their leaders have indicated a high interest among their population in joining the fight. If the enemy gets through Greece and puts Italia under threat, they will be even more likely to sign up. I think we might be able to assemble a large enough force to counter them out of Italia alone, although it will strip the country dangerously bare and will be the only large mobilization we'll be able to manage from there."

"But like you said, that takes time, which is why what we really need is to get the Greeks themselves to cooperate, instead of offering themselves up as victims to the easterners. We need them to hold the line to give the Italians time to mobilize and train properly."

"Even with advisors and our arms, I'm not sure they will be able to hold out against the eastern armies alone. Unless they get over their infighting and work together, one city-state, no matter how well armed, is not going to stand up to a fully rifle-armed army."

"I know, but I don't see what other choice we have. Besides, there's also the worse possibility that some of the city-states will see themselves with a better chance of survival by joining the easterners instead of fighting them, giving the easterners a secure base to fight from."

"A distinct possibility, and one I'm not even sure our presence will be able to prevent. But I think you're correct, and there are very few options left open to us. It's worth a try."

"I'm very glad you think so because I want you to lead the mission to Greece," Lucilla said.

She kept her tone even and confident, but inside she was nervous. She knew what the response to this request was going to be, and she did not relish it.

To say he was surprised was an understatement.

"Your Majesty, I ... I can't. I'm too old for that. My place is here, advising you, not traipsing across Greece."

"And there's nowhere I would rather you be, if I had a choice. Unfortunately, I do not. You yourself just said how fraught this mission is going to be; how difficult it will be to convince any of the city-states to not only join our cause in defense, but work with the neighbors they've spent generations hating. It will take someone with experience and a deft hand to even give us a slight chance of success. Every person we have who is experienced in this kind of high-level diplomacy is already in the field. You are quite literally the only person left in my government who fits those qualifications."

"I appreciate your assessment of my abilities, Empress, but even if I wanted to go, I'm not in the physical condition for such a journey. You know that."

"I know it will be difficult. Llassar said much the same thing to me when I asked him to handle Sardinia. But, like with him, I need you, Ramirus. This is not only critical to the fate of the alliance, but to our very Empire. I don't expect you to do this alone. I am going to send Gaius with you as an aide. Besides being trained by Faenius, he's young, strong, and eager to learn. He'll handle much of the physical work, leaving you to deal only with the negotiations. He will make the task bearable for you while having a chance to gain experience in diplomacy. The fact that we have run out of anyone with experience in this type of negotiation makes it clear we have not put enough emphasis on this. We are no longer a small Empire on a small island. The number of independent political bodies grows yearly, and we need to have relations with them, which means training our next batch of new diplomats. I can't think of anyone I'd rather have teaching these young men than you."

"What about if the Greeks agree? I agree Gaius is a good lad, but he is not a military man. They will need to immediately begin training in our tactics, and they will have almost no time to learn them. If we had Llassar or even Cormac, or if one of the legates was not in the field and able to handle that end of the burden, it might give us a chance. Neither I nor Gaius, however, have the training to teach the Greeks what they need to know about fighting."

"I'm aware, which is why I was planning on sending Modius with you. He's been working closely with the legions, learning the new tactics we've been developing to deal with these easterners while protecting ... well, me. But his starting point was our current tactics. Since it seems the easterners have adopted our own strategies, he has been learning everything about how our legions fight. While not ideal, he's been in service for decades and is our best option, with all of our legates in the field. He'll also lead the security detachment of praetorians we send with you, although Gaius is able to do that as well. With the two of them, however, you should be able to delegate those tasks you do not feel prepared to handle yourself and focus on those you do."

"Have you told Modius of his new assignment?" Ramirus asked skeptically.

"Not yet, but leave him to me. He won't be happy, but he'll understand the reason. Besides, it's not like I leave the palace complex very much these days anyway, where I have dozens of guards at any one time."

Ramirus made a non-committal noise, clearly not believing what the Empress was selling.

"Please say yes," she said, using the voice she used as a young girl, trying to convince him to back whatever argument she wanted to make to her father. "I need your help."

Ramirus sighed heavily. "You know there's nothing I could deny you. Yes. Fine. I'll go."

"Thank you, old friend," she said, taking his hand in hers.

He patted her hand gently. She tried to hide the sadness the moment caused her. She knew this was necessary, for the war and the future of the Empire, but she had yet to acknowledge, even to herself, how difficult it was going to be without her old friend at her side.

"Good morning, my friend," Hortensius said, walking into the small dockside building Lucan used as his office.

It was very different from how both Hortensius himself and Sorantius kept their own working spaces, which they'd all but overfilled with remnants of every project they had completed, were currently working on, and even ones that were just ideas. Lucan, by contrast, had no paperwork or anything else that would indicate there was any project currently in the works aside from the dozen caravels currently under construction and the rectangular box floating in the harbor.

That box, however, was the reason Hortensius was here. It might have seemed innocuous and even strange to uninformed observers, but it was the test platform for the new ship-based boiler and high-pressure conduit system that would be the center of the new river boats. Essentially, the size of the boiler on a train, but with limitations the train didn't have, the biggest of which was protecting the boiler.

Boilers were susceptible to exploding when punctured and these ships were being designed to go into combat, where they would be shot at by rifle and cannon. Something trains, in general, were not expected to handle and so had no serious protection against. The biggest problems they'd faced, so far, were how far they had to go in protecting the boiler, the weight for the ship as far as armor went, since every stone meant the vessel was a deeper draft, and dealing with exhaust on the boiler, which would be a natural weak point for any protection they set up.

"I'm glad you're here," Lucan said, frustration clear on his face as he looked at the diagrams nailed up on the wall of the office. "We're still having problems with pressure drops and the build-up of pressure in the boiler. It's not catastrophic, but it could become a real problem once we start working on the ancillary systems."

"Hmm," Hortensius said, stroking his beard as he joined the shipbuilder, looking over the schematics. "Have you identified the cause?"

"No, and it's frustrating me. Your assistants have been looking over the boiler, and they assure me everything is working as intended, but after just a few hand spans from the boiler, the pipes start to lose pressure. Anything over half the length of the boat and there won't be enough to do anything. Which is why I feel it's definitely in the boiler itself."

"I see. It does sound like it, but my guys have been working with the boilers for a while, and know them pretty well, even if they're scaled down. If they say it's not the boiler, then there's a good chance it's not. If it's losing pressure over that short a distance, it could be the connection points or something with the piping. We'll have to investigate it. Has it caused any kind of buildup in the boiler itself?"

"I don't think so, at least not that your people have told me. I'll be honest, I'm struggling to keep up with all of these changes. Give me sail and timber any day."

"I understand, but we have to move with the times. I felt much the same when the Consul came to me eight years ago to tell me the way I had always done my businesses was wrong, and that there were better ways to do it. You managed to accept the idea of large, sail-driven ships when everyone else was stuck believing that the only way to fight on the sea was on a galley with oarsmen. This is the same type of change. Just give yourself time."

Lucan shrugged, but Hortensius could tell his words helped. These were challenging times, and the manufacturer knew sometimes they just needed a little reminder of everything they'd already accomplished.

Hortensius was about to change the subject, to talk about the protected crankshaft, which is what he really wanted to talk about. He was concerned about its housing, specifically. It was longer than anything at either of the factories or any of the train design, which would have been a challenge all on its own, but the fact that the ships would be under fire made it even more complicated. Already, the steam engine was in the center of the ship and below the water line to protect it from incoming fire, which would put the crankshaft along the bottom keel, which led to concern that if the ship ever ran aground, it could bend or damage the shaft, and cut power to the engine entirely.

He, however, never got to ask his question.

"Master Lucan, there's an odd vibration coming from the test platform, I thought ... Ohh, Master Hortensius, I didn't know you were here," one of his assistants said, coming into the office.

"How bad is it?" Hortensius asked.

"Not terrible, but it seems to be oscillating, which is unusual. We wanted to cut the boiler, but we're in the middle of an extended duration test, and would have to start the test over, so we wanted to check with Master Lucan first."

If the vibrations weren't too terribly bad, it was a reasonable decision to proceed. They ran every boiler through a long high-pressure test, keeping the fires stoked and the pressure up for at least twelve hours to ensure the tank didn't have any cracks or faults.

Vibrations were somewhat normal in any operating tank, but this was one of his more experienced men, so if he said the vibrations felt wrong, he was probably right.

"Then we'd better ..."

Hortensius never got to finish that sentence, as they were drowned out by an earth-shattering boom that shook the pier and Lucan's small office.

All three men sprinted outside, and then froze at the sight before them. The rectangular box had a massive hole in its center and was already starting to list to the side while debris was raining down from where it had been thrown into the air. Also, there were almost a dozen men in the water, some flailing about and others floating ... completely still.

"Run to the hospital. Tell them we need every healer they can spare. Now!" Hortensius ordered his assistant, who gave one last look at the remains of the test platform before running off.

"Let's get those men out of the water!" he began yelling at the stunned workers. "Move. We don't have time to waste."

This was a disaster, but he would worry about that later. For now, there were people to save.

Carthage

"... another riot in the western market. Injuries were kept to a minimum and five arrests were made," Claudius said, standing in the small room designated as Cormac's working office.

Technically hers too, Medb thought, but appearances must be maintained, and he was now in charge of the province until the Empress appointed a new governor. She was just his wife.

"Do what you can to keep the damage and loss of life under control, Tribune, but prepare your men for larger operations very soon," Cormac said.

"Yes, Governor," Claudius said, bowing before he left the office.

"I would have thought the people would have calmed down now that the tax collectors have been stripped of their power and Eoghan arrested," Cormac said, frustrated.

"If left on their own, I suspect that would be the case, but I don't think this is happening on its own. It's telling that the market where this happened is close to the richest part of town where Eoghan's supporters live. The people there were less affected by his tax collectors than poorer areas of the city, which have, in fact, calmed down since his arrest."

"You think they are pushing people to riot in retaliation for his firing? For what purpose?"

"I do. It's not in the books, but reading between the lines, it seems clear they were getting their money's worth from him, or at least thought they were, and aren't happy to see him gone. As to why? The easiest answer is for some kind of revenge; but with people like this, money is normally at the root. So, I suspect they hope that if the unrest continues or worsens, you will be recalled and someone new will be put in that they can try to corrupt like they did Eoghan."

"You don't think whoever the outside player your spy has mentioned is behind it?"

"Possibly, but none of the unrest so far has been in the sections closest to the wealthy areas of town. They've all been in the poorer areas. They have also either exploited existing tensions or the unrest has come with a message about returning the previous regime. You heard Claudius's report. There have been attacks, but they seem almost unmotivated. People aren't demanding anything; they aren't putting up propaganda or anything else that would indicate a motive. They're just attacking guards and causing destruction. It is unrest for the sake of unrest. It feels different to me."

"You are more of an expert in these things than I am. All I know is, it's working. We're not going to be able to keep reacting passively, responding to the unrest. Especially if it isn't tied to anything specific, and is being pushed by elements not addressing specific anger or resentment. We're going to have to be more proactive."

"What exactly are you thinking when you say more proactive?" Medb asked, suspicious she already knew the answer.

"Martial law, most likely. We've tried increased patrols, checkpoints, random stops, but none of them are working. This city is just too big and there aren't enough praetorians to keep it tightly controlled while letting the city operate as normal."

"You know that's a risk, right? It will give ammunition to the people riling up the populace, something to point to and say 'see what the Britannians are'."

"I know, but I'm not sure what choice I have. We can try and work with the people, maybe set up some way for the locals to voice their opinions, but until we weed out the bad elements, we're going to keep losing ground."

"If you're dead set ..."

A sharp knock on the door stopped her from completing that sentence.

"Come," Cormac commanded.

A messenger hurried in. Medb thought she might recognize him as one of the men who carried messages from the docks.

179

"A message from Kalb, Governor, just arrived on one of the imperial message boats."

"Thank you," Cormac said, taking the note and dismissing the man.

That actually didn't tell them much. Since Kalb was the closest point to North Africa, most telegraph traffic bound for North Africa went to it and then was sent by messenger boat to Carthage. Which meant the message could be from anywhere on the continent or sent by another messenger boat from Britannia to Gaul before being retransmitted down to Kalb.

It made Medb smile slightly to think how inefficient that system was, considering it wasn't that many years ago it would take a day for a message to reach the borders of her small kingdom, and another day to get a reply. How quickly they adapted.

As she'd suspected, this one was from Britannia. The contents, however, were a complete shock.

"The Empress is requesting your presence in Sardinia to assist Llassar," Cormac said, handing the message over. "He's reported that an outside group is interfering with the unification, keeping the Sardinians from joining the rest of Italia. She wants you to uncover whoever's behind it and remove the problem."

Medb read it quickly. Then reread it.

"It's interesting timing," he said. "Could these be the same people causing problems here?"

"You know I'm not going to make a guess like that without being properly informed, Cormac. I won't know anything until I get there and see the situation for myself."

"But it's possible, isn't it?"

"Possible? Of course. The timing, at least, makes it worth considering, but coincidences happen and there are a lot of forces in play at the moment, so it doesn't do to jump to conclusions. Gathering intel with preconceived notions just confirms what you're looking for instead of telling you what's really happening."

"We've been sending back reports. Doesn't the Empress know how precarious things are here right now?"

"She almost certainly does, but she also knows we're on top of things here and she has faith in you to handle the situation. You weren't sent here as an excuse to bring me along. You showed at the end of the war that you're capable of dealing with these situations on your own."

"I had Llassar with me that time," he pointed out.

"That was also five years ago. You've grown significantly since then. You already have a plan. I'll be back as soon as things are sorted there; until then you and Claudius can manage things here. He's a good man. Use him. He can run our informant for the time being, and if something notable is uncovered, you can call me back. Although don't ..."

"Talk about your informants by messenger. Yes, I know," Cormac said.

Even if she hadn't gone over her rules for running an informant when Geral was recruited, she made a point to turn every opportunity into a teaching moment for him. Even in their personal moments. Some people talked about the fates and their futures as pillow talk, others about their fears and aspirations. Medb talked about leadership and complained about incompetence.

She knew he found it endearing, and maybe she would have done it naturally, but she'd also been slowly preparing him to be the leader he needed to be someday. Cormac was smarter and more diligent than any man she'd known, but even he needed some direction.

She turned to leave, but Cormac's hand shot out, catching her wrist. In one swift motion, he pulled her down onto his lap, eliciting a small noise of surprise from her, before she smiled at him. She liked this side of him, when he took control. He was also smart enough to only do it at the times she approved of, and not when it would be inconvenient.

"I'll miss you," he said into her hair as he pulled her into an embrace.

She leaned into him, relaxing as she felt his strong arms tighten around her. Tilting her head up, she captured his lips in a passionate kiss, allowing herself a moment of vulnerability.

"Keep your wits about you," she said softly as she pulled away. "You're still sitting on one of Hortensius's powder barrels."

"You too," he said.

Chapter 16

Eastern Germania

"It's good ground for a fight," Ky subvocalized, watching his men set up their positions in the undergrowth just where it began to thicken after thinning out at the creek that marked the front of his lines.

It wasn't a steep hill, at least not enough of one to give his men a high-ground advantage, but the creek had just enough water in it to keep the enemy from using it as cover and would slow them down as they climbed onto its muddy banks.

"It should suffice, and the widening upstream should keep the enemy from trying to march around your position."

"That isn't likely to happen anyway. They've been chasing us for a week. Long enough to give them target blindness. They want to get at us, and they want it badly."

"It does not do to attempt to psychoanalyze the enemy who, if they are proficient enough in maneuvers and strategy, will see the reason you chose this as a place to fight, and might maneuver around it."

"Maybe, but the way they have increased the aggression in following us says they want to bring us to grips. They're looking for payback for that last fight, and now that they've been reinforced again, they think they can get it."

"Perhaps," Sophus said.

Another human mannerism the AI had picked up over the last few years. Eight years ago, it would have either just stopped arguing or deferred to its human, but now it always had to get in the last little word, usually to hedge.

"Positions secure," Bomilcar said, walking over from the lines. "The men are dug in and ready. Are you sure these holes are a good idea? They will limit our movement."

"I know, but standing out in the open, against rifles and shell fire, is costly. Even with our last victory, we saw that. We lost enough men and even in defeat the enemy is still larger than us."

Knowing about how line infantry tactics worked had been one thing, and it had been effective against the Carthaginians, but it only took one full clash with the easterners to see it for the folly it was. They could not withstand that level of losses, and even if they could, Ky was not willing to continue accepting them. Line of battle in the field against similar arms might have been a viable strategy, but it wasn't the best one.

Of course, Sophus had shown Ky other options. They might be better in the short run, but as the enemy adapted, they would end up in an even more brutal form of warfare.

The problem was that the enemy was clever and was adapting its strategy fast, some that they didn't even need to copy from the Britannians. It was the obvious evolution of this style of warfare, and the worst option would be to let the enemy get there first and dictate the flow of battle. There were honestly no good options, but this was the best one. When the enemy adapted, they would adapt with them.

"It just feels like we are turning every open battle into a siege."

"It can become that, and will if the enemy adopts our plan, which will push us into an even more static posture. My hope is that we win the war before that can happen. There are counters for how to deal with a static war like that, but they require a significant leap in technology that will take us some time to achieve."

"Just how much do you know that you haven't told us?" Bomilcar asked, an odd expression on his face.

"The real question is how much do I know that we can actually act on, which is the important part. Everything requires a previous step, which requires a previous step, and so on, seemingly forever. I've already started working with Hortensius on the steps for what comes next, to allow us to change the battlefield again in our favor, but until then, we have to go with the best tactics we can with what we have. Which means, for now, rifle pits and pulling the enemy in to fight where we want them. Are the skirmishers out?"

"Yes. Across the creek and up on the far rise. The cavalry is out too, although spread out like they are, I'm not sure what good they can do. Too thin for any charge to work, especially in these woods."

"The day of cavalry charges is at an end, my friend. They might still work a bit when cleaning up during a rout, but for now they're better used as fast scouts and that's it. We may start working on a change in strategy where they become essentially infantry on horseback, riding to a fight and then dismounting when they get there to fight as normal infantry, but fighting from the saddle is a thing of the past. Massed rifle fire just makes it impossible for anything else to work."

"I know. That much, at least, has been obvious. I'd hope that when we catch their scouts in the open, however, they might still have value."

"That would still be more one on one anyway. Massed cavalry against a single scout, which is what you'd get, would be a waste of manpower."

Bomilcar only nodded. Ky knew it was hard for him. He'd already given up one way of war, adapted to another, only to be told that way was also obsolete. He must feel like he could never catch up.

"We should get ready. Our scouts are pulling back and the enemy should be in sight in the next fifteen minutes, give or take," Ky added. "Pass the word that our scouts are returning."

He'd been watching the enemy movement for the better part of an hour as his scouts crept as close as they could to observe them. Some had gotten away successfully, others had been seen and paid the price. It pained Ky to see that, especially since their loss wasn't strictly necessary. While it was good for the legions to practice proper scouting in preparation for when he wasn't around, when he was, he could see the battlefield much clearer than any detail a scout would provide.

But finding the enemy wasn't the main goal of the scouts or the skirmishers. He needed the enemy to find him and come where he wanted to fight. To pull them in.

The cavalry had already done its job, and now the skirmishers were doing theirs, taking shots at the enemy line and falling back. The enemy had been pursuing them for long enough, and with enough small clashes whenever it seemed like they might decide to turn and make for strategic targets like villages or mines, ensured that the enemy was invested. They wanted to catch and destroy his army.

Which is what Ky wanted them to focus on.

The scouts came crashing out of the tree line, jogging toward his men, which is why he'd passed the word that they were coming. Every one of the legionnaires knew the running was over and they were about to face the enemy again, and Ky could feel their nerves.

A few minutes later, the skirmishers began to come in, splashing through the creek, running as if for their lives.

Which essentially they were.

"Here they come," Ky said. "Hold the men steady. Fire at will. Target large bodies."

The orders had already been passed out, and the men knew what they were supposed to do, but Ky wanted to say it again. At least they didn't have to worry about the men firing too early at targets far enough away that they had a poor chance of hitting them. The trees got thick enough away from the creek that by the time his men could see the enemy, the enemy was close enough to shoot.

True, trees would also help protect them, but if the enemy held together in compact rows, it would be alright. His legionnaires only had to aim for the massed body of men.

Better yet, clearly, they had no idea where his men were, because they came running out of the forest in clumps, not in fire lines, taking potshots at his skirmishers as they tried to make it across the creek. And then his men jumped the gun. Only a few at first, shooting here and there at individual pickets chasing his men, but those few quickly became an avalanche as all of his men's pent-up frustration was let out.

Thankfully, they'd waited until practically all of his own skirmishers were across the creek, but it was a wasted first volley. The enemy seemed confused at first, maybe thinking there were other skirmishers, with some of them rushing forward, some trying to hold and fire back, others falling back to hide behind trees.

The next men out of the trees were organized front-line troops spread out into firing lines. Almost as soon as the first bullets from his men hit them, they stopped and began to let off volleys. They went too high, missing his people almost entirely, and confirming that the enemy really wasn't sure yet where his men were.

The dark wool tunics and pants that were the standard uniform of the legion weren't exactly camouflage, but in a forest with dappled light, it did help hide them a bit. The enemy had marched to the bank of the creek, putting themselves in what was almost a clearing, which made it harder to see into the tree line opposite.

They kept firing, stacking up on the bank, the eastern officers shouting and trying to keep their men organized as they worked out what was happening. Finally, someone figured out that they weren't just facing pickets, but had found the full Britannian line. And that their volley fire wasn't having a noticeable effect. They could see the smoke rising from the tree line and knew that was their target.

They ran forward, jumping into the creek and then struggling on the other side in the mud and slime, even as his men continued to fire into them, the shallow water began to fill with bodies. The first impact was fast and short. His men were organized and in firm ranks, standing up from their firing pits while the enemy had to climb over the small barricades of stone and wood his men made for themselves. The enemy was rebuffed almost as soon as they hit his line, their morale already down from the fire they'd taken as they crossed the stream.

More lines began to emerge from the opposite tree line as the enemy became committed. Bomilcar had been waiting for that and the Britannian artillery opened up as shells began to scream into the enemy line, smashing into men and trees alike.

Several more times, the enemy pushed into his center, waves close enough that they were starting to be less mauled in the time it took for them to get into melee range. The fighting had also extended, as the enemy line began to stretch out, maybe trying to find his flanks. And then the enemy artillery opened up. They clearly didn't have the full sense of his line, and it wasn't as well targeted as his own, but it had a chance of seriously hurting his unit cohesion.

"Signal the artillery commander to focus on counter-battery fire.

There was a slight pause in the firing of his own canon, as his gun captains began to adjust their targets. It was only a few minutes at most, however, with that said, his men had done what they were told and already plotted out the enemy firing line, knowing Ky's order was coming.

The exchange of artillery fire grew more intense as the Britannian gunners zeroed in on the eastern batteries. The enemy returned the favor, pulling more and more artillery from both sides off the infantry as each tried to silence the other. The tree line and lack of explosive shells on either side meant very few of the rounds were causing damage, at least not enough to silence the other side's artillery.

The enemy saw this, too, because they began to shift their forces. By now, they'd engaged up and down his line, following a rough pattern with the enemy staying in the opposite tree line, albeit with less cover, and occasionally making a charge forward to try and break through his lines. That balance was slowly shifting as the enemy moved more of their forces to his left flank, spilling further and further over, clearly trying to roll him up.

Marcus, whose legion was on that end, saw it as well and had started to bend the edge of his link back, making it harder for the enemy to get to the end. Even with that, after almost an hour of pounding away, with repeated charges, the left flank was looking weak, the casualties starting to build up as his line thinned out.

"Send in the reserve cohorts to shore up the left," Ky ordered.

"That's all the reserves we have," Bomilcar said. "If they make a push somewhere else, we won't be able to stop it, and we're more exposed than they are."

"I know, but if Marcus rolls, we're in trouble. Besides, this also looks like their reserves. They clearly think the left is where we're weakest and where they'll get a breakthrough. Send them in."

Bomilcar nodded and turned to find a messenger. It didn't take long for the reserves to get there, and just in time as more of the enemy slammed into the line, trying to break through. The fighting turned into intense hand-to-hand several times, but his men held strong. Early in the afternoon the enemy started thinning its center and the forces across from his right flank, which had taken to just exchanging fire with his men, and sending those forces to the battle on the left.

Ky watched the shifting and considered. He was about to order his own center weakened, shifting men to the right to try and counter-flank the enemy now that those forces had been so depleted when the enemy made a mistake. Part of the center line also began to shift to the left, but the part next to it held position, opening up a hole in the center.

"Push the center forward. Now!" Ky shouted, riding his horse toward the front line. "Cavalry forward. Follow them through!"

Bomilcar was shouting the orders already, sending the fourteenth cohort, which was at the center of their own line, surging forward. A moment later, the cavalry who had been holding, waiting for the end of the battle, rode forward, crashing into the breach and moving behind the enemy. They wouldn't be able to hold anything open and they needed to move quickly to prevent being torn apart, but they would create chaos, and hopefully keep the enemy from reinforcing where they needed to until it was too late.

"Consul, we're spreading our line too thin, creating a bulge in the center," Gordianus said. "If they press in reinforcements, our men could be isolated and destroyed."

Ky looked down at the line, and Gordianus was right. The cohorts on either side of the fourteenth had partially followed to hold cohesion, but that meant the entire center of his line had created a dangerous salient the enemy could exploit once the seriousness of the situation hit them.

For a moment, that thought was pushed out of his head as his line, led by the cavalry, pushed through the hole in the enemy line before they could close it back up.

"Signal the right wing. I want them to trim to the left by four centuries."

It was a maneuver they had practiced, where the cohorts would send parts of their units left or right, weakening their line, but allowing the next unit to send more as it repositioned sideways, and so on and so on, until entire units could be freed up. Shifting by five centuries meant the far right unit would have to stretch only by one century, which had an added-on effect the further it stretched.

The men were thrown into the sides of the salient just as the enemy tried to push back and get men in to close the breach and pinch off the salient. They also could only pull from their left, the ones facing the Britannian right, which had been lightly engaged all morning, as opposed to the left wing, which was still in heavy fighting.

"Should we ..." Bomilcar said, seeing the salient starting to get squeezed.

Ky held up a hand. He wasn't looking at the salient. He was looking at the drone feed, which was doing a rough count of how many soldiers were moving toward the salient, and how many were left.

"They're over-committing, amplifying the mistake. Tell Marcus to hold. He has to keep the left engaged," Ky said to a signalman, who ran off to send the message.

"You think they're going to weaken the right?"

"I do. In fact, they're already doing it. Prepare orders. I want the right to now shift from the salient to the right four cohorts, which I want to overextend. As soon ... and I mean as soon, as they pass the edge of the enemy, they are to wheel and attack. I want them wrapping around the flank. I want—"

"They'll extend with us," Bomilcar said.

"They won't be able to. They're sending too many men to the center. Which is why we wait. Just a little longer."

"Our men could be squeezed out by then and cut off."

"I know. It's a risk, but it could end the battle," Ky said, almost offhandedly, his entire attention focused on the right wing.

Numbers counted down in his vision. Would they do it? Would they strip their line that much?

"Send the order," Ky commanded as it got close enough.

It wouldn't be instantaneous. The order went out, and again a shimmy happened down the line as his men passed to the right, thinning out even more. And then they were over the edge and wrapping around, their rifles shooting down the enemy line, tearing into them.

The enemy reacted quickly, unfortunately, rolling back with them.

"Keep pushing the right flank. Roll it up. Roll it up," Ky commanded, riding up and down the line, as animated as he'd ever been.

The enemy continued to fall back. It wasn't a rout, but they were bending far over, until finally they peeled part of the forces trying to close the salient, allowing it to join the right flank, extending it far. The Britannia cavalry commander saw his chance and rode hard for the enemy artillery, that had already started pulling back as soon as they saw the line collapsing in on itself. They'd hopefully get some of those pieces, but Ky was less focused on that.

The entire enemy line was pulling back, almost congealing. Ky could see where they were going, a series of hilltops to the far rear of the enemy line. It was a good defensive position with enough escapes that it was unlikely they'd be able to surround the hills, and attacking up them trying to rout the enemy would be a losing battle. It would cost him men and wouldn't get him to the enemy.

"Pull back. Shell the hill, but otherwise let them run," Ky said.

"Are you sure, Consul? We could end them now?"

"We can't, and our units are now mixed up. We would be giving them the high ground and forcing ourselves to charge uphill. We did the damage we needed to do. Keep the men in line until they run and shell the hills to force them to go, but otherwise, it's not worth it."

Bomilcar looked like he didn't want to agree, but saluted and rode off. Ky could see his point, but he had a bigger problem. He'd shifted tactics, again, but the losses were high. There was an obvious next step.

But should he take it?

Chapter 17

Carthage

Summer in Carthage was dreadful, especially for someone like Cormac, who had grown up in the cooler and much wetter climate of Ériu. Cormac had thought it was warm there in the summers, but he now realized it was nothing compared to Africa.

Even Hispania in the late summer could not compare to the oppressive heat here in Carthage. He was glad, at least, for the new standards for the uniforms of military officers, which he still styled himself as at least in dress, regardless of the fact that he spent little time with the legions themselves. The wool uniform might be a little stuffy, but it was still worlds more comfortable in the sun than heavy metal breastplates, that would become unbearably hot while cutting into his shoulders, no matter how much padding he used.

It was going to be a long day, so at least comfort wasn't one of the things he was going to have to deal with. Standing on top of the steps, Cormac looked out at the sea of faces from all walks of life in Carthage. Every one of them was angry.

He had tried to keep today's news, at least the topic of it, secret, but word had leaked out. The palace, although run by the Britannians and with a heavy Britannian staff, was still full of Carthaginians. Running a government took manpower, and only so much could come from the home islands. The rest was made up of vetted locals, but even with vetting, not everyone brought in was completely trustworthy. People could be very good at hiding connections and intentions. His wife had made sure he learned that lesson.

The place leaked like a sieve. It made Cormac wonder how Eoghan had ever thought he would keep his graft a secret.

There was nothing to do about it but start, unfortunately.

"Citizens of Carthage, I stand before you today with a heavy heart and a solemn duty. The unrest that has gripped this city can no longer be ignored. It is with great reluctance that I must announce the implementation of martial law, effective immediately."

Even though it seemed most of the onlookers knew what he was going to announce, shock still seemed to ripple through the crowd.

"What does that mean for you? A curfew will be strictly enforced from sunset to sunrise. Anyone found on the streets without a pass from the palace or an official escort will be detained and investigated to determine if they are part of an insurgent group. This will be inflexible, so if you need essentials, you must get them before the sun goes down, or you will be held accountable for your flaunting of martial law. Furthermore, to limit large gatherings, all but three markets within the city, which we will designate, will be closed. The three markets that remain open will operate under strict regulations. They will be cordoned off, and only a limited number of people will be allowed in at a time, where they must do their shopping quickly and leave, and no one is allowed to gather at the entrances of the markets to wait for their turn. We will be testing different systems to find the one that will allow the most people in throughout the day, but these rules are immediate and go into effect as soon as the other markets are closed. Any illegal markets that spring up will be swiftly dealt with. Vendors and patrons of these unauthorized markets will face arrest, and all goods will be confiscated without exception."

The mutterings got louder, as people became more incensed at hearing the specifics of their new limitations. Cormac had established a ring of praetorians around the area, in case things went badly, but for now he held them in place. He didn't begrudge the citizens their anger, only required them to follow the rules they were given.

"Finally, there will be no public gatherings of any type unless authorized by the provincial government. Any groups larger than three people are forbidden to gather on the streets, and homes may not house more than three guests beyond their normal occupancy. Shops may remain open, but they must also abide by the three-person limit inside their stores. Those shops that break those limits will find their businesses closed, and homeowners who break the limits will be evicted from their homes permanently. Repeat offenders who continue to break curfews or assembly rules will find themselves detained."

Again, a rumble rose throughout the crowd. Cormac knew that, between this and the closed markets, it was going to make life in the city hard for most of its residents, but it was the only thing he'd been able to think of to limit the crowds that had been causing violence. The graffiti and plotting were problems, but they did not directly destabilize the city. The rioting, on the other hand, was getting out of control.

"Down with Britannia! Carthage for Carthaginians!" a man near the front shouted.

Two men next to him picked up the chant.

"Guards! Arrest those individuals immediately!" Cormac said, pointing at the men.

The praetorians swept in, pressing against the crowd, as three of them came around front to grab the shouting men. This was what Cormac had feared, since this kind of demonstration could turn the entire gathering into a mob.

Thankfully, no one tried to pull the men deeper into the crowd or protect them, and after a minute, the men were hauled away, still shouting.

"Let me be absolutely clear; we will not put up with any foolishness. We will try to protect the people of this city and allow them to go about their days without harassment, but any instances of violence, the carrying of weapons, or damage to public property will be met with swift and severe consequences. These measures may seem harsh, but they have become necessary due to the lawlessness that has overtaken this city."

The crowd made noise, but after the arrest of the three men, no one acted out.

"I understand these measures may seem severe, but I assure you, they are not the only changes coming to Carthage. The taxes instituted by the previous governor have been abolished. I know that some have heard about this already, as we ended them the day the governor was removed from his position and arrested, but we are announcing it again, now. In addition to their end, the special tax collectors appointed under his rule have been removed from their positions as well."

This at least got something of a positive response. The tax collectors were universally hated by everyone in the city. No one would miss them.

"Moreover, the Britannic Empire acknowledges the wrongs inflicted upon this city and we look to make amends for that. Our goal is to see that Carthage is once again the shining jewel of the Mediterranean. But we cannot achieve this goal if the city descends into chaos. The restrictions I've outlined are temporary. The sooner peace returns to Carthage, the sooner we can lift these measures, so it is up to all of you to ensure the lawlessness and wanton destruction of property that has been occurring of late, ends. With the return of reason to your city, we will return freedom and peace to you."

There was some grumbling, and Cormac knew that asking them to inform on their neighbors was a hard sell, but some would do it, if for nothing else than to end the restrictions. Medb was right, though. There was a chance this would backfire and unrest would grow instead. Unfortunately, he saw no other option to stop the unrest in the city.

He just hoped she was wrong and it worked.

Port Vikhavn

Valdar and a few guards lent to him by the garrison made their way up to the village, a few hours' walk from the port, where the major tribe in the area was based. Actually, it was more accurate to say where the current major tribe in the area was based. The Ikondi tribe had not been the largest of the tribes in the area when Valdar had first arrived, but they had been the ones closest to the estuary where his ships had sailed in and the ones most open to working with the foreigners.

The first year, it had taken a lot of work to get the port up and running and to find food for the people there. Not only did the Ikondi help build the port and provide food for its people, they also protected the men he'd left there to establish the port from other tribes that had preferred not to let foreigners establish themselves in the nearby lands.

It was because of that protection that the commander of the garrison had given the tribe the first shipment of muskets and taught them how to use them. The Ikondi wasn't a small tribe, but they were struggling to deal with all of the enemies they'd made defending the Britannians. Had things continued to progress, there was every chance they would have been forced to step aside or have fallen with the Britannians in those vulnerable early months.

They had taken to the weapons well, and by the end of the first year of the port's existence the Ikondi had crushed or absorbed most of their neighbors, pushing the remaining few into conflict with tribes deeper in the continent.

All in all, it had led the Ikondi to be amenable to the Britannians, and the Britannians to them. There had been a few difficult points, as happens any time two peoples are in close contact, but they had managed to work through them. Mostly because the port really did need the locals, if only to supply foods and other usable goods that would be expensive and difficult to continually ship in, and the locals needed the Britannians to supply the weapons that gave them superiority over their neighbors.

Valdar arrived at the chieftain's hut, which was now closer to a Roman-style house, another thing they'd taken from the Britannians, and stood outside waiting, head patiently bowed, not facing the door, as was the Ikondi's tradition to show respect and deference to a chieftain.

He didn't have to wait long.

Ekoko was a decent sort and didn't abuse his rights. At least not against the Britannians. Valdar had to stand only for a minute, which was the traditional time the chieftain's guards made him wait, for honor's sake, before they ushered him inside. He found the chieftain inside with one of the small books that had been produced using the new printing presses put into service shortly after the war.

This one was a 'primer' as the Consul called it, teaching children how to read Latin, Caledonian, and Ulaid, as well as Scandi and several other languages of the continent. Valdar had to admit, they made it easier than how he'd been forced to learn as a child, through listening and repetition with his mother.

"Admiral! It is good to see you again. I trust your ship repairs are going well?"

Latin had been growing in popularity, mostly because of trade with the port and its visitors, and no one had worked harder to learn it than Chief Ekoko, who frankly spoke it better than Valdar himself did.

"Yes. Most of our ships are repaired as well as they can be until we can get them back to the docks in Devnum."

"You should consider building one of those … dry docks, I believe it is called, here. So that we may make ships for all."

Valdar smiled. Ekoko had already seen the small stream of trade here, and how that had enriched his people. He'd made numerous trips to the port and talked to the sailors and men who came through, hearing about Kalb and Devnum and all the great trade and wonder that went through there, and wanted it for his people. He was convinced, probably rightfully, that if the Britannians built out this port more, and put more of their resources through it, his people would see some of the wealth from it.

Already, many of his people had started going in to work at the docks, paid in wages that they then used to buy goods from the few merchant houses based out of the port. Those goods then made it back into the villages, which only increased the need for Britannian goods more.

"I know, and if we ever do more work around the coast or set up a more permanent presence, it might be possible, but this is just an outpost on the edge of our Empire, and we do not want to infringe on your people more than we already have."

"Yes. Always thinking of us. Your generosity knows no bounds. So, what is it that my people can do for our Britannian friends?"

His tone was sarcastic, but not actively mean or angry, although it was often hard to tell exactly what the chieftain was thinking.

"I come bringing news of the enemy we told you about almost a month ago. Our scouting ships have spotted them making their way north, finally. It seems as if they've finished their repairs and have decided to bring the fight to us. Our best guess is that they will be here in a few days' time."

"They are weak if they must repair all of their vessels in order to attack you again, instead of pressing the attack. You had your men ready to fight again in just days, and most of your ships ready in half the time they have taken, according to what the people at the docks have been saying."

"It's not that simple. These ships are hard to repair while they are underway, and even those repairs are limited in effectiveness. While we at least had a port here with supplies and were within a few weeks' sail of a supply run from Kalb, they are months' sail from home and, as far as I know, have no relief supplies. They would have had to repair under sail or beach their ships. Both time-consuming processes."

"And you still think they have a larger number of ships than the impressive fleet in our harbor?" the chieftain asked.

Valdar repressed another smile. It was always 'our harbor,' regardless of the fact that his village was several hours from the port. He knew that, in his heart, the chieftain partially considered the Britannian port part of his domain. For now, it was an unspoken thing, but it could change the entire nature of relations in this part of Africa if that shifted.

"Yes. Even with our reinforcements, they have a larger fleet than ours, and their fleet is made up of ships entirely the size of our caravels while a third of ours are the smaller schooners with

197

their lighter load of cannon. And that's assuming they have not managed to be reinforced in the time since we engaged, and that is what they were waiting for."

"I see. So what can my people do to help our friends, the Britannians?"

"We should be able to handle the initial assault, which I think should be a straight-up assault on our port. That's how they handled our other port they assaulted and the battle we had with them consisted of very straightforward tactics, them preferring trying to overpower us to finesse. If that's the case, we should be able to repulse their attack. Our forts are over-armed at the moment and can throw a massive weight of fire at ranges that should outperform any shipboard cannon they have. The forts can also take a significant pounding while a ship can only afford a few solid hits before they are in great danger. Should they get past the forts, well, then they will have my ships to worry about. So, other than keeping your people on land when they begin their assault, I don't see much of a need for additional effort. My real concern is that once they realize a direct assault is futile, they may attempt to land forces outside the range of the cannon at our forts, either north or south along the coast. From there, they could march overland to attack the port from the rear."

"And you do not think you could defeat these people? Even with your fine weapons?"

Another thing the chieftain often mentioned was that the Britannians never shared the rifles with his men, who had figured out from both talking to the legionnaires stationed there and seeing their target practice that the weapons the legionnaires carried were significantly better than what was sold to his people. Again, he didn't do more than hint at it, but the port commander had already warned Valdar not to get too comfortable with the chieftain, who was much more crafty than he let on.

Valdar tended to agree, but he also thought that Ekoko was too clever to try and take over the Britannians' holdings, at least by force. He might seek to get an edge but was smart enough to know that he needed continued Britannian cooperation, if only for expendable things like gunpowder, if nothing else.

"Just as their ships rival ours, so do their weapons. They will be armed much the same as we are. They aren't numerous, and maybe less numerous than us, but we have to guard two forts that require a day's march all the way around the estuary to bring in reinforcements, meaning one of the forts could fall. Should that happen, it's likely the port would go with it."

"You will, of course, not stand alone," Ekoko said, his teasing tone from before gone. "These are the lands of the Ikondi. We know every trail, every rock, every stream. If the invaders try to sneak past your defenses, they will find us waiting for them."

"Thank you, my friend. I would not ask such a serious thing of you if our need wasn't dire."

"There is no need for thanks between brothers," Ekoko replied, clapping Valdar on the arm. "The Britannians have brought prosperity to my people. We will stand with you against any threat."

"Good. We don't want you to stand unprepared. I know it's not the firearms you'd like, but in this last shipment I have arranged for more muskets and gunpowder for your people and will have them delivered shortly. I've also instructed the commander of the port that all limits on the amount of muskets and gunpowder you want to buy are lifted, if the port has the supplies to spare, of course."

"Your generosity is appreciated, as always."

There was a little disappointment there, Valdar was sure, but he also sounded appreciative. Having enough muskets to arm every man in the tribe would give him an even bigger advantage against his neighbors. Valdar had not wanted to upset the local polity this badly, but he had little choice, since it was that or die. And who knew what the easterners would do in their stead?

"I'm sorry it can't be more, but I will talk to my Empress about you. About how loyally you stand with us."

"I would appreciate it. Tell this Empress of yours that we wish nothing more than to be your friend. To show that, we will ensure your people remain undefeated in our lands. These people will leave or they will die screaming."

Valdar had no doubt that the chieftain meant it.

Caralis, Sardinia

Medb stepped off the ship onto the sunbaked docks of Caralis, glad to be on land again. With Sardinia isolating itself and not trading as widely as some of the members of the Western Alliance, and so much of that trade now diverted to war supplies, there were not very many ships that sailed from Carthage to the island. She had been forced to take a ship to Kalb and then one of the messenger ships set up specifically to support Llassar's mission. A small schooner, trimmed down and light, designed for speed and not comfort, she had been assigned to the first officer's tiny cabin. If she could stick to trains and avoid ships for the rest of her life, she would gladly do that.

She had never been to this island, let alone this small port city, which meant she had little to no idea where to go. The boat captain had known that Llassar was operating out of the offices of the small trading factor that one of the Britannian merchant companies had set up here, although the reason why any of the Britannian merchants would want to operate out of this place, she'd never understand.

Sardinia had little in the way of natural resources or manufacturing that they could not get closer to home and, because they were not part of the Western Alliance, any trade through here was subject to the tariffs that helped pay for the Empire and the war.

Even the city itself felt out of place from what she'd grown used to. The places she'd traveled since the end of the war, Carthage, Gaul, Hispania, even Egypt, had begun to adopt some of the Britannian customs and style. Here, however, looked like you were entering a Carthaginian port right after it had been liberated. The city felt like it was trapped in a moment from five years ago, not changing with the times.

No telegraph wires, no sounds of steam whistles or trains. Really no indication of the modern technology Britannia had introduced to the world.

Seeing a guard, still wearing armor and carrying a pike of all things, Medb made her way to him.

"I'm looking for the Britannian trading house. I'm to understand it's somewhere near these docks," she said in Latin, still the common language of Italia, and she hoped the island.

The man looked her up and down, almost sneering, and in a thick Punic accent, he said, "Over there."

He pointed to the rough set of buildings off to one side of the port. They were small and run-down looking and none seemed attached to a warehouse. It was clear, however, that he had no intention of clarifying his answer or giving more specifics.

"Thank you," she said in Phoenician, getting a small eyebrow raise from the man, but little more.

She made her way across the docks and past larger warehouses to the collections of doors. Thankfully, a few had signs set near the doorways to tell passers by what business they were looking at. Most were in Phoenician, but one was in Latin, and was clearly the place she was looking for.

Walking inside, she found several men sitting around a small table, examining what looked like figures on paper, another sign of the Britannians' influence, who preferred the new ways of accounting to the tally system still used by many other cultures.

"Llassar?"

"Who are you?" one of the men asked with a rough Roman accent.

Roman merchants were common, but usually represented land-based concerns. The Scandi immigrants in Britannia had all but captured that section of the economy, with most ship masters and dockside accommodations run by them.

"I was sent by the imperial government. He's expecting me."

Her tone made it clear she was not planning on handing out other information, and he would be a fool to push for it. As usual, he backed down. Men, especially outside of the large cities, just did not know how to deal with an assertive woman, making it easy to put them back on their heels.

She raised an eyebrow when he didn't answer right away.

"Through there," one of them said, jutting his chin at a doorway.

"Thank you," she said, and left them to their accounting.

The whispering started before she'd made it to the closed door, but she didn't care.

She knocked on it as she opened the door, finding Llassar sitting at a small table, looking through papers as well, although these looked like letters of sorts.

"Medb," he said, standing and offering his hand. "I'm glad you made it."

Closing the door, she took his hand, placing her opposite hand over his. She liked Llassar. He wasn't an idiot for one, and for a warrior he wasn't completely ruled by his emotions. He'd also made himself into a fair diplomat, although he still saw situations very directly and had trouble when it came to things that were not cut and dry. Which is almost certainly why he'd sent for her.

"I heard you were having trouble getting unification pushed through."

"You could say that, although I'd say there are people blocking unification," he said, offering her a chair. "Everyone seems to agree on the benefits and want what the mainlanders are offering, but there are holdouts, and I think they are not doing it for ideological reasons."

"Why?" she asked, sitting across from him as he settled back into his own seat.

"For one, it's who's behind the problem. Most of the city and port leaders agree that it's in their best interest and it's the landholders who are fighting it. But looking at what's being offered, the landholders have so much more to gain than the cities and ports, so if anything, it should be the other way around. The other reason is, it isn't something that came about naturally. From talking to leaders who want to see unification go through and from the few meetings I've been able to arrange with the landholders, it seems clear that there is one man in particular named Nuraian who's influencing the rest to follow his lead in blocking unification. They look to him whenever their reasoning is challenged, and he most often speaks for them. While that is somewhat natural, considering his position in the overall hierarchy of the area, it feels like there's more to it."

"Which is why you say you think there's outside influence?"

"Yes. I just don't know how to go about proving my suspicions. If I could, I think I can use that to convince the others to abandon him, as their biggest reason for not wanting unification, in actuality, is how fiercely independent the island is. If he was seen to be in someone else's pocket, he would lose face with them, and I think they'd abandon him."

"Perhaps," Medb said.

It wasn't that she disagreed. If he'd studied the society as closely as he did most of the societies he visited, then he'd probably know if that were true or not. It was more that she distrusted endorsing any conclusion before she had enough information to support it. Keeping an open mind to the data, as the Consul sometimes called it, made her more willing to accept the answers it supported. Something the Consul called target lock, a phrase she still did not understand.

"Have you noticed any recent changes in trade patterns or economic activities that might explain the landowners' resistance to unification?"

"Now that you mention it, there's been a surprising amount of trade with a Britannian trade house on one of the Gallic coasts. It's unusual, given the tariffs and the island's typical isolationist tendencies," Llassar said, leaning back in his chair, rubbing his chin thoughtfully.

"Is the trade going back to Britannia?"

"I believe so. They have heavy rail use, from what I understand."

"Is it connected to this trade house?" she asked, waving at the building around her.

"Yes. They're the only ones operating on the island, from any of the ports, but Caralis is the most northern port, closest to Gaul, so it makes sense they would trade with someone located here."

Some pieces fell into place for Medb, but she did not want to say anything yet. The closer to her chest she played her cards, the better.

"I see. I think I have some places to start, but I'll need to dip into the funds you have on hand. You'll probably have to send a messenger boat to Kalb for more. We don't have the personnel here to use our own manpower, so we'll have to buy the people we need."

"I'll make the necessary arrangements."

"I also need you to find out which Britannian ship captains are doing business here. And after we're done here, I'd like you to meet with the Britannian trade factors. Was it those men, or someone more competent?" she asked, pointing toward the outer room.

"Someone else. He doesn't come down to the docks much. I can arrange both."

"Good. Let's get started then. The sooner we unravel this mystery, the better. I still have matters to attend to that I left unattended in Carthage," Medb said, standing.

Llassar rose as well, saying, "I appreciate you coming in spite of that. I've already arranged lodging for you, and I will take care of those other things."

She smiled at the aging Caledonian. Competence; it was such a rare quality, and still one she admired. It should make this, if not easy, at least bearable.

Chapter 18

Camp Banwīhraz, Central Germania

Ky walked past the two guards on duty outside of the large tent with the prison camp commander, Sellic, glued to his side as his other lictore joined the legionnaires on guard outside. Sellic had on his guard face, but even without the serious expression, Ky would have known how annoyed the man was.

He, and the other lictore commanders, had lobbied hard against Ky's plan to leave the army for almost a week as he traveled back from the front by horse and then train to the large prisoner camp. Their concern hadn't been for Ky leaving the army, of course, which was in Bomilcar's competent hands, but for Ky being inside a fenced-in area with hundreds of captured, and mostly injured, easterner prisoners.

He understood their concern, but he also knew how important this was.

He actually should have made this trip after the first large battle when they'd been left with the field, and injured prisoners. That had still been a precarious time for the legions, however, and Ky hadn't been able to leave them. Morale had been low after a month of retreating, and they'd needed to aggressively follow up on their victory to show the men that they were not fighting an unbeatable enemy.

After several more battles, the tempo of operations had slowed down. The enemy had pulled back, most likely to reinforce itself. He'd learned from Britannian sources in Greece that the enemy's rapid progress in that region had slowed significantly as the size of the forces being seen had shrunk. Instead of thousands of soldiers marching into Greek cities and putting them to the torch, now the attacks involved hundreds. Ky's only thought was that a lot of those men, who'd been having an easy time of it, had been sent to join the army facing Ky.

Whatever the reason, Ky and Bomilcar had agreed that their men needed a rest. It also allowed the time for another legion to join the army, along with some reinforcements from the training camps to replace the steep casualties the legions had suffered.

In addition, it gave Ky a chance to finally make his way back to where they'd been holding all of the easterner prisoners and conduct his first interviews. They still knew frighteningly little about who the easterners were, aside from the obvious physical characteristics that marked them as being from Asia.

Unlike when fighting western armies, where regions had been in contact for centuries and there was at least some exposure to the various languages, before this new war began, no one in the west had ever met an easterner before. Or at least had serious contact with one of them. All of the trade that had come from that side of the world, before it had suddenly stopped at the end of the Carthaginian war, had been through intermediaries, who themselves had gotten the goods from other intermediaries. Ramirus had searched the Empire and their allies for years and had not been able to come up with anyone who'd had face-to-face contact with their new enemy.

Now that they had contact, in the form of prisoners, every report from the men charged with guarding them only talked about the language barrier and their unusual customs. There had yet to be one interview with any of the captured easterners, which was desperately needed since they still knew almost nothing about the enemy they faced.

Which was why this trip was so necessary, in spite of the small risk of being inside a prison camp with several thousand bored and angry enemy soldiers.

The inside of the tent held almost as many legionnaires as prisoners, which seemed excessive considering the state of these men. All six of the selected prisoners were injured to some degree and each looked excessively thin. Ky knew from reports that most of the men captured had one degree or another of malnutrition, and most had in fact gained weight since being in Britannian custody.

Ky had his suspicions of why this was, but he really needed first-person interviews to find out for sure. And to do that, he needed to get their language. There were those among his people gifted with languages who'd started to try and decipher the easterners' tongue, but that would take too long.

Ky needed answers, and he needed them soon.

"I am Consul Ky of the Britannian Empire. You are being held as prisoners of war. As soon as this conflict is over, you will be returned to your people. Do you understand me?" Ky said, stopping and standing in front of the men.

He received only blank, uncomprehending stares in return. Ky tried it again, using the language files Sophus had downloaded to speak the oldest form of Chinese, the language of the most populous country in Asia. At least at the point where Sophus's records cut off, and the one Ky had suspected all along to be the origin of their eastern enemy.

This time there was almost a flicker of something. Not recognition, exactly. Closer to a recognition of possible recognition. Some of the sounds must have been right, but the ordering wrong enough to make it sound like gibberish.

At least it told him he was in the right area.

Ky tried again, using what he would have thought of as universal hand signals to get across the idea that his name was Ky and that they were being held prisoner but would not be harmed.

The men still stared back, although this time Ky was certain they understood at least enough of what he'd said to get the point. This was the other thing the reports had suggested. That basic, non-verbal communication was possible, but that the prisoners were reticent to respond even if they clearly understood.

Which was not uncommon for prisoners.

"Like I said, they just stare," the camp commander said.

"So how do we get men, who we can't speak to, to talk, when they don't want to?" Ky mused sub-vocally, more out of habit than actually asking the AI.

"Intimidation is the most common tactic in these types of interrogations."

"How, exactly, do you intimidate men you can't talk to?"

"There are multiple options available. Physical acts, both demonstrative and against the person in question, and nonverbal intimidation, are the most likely paths."

"So, just torture them and hope they scream enough words in their language for you to begin to decipher it?"

"That would be ineffective. A better choice would be to play on the psychological fears of the subject."

"Which would require us to be able to communicate with them. Quite the circular logic you have there," Ky said, more frustrated at the situation than the AI.

"There are some predictive choices that can be made without communicating with the prisoners. We believe these people are from areas around modern-day China, Korea, or one of the Southeast Asian countries, although physical markers are most suggestive of mainland China itself. Using that assumption as a baseline, China had significant writings from this time, some of which survived and made their way into more modern retellings. Some of these include their superstitious beliefs in malevolent forces that they believed affected their lives. Some of these forces exhibited inhuman capabilities that your own physical enhancements are capable of replicating. Soldiers in militaries, such as these, in this time period, were not voluntary but rather conscripted, and conscripts almost inevitably came from the lower, and less educated, sections of society. Should you exhibit these superhuman feats, it is probable that they might make the connection on their own with these malevolent forces and believe you are one. We have seen much the same in both Rome and Germania, where popular belief still exists that you are somehow connected with positive supernatural forces."

"So I pretend I'm a demon and scare them into talking?"

"I believe that is what I just said," Sophus said.

If Ky didn't know better, he would think the AI was annoyed at the questioning.

"So how do I do this?"

"The best option is to try and emulate the god-like warrior Erlang Shen, who is known for his immense strength and bravery. He is also known for having a third eye, but it is possible that it is metaphorical *but not physical. However, even if not a specific deity, showing feats of strength and simple nanite repair of abrasions should be enough to frighten them, although some physical intimidation may also be required."*

"I see," Ky subvocalized and thought, while Sophus helpfully flashed across images and information about the mythological figure across his eyes.

It seemed silly, and Ky was not an actor, but it was worth a try.

Ky reached down between them, keeping eye contact with the man in the center, taking the thick metal chain connecting the manacles together, Ky slowly and easily pulled it apart, the thick iron cracking and then snapping as it broke. Ky never blinked. Taking the now broken end of the chain in his hand, Ky folded it over and then smashed it in a fist, partially flattening the metal before releasing it.

The men's eyes went wide looking at it, and Ky even heard one of the legionnaires gasp.

Ky then reached up and traced out an eye on his forehead, making sure he had their attention, before pulling out his knife. The men flinched back, probably fearing that Ky would then stab one of them or otherwise torture them. Instead, Ky raised his palm and ran the edge of the knife across his hand, causing a red line to appear as the skin split and blood began to seep out.

Ky had made sure the cut wasn't deep, so that it would heal quickly, but deep enough that they could tell what he'd done. Ky held the open wound in front of them, holding his hand steady as Sophus redirected more nanites than were necessary for such a wound to not only staunch the bleeding and close it, but to do it more quickly than was necessary, or would have been done under their own programming.

Their fear turned into astonishment as the wound began to close until it was as if he had never been injured at all.

"Ky," Ky said in an inhumanly low voice, pointing at himself before pointing at the prisoner.

The man said nothing.

Ky repeated the gesture, and again to the man next to him. Finally, one of the men got the idea and said, "Shan."

Ky made the same gesture. For a moment, he didn't think the man would understand, but Ky kept doing it, staring at the man hard. He got the idea because the man started to babble nervously. It was clear he wasn't sure what Ky was asking, but that he was trying, just saying anything that came into his head.

It was enough, as Sophus began to build a database, cross-referencing with known words in the language. The more the man spoke, the more the database began to build. Ky gestured at the men around him, making the same 'more' gesture. Not all, but some of them began to speak as well.

Ky had been right, it was some form of ancient Chinese. As with Latin, what they had in the databases was not enough to understand on its own, but knowing that was enough to build out the database faster.

Ky kept them going for several minutes, occasionally tapping a man in the chest hard to get him to continue. They rambled, muttered what seemed to be prayers, and seemed to beg for their lives.

The longer they talked, the more Ky began to understand as Sophus's translations expanded.

"Mercy, great spirit!" one of them said, although spirit might have been wrong, with Sophus only giving it a seventy percent chance of accuracy. "We are ... men! Spare us ...!"

More and more words began to connect and translate until Ky felt he had enough to make out what they were saying.

"Who are you? What is the name of your homeland?"

The men looked confused for a minute, and Ky thought perhaps they didn't understand him.

"What is the land you're from called?"

They looked at each other again. Maybe wondering why a great spirit wouldn't know its own people's land. Their fear, however, was greater than their confusion.

"TianYou."

"There is no known Asian country with that name in recorded history, however the phrase itself is out of ancient China to the effect of 'blessed by heaven' and does invoke several ideas common in Chinese history."

"But it didn't exist in real history?" Ky asked.

"No, Commander."

"So this is some alternate version of China? I get things are different here, but even with the Romans losing the Punic wars, the basic makeup of the countries, who the players are, remained largely the same. Why would an Asia be different, and have a completely new political faction?"

"There is not enough data to answer that."

"What is TianYou?" Ky asked the prisoners.

"TianYou is ... and ... beyond the ... in all directions."

"Who is in charge? Who rules over you?"

"Our emperor rules over all. He is ... he has been appointed by his fellow gods," the man said, finally with enough information that the sentence as a whole was translated.

"Why are you attacking us? What reason has your emperor given for this war?"

The men exchanged nervous glances.

"We ... we don't know, great spirit," one of the men said. "Our lords came to our farms, told us we had to fight a great enemy, taught us to use the fire weapons, and marched us across the earth to this place."

"Your lords? Who are these lords?"

"They are the emperor's chosen. They command us in his name," another prisoner said.

"Tell me about your emperor. Who is he?"

"He is ... the emperor," one of them said, as if that explained everything.

"Have any of you seen him?" Ky asked.

The man named Shan shook his head vigorously. "No one may set eyes upon the emperor, great spirit. He is too exalted for mortal gaze."

"These weapons of yours, how are they made?"

We do not know," one of them admitted. "We're only farmers and laborers. We were taught only to operate them."

Ky sighed. He hadn't expected much, but this was even worse than that. He was not going to get anything useful out of them. They were just conscripts and wouldn't know anything they weren't told.

"Fine. Tell me about your day-to-day lives in TianYou. What do you eat? How do you spend your time? What are your villages like?"

The men looked confused, but as instructions go they'd at least been given one they could carry out. While it would give him some better understanding of the culture they were up against, which he would send to Lucilla, the main goal now was to crack their language, which would allow more interrogations in the future and give Ramirus and Medb a little better chance of finding out what was really going on.

Or so he hoped.

Fort Dún Mara, Port Vikhavn

Valdar leaned against the battlements of Dún Mara, the northern fort guarding the entrance to Port Vikhavn's estuary. The final scout had returned early that morning, warning that the enemy fleet was coming soon, and it was massive.

They hadn't been wrong. Their sails practically filled the horizon as they approached, bunching around the outer island across from the mouth of the estuary. Valdar tried to count as many of them as he could through the spyglass, but between the depth of the fleet and the island blocking many of them, it was hard to get a real gauge of what he faced. What was clear to him was that they'd significantly reinforced since their last fight, which also helped to explain their month-long delay.

The month-long delay made sense to complete the needed repairs, but even more so if they'd waited for reinforcements from the east. Valdar had never sailed that far, but knowing how long it had taken to sail around the cape to the Sea of Reeds, the timeline didn't seem out of the realm of possibility. Of course, they could have established a port closer and been amassing reinforcements there as well, an idea that filled him with dread. If they did survive this battle, he would have to continue his exploration around the continent to see if it were true. It is what he would have done in their place.

In fact, it is what he did do.

They were like a great wave of locusts, swarming around just out of range of his guns. He could feel his men on edge. Even without a spyglass, it was impossible to miss the mass of sails forming up against them.

"They're forming up," Valdar called out, seeing the tell-tale signs of their fleet getting into position. "Signal Leonis to man their guns and fire when the enemy reaches medium range, and don't let up until they flee."

The twin forts guarding the estuary, Arx Leonis and Dún Mara, had spent the month reprieve given to them by the enemy well, training with the new cannon delivered to them, taking ranges using the outer isle as markers, and spending some of the large resupply of shell and powder on target practice on floating barrels. The men were as prepared as Valdar could make them.

He just hoped it would be enough.

Valdar watched as the enemy fleet began to move, the first wave of ships breaking away from the main group and heading straight for the mouth of the estuary. They were in a long line and swept far out to the south before turning and heading in a line north.

They were going to sweep the mouth of the estuary, giving the entire wave of ships, possibly as many as he had in total, broadsides at the forts, in an attempt to break them.

They were in tight formation, the ships sailing close to one another. It would allow them to pound his forts without a break, putting out a significant amount of fire in a short time frame, but it would also make them easier targets, with less chance for his men to miss a ship by shooting too far left or right. It was a calculated risk by the enemy, one he might have taken as well.

Ships did not do well against forts. A fort could take dozens, maybe hundreds, of hits before being compromised. A ship could be felled in one shot and was unlikely to survive dozens.

It also gave him the first shot, since his cannon had a wide angle of fire, being able to turn in their battlements, while ships were locked in broadsides. They would have to wait to give the forts a proper broadside, he would be able to shoot into their line first, and Arx Leonis took advantage of that, the centurion placed in charge of it knowing his job and firing as soon as they reached the appropriate range.

The fort's cannons belched to life in staggered succession, each waiting for the range to close to the correct spot. Plumes of water sprouted around the lead ships, with a few balls slamming into them. They fired again, with more shells hitting targets, and the lead ship began to veer off, listing a little bit. If Valdar had to guess, they were going to try to beach the ship on one of the outer islands, or at least get close, before the ship slipped under the waves.

The rest of the line continued on, saved from most of the fire by their lead ship, which had taken the brunt of the damage. Then it was their turn to fire, as their first broadside thundered and cannonballs screamed into the jungle around the fort, cutting trees in half, or smashed into the solid rock face of the fort, held in place by massive mounds of dirt and timber. They might as well have been pebbles thrown against a house, for all the good they did, but they continued to try.

The fort and the ships exchanged fire, each smashing cannon-balls into the other. Some of the rounds the fort was firing had been heated red hot before being loaded, with the effect of setting canvas and pitch ablaze as they landed. By the time the ships passed the mouth of the estuary, another ship had twisted out of line, burning, with nearly every other vessel in the first wave somehow damaged and weakened.

Leonis had taken some damage. One of the cannons had been hit by a lucky shot and sent flying, and there were dents and gouges all along the fort's wall, but it was far from finished, and still going strong. The men had even almost got a new gun in place where the destroyed cannon had been.

And now it was his fort's turn.

"Ready!" the gun captain called out, sighting down a mounted looking glass that had been marked with specific ranges on it. "FIRE!"

The first cannon roared as it sent a shot downrange. Whether by luck or training, it hit true, the ball smashing across the deck of the now lead ship, wiping out men and material. The rest of the cannons followed moments later. There was a good breeze that was carrying the billowing clouds of smoke away, making it possible to see well enough to aim, although even with that, it was sometimes difficult to make out the targets they were aiming at.

More ships began to go beneath the waves, some right in front of the ships following close behind them, causing a series of collisions that damaged more ships.

By the time the line of ships finally crossed out of his range, four ships had sunk, another one beached itself on one of the outlying islands, and ten were damaged to the point where Valdar was surprised they remained afloat, with holes below the waterline and damaged main masts.

After almost two hours of continuous cannon fire, it was almost eerie to have silence again. Well, silence from the cannons. Corpses still bobbed in the water, or men swam for their lives and the handful of injured men in the fort were tended to.

"They'll be back soon. Start on repairs and bring up replacement ammunition. Have the cooks feed the men while there's a lull."

His men knew their job, but after an intense fight like that, sometimes they tended to mill around a bit, unsure of what to do next, still rattled by the gunfire and death.

The enemy fleet, or all of the ships that could, retreated beyond the outer islands. For a moment, Valdar hoped they might give up and decide to continue north toward the home islands. While that would have forced Valdar's fleet to chase after them, it would also put his fleet between the easterners and resupply and put a second, not quite as large but still formidable, Britannian fleet on the other side of them, sandwiching the enemy fleet between them.

Lucan, in addition to working on the river boat prototype, had increased production on ships and had added two drydock slips to Kalb, which would have their first ship out within the next few weeks. That should give them enough fighting ability to smash the enemy between them, in a weaker position.

He wasn't so lucky, however.

Instead of fleeing south or charging north, they just hung outside the outer island. Were they hoping to blockade him? Starve him out?

They might not know the connections he had with the locals, so maybe they thought they could starve him out. That seemed like an interesting strategy, since even if he was on his own, it would take weeks to accomplish that, during which time he could sally out and harass them before retreating back.

It wasn't a strategy he would have taken.

After an hour break, their ships began moving again, another batch forming into a long line, which meant they were coming in again. It seemed like a pointless endeavor. With the amount of damage they'd done on the first pass, it would be weeks, and a lot more ships than they had, to put either one of the forts out of commission, let alone both.

"Signal the fleet and Leonis that they are preparing to come again and to stand ready. Leonis is to follow the same strategy as before."

The message flags began to fly, and his men scrambled back to their guns from where they'd been lounging, taking advantage of the break. Valdar, however, continued to watch the enemy.

Their ships didn't form one long line this time, but a line of three abreast, which would be insane for another sweeping pass. The outer two lines wouldn't be able to get shots off, but his men would be able to hit along all three at first, and then as they passed, the inner lines would be there to absorb shots. It was a terrible formation, and while a tad bit too direct in their tactics, the enemy had yet to show themselves to be stupid.

Instead of sailing south, or even far north, to get in position for a run-up, they cut hard around the outer islands and then turned hard, making a straight line for the mouth of the estuary.

They were going to push their way through, hoping they could get either tangled with his ships or deep enough to be out of the range of the guns. They couldn't, but they could go at the port, giving Valdar the option of shelling his own people or letting them have it.

"Signal the fleet. They're going to try to punch through. Prepare the reception committee," Valdar ordered.

This had always been an option. One, in fact, that Valdar had thought even probable, and he and his officers had discussed in depth what to do when they did try it.

As soon as the ship sailed within range, his cannon opened up. Unlike last time, they were head-on the entire way, essentially crossing the T with two forts.

"Fire!" Valdar's command rang out, and Dún Mara's cannons thundered in response, the heavy iron balls screaming through the air before crashing into the advancing ships. The lead vessel in the first column took a direct hit, the shot tearing through its bow and sending splintered wood and bodies alike into the sea. The ship shuddered under the impact, its momentum faltering as the crew scrambled to right her course.

Arx Leonis joined the fray, its own cannons unleashing a barrage that caught the first ship in the line third line. The enemy vessel lurched to one side, its sails catching fire as a heated shot ignited the tarred canvas. Men scrambled to douse the flames, but it was already too late. The ship, ablaze and out of control, veered sharply toward the rocky outcrop at the mouth of the inlet, breaking apart on the rocks and beginning to burn to the water line.

"Keep firing!" Valdar urged, his focus shifting to the third column of ships.

Another ship in the lead column shuddered under the impact of the cannon fire. This one, too, began to list, its hull breached below the waterline. The frantic efforts of its crew to plug the leaks were futile, and within moments, the vessel began to sink, its stern rising into the air before disappearing beneath the waves.

The gun crews worked feverishly, reloading and firing as quickly as they could. Not that they were going to be able to stop the inevitable. Finally, the enemy ships entered range and again opened broadsides, blasting away at the forts. Valdar could see their strategy now. The three lines meant that the center line couldn't fire at all, but they were also mostly protected with how closely the other two lines were sailing. They were allowing two-thirds of this wave to be chewed apart by the forts just to get the last third into the bay unscathed.

The fact that this was almost a third of their fleet spoke volumes about what the easterners were willing to throw into victory. The waters of the estuary inlet became a graveyard of shattered timbers and floating debris, as more ships sank. Despite the carnage, their plan was working so far. The middle line was going to mostly get through unscathed.

"Signal the ships. They're going to make it through."

He knew the captains were watching and would be ready, but he still wanted to give them a moment's warning. The enemy had a good plan, but it was never going to work.

His fleet was set up in a crescent formation, so that every ship could get a shot off. As the enemy broke through, they got pounded again, the lead ships breaking up almost as soon as they crossed into the harbor. The captains had timed it well and dozens of rounds smashed into the ship as it cleared the smoke and debris of the inlet channel.

The rear guns of the fort added to the death. Broadside after broadside tore apart enemy ships until sinking so many that the inlet itself became blocked with their burning hulks. Some of the remaining ships raised a white flag, surrendering. Others tried to turn and escape. All but the back few ships in the sortie failed. There were just too many ships, too many wrecks, and not enough open water. Of the initial twenty or so ships that had made the run to try and smash into the harbor, only four made it back out, running back to their fleet, limping as they did from the pounding the forts gave them on the way out.

"Send out the boats to pick up survivors," Valdar commanded. "Take them prisoner and turn them over to the port commander. We'll figure out what to do with them and how to question them soon."

He had other things to worry about at the moment. The enemy's attack might have failed, but it succeeded in locking his ships in the port. The mouth of the estuary was choked with the wreckage of sunken ships, their masts jutting out of the water like tombstones. None of his ships would be making their way out to the ocean until this got cleaned up.

Chapter 19

Devnum

Hortensius made his way down the docks again. The non-stop travel was a reminder of how time was catching up to him. It felt like only a few years ago that he was just opening his first factory, working constantly, getting it running and profitable through sheer willpower alone.

He still had that same willpower, but his body was starting to let him down, his hips screaming at him during the long walk from the train station to the docks. While he found the entire ship project interesting from a technical standpoint, he would be happy for the day when he could just stay at his factory and stop the endless travel back and forth.

"Lucan!" Hortensius called out as he shuffled his way to the slip where the shipmaster was looking over the rebuilt steamship prototype.

"Hortensius, my friend. Thanks for coming down. I know these trips are wearing on you, but we got the engine and propeller in place and started the tests, and I thought you'd want to see it. It's a little early in the process, but after the last incident … well, I wanted to make sure we both had eyes on it to make sure the flaws were ironed out."

"Of course, of course. It is unfortunate, but this is how we learn the hard lessons. Thankfully, for this catastrophe, I believe we've identified the root cause."

Lucan held out his arm to take some of Hortensius' weight, the two walking out onto the platform and down into the still open shell of the test platform, allowing him to look down to see the still gleaming copper pipes and rebuilt boiler.

"The issue stemmed from the thin, high-pressure lines we initially used," Hortensius continued. "They allowed excessive pressure to build up and feed back into the boiler, leading to a catastrophic failure, and we've implemented some additions to the design to fix that."

"Your man mentioned that but didn't go into specifics."

"We've implemented thicker, reinforced pipes capable of withstanding higher pressures and incorporated a series of pressure relief valves that should allow the boiler to shed any backup and prevent that buildup from occurring again. Of course, my team will continue to monitor the system to make sure it really does fix it."

"If we're releasing steam to protect the boiler, how do we keep the pressure up? Won't it just bleed all the power away?"

"It shouldn't, since it should only release the steam in over-pressure situations, which would only happen if something else had failed, but that is possible in a combat situation, which could lead to a loss of power during combat."

"That isn't ideal."

"No. Although neither is the boiler exploding during a combat situation."

"That's true," Lucan said, frowning down at the ship.

Hortensius knew the shipbuilder would prefer to stick to wood and sail, things he was more comfortable with.

"The only real fix for this is training," Hortensius said. "I think it's clear every ship is going to need an engineer, which in this case just means someone trained on the system, inside and out. These men will be taught not just how to operate it, but to recognize problems and perform field improvements. It will make getting ships out of the slip harder, of course, since proper training can take as much time as building one of these, but I think we can set up a program to do it."

"We should really start that now, then. The Consul has already asked about the new river ships twice this month, and I imagine those requests will become more frequent as the year draws to an end. If we want these engineers of yours trained properly, you need to start *now*. Unless you plan on parting with some of your people."

"Ha, you know that is out of the question. I'll begin working on a program now and see what volunteers we can get for it, since I'm sure that the training will also need some fine-tuning as we get into it."

"Good. Then I'm extra glad you came out today because that could have been a major delay point in this entire project. You know, I must admit, this experience has given me a newfound appreciation for the risks involved in our work. I know you talked about how much harder the accelerated timeline made everything, but ... I hadn't put that together with the safety risk before."

"Yes. I think it takes the first big failure for all of us, before we realize just how big the costs can be if we make a mistake in haste."

"Yes," Lucan said in the tone of a man remembering his own failures, before shaking it off. "Well, so far, it seems the design is working better, but we'll see once we get the entire ship built around it. I also wanted you to come by and talk about the propeller design. We got the bent one pulled out and had to make some design adjustments for this new one, as well as adding in the new protective shell you designed, which I have some concerns about."

"Really? I thought it was actually ingenious when one of my designers brought it to me. It wasn't in the Consul's original plans, but the small-scale river testing we did showed that the housing would allow enough water to pass through to not impact momentum and would protect the blade and shaft from debris and even small impacts with shallow riverbeds, should they occur."

"And our testing shows the same. My concern was twofold. One was clogging. The way it allows water to pass through is great, and will probably work well on the ocean, but in a river, with silt and debris, clogging will be a problem. I've talked to some of your guys about using some of the cabling equipment you designed for other areas and making some kind of metal weave to put over it, to keep that stuff out of the flow, but that has its own problem. It's easy to see the pressure created by the water coming through will hold the debris in place, clogging the mesh. The more it gets clogged, the less water that comes through and the less propulsion we'll get."

"That is a good point," Hortensius said, pressing his lips together in thought.

"I do have a suggestion, however."

"Really? I'm all ears."

This was the part Hortensius liked the most about collaboration. The bouncing of ideas off of each other, sharing thoughts. It got his heart pumping.

"Instead of the opening at the rear of the intake, what if that was closed and pointed, because it's also adding drag to the ship, and instead we put these almost gill-like inlets down the length of the shaft housing to allow water in, smaller and still with the metal weave protecting from debris, but with enough of them, and each only providing a fraction of the flow, so that any one of them, or several of them, getting clogged wouldn't impact the overall water flow."

Hortensius nodded along as Lucan spoke. "That's interesting. That's very interesting. If it's not a flat, wide surface, or even the curved one we had, and if we angled it out instead of in, the pressure of the water moving along the housing as it cut through the water would push the debris that did try to clog in the vents. That could very well work."

Lucan beamed. "I'm glad you approve."

"I do. You know, this is where it shows how much practical experience matters. The theory of all this is workable, but you have real experience with water. A lifetime of it. Which really helps you see other ways to do things that we didn't think of. We need more of this. I should probably look at bringing in experts for whatever area a project is impacting for the other stuff we're working on, who've used the design, or previous or similar designs, in the field enough to see the pitfalls we haven't thought of."

"That's probably not a bad idea," Lucan said, clearly happy he'd been able to contribute.

Hortensius, however, was already working out the venting idea. They were very close to being able to actually build one of these river beasts. He still didn't see how well these could help them in the war, considering the rivers mostly ran west to east and not across the enemies' path of advancement. What mattered was that the Consul did see.

Besides, this was a test platform for the ocean-going ships all along, which meant they were closer to that now than ever before.

Pella, Macedonia

The journey to Greece had been long, and Ramirus's very bones hurt. The first two-thirds of the journey had not been that difficult, mostly done on long stretches of rail in fairly comfortable passenger cars, with the exception of a short boat trip across the channel.

The real trouble had been once they'd reached the edge of Italia, where the Britannian rail lines ended. From there, they had traveled by horseback over rough paved roads, across mountains and hills. Ramirus realized how much he'd grown used to living in a more modernized society, since this would have once been his normal transportation when he traveled beyond Devnum, and now he hardly ever mounted a horse. That had also been almost seven years prior. He was so much older now.

Finally, they'd made it to Pella, the once-grand capital of Macedonia. The city's faded glory struck him immediately. Not just that it had faded from its glory days under Philip and Alexander, before the rise of the Carthaginians, although it certainly had lost the splendor it held at the height of the Hellenistic age. Again, he was forced to realize how much the Consul had given them and how it had affected nearly every aspect of his life.

Since leaving Gaul and even Italia, which had started to adopt some of Britannia's cultural and technological changes, every city they'd traveled through in Greece had been run down, rough, and difficult. He noticed the lack of steam whistles and telegraph lines and the very people looked generally sicker and more malnourished than his, or any of their allies, did.

It wasn't completely devoid of Britannian influence. Here and there, a hint of smuggled-in or purchased products could be seen. Steel fixtures that looked much newer and cleaner than the steel around it, cut with a much cleaner edge. A small steam-powered water pump in the corner of a square, chugging away next to a well of some sort, the presence of which once again proved that items marked as only for sale to allies didn't always seem to stay that way. They still made their way out of allied hands, resold to people not part of the alliance.

That, however, wasn't the most notable thing about the city. The most notable thing was the people. Ramirus had traveled through city after city on the long journey across the continent, and once they passed the bounds of Britannian influence, he had noticed how each step further east he went, the more subdued the people seemed to be.

The citizens of Pella hurried about their business, not stopping to talk to their neighbors in most cases, and those that did, did so in hushed whispers. There was a tension that seemed to hang over the entire city. The only exception to the fear of interacting or even noticing their neighbors seemed to be his party, which stood out, followed by a squad of praetorians carrying the long Britannian rifles, escorted by guardsmen still in armor with swords, spears, and the occasional Britannian musket.

People's eyes followed them as they passed toward the somewhat small palace at the center of the city, all that remained of Philip's once-powerful home.

They were led inside to something more like a teaching amphitheater than a meeting room or a forum. Already inside were dozens of men in various types of dress, although it was all still unmistakably Greek. Another difference from the Britannians, who'd shed their traditional togas for more comfortable and versatile pants and tunics that the Consul and the legionnaires had adopted. Looking at the draped clothes the Greek dignitaries wore, Ramirus suppressed a frown. He did not miss the days of dealing with all of that fabric. It might not be the greatest invention provided by the Consul, but it wasn't far off either.

He knew some of the men by description or style of dress; the others, Ramirus could only guess, but it did seem as if the majority of the various Greek kingdoms and city-states were represented.

A heavyset man with graying hair at his temples rose as Ramirus's party entered. "Welcome, emissaries of Britannia. I am Aristides of Athens. We have gathered, as requested, to hear your words. Though I must say, many here question the wisdom of entertaining Britannian overtures at this time."

He spoke Greek, as they always did. It was standard for negotiations to take place in the language of the larger nations, and Latin had become the default language of the majority of Britannia's allies because of that. And yet, the Greeks saw themselves as perpetually above everyone else and refused to 'stoop to the level of barbarians.'

Ramirus inclined his head respectfully and replied in the same language. "We appreciate your willingness to meet, despite your reservations. I assure you, what we have to discuss is of utmost importance to the future of all our peoples. And I thank you for your warm welcome. I am Ramirus, emissary of Empress Lucilla Germanicus and the Britannian Empire. I know we have spoken to most of your representatives in the past about various alliances and treaties to enable our two peoples to work together, and also with the men you sent to the council where the great western alliance was formed. At that time, war was a possibility, a far-off worry, and your people chose not to join those of us who began to prepare for its coming. Now that the war is here and your own borders have been violated, we have returned to once again ask you to stand with us against this enemy from the Far East that hopes to become our overlords now that we have freed ourselves from the Carthaginians."

Straight and to the point, as he had found was always the best way when dealing with the Greeks. Otherwise, they would pull everything down into pointless debate on topics of little importance, completely missing the reasoning of the original offer.

It took them no time to begin to do that once again.

"We cannot simply bow to Britannian demands!" cried out one man.

"What of our sovereignty? Will you make us mere puppets?" yelled another.

Across the entire gathering, men began to shout reasons why they didn't want to join the alliance, as if nothing had changed. As if Britannia had marched in and offered demands without reason.

For several minutes, Ramirus stood there and let them vent their frustration. Waiting for a pause in their commentary but otherwise ignoring their objections. Finally, Ramirus raised his hand, thankfully quelling the cacophony for a moment.

"Gentlemen, before we continue down this well-worn path yet again, how have these lines of questioning protected your people? Are your cities still safe, unthreatened? Your colonies thriving, unconquered? Does denying the reality of your situation protect your people in any way, or does it hand them to your enemy?"

That, at least, had an effect. It was as if he had personally walked up to each man in the room and slapped him in the face. Again, there was an outcry, men demanding an apology for his words, as if that was what was hurting them and not the armies marching even now across their lands.

"I am sorry if my words struck you as callous, and I did not come here to cause offense, but we have heard word of how poorly the situation fares for you. Of armies marching into Thrace. Of your people dying. Now is not the time to bicker and squabble. Now is the time to come together and stop the enemy before another foot of ground is taken. I know your people understand it. I could feel their fear as we made our way through your cities for this meeting. They are afraid of the horde already killing fellow Greeks, with promises to kill more before they are done. Aren't you duty-bound to address your people's fears? To see to their safety?"

For a moment, no one answered. Really, what could they say? Everything Ramirus had said was true. Their people were in danger, were already dying. And yet still they argued.

"Pretty words, Britannian," a voice called out from the back. "Considering your failures to protect those who did agree to your terms."

Ramirus turned to face the speaker, a tall, lean man with a neatly trimmed beard. "And you are?"

"Lysander of Thrace," the man replied, rising to his feet. "While you speak of fear and duty, we've heard reports of your struggles in Germania. How can you protect us when you can barely hold your own lines?"

Murmurs of agreement rippled through the crowd. They were so ready to believe any word that reinforced their own biases. Ramirus could feel the situation slipping away from him.

"The war in Germania is complex, but the easterners have been retreating for weeks now, losing two major battles to our legions."

"And yet they still stand on the soil of Germania, whom you swore to protect. We hear even now, more of the easterners march to counter your forces. There is a better way," he said, looking now to the men around him. "The easterners have offered terms. Favorable ones."

"You can't seriously be considering capitulation," Ramirus said, even as a wave of relief seemed to sweep across the men as they took in the news and began to whisper among themselves.

"And why not? The easterners offer protection, trade, and autonomy. What does Britannia offer but more war and uncertainty?"

Ramirus watched in dismay as several Greek leaders nodded in agreement. The atmosphere in the room had shifted dramatically. What had begun as reluctance and skepticism was now morphing into genuine interest in surrender.

"This is madness," Ramirus said. "Moments ago, many of you complained that our offer, which came with no claim over your territory, no financial burden, nothing more than your participation in your own defense, was an affront to your sovereignty. And yet to a people who have already killed your citizens, who move to burn your cities, offers you subjugation, you see some kind of salvation. What kind of insanity is this?"

"You have a point," Aristides said. "But you do not offer guarantees. Unless you plan on attacking Greece if we choose to capitulate and surrender?"

Ramirus didn't answer, mostly because he couldn't say, and definitely couldn't promise, anything if they sided with the easterners. The debate went on for twenty more minutes, and nothing changed. Some of the assembled leaders, mostly those farthest from Asia Minor, were on the fence, unsure of what they wanted to do, but many of those closer to the east, which was a majority of the major states, seemed to be siding with the Thracians and could not be budged.

They were reacting out of fear, spurred on by their previous choices made out of apathy and fear of doing something when they could have done nothing. It was one bad choice after another compounding the impact with each one.

They ended with an agreement to meet again and an offer for Ramirus to stay in the city, which he accepted with the hopes that he could convince at least some of them to see reason.

He needed to send word to the Empress right away and wished a telegraph line had made its way all the way here. She needed to know things in Greece were much worse than anyone feared.

Chapter 20

Sardinia

Medb was back in a dark room, the windows shuttered against the outside world, partially for secrecy but also to keep the noxious smell of fish and salt out of her nose. She'd never loved ships and tried to stay on dry land as much as possible, but she hadn't realized her dislike of it would translate to docks as well.

Of course, she rarely spent much time at them, aside from getting to and from whatever ship she'd been forced to take. Now, not only had she been forced to spend a week stuck here, but she'd made arrangements to stay in a less than savory place far down from the Britannian mission, above a fishmonger's warehouse.

The smell was putrid. The warehouse was also extremely busy, doing a very lively business. She knew that others in her profession would have frowned on such a thing. After all, how could you conduct secret meetings in a place with so many eyes? Ramirus, however, had given her very good advice when he'd started teaching her the intricacies of the trade.

"People see what they want to see and only really notice things that are out of place. So a quiet building, with no one around except for one room with people coming and going would draw suspicion, but a place with strangers coming from all over the city to buy wares and both fishermen and passing traders stopping to do business meant that there were always people around, always going in different directions, with so much happening that it would be hard to track where any one person was headed.

So her little rented room, arranged by intermediaries renting it to use temporarily for managing a flow of workers into the harbor during the particularly busy shipping season, which this was, would gain little notice. She'd also made sure it was down a long hallway, around a corner from any open spaces, in a building where the layout meant no other doors were around the same corner, which meant no through traffic and nothing for people to notice if they had noticed the influx of people through her small room.

And people certainly influxed. She'd used a Britannian porter Llassar had befriended early on for the first stages of her plan, but that had just been to hire people more suitable for the work she needed to do but couldn't do in person. Unlike Llassar, who was the face of Britannia here, she wanted to leave her options open, based on what she found, which meant operating in secret.

Speaking of more suitable people, a knock at the door told her one of those men had finally finished his latest task.

"Come," she said, not getting up.

The door opened, revealing a nondescript man that Medb knew was much more deadly than his plain exterior indicated. Which is exactly what she liked. Some people would go for the big brutes, a scar over one eye, speaking to a career of life-or-death situations, and those men had their places, but for her money, they stood out too much. Men like Melsar were much better for most of the work she needed.

In front of Melsar was a nervous-looking man, suggesting her associate had found it necessary to prove his bona fides to him. Good. She wanted this man nervous.

"Thank you, Melsar. Wait outside, would you?"

The beady-eyed man grunted an acknowledgment and closed the door, leaving Medb alone with her new guest. The smaller man's eyes darted around the sparse room, his fingers fidgeting with the frayed edges of his tunic.

"What do you want with me?"

"What I want, Berith, is to have a little chat about your financial situation."

"What financial situation? I don't even know you, how do you know ..."

"I actually know quite a bit about you, Berith. I know that you are single since your wife left you and ran to the mainland. I know that your brother stopped talking to you after you borrowed money from him and then failed to pay him back a year ago. And I know about the debts you were supposed to pay back with that money but used for more gambling instead. Money you still owe Nurakes."

"Did Nurakes send you? I told him …"

"I do not work for Nurakes, but I did have a nice conversation with him about your situation. He was very concerned about how far behind you were on paying him back, and I think he was considering fairly extreme tactics to get that money back. Lucky for you, I convinced him to sell me your debt instead."

"What … Why would you do that? If you know I couldn't pay?"

"Because I don't want coin from you, Berith. I'm after something far more valuable than that."

"What … what do you mean?"

"Information," Medb said simply. "You tell me what I want to know, and I'll consider your debt paid in full."

He looked surprised, probably trying to figure out why anyone would come to him for information.

"What kind of information?"

"Information about your master, Nuraian."

Another look of surprise. Whatever he had been expecting from Medb, that was clearly not it.

"Nuraian? He is just a businessman. What could you possibly want to know about him?"

"You are not so naive that you believe that, Berith. I think you know there is more to it than that. You are in his house. You see the people he has coming in and out of it. Nuraian has been quite involved in Sardinian politics recently, with all sorts of people around, talking to him. Lots of people from the cities, other farmers. I would like to know what he is so interested in, and I would like for you to tell me."

"I … I only keep his house, do repairs. I do not know anything about his interests or business dealings."

"Come now, Berith. We both know your position gives you far more access than most. You are around; you see who comes and goes. You are exactly who I am looking for. I know about his normal business interests, but what I want to hear about are the unusual people who started to come by his home over the last six months or so. The types of people you do not remember seeing before then."

Berith blanched, shaking his head vigorously. "No, I cannot ... I will not betray my master's trust. He would have my head!"

"And what do you think I will do, Berith. That was a lot of money I paid to Nurakes for your debts. Do you think it is only your head I will take? Should I call my man back in here and give you a taste of what you could lose?"

He did not say anything right away, just looked from her to the door and back again.

"No," he finally said sheepishly.

"Then tell me what I want to hear. Has there been anything unusual happening at your master's house recently? Something out of the ordinary, more visitors than normal, or visitors that perhaps stood out a little?"

"Yes, there has been an increase in shipments. A lot of wagons coming in full and leaving full, although always covered. Sometimes dozens in a day, although we are not allowed to go near the area where those goods are being delivered to and held."

"What about the people bringing those goods in? Were they foreigners?"

"Yes," he said, clearly a little surprised at her guess.

"Greeks? Egyptians? Maybe more unusual types from further east?"

"No," he said, confused now rather than surprised. "Mostly Britons speaking Latin, which I do not know well, so I couldn't really make out what they were saying. If I had to guess, though, I'd say they were Romans from their dress."

Medb kept her face neutral. That it was a surprise to her as much as her earlier questions were a surprise to him was not something he needed to know. Details like that were best left unspoken.

"I see. And you have no idea what they were bringing?"

"No, but it seemed important."

Medb studied him for a moment, considering whether to push him further. It would be useful for him to sneak into the area where the goods were held, perhaps get a peek at them. She almost instantly discarded that idea. He was much too jittery to be given a more strenuous task. He would almost certainly be caught easily, and she needed more time before she did anything to alert Nuraian that she was looking into him.

Better to leave things as they were. Just knowing the men were Britons was enough to give her a place to start looking.

"Thank you for your help, Berith. You are to keep this meeting to yourself," she said, making sure he saw the look in her eyes and took her very seriously. "Not a word about talking to me. To anyone. Unless, of course, you want a visit from my man."

Berith nodded vigorously, eyes going back to the door again. "No, my lady. I mean yes. I mean, I won't say anything. I swear it. But ... my debt ...?"

"If the information you've given me is accurate, and if you keep your mouth closed, your debt will be settled. But cross me, Berith, and you'll wish Nurakes was the one you had to worry about."

"I won't."

Medb dismissed him with a wave, watching as he scurried out of the room, leaving her alone with her thoughts. Romans in Sardinia.

That was interesting.

North of Port Vikhavn

Li Shu crept through the dense jungle, his cotton tunic clinging to his sweat-soaked skin. He hated this place. It was hot and wet, the air feeling like porridge around him, his nostrils filled with the smell of decayed vegetation mixed with salt water.

It was beyond foul.

He had been happy to finally be allowed off the ship the officials had crammed so many of them into. They weren't sailors and Li had never even been on a ship before a few months ago, when they sailed him what seemed like around the entire world. He had been forced to hide below decks while the ships were being ripped apart by cannon shells and men sent to the bottom of the sea, drowning.

Now, he was not so sure the ships were all that bad. Insects kept biting him, tearing at his skin. Worse, they were lost. He knew it. They had changed direction multiple times and he could swear they had even gone backward a few times, although it was very hard to tell. The jungle was very thick, and he couldn't even really see the moon or stars with what light they did cast becoming scattered through the trees, creating shadows everywhere.

They had stopped again with their leader, who was in the rear as was befitting his station, talking with several of his senior men. They were arguing, each pointing in one direction or another. Li didn't like being in this small clearing. It made him feel exposed.

"We've been wandering for hours," Wei, a man standing a few steps from him, said. "He's lost again."

"Quiet," someone hissed. "He'll hear you."

"I don't care. We should run back to the beach and leave this cursed place."

"And face execution? No thank you."

"Silence in the ranks! The next man who speaks dies where he stands," the commander said, his voice a little louder than Li would have liked.

They all fell silent, but Wei wasn't wrong. They were nowhere near the cursed westerner fort. A rustle in the underbrush caught Li Shu's attention. He raised his musket instinctively, but couldn't pinpoint the source of the noise. Several other men followed suit, although he was pretty sure they were mimicking him.

Everyone was nervous and on edge.

"I saw something in the trees," a man said, pointing off to the right.

"It's an animal, you idiot. Be silent," the commander said, before going back to his argument.

It probably was an animal. They had nearly opened fire several times already, mistaking wildlife for the enemy. They all knew they had to be quiet. Firing a rifle would certainly let the enemy know they were there, but it had been very close at times. There were animals everywhere it seemed, and they all sounded like an army sneaking up to kill them.

And then the night erupted into chaos. It took a second for Li's brain to register what was happening as tongues of fire leaped out of the jungle all around them, as if they'd angered a nest of dragons that spewed their displeasure.

It wasn't dragons, though. It was firearms of some kind, and the shots were coming from all around them. Bullets ripped into the tightly packed men, sending some of his comrades crumpling to the ground.

"Ambush!" someone screamed.

"Form a line! Return fire!" the commander shrieked.

It took a moment for the under-commanders to shake their men out of the absolute shock they were in and get them moving into formation. Li scrambled to obey, his fingers fumbling with his weapon as he tried to align himself with the others. The air was already clogged with the acrid smoke from the weapons firing at them, the hazy fog making the jungle even darker, which Li hadn't thought possible.

"Fire!" the under commander shouted.

Li and the other men in line let loose a thundering volley into the darkness in front of them. There was no musket fire from in front, but it continued to come in from the sides in sporadic shots.

"Did we hit anyone?" Wei asked.

As if in answer, tongues of flame leaped out of the forest in front of them again, proving that at least some of the attackers in that direction were still alive. The man beside him crumpled, clutching his chest.

"Again!" the commander bellowed. "Fire another volley!"

Li finished reloading and lifted his rifle. He didn't even wait for the others, firing into the darkness. A few of his comrades did the same, while others just stood there in shock, not even having reloaded. If the first volley had been ineffective, this one was almost certainly not going to stop the assault.

Li started to reload again.

Instead of more fire, however, the jungle suddenly came alive. Dark figures erupted from the undergrowth, brandishing wicked-looking spears and blades. Li lifted his rifle as several ran for him, but he was panicking. He squeezed the trigger hard, jerking the weapon up, the shot going wild.

"Demons!" someone screamed. "We're surrounded by demons!"

Panic spread through their ranks. Li Shu watched in horror as his comrades fumbled with their weapons, unable to reload fast enough to meet this new threat.

A man was charging right at Li, and there was no time to reload his rifle. He barely managed to bring it up in time to deflect a vicious downward slash of the blade in the man's hand. The impact jarred his arms, nearly causing him to drop his rifle. Acting on instinct, more from learning to use a staff and spear as a child and young man than from the incredibly short training they'd been given on how to use the rifles, Li swung out with the butt of the rifle, catching his assailant in the jaw.

The man staggered back, momentarily stunned. Li Shu seized his chance. With a desperate cry, he lunged forward, driving his bayonet deep into his attacker's chest. The man's eyes widened in shock, then glazed over as he slumped to the ground.

All around him, men began to fall as his entire group began to come apart, any sense of cohesion gone. And then they lost the commander.

Li turned to see what the orders were when a spear came out of seemingly nowhere and embedded itself into the commander's chest, impaling him. The man had the nerve to look surprised as he died, as if he hadn't led them straight into this trap.

With his death, all semblance of order evaporated instantly. Men scattered in all directions, running for their lives.

"Back to the boats!" someone shouted.

It was as good of a plan as Li had heard, except he wasn't even sure which direction the boats were in. He began to run.

He passed a small group huddled behind a fallen log on the edge of the clearing, desperately trying to mount a final stand. Li ignored them. They were doomed. The only way to survive was to get away, and any thought of helping his compatriots was overwhelmed by his desire to live. He plunged into the undergrowth, branches whipping at his face as he ran blindly.

He could hear the men predictably dying behind him. The sounds spurred him on to greater speed as he put as much distance between himself and the carnage as possible. The sounds of terror and death began to fade, but Li didn't stop running.

At least, not until his foot caught on an unseen root, sending him sprawling. Li scrambled to his feet, mud and rotting vegetation clinging to his clothes.

He stood there for a moment, the jungle suddenly silent around him. He had no idea which way he'd run away from the fight or which way he should go now. He didn't want to just run back into that carnage, and he didn't want to be lost in the jungle forever.

He was lost. In the darkness, every direction looked the same. The launches, their only hope of escape, could be anywhere.

A twig snapped nearby. Li spun, bringing his rifle up. His eyes darted wildly, not that it helped. The jungle was inky black, and anything more than a step away from him was lost in the void.

Another crack, closer this time. He whirled, weapon at the ready. And then he saw the eyes. The only thing he could make out in the jungle. Two white, human eyes right next to him. And then the smile, the white teeth showing in the darkness.

What Li didn't see was the blade crashing down toward him until it bit deep into his skull, ending any further thoughts or fears.

Outside Factorium

It was unusual to be in a carriage again. She had grown so used to the jostling experience of the train rides that she thought she didn't really even notice how uncomfortable it was any more, and she had only really traveled by train or boat for years now. Ky complained that those could be more stable experiences, and she had almost started having that same attitude every time the train jostled or shifted.

Being in one of these again, however, pulled over a rough, uneven dirt track that shouldn't actually be called a road, made her want to take back every one of those thoughts. Twice, the wagon had shifted so precariously that she had sworn it was going to topple over onto its side and once she had banged her head hard enough that she could feel a knot forming.

Hortensius, however, had said this was the most important demonstration he had given in years and that it was critical for her to be there to approve the final steps of the fuse project so he could start producing new shells and get them to the front before the winter set in.

So, in the carriage she went.

Thankfully, the ride from the Factorium station to the testing grounds was not a long one. As the carriage pulled to a stop, she could see a gun set up on a concrete slab in the middle of the field, with protective concrete buildings behind it and a big open field in front of it.

Hortensius and a small army of assistants were gathered around the howitzer, but the manufacturer turned and hurried over as soon as he saw her, intercepting her by the concrete observation bunkers.

"Your Majesty! Thank you for coming to witness our final demonstration," Hortensius said, out of breath but still bowing. "I believe you're going to be quite impressed with what we have to show you."

"I'm certain I will be," Lucilla said, smiling at her old friend.

"While I believe this should be safe, I think it best if everyone uses the bunkers today. Our last test had some ... explosive results on the test platform and I'd hate to see anyone injured by our work. Or at least any of our people injured."

There was an odd sound to his voice and Lucilla wondered if it ever bothered him, working on weapons designed to kill people. He was a true Roman and she knew how seriously he took his part in protecting the Empire, but he was also one of the gentlest souls she had ever met, and he would not hurt a fly.

It, in turn, made her sad, the things the world made of them.

She allowed him to usher her and her guards into a bunker, while he returned to the gun and spent a few minutes performing his last checks, before he and his assistants all came into the bunkers themselves, with Hortensius joining her in the central bunker.

One poor soul was much closer, in a small trench, with a long pull rope that ran to the gun to set it off.

"It looks like we're all set," Hortensius said as he entered the bunker. "This first shot will use the impact fuse. If it works properly, it will explode when it hits the ground, both creating a destructive blast that is capable of destroying fortifications or other obstacles, as well as people, of course. The shell casing itself actually rips to pieces as it explodes, each piece becoming as deadly as bullets. Jagged and sharp, the explosion expels those pieces at a high rate of speed, increasing the impact and affecting uncovered targets well away from the blast radius."

"Ohh," Lucilla said.

That was not in Ky's instructions, which had mostly been technical focusing on how to build it. She had understood those and the purpose of having it explode, since a hard shell would generally only injure those impacted by it and maybe people a few steps away as it sent up dirt and debris, but that was it. From what she had read, an explosion would have a chance to affect everyone in a radius around the explosion. It had not occurred to her that the metal casing of the shells would also become weapons, but giving it some thought, it made sense.

"I'm looking forward to seeing it in action," Lucilla added.

"Yes. Yes. These glasses have been set to give you a better view of the impact area," he said, pointing to several brass spyglasses fixed into a viewing slit.

Lucilla moved up to one and peered through it. Another invention that she didn't use much, but found fascinating every time she did, as it brought the pock-marked landscape close enough that she felt like she could reach out and touch it. It also helped that the ground had been chosen well, with the bunkers on a slight rise behind the firing platform, making the testing grounds themselves visible with no obstructions.

"Yes. This is excellent."

"Good," Hortensius said before leaning up to the small viewing slit and yelling out to the man in the trench. "Fire at will, please, Bodvoc."

The man gave a wave and yanked the line. Lucilla was prepared for it, and yet the boom of the cannon took her by surprise. She stared intently through the looking glass as the shell arced through the air and then came plummeting back to the earth. When it hit, there was an impressive plume of fire, followed by a booming sound and then a shaking of the very ground they stood on. When the smoke from the shell cleared, a large hole was cut into the ground.

It was an impressive display.

"My goodness."

"Yes, the destructive force is something," Hortensius said.

"It's all thanks to you and the Consul. That last change you gave us was quite impressive, especially using the initial shock of being fired by the cannon to activate the fuse without the need for the extensive safety system we had been building into them."

"What about on different terrain? Say if there's dense vegetation that cushions its fall. Will the shell still go off?"

"Yes. We've tested it against a variety of surfaces and found that it will detonate reliably on impact with any solid surface, be it fortifications, rocky ground, or even dense vegetation."

"You've done exceptional work, Hortensius. I'm proud of what you've accomplished here."

"Thank you, Your Majesty. But we're not done yet. If you'll allow me, I'd like to show you that surprise I mentioned earlier."

"A surprise?" Lucilla asked.

That was unusual. Hortensius was a brilliant man, but everything that had been invented had come from Ky, usually through her. It was a surprise sometimes what the end result actually looked like, and Lucilla didn't always completely understand what the diagrams and instructions were telling Hortensius, but she still had some basic idea of what the result was going to be.

So an actual surprise would be ... well, a surprise.

"You'll see in a moment, Your Majesty. I think you'll find this quite impressive."

The crew finished their preparations and retreated to the safety of the bunkers. Once more, the lone figure in the trench pulled the firing cord. As with the last time, she looked into the spyglass trained down-field as the shell arced high into the sky, expecting it to come crashing back to the earth, as it had the last time.

However, just as it reached its apex, something unexpected occurred. The shell suddenly erupted in a brilliant flash, far above the target area.

Lucilla blinked in surprise, momentarily stepping back from the spyglass, thinking something had gone wrong. "What in the world?"

Hortensius, who was smiling, waved her back to look as a second shell was loaded and fired.

"That is what is supposed to happen, but you missed the most important part. Watch all the way through this time, Your Majesty."

Again, the shell arched high in the sky, and again it exploded well before it ever touched the ground. This time, she continued watching as, across a wide swath of land, puffs of dust began to spring up, very dense in a circle more or less under the shell but spreading out for quite some distance as something peppered the ground.

Stepping back again, Lucilla said, "Alright, I'm thoroughly impressed. Now, explain what I just saw."

Hortensius nodded eagerly. "This, Your Majesty, is what we're calling an airburst shell. The impacts you saw were from hundreds of projectiles in the shell that are launched out when it explodes, raining down on targets below it, followed by fragments of the shell, afterward, of course. While this would cause little damage to a structure as such, it would be highly effective against infantry hiding behind a barrier or men caught in an open field. More so than the standard explosive shell. What happens is when the howitzer fires, the recoil triggers a ruggedized spring mechanism inside the shell. This mechanism sets a simple, reliable timing system in motion. As the shell travels, the spring slowly unwinds, moving a reinforced metal disc that controls the delay. Once the preset time is reached, the mechanism releases a pin that strikes a percussion cap, which then ignites the explosive charge, causing the shell to detonate, which expels the shot that fills the front of the shell downward."

"And this happens while the shell is still in the air? Can you control when it explodes?"

"Yes. This starts when the shell is fired and, ideally, the timing is right so it explodes before it hits the ground, since the gunpowder load is much smaller in this shell to make room for the shot. The gunner sets the timing in the number of beats between firing and explosion, which loosens or tightens the spring mechanism so it goes off sooner or later, depending on the setting. The gunners will need some training to understand timing, but it is possible to work out with some fairly straightforward math."

"Do we need new guns to fire these?"

"No, that's the best part. These will work in our existing howitzers, and even our straight-firing artillery, although impact and detonation will become more unpredictable than in arching style artillery."

"This is truly remarkable work, Hortensius," she said. "I want both types of shells put into production immediately. How soon can we get them to our forces on the front lines?"

"Soon. We're almost done setting up the production lines and have already begun stocking the raw materials to decrease the time it takes to get started. We wanted to get your approval first, however."

"Consider it given. I want these shipped to the front as quickly as possible. The sooner the legions have these, the better."

Chapter 21

Pella, Macedonia

Ramirus stood by the window of his temporary quarters in Pella, his eyes fixed on the bustling streets below. It had been a less than productive several weeks since his first meeting with the Greeks. They had only grown more stubborn and contrarian since. To the point where he was pretty sure they were not negotiating on an even field and had sent young Gaius to keep an eye on some of their Greek friends to see what was really going on.

As if he thought him into existence, there was a quick knock followed by Gaius being let into the room by Modius, who'd taken to guarding him as closely as he had the Empress. Ramirus thought he was an easier charge, however, since he was not as adventurous as their leader. He, for instance, rarely felt the need to be out doing things for himself, as opposed to dispatching subordinates and hired hands to do the more physical work for him.

"What did you find?" Ramirus asked as Modius shut the door.

"You were correct; I apologize for not having more patience."

Ramirus smiled at the young man. He was a sharp lad, who'd done excellent service for the Empress, both organizationally as her aide and keeping her safe. He was, however, young and had the failings young men have. Most notably the inability to wait and let situations play out before acting, always wanting to be doing rather than waiting to do a thing right.

"That is fine, Gaius. I just hope you remember this for the future. Now, in what way was I correct?"

"The Macedonians and the Thracians have had visitors. They were well-bundled to conceal their identities and came in late at night under the cover of darkness, but I managed to finally see one of their faces. They match the descriptions we've had of the easterners. It was unmistakable."

"I was afraid of as much, but it explains their attitudes. This complicates matters significantly. We may have to inform the Empress that we've failed and set up defenses along the Italian border. If they are already in the pocket of our adversary, abandoning all of Greece might be our only option now."

"Sir, is that not premature?"

"I …" Ramirus began to say before a knock at the door interrupted them.

Ramirus waved Gaius to see who it was. Even with Modius outside, who would surely have prevented someone with the intent to harm them from getting that close to the door, at least without a struggle loud enough to hear, Gaius's hand was on the dagger at his waist.

Cracking it slightly, he whispered to the guard on the other side of the door before half closing it and turning back to Ramirus.

"There are representatives from Illyria, Epirus, and Corinth here who say they need to speak with you."

"Then let them in," Ramirus said.

Gaius stepped back, pulling the door fully open, and three men who Ramirus had spoken to individually several times, but not collectively, entered. All had been in the cautiously neutral category, so far as Ramirus was concerned. They hadn't been as hostile to him as, say, the Macedonians or the Thracians, but they also hadn't welcomed his proposals with open arms either.

"Welcome, gentlemen. To what do I owe the pleasure of your collective company?"

"We hope to have a moment of your time. We have … concerns and thought it time to talk plainly about them."

'It's about time,' Ramirus thought.

What he actually said was, "Then please, take a seat and tell me what is troubling you. I must say, I am surprised to see the three of you together. I did not get the impression Corinth did much trading with either Illyria or Epirus."

"We share some common interests, the most pressing of which is why we came to see you," the man from Illyria said. "We have ... concerns. Specifically about some of our neighbors."

The man paused, exchanging glances with the other two. Clearly, they were nervous, although Ramirus could not tell why. Greece was never a tightly knit region, with its various kingdoms and city-states fighting among each other as much as they cooperated. Going against some of those neighbors now should not be that large of a stretch for them.

"We believe some of them have been in talks with the easterners and are not only considering turning their support in that direction, but are in the process of finalizing the details of it. While that concerns us, the fact that it is the Macedonians, Paeonians, Thessalians, and Thracians is what drives us here. Together, that group makes up the entire northwest of Greece. For now, we hold the easterners at the Dardanelles, since it is slow and difficult for them to get large numbers of men across easily, at least while you hold the sea. If these kingdoms go to their side, especially the Thracians, it opens all of Greece to their threat. We will be left helpless."

"Yes, I am aware of this."

"You are!" The man from Corinth said, more as a stunned statement than a question.

"Yes. We've recently become aware that several of your neighbors have been meeting with representatives of the eastern invaders. Although I hadn't realized it was so many of them. I'm not sure that this should come as a surprise to any of you. They have made it fairly clear that they think continuing to fight will only end in failure."

"We were aware they were considering it, but to think they would go this far without telling anyone or discussing it with the rest of us was ... unexpected," the man from Epirus said.

Ramirus had to fight to keep his face in check. Could they be that naive? None of them, not even the powers these men represented, worked well with their neighbors. They would regularly backstab one another for the slightest advantage. To think that this time would be different was wishful thinking. Terrified men who hoped for a sudden, unexpected reprieve from the doom at their doorstep.

"What's done is done," Ramirus said. "What matters now is how you respond. If the northwestern powers have given over, then the front will be extended and hard to defend. Are you the only ones willing to fight for your people?"

"Athens, Argos, and Sparta remain undecided, but they might be swayed to our cause," the Corinthian representative said.

"I think if enough come over, especially Athens, the rest will join with us. With Athens and Corinth, most of the states would be otherwise cut off from an easy partnership with the easterners or the northwestern kingdoms. Their position would be precarious," the Illyrian representative said. "Even with them, ours is equally as troubling."

"Our offer still stands, even if for only a few of you. Let me be clear. If you join the Western Alliance, Britannia will fight to protect your people and your lands. This is not a hollow promise, but a solemn commitment."

"And what exactly would this commitment entail?"

Ramirus managed to just hold in the exasperated sigh. Even at this late moment, when they come to him, tails between their legs in fear, still they haggle.

"It means full integration into our alliance. There are no half-measures in this. You'll be expected to contribute troops and resources. In return, we will allocate troops to help you as well as ensure your forces are trained and armed to the same standard as any other member of the alliance. With Italia on the verge of joining the alliance, we will have the manpower to bolster your defenses and protect the entire border with the traitor states. We're also prepared to defend the entirety of the Middle Sea, including the Aegean and Ionian."

"That's all well and good, but can we truly withstand a direct confrontation with the easterners? Even with your support, their numbers are vast and they match you in arms," the Epirus representative asked.

Ramirus could see they were worried. They wanted to fight, but their fear could still drive them into the arms of the easterners, just as it had the Thracians and Macedonians.

"It's a valid question. The easterners are formidable, no doubt. But our alliance has advantages they can't match. The easterners are, as far as we can tell, copying our technology, and already our philosophers have new weapons in the works that will once again tip the balance in our favor. Their equality in arms will not last. I can't stress enough, however, that you can't wait for that to happen. It is important to act now, before they make inroads. This is a unique moment for the Greek states to stand united and prevent the easterners from gaining a foothold on your soil."

The men exchanged looks, clearly still unsure. Greeks. Always haggling until the last moment, never willing to commit until they knew who was going to win. In the last war, they only turned against the Carthaginians in the last months, with Britannian armies at the very doors of Carthage itself and nearly all Carthaginian forces pulled from their borders.

And even then, it was only by proclamation.

Gone were the Greeks who stood up to Xerxes. Gone were the forbearers of Philip and Alexander. These were a shadow of the men that came before them.

"Gentlemen, I cannot stress enough the importance of immediate action. Every moment we delay gives the easterners more time to gain a foothold in your lands. Now is the moment to prove you are who your ancestors were."

"But surely, if we wait, we might gather more support ..." the Illyrian envoy started to say.

"No," Ramirus cut him off firmly. "Waiting only serves our enemies. The longer we hesitate, the more attractive their offers become to those who fear the coming storm. If you mean to stand with us, then you must do it now. Otherwise, we will have to pull back to lands that do wish to defend themselves. We will do our best to supply you with what you need to fight off the easterners, should you choose to fight, but once the line is crossed we must do what we have to for the good of the alliance. You can be part of that and get our full support ... or not. It's your choice."

"And if we fail?" the man from Corinth asked.

"Then we fail together, but I assure you, the alternative is far worse. Do you long for a return of masters from far away to answer to? Do you miss the Carthaginians that much?"

Silence fell over the men. The men exchanged glances again, but they knew they had no choice. They couldn't dither or dally any longer. It was time to shit or leave the latrine. Ramirus knew he needed just one of them to agree, and the others would follow. They were just too afraid to be first.

Finally, the Illyrian envoy spoke. "You're right. We cannot simply wait till they come for us. Illyria will stand with the Western Alliance."

As he predicted, the other two followed.

"As will Epirus."

"And Corinth. May the gods have mercy on us all."

Ramirus allowed himself a small smile. "You've made the right choice, gentlemen. Britannia will honor its commitments. You will not stand alone against this threat."

"What now?" the Epirote asked.

"Now," Ramirus said. "We must move swiftly. Your task is twofold and equally critical. You need to go to your leaders and make sure they agree with your decision, and convince your people this is the right course. They must understand there is no halfway commitment. Equally as important, you must reach out to the other Greek states not yet in the easterners' pocket. Athens, Argos, Sparta – all must be swayed to our cause before the Macedonians and Thracians can convince them otherwise. The enemy thinks they have some time, that their agreements are a secret. I also get the sense that they have not finalized their terms. We have seen easterners sneaking in and out of the secret negotiations, which means they are on the verge of turning, but have not done so yet. We can move faster, and rally the rest of Greece behind us, before they know it's happening."

"That will be no easy task. Many will be reluctant to choose sides in this conflict."

"Then make them see there is no true neutrality," Ramirus countered. "If the south remains divided, it will doom any hope of a unified Greek response. Even if that unified response only encompasses half of Greece, it's far better than scattered, ineffective resistance. Stress the urgency. Emphasize the threat. Make it clear that this is not some distant conflict, but a fight for the very soul of Greece."

The men all nodded their understanding. Now that they'd committed and fallen in with the Britannians, they had their rudder again. A new north star to guide them.

"Good," Ramirus said. "Time is of the essence. I suggest you begin your efforts immediately. The fate of Greece may well rest on your ability to rally your fellow countrymen."

He just hoped he didn't over-promise. A line from Thessaly to Thrace was long and would be difficult to fight.

Sardinia

Medb watched the tavern for a few minutes, waiting for the right moment to go in. She had already sent a few of her henchmen in for drinks and knew the man she was looking for had a table in the corner, which was perfect. What she needed was for it to be crowded enough that people wouldn't really notice one more person at his table, yet not so crowded that there would be lots of ears to overhear them.

It hadn't been difficult to find the man. There weren't that many Britannians in Sardinia, and the more she found out about him, the clearer it was that he was a Roman, who were not nearly as common as Scandi transplants or even Caledonians, who made up the second largest contingent of merchants in the Empire.

What had surprised her was how small-time Marcellinus was, considering his double-dealing. He did spread a fair amount of money around, from what she could find, but as far as volumes of shipments went, it wasn't much and every manifest suggested it was fairly mundane. A second surprise was that much of what he traded seemed to be goods from neutral ports to other neutral ports. She couldn't do a full accounting, at least not in the time she had available to her, but it seemed at first blush that what business he did with the Empire stayed in the Empire and what business he did with neutral ports stayed with neutral ports.

Most merchants from the Empire tended to sell the more advanced Britannian goods to regions that needed them, which had been Gaul, Northern Germania, and Scandi. But as those kingdoms were allowed access to knowledge of how to make some of the more basic goods and raw materials, mostly so the Empire could outsource some of its more basic production needs to free up its own factories, that trade had shifted to kingdoms around the Middle Sea.

That trade was all, however, from Britannian ports to neutral ports, which this man seemed to be avoiding.

Medb pushed off the thought. 'She'd know soon enough,' she thought as she headed into the tavern, which had reached about the right level of occupancy.

Marcellinus wasn't alone. He was engrossed in conversation with a group of what she assumed were locals, although one looked out of place, like he was wearing borrowed clothes. So many of them were foreigners not wanting to stand out. Without getting closer to hear accents, it was impossible to tell. They could be Italians or Greeks or even Egyptians. It didn't matter. They were incidental. Who she needed was Marcellinus.

Medb found a secluded spot where she could observe without drawing attention. It was only partially successful, with two men coming up to her, trying to talk to her. Normally she would have eviscerated them, but to keep from drawing too much attention to herself, she had to humor the drunken fools.

It was exhausting.

By the time she got rid of the men, Marcellinus was alone and the questionable men were gone. Medb saw her opening and pushed off the stool she'd been sitting on and made her way to his table.

"Mind if I join you?" she asked, not waiting for an answer before taking the seat across from him.

He looked at her, the brief moment of annoyance turning into recognition and surprise.

"You have done quite well for yourself here, Marcellinus," she said, as if they were old friends. "It's not often one finds such competence in these backwater regions."

"I ... thank you, my lady. But I must admit, I'm somewhat confused."

"Confused? About what?"

"About why you would be here, talking to me. I heard you were here, in Sardinia, but none of us could figure out why. Everyone knows you're the Empress's hatchet woman. That you're sent to deal with problems she wants taken care of but doesn't want her own hands bloodied with. As you said, this is a backwater, so why would one of the Empress's trusted advisors be here."

"Trusted advisor goes a bit far," Medb said. "It's true, I do get sent to do some of the Empire's dirty work, but it's because everyone already sees me as corrupt. Something ... other, so if I'm asked to do something that would be otherwise distasteful, the Empress can say I went too far or just let people assume the rumors they've heard about me are true. And what choice does a lapdog have? Married to my mortal enemy and threatened with death if I don't comply, I am simply surviving. With you Romans hating me for not being Roman and everyone else despising me for doing Rome's dirty work, is there any surprise that there are so many rumors about me? You should ask yourself how many of those are true?"

"That sounds like a difficult life," Marcellinus said.

"You have no idea. When whatever thankless task I'm forced to do is finished, I get to return to the loving arms of my idiot husband and cater to his childish urges. If that's what you mean by being the Empress's trusted advisor, then sure, that's exactly what I am."

Marcellinus gave a snort of laughter in response.

"I heard you were here to work with the Caledonian?"

"He needed someone to step and fetch for him while he tries to convince the Sardinians to give up their objections to unification and join it. I guess they feel something about my reputation will help, so they show me off like a prized pony, as if my presence somehow proves the Empress takes this backwater seriously," she said, gesturing broadly at their surroundings. "As if anyone could take a place like this seriously."

"There are virtues to a place like this, you know."

"I find that difficult to believe. What could this place possibly offer?"

"Well, for one, I'm making an absolute fortune here. This port isn't part of the Empire or its allies, which opens up ... opportunities."

"Opportunities?" she said, leaning in, pressing her chest into her folded arms, which had the added benefits of lifting her bosom up.

She was watching his reactions closely, catching his eyes each time they dipped to the low-cut neckline she'd chosen purposefully. From what she'd heard, Marcellinus was a free spirit and made frequent visits to the port's prostitutes. She hoped his lascivious character held true. His eyes said it did.

"Well, for one, the trade routes here are well placed. With the amount of traffic through the Middle Sea, from Kalb to Southern Gaul and all the way to Egypt, Sardinia is a well-positioned stopping place for both offloading to smaller ships to travel to a variety of destinations and selling to smaller merchant factors who operate on a more regional basis."

Marcellinus looked pleased with himself, looking to Medb to be surprised or impressed, if she guessed correctly.

"I would think, with as small as the Middle Sea is, transshipment points would be less than necessary. Even the regional merchants could easily sail as far as Kalb, without the need for a middleman, and from what I've seen of Sardinia's own production, there is little available here that is not also available on the mainland. Maybe at a cheaper price, but that leaves little room for markup for a middleman, at least if you want to maintain a competitive advantage."

Marcellinus's smile faded as he eyed Medb. "That's surprisingly astute for someone who spends most of their time on land, an unappreciated castoff used by the Empire."

"The Empire might not appreciate me, but that is not the same thing as not having value. I would have thought a smart man like yourself would have seen that. Now, from what I've heard, you're much too clever to play word games. So what is it about this place, really, that makes it worth the effort?"

Marcellinus didn't say anything for a full minute, just watching her, considering. This was the moment in every ruse where things hung in the balance. He was deciding which way he would go. Yes, there would be other moments, smaller ones, where he would wonder if he should say more, if he should trust her, but they would all be made easier by this first one.

She met his gaze evenly, keeping her eyes soft, a slight amused smile on her face. A hint of intelligence, but not so much that he couldn't still feel superior. A taste of admiration that suggested there was more to be won, but not so much that it felt forced or unbelievable.

As with so many men before him, he blinked first.

"Sardinia is, for the moment, a neutral port. Not part of the Empire, its protectorate, or one of its allies. Goods through here don't need to rely on Britannian hulls, and so there's no need for Britannian taxes."

"But surely you aren't just transporting raw materials and the simple goods made here to other neutral ports. Competing with Egyptian and Greek merchants seems like it wouldn't keep you in the well-curated style you clearly enjoy. There's more to it than that, surely?"

Marcellinus tugged on his embroidered tunic, smiling a little. "There might be."

"Be coy then," Medb said, leaning back in a faint pout, lifting her crossed arms so they covered what was so recently on display. "I'd hoped I'd found the one man on this godsforsaken island interesting enough to talk to."

"It's just that you can't be too careful. But just imagine what military supplies the Empire has that other kingdoms want. If a smart man found a way to get those from the Empire and to divert those shipments to other parties, well, a smart man could do very well for himself. And you did say I was a smart man."

"I did," Medb said, giving him a conspiratorial smile. "But how would someone manage that? I know for a fact the Empire is watching for just that kind of thing. There have been several merchants in the past caught and punished harshly, in fact."

"It wouldn't be easy, that is certain. But if shipments were traded from one Britannian port to another, and customs officers were paid to look the other way as boxes were switched out, well, things can happen."

"That's very interesting. Very interesting. Wouldn't that be hard, especially now with so much focus on Sardinia? Assuming someone was to do that here, of course," she said, giving him a little wink. "With Llassar sniffing about, I imagine the risk goes up significantly."

"You have no idea."

"I have some," Medb said, and then paused as if she was considering a weighty question.

"What?" he asked, almost genuinely concerned.

"Marcellinus, you are a clever man, and one who sees opportunities, that much is clear. I also know you have to play your hand close to your chest, because of the times we live in, so I will be the first to risk, to show you I am serious, and speak plainly," she said, looking over her shoulder slightly, as if she was seeing if anyone was close enough to hear her, before dropping her voice to a conspiratorial whisper. "I might have a solution for you. I am returning to Carthage soon. It's the perfect place for a man of your … talents. True, it's a protectorate, but it's so delightfully corrupt, it might as well be unwatched."

"I'm not so sure. I tried dealing with Eoghan once. Found the man utterly insufferable."

Medb laughed, a rich, throaty sound. "Oh, I couldn't agree more. But things have changed. My husband controls the city now and I control him. He could ensure your shipments remain … unexamined."

"Young men can often act in opposition to their self-interest when their egos are on the line."

"I can deal with Cormac. You would not be the first merchant who found a convenient home in our new city. I'd expect a cut, of course. But I am the reasonable sort. And who knows? Perhaps we could find other ways to … collaborate. There's a fortune to be made there, you know."

His eyes dipped to her chest again, for a second.

"We'd have to work out those details."

"Of course. Of course."

"When do you leave?"

"Soon," Medb replied. "You could come with me. We could make quite the team, you and I."

The merchant's face split into a wide grin. "My lady, it would be my pleasure to offer you passage on my ship."

Medb's smile, for once, was genuine. "Wonderful. This will be fun, Marcellinus. I can already tell."

He raised a mock toast to her, smiling, a faraway look in his eyes. Medb returned the smile, much more genuinely this time.

Although for far different reasons.

Chapter 22

Temporary Legion Hospital, Eastern Germania

Ky stepped off the small military train and was immediately stopped by multiple soldiers who wanted to reach out and touch him, or wish him well, or just get his blessing.

Their level of adulation still made him uncomfortable, but he understood that in some ways they needed it, so he did his best to give them what they wanted, offering them the most hopeful words he could to soothe their worries as best he could.

The only thing that made this time different was that every one of the soldiers greeting him was injured in one way or another. Ky hadn't been to the far rear, to their medical camp, in more than a month, something that bothered him greatly. During less critical moments of the campaign, he liked to come back and visit with the injured men, see how they were faring, and try to buoy their spirits a bit. The last month, however, he'd had even more reasons for wanting to come back, as the men the physician Hywel had trained on the new procedures and a large shipment of supplies and equipment to perform them had arrived at the rear hospital that served as the recuperation and recovery center.

Some of these techniques would move to the front-line medical stations, of course, since often amputations couldn't wait for an ambulance carriage and then a short train ride to the temporary rear hospital. That would take time, however, as those physicians had to cycle through the rear facilities to be trained in the techniques while not actively under fire or being deluged with wounded that all needed immediate treatment.

Unfortunately, he'd been unable to come until now. After their last defeat, the enemy had begun pulling back from them. Not fully retreating, but every time they advanced to make contact, the enemy would pull their line back. If his forces slowed their pursuit, they would start lining up again. It was clear they were waiting for something, and that something had to be reinforcements. Ky had received another legion and replacements for the men they had lost from the training camp in Germania while the enemy had been bled badly in their handful of engagements.

It was only a matter of time until they got more men, and Ky had been focused on getting them to grips before that happened, in order to cause as much pain as he could before the odds unbalanced again. Unfortunately, having knowledge and abilities that gave his side an edge did not mean the enemy was incompetent. The drone gave them an edge in scouting, but the distances in this area of the world were long and the enemy did excellent scouting with what they had available, reacting quickly any time their scouts or skirmishers came in contact, quickly withdrawing.

For a month, he'd chased them over mountainous regions that would, in another future that would never happen, be the countries of Ukraine and Belarus. The entire time, they'd stayed a step ahead of him, always just out of reach.

Finally, he'd decided to change tactics and let the enemy wait for their reinforcements. His legates had been unsure about the decision, since wisdom dictated that if they were to fight, they should fight when the enemy was the weakest and they were the strongest. Ky, however, was not sure this style of warfare was the one they should be fighting at all. He knew the lessons of what happened when rifled firearms made their appearance, and the tactics stayed in the Victorian model. He'd known it, but still gone into battle with those tactics, and seen his men mauled even in victory.

It was time for a change, and the breather the enemy asked for while they waited to reinforce would suffice for him as well. They may come back rearmed and reinforced, but they would meet a surprise when they did.

He'd gotten a skeptical Bomilcar to work on what needed to be done, and then set off for the rear to see the new techniques in person before things heated up again.

Ky made his way to the largest of the sprawling tents with the caduceus symbol marking it as a primary center of healing, one of the few symbols that transcended the ancient world and stood for the same thing thousands of years later in his time.

The inside of the main area in the front part of the facility was huge and filled with row after row of cots. There was a sickly smell in the air, but it was not as bad as some of the field hospitals Ky had been in when he first arrived, where men were left to fester in their own fluids and disease ran rampant. Now, dressings and beddings were changed regularly and there was a slight tinge in the air from the antiseptics used to wash down every surface.

He was glad to see they were being so diligent at it.

A man in a clean, full-body tunic that clasped in the back and a thick leather apron approached Ky. It was similar to what most of the men and handful of women walking between the cots were wearing and was the more or less de facto uniform of physicians in the Empire. It wasn't perfect, but the over-tunic allowed them to quickly change when they got dirtied so they could be boiled and sprayed down with antiseptics, while the leather apron would stand up to higher levels of antiseptics and harder sterilization.

It wouldn't stop all transmission of bacteria, just as the cloth masks they wore when dealing with infectious patients wouldn't stop everything, but it was better than just wearing the clothes that they wore around outside the tent or that had become soiled with fluids from multiple patients throughout the day.

When it came to keeping the areas around the patients clean, especially those with open wounds, incremental precautions were better than no precautions.

"Consul," the man greeted, inclining his head respectfully. "I'm Veturius. I was sent as head of the team from Devnum to train everyone on the new procedures we've been working on. We've been hoping you'd be able to come see us."

"I'm sorry it took me so long to make it. The reports I've seen have been stellar, however. Did you train under Hywel?"

"Yes. I was part of the first volunteers he brought in to train and assisted in our first amputation, and several of the smaller surgeries we did since, including leading on seven procedures before I volunteered to come out here. Not a lot to your years, I'm sure, but I was primary on more procedures than anyone other than Hywel himself, so it made sense for me to be the one to come out."

"I'm sure everyone here is glad of that experience. I've seen the instructions Hywel put together for the procedures and the training you're going to be doing, and it all looks excellent to me. I'm not here to second-guess your work, but I wanted to see what was being done in person, since I've only been able to rely on reports over the telegraph to this point. How are you finding it, both the things you learned and putting it into practice here?"

"Good. I was a healer before I volunteered, so I can say with some confidence that they're making a world of difference. We're saving limbs and lives that we would have lost before. People are surviving wounds longer and even recovering. I was notified just before you arrived that we are receiving some injured any time now. Do you want to observe our work?"

"I do. If I'm going to be near the procedures, I should probably scrub in as well," Ky said.

As with nearly every industry that had been rapidly advanced, Ky had been forced to introduce words to describe things never considered before his arrival. Strangely, many of them traced their lineage back to Roman itself, sometimes creating confusion due to the circular etymology. It was one of the strange things about time travel that those who made entertainment about it never considered in their videos and stories.

"Of course, Consul. We'll need to get you properly set up. I don't know if you've ever cleaned with this antiseptic powder we've started using, but I should warn you, it does wear on your skin. We've had to start rotating those who use it to be properly sterilized to spend days just working the ward to give their skin time to recover."

"Just the coverings will be fine. My skin doesn't harbor germs. It's one of my ... adaptations."

The physician's expression wavered between impressed and skeptical, but he didn't argue aside from a moment's hesitation. Saying outlandish things without being called on it was one of the few benefits of the pedestal his people put him on. One he'd give up if it meant no longer having to constantly perch on it, but if he had to, he'd at least take the good with the bad.

"Ohh. Uhh, in that case, follow me."

Veturius led Ky through the connected tents, away from the ward filled with cots and recovering men, and into a connected one where the canvas walls had almost a glossy sheen that Ky knew came from regular scrubbing with less diluted acids and other antiseptics. The air carried a sharp, chemical odor.

"We've done our best to maintain a sterile environment," Veturius explained, gesturing around the tent. "As with our overgarments, we change the tent material frequently, having the old ones boiled and treated with antiseptics. It is a demanding process, so we usually only manage it once a day. It's also why this section is double lined, so that there is still a barrier as we change out the floors, walls, and even the ceilings. Although reuse is severely limited. Chemicals we use eat through the canvas rather quickly. And to be frank, I'm not entirely certain how sterile we're actually getting these portable units. A permanent structure with less porous surfaces would be ideal."

"Your concerns are valid," Ky acknowledged. "It's not as sterile as we need it to be, but it's what we have to work with in the field. Even these measures will significantly reduce infections. And penicillin will help combat what does get through, for the most part. Sadly, we'll still lose some men. It's still a vast improvement over what was used before."

"True. I think …"

Their conversation was cut short as a commotion signaled the arrival of the patients Veturius had been warned were coming. The physician led Ky to a side chamber of the winding, interconnected tents, where a portable metal table had been set up, one of the many pieces of equipment designed and set to the front. Several large buckets for catching limbs and blood sat next to it, ready for the gruesome task.

Veturius wasn't doing the procedure himself but rather standing over the shoulder of a man who was, giving pointers and instructions as he went. The procedure itself was well done, exactly to the specifications set down by Ky in his original instructions and adapted into practice by Hywel. The ether did its job, putting the man under, and was monitored closely throughout the whole procedure. Ky knew from reports there had been failures, men who were put under and were not able to wake again. He'd known that would happen before he ever gave Sorantius instructions for making it, but it was still much better than being awake as a limb was sawed away and debrided, and the wound stitched closed.

After watching the amputation, Veturius showed him several minor operations involving the removal of bullets. That was much trickier since any cutting into a patient introduced new wounds and vectors for infection. They'd settled on removing bullets and shrapnel if they weren't too deep or too close to organs. Unfortunately, many injuries involved the perforation of major organs and all they could do was administer medicine for pain and hope the body did its own work.

They were still a long way from internal stitching or repair of organs. It would come, but it seemed unlikely to Ky they would reach that level for several years, and maybe as much as a decade after that to get beyond the most rudimentary levels.

Even without that, cutting away dead muscle and tissue and removing bullets would save many of these men's lives.

Ky only stayed for a few procedures. Their focus needed to be on the patients themselves and on training the field medics who were currently learning all of these procedures so they could take that knowledge to the forward aid stations.

Ky returned to the recovery ward, stopping at beds here or there to see how the wounds responded after the procedure, which was as important as the procedures themselves, as far as infection went.

He was happy to see that most of the bandages were clean and mostly free of seepage outside of the innermost bandages.

"How are you, soldier?" Ky asked as he stopped by one of the men whose right leg ended in a thick white bandage just at the knee.

"Consul! I ... I'm honored, sir. The pain's not so bad, but the fever's been rough."

"Do you mind if I look at your leg?"

"Of course, anything you could do, Consul. I'd like to get back to my friends."

Ky gave the man a sad smile. The soldier in him understood the feelings that, by being wounded, you were letting your squad mates down. He knew the man would probably agree to go back to the front again, even if he couldn't stand on his own. Ky didn't have the heart to tell him he would be going home, never to walk again, unable to see his friends until after the war's end.

For some soldiers, death might be preferable.

Ky patted him on the shoulder before bending down to unwrap some of the bandage to look at the leg. The amputation was below the knee, which was good, since infection and postoperative complications were much less likely in partial limb amputations than full limb amputations. The wound was still red and angry, with blood and a small amount of pus seeping through the stitches.

Ky reached up to Veturius, who handed him a clean cloth that he had dampened in boiled water and allowed to cool before handing it to him so that Ky could wipe the wound clear. The cuts looked good and already he could see some of the folds knitting together, the body taking over closing the wound for good.

Veturius waved over another physician, who respectfully replaced Ky to apply a clean bandage while Ky and Veturius stepped back for a moment.

"We did this one five days ago. A slight post-op infection but he's responding to the penicillin well. I believe he should recover."

"Good. You've done excellent work here, Veturius, and the legions will be stronger for your effort."

"I just wish I could do more."

"I know," Ky said with a sigh. "I know."

Before Ky could say anything else, a commotion near the entrance of the tent caught his attention. Several attendants were blocking the way of a man wearing somewhat muddy clothing, who was arguing with them, agitated and clearly wanting to enter the tent itself.

Ky understood the attendants' duty. They had strict rules for the cleanliness of anyone coming into the ward, for health reasons, and this man had clearly just come off a horse that he'd ridden hard through some fairly rough territory. The man was dressed as one of their forward scouts, one who'd clearly been in the field until very recently. If he was here to see a patient, Ky would have thought he would have stopped to get cleaned up along the way.

Ky excused himself and joined the small gathering.

"Is there something wrong, Optio?" Ky asked the man.

"Consul. General Bomilcar sent me to report what I saw directly to you. I've been watching the main body of the enemy for over a week. They've brought forward a very large group of reinforcements. They didn't look ready to move yet, but I was told if their force grew beyond a set point, to report back."

"You did the right thing."

Bomilcar was right to send him. If they weren't moving now, Ky imagined they would be soon.

"Go to the barracks here, get cleaned up and get some rest before you head back to the army," Ky said, patting the man on the shoulder before turning to Veturius, who'd followed him to the commotion. "I'm afraid I'll have to cut our visit short, Veturius. Duty calls."

"Of course, Consul," Veturius said with a slight bow.

"Keep up the good work and get ready. I think this might mean you're going to be much busier very soon."

Devnum

Lucilla hadn't been to the docks since the last demonstration, after the riverboat disaster, and the test ship hadn't even had a top on it, so she was quite surprised to find what she assumed was a completed vessel sitting dockside, with a smiling Lucan and

Hortensius standing in front of it, both men looking amazingly pleased with themselves.

"Your Majesty," Hortensius said, bowing deeply. "Thank you for coming."

"How could I not? After the last setback, I am honestly surprised with how quickly you managed to get this project finished and had to see it for myself. Your timing could not be better. The latest word from the front is that the enemy has been reinforced and is preparing to march, and the Consul has been asking for your monstrosity."

Monstrosity was as good of a description for what they had made as anything else. Unlike the tall, wooden-masted ships that had carried Britannia through the war, this thing was short, low to the water, and almost like an elongated triangle with the bottom side in the water and the point at the top. Except there was a flat bottom part that flared out just above the waterline, which was big enough for dozens of people to stand on it, if they were packed closely enough together.

It was as ugly as it was long, with three smokestacks rising out of the center, although well separated and square open ports all along the side, each of which looked to have a cannon in it. There were five on each side which she thought would make it quite formidable, especially coupled with the new exploding shells, allowing it to put out quite a lot of fire.

"It's certainly ... distinctive," she said as diplomatically as she could, getting a chuckle out of Lucan.

"There was a feeling that function should come before form," the shipbuilder said.

Hortensius gave the man a look and it was obvious this had been something of a point of contention between the two.

"Well then, show me your creation; tell me what we can expect from it. There seems to be a good number of cannons on each side."

"Indeed," Hortensius said. "With five on each side, it should be able to produce a significant amount of fire. What's more, we've designed them to extend further out than traditional ship-mounted guns, which allows for elevation adjustment, granting us greater range when providing support fire. In direct engagements, we can retract them for more traditional line-of-sight firing."

"Wouldn't they be vulnerable to fire from rifles on the shore, though, assuming they're dealing with a land-based opponent? Those gun ports are not huge, but if I had a weapon, I would be aiming directly into it every time."

"That is an excellent observation, and a problem we saw as well," he said before waving at someone inside the ship through one of the gun ports.

She'd seen a chain coming down from the top corners of the opening to what looked like the flared-out flat bottom and had wondered what those were for. As she watched, the chains were pulled in, bringing up a square, flat metal plate that completely covered the opening, slamming closed with a satisfying clang.

It was quite clever.

"With the cover locked in place, the gunners have time to reload the weapon inside in safety. There is, of course, still the danger when it is open so the gun can fire, but there is just so much that can be done to limit the danger to the men inside."

"With the gun pulled back that far, is there room to reload the weapon? It looks much narrower than the caravels."

"Yes. It's hard to see, looking at the ship head-on, but the ports on either side are not across from each other, but staggered, leaving the full width of the ship for movement of each cannon, which sits on a cart mounted to rails on the floor, instead of a traditional gun carriage. There is plenty of room for the crew to work their weapon."

"Again, very clever."

"We've tried to think of the various ways the ship could be put in danger and build in features to allow that danger to be mitigated to some degree," Lucan said. "Things such as the protective housing around the propeller and the spaced-out, multiple smokestacks for the coal furnace smoke."

"I saw that and was wondering, since I thought the ship had just the one connected to the boiler."

"It does, but if the smokestack is damaged in combat, it could send a staggering amount of smoke into the ship itself if the exhaust pipe is blocked. While we've kept these as short as possible and armored them, we recognize they could still be vulnerable in combat, especially with how large and prominent of a target this ship will be on the water. We armored it, which should help some, but there is not enough armor to protect it from a direct cannon shot. At least with it still being functional. Instead, we made three branching smokestacks, so that if one gets knocked down, the exhaust still has a point to escape. Again, not foolproof, but it does add some additional redundancy."

"That's good thinking, although it does give me pause. Is the rest of the ship as vulnerable to direct cannon fire as the smoke-stacks?"

"No, Your Majesty," Hortensius said. "The ship itself is metal plating backed against a solid timber frame, making it more solid and resilient. The plates are very thick. It would take repeated and continual impacts at the same point to punch through, which would be more spectacular marksmanship than we've managed with our own artillery. Even if they copied our fused shells, it is unlikely the explosion would be enough to penetrate the metal. Except for lucky shots or catastrophic failure in the metal, this ship is all but invulnerable to direct fire."

"*That is not a correct assessment,*" Sophus said. "*It is possible to design a penetrative warhead which is specifically engineered to punch through metal plating. He is also not considering the possibility of vastly larger caliber artillery capable of firing munitions large enough to rupture even thick metal plating. Given the weapons currently being fielded, however, his assessment is correct.*"

Lucilla ignored the voice in her ear. Sophus had a habit of chiming in with information that was, while factually correct, not particularly helpful to the conversation at hand.

"Does this not make it heavy enough that it will drag on the bottom and get stuck?"

"The armor does add considerable weight, which is why we have the flared-out design, for a larger base to allow for the maximum amount of displacement," Lucan said. "We are still finishing the paddle wheel design, but it is much less armored and more vul-nerable than this version of the river ships, since its focus is on remaining shallow drafting, which is why we wanted to get this one done first. Navigating more treacherous or confined areas will require skilled pilots familiar with local geography, but we believe the trade-off in armor protection is worth it, especially given the intended use in combat situations."

"Gentlemen, I must say I'm impressed. This seems to be everything promised and more. We need to get several of these into production right away. We received word from the front that the enemy is on the march again after pulling back from their losses, and Ky has been asking when he would have these available. I know this was made as only a test platform, but I would like to send it forward as quickly as possible since it seems unlikely any of the purpose-built vessels will be ready before the current offensive gets underway."

"We thought you might say that and we have ... concerns," Lucan said.

"About the vessel's ability in combat?"

"No, Your Majesty. We think it will operate fine once it's in place on a river as intended. Our concern is getting it there. If you notice how low it is to the water, I'm fairly certain this will be a major issue crossing the open seas. The gunports and other venting are not watertight and will likely lead to the ship flooding or foundering in even moderate seas."

Can it cross the channel at all, or are you saying we'll need to build dry-docks closer to the rivers there?"

"It's possible," Lucan admitted, though his hesitation was clear. "But it won't be ideal. If we do try to send it across the channel, we'll need to carefully plan the journey, and even then, there's a significant risk."

"But you can get it across."

"I believe so, Your Majesty. If we cross the channel and then hug the coast, we should be able to get it into the Serpentine Sea, and onto one of the large north-to-south river systems for transition deeper into the continent. My concern is rivers beyond the channel and traditional Scandi waters, and how difficult they will be to navigate. To get a ship into places like Italia, Hispania, Greece, and especially Africa and positions further east seems all but impossible."

"Then we will figure that part out. If we need to build dry-docks in those areas, we will. For now, at least, if we can get ships up and around the coastline and into the areas where they are needed for the current engagement, that's what we need to do. If you want to start work on a dry-dock closer in, on the appropriate river systems or just in the Scandi Sea, then that's fine, but I want the other ships started now. We can't delay until we have the perfect situation."

"Yes, of course, Your Majesty," Lucan said. "We'll take care of it."

"Good. I know you'll get this figured out and that you'll tell me what you need from me to make this work. I just hope this boat can get to Ky in time to do some good.

Chapter 23

Carthage

"And then," Marcellinus chuckled, "the fool actually believed me when I told him the crate was full of salted fish! Can you imagine?"

Medb gave a throaty laugh, pulling her arm slightly against his so her body brushed his side slightly. He joined her laugh as they made their way slowly up the palace steps.

"And he believed it? You must have nerves of iron to face him and not break. I just … how can they be so gullible. You really are quite something, my friend."

"You aren't half bad yourself," he said, putting a hand on top of the one cupping his bicep. "With your connections and my … let's call it business acumen, we'll have this city in the palm of our hands before the year is out."

"Ohh, I have no doubt. We make quite the pair."

"Indeed, though I must admit, I find myself wishing our journey here had afforded us more … intimate opportunities to solidify our partnership."

The look in his eyes made it very clear what he meant, as they dipped once again to her well-sorted cleavage.

Medb squeezed his arm, her laugh low and throaty. "Patience, my dear Marcellinus. Good things come to those who wait."

They walked past the guards and into the audience chamber itself, which was more or less empty aside from her husband, on the much simpler chair that had been brought in to replace the throne used by Eoghan, and a few guards attending him.

Medb stopped at the foot of the dais that he sat upon, releasing Marcellinus's arm.

"Husband," she said as she curtsied. "I have returned."

Cormac sat rigid, his hazel eyes fixed on the pair, not returning her greeting. Marcellinus looked to her a little worried, but the small smile she gave him seemed to give him a small measure of courage.

"My lord Cormac, it's an honor. I'm Marcellinus, a humble merchant eager to contribute to your grand vision for Carthage," he said, giving a low bow.

"I'm sure you are," Cormac replied, his tone as cold as his stare. "Guards, seize him."

Cormac didn't break eye contact as men materialized at the merchant's side. Marcellinus's face was locked in shock, his mouth opened, all but frozen in place as the guards grabbed his arm on either side, much as Medb had done moments before, but much less gently.

"What? What is the meaning of this?" he sputtered, struggling against their grip. "Medb! Tell him there's been some mistake!"

Medb looked to Marcellinus one last time, the humor completely gone from her eyes, replaced by the same cold stare her husband was giving him.

Facing Cormac, she began to slowly ascend the dais, each step purposeful and deliberate. As she reached him, she leaned down, pressing a kiss to his forehead, her fingers gently running through his hair. Cormac looked up at her and for a brief moment, both of their eyes softened as she gazed at him with true warmth before her mask slipped back in place and she straightened, looking down at the stunned merchant.

"This," Medb said, her voice cold and heartless, "is your arrest."

"On what grounds?" he sputtered, looking frantically between Medb and Cormac, trying to pull futilely against the guard's grip. "This is madness!"

"Treason, for starters," Medb replied.

"What? I would never ... Prince Cormac, I don't know what you've been told ..."

"Marcellinus, you stand accused of selling proscribed weapons, avoiding imperial taxes, supporting rebel factions, and plotting to use Empire resources for your own enrichment," Cormac said as if the merchant hadn't even spoken.

The color drained from Marcellinus's face. "This ... that is absurd! You have no proof! Tell him, Medb! You ... this can't be true. We ..."

He stopped, seeing the look on Medb's face as she reached into a pouch sewn into her dress and pulled out several rolled pages, the edges jagged as if they were ripped from a book, and handed them over to her husband.

Cormac looked down at them, his eyes moving left to right as he read everything.

"Two hundred rifles and fifty barrels of gunpowder to someone named Nebamun. Sounds very Egyptian, which is a country not allowed to buy those weapons, which is probably why you declared it as farm implements. Ohh, this is interesting. A five thousand denarii payment from Zamaris. That name has come up several times recently when dealing with some of the more organized pro-Carthaginian factions in the city. I wonder what he could have possibly been paying you for. Do you have any explanation for that?"

Cormac looked up from the document at the merchant's face, his mouth moving wordlessly like a fish.

"I thought not," Cormac said, putting the documents into his own pocket. "These do seem like a fair amount of proof, though. Enough to pass judgment."

"I ... you can't ... I'm not ..."

"Guilty?" Cormac said, interrupting him. "No. I think you are. All of your possessions and holdings are now forfeit to the Empire. Ships will be dispatched with orders to the navy that any vessel bearing your name is now the property of the crown. Your officers and factors face arrest warrants, pending proof of their innocence."

"You should also send word to the capital," Medb said. "I understand he has quite a few holdings there. I believe his properties, and his family's properties, should be seized. I'm sure the Empress would agree that the proceeds from the sale of them would do well in funding the war effort and taking care of the men wounded in battle."

"Excellent thinking, love," Cormac said, patting her hand.

"My ... my wife," Marcellinus stammered, finding his voice at last. "What about her?"

Cormac's cool facade slipped for a moment, letting some of his annoyance through. "Now you show concern for your wife? Curious, given your eagerness to bed mine."

Marcellinus looked from him to Medb and back again, his eyes wide and full of fear. Was he so stupid he thought she hadn't told Cormac everything? Even now, when all of his secrets were being laid bare, did he still think that would be hidden?

"She'll have to crawl back to her family. Let her try to salvage some dignity after choosing such a poor excuse for a husband."

"What about me?"

"You," Cormac sneered. "You are to be executed tomorrow morning. You will finally get to do something noble for your Empire, serve as a warning to any who'd dare steal from the Empire in these times of war. Take him away."

Marcellinus looked like a frantic animal as he tried to wrench free of their grasps and make a run for it. The entire attempt was pathetic; his screams could be heard fading down the corridor after they dragged him out of the room.

Medb looked down at her husband and smiled, happy to be with him again.

Port Vikhavn

"I believe they've decided to give up on taking the port," Valdar said, looking around the room at the gathered men.

It was an eclectic bunch. Ship's captains, the majority of which were Scandi or Germanic immigrants, side by side with the Roman port commander and some of his equally Roman officers, next to

Chief Ekoko of the Ikondi tribe and a few of his men. Each was dressed according to their customs, making for a motley bunch.

There was a comfort in that, even with the serious tone Valdar had set for the meeting. In the month that they'd been penned up in the estuary, the enemy had tried one more seaborne and three more landborne assaults, all of which had failed devastatingly.

So much so, that their total number of ships had finally gotten close to parity.

That, however, was not without its cost, which this meeting would hopefully address.

"The men our friend Chief Ekoko has managed to get on the outer island to keep an eye on their fleet have reported an uptick in activity. The enemy's been making repairs to their ships, with a lot of focus on repairing damaged masts and sails and replacing rigging. The kinds of things you'd see focused on for longer ocean voyages instead of the short assaults they've been trying."

"You think they're planning on sailing north?" Captain Fabius of the Aeolus asked.

"That's exactly what I think. They've realized they can't break through our defenses here and have decided to try their luck elsewhere."

"I thought they wouldn't bypass us because we'd be able to sail out and come up behind them."

"That remains true, but watching their pattern lately, they're sitting on the two lines we would have to take if we were to sally out of the port. We're protected here, but that protection has become a double-edged sword, locking us in here as much as it's keeping them out there."

"Then how do we deal with them?" one of the other captains asked. "You just said they're sitting on the lanes we would need to sail out of here, and I'm not sure we'd be able to get into appropriate lines before we got to them, meaning any assault would be scattered and weak. We'd be torn apart."

"It's worse than that," the port commander said. "We're dangerously low on powder. If we do mount an assault on their lines, we'll have to pull the majority of what we have in the forts and might even have to borrow some from the chief's stores. If your assault were to fail, I'm not sure we'd have enough powder and shot to repulse another attack on the port."

"I know it puts us in a tough spot. We can't sit here and let them sail for our homelands, and we can't sally out of here without putting ourselves at serious risk. What we can't do is remain inactive, refusing to make a choice. Whatever we do, it must be decisive."

"I believe the admiral is hinting that he has a plan to address your troubles," the chief said.

Valdar smiled at the man. He might be considered backward by many of the people in the Empire, but Valdar would never make that mistake. He was a shrewd man, who both understood how to read people and paid close attention to situations.

It had served him well, allowing him to become chieftain in the first place and then recognize the value of their visitors five years ago, and turn that to his advantage when other tribal leaders had only seen a threat.

"The chief is, of course, correct. I do have a plan to even those odds, but it's going to be risky. I want you to assemble your carpenters and sailing masters and take all of the extra anchor chain, along with any similar chain we might have in the port, and wrap the ships' hulls in that chain, from the deck to the waterline, finding ways to affix it so it stays put even when pounded by shot and shell."

"Chains, sir?" Captain Fabius asked. "I don't follow."

"During that last assault, I was watching when a shell came in high on the deck and hit the anchor chain, and then glanced off instead of plowing through it into the timber. I think the chains could work as an impromptu armor plating, like what the Consul and shipbuilders are working on for those river ships they were discussing before we sailed out. We have to talk about how far apart those rows should be placed and if just one layer is needed, and as I said, how to get it to stay on the hull, but it should, I think, give us some protection and allow us to fight longer."

"We've got a fair amount of chains stored in the fort's warehouses," the port commander said. "And that apprentice of Hortensius – what's his name, Aulus? – he's got a small smithy and workshop. We could probably produce more, given some time."

"Time is not something we have a lot of, but if he starts now, by the time we've used up what we have, it would give us just a little more. How many ships can we reinforce?"

The commander thought for a moment and said, "It depends on how it's spaced apart, but seven, maybe eight, at the most."

Valdar's expression remained neutral, but inwardly he felt a flicker of disappointment. He knew it wasn't going to be enough for the whole fleet, but he was hoping for more.

"Then that will have to be what we have."

"Admiral, even with these chains, our ships won't be impervious. We'll still be vulnerable to concentrated fire," Captain Einar, one of his most experienced captains, said. "With only eight protected ships, we are not going to be able to defeat enough of their ships to stop them from sailing north or taking the port once we fire off the last of the powder."

"You're right, Captain," Valdar agreed. "The chains will help us survive longer and hopefully get into a decent fighting position, but won't make us invincible. They're a calculated risk, giving us a fighting chance where before we had none."

He could see his words had not filled the men with confidence, as they all looked to each other, worried that Valdar's plan would mean disaster for them all.

"Before you all look like I've doomed you to an eternity on the ocean floor, I should say the reinforced ships are not our entire strategy. They're a crucial part, yes, but not the whole plan. What we're creating here is a diversion, gentlemen. Well, less of a diversion and more of a wedge to push the enemy where we're going to need them to go. Which is also why I asked Chief Ekoko to join us. I know you have already done much to help us, my friend, but I need to ask for your assistance once again."

"My men stand ready, Admiral. Your people have done well by mine, and we are not only willing, but joyful to return that in kind."

"Good, I'm glad. I should tell you this is going to be risky. More than ambushing lost sailors in the jungle."

"My people are mighty warriors and unafraid. We will do what needs to be done."

"Good," Valdar said. "Very good."

Factorium

Lucilla was tired. The last week had been a whirlwind of trains, carriages, and horses as she made a tour through Caledonia, trying to remind the people there that they were valued members of the Empire, and not just an appendage that absorbed its men for fighting in far-off lands.

It had been a high holiday for their culture going back into far memory, before her own people had even come to the isles, and it was important for her to be seen celebrating those traditions with them. She might be Roman, and not Caledonian, but she was still their monarch, and they needed to know that she respected their way of life, and didn't demand they simply conform to Roman traditions.

That had been part of the thinking. There also had been some voices of late, a small but very vocal minority, that had complained about the Empire taking Caledonia's sacrifice for granted. They felt that since the Empress was Roman, and with a member of the Ulaid royal family living in Devnum and in line for the reins of power, it put Caledonia, who had no direct connection, behind the other two Empire members.

She'd spent much of her time, in between hosting celebrations and attending ceremonies, in talks with Talogren, who was aging rapidly and considering the legacy of his people after he was gone. She wasn't as close with the Caledonians as she was with the Ulaid or her own people, but she respected Talogren and didn't want to see Caledonia fall to pieces once he was gone. This would be the first transfer of power inside the Empire and a test to see if this new nation of theirs could outlast the generation that had created it.

This would be the first of many trips she would take to the north and her meetings with Talogren had gone well, but the time away had created a backlog of other work for her. Between internal politics and massaging the still vulnerable western alliance to get each of her new allies to continue to give to the war effort even as six months of war had passed with nearly no gain aside from holding the eastern armies to the outskirts of Germania, she had what seemed to be an endless amount of work.

Work that had to wait a while longer. She'd found a telegram waiting for her when she returned, requesting her presence in Factorium to assist Hortensius in the metal cartridge program, which he'd finally been able to devote some resources to now that the fuses were past the development stage and into production.

She didn't begrudge helping her old friend. After all, she was only one of two people with access to Sophus, who was the fount of all of this new technology. She just wished there was a way she could do it from the palace, over the telegraph lines.

She knew, of course, that wasn't possible, so she once again found herself walking into his factory, the intense heat of the building surprising her, as it did every time.

"Your Imperial Majesty," a young aide greeted her almost as soon as she walked through the door, bowing low. "Hortensius is expecting you in Workshop Three."

Lucilla waved the man to lead on, following him through the maze of people and machinery. She had never *not* been lost here. Every time she saw the building it had been expanded again. She vaguely knew he'd taken to numbering the add-on expansions on the main factory, but for the life of her, she wouldn't have been able to find Workshop Three without a guide, which is probably what led to Hortensius having one waiting for her when she arrived.

The machines in this new section were very different than the ones she'd seen before. They were huge with a massive iron top section, held above a steel bed on thick steel guide arms, with a wheel on the side that would force it down onto the metal sheet below, pressing it into shape.

She knew what the machines did, of course, because the design had come from her own hand, directed by Sophus, who liked to explain what she was writing, in between her actually writing the instructions or drawing diagrams.

She found Hortensius next to one of the behemoths, looking at a piece of metal in his hand.

"Empress," Hortensius greeted her with a quick bow. "I know you're very busy, but I'm delighted you could come. We have an issue with the new metal casings that we have not been able to get past and could greatly use your assistance. While I know you defined the process for us, I'd like to show you our progress on the metal cartridges before we discuss the challenges we're facing, so you can see it all together."

Lucilla smiled. She knew he was being diplomatic. He was one of her closest advisors and she was sure he had figured out a long time ago that the information she passed on to him did not come directly from her, and that she often did not fully understand the things she'd explained to him. She almost certainly needed to see it in action, and it warmed her heart that her old friend knew that.

"That sounds like an excellent plan to me."

Lucilla followed Hortensius to a table next to a furnace with stacks of thin rolled brass sheets cut into discs.

"The process actually started off quite well," Hortensius began, picking up a small brass cylinder. "We begin with these brass discs, as the Consul's process recommended."

Lucilla nodded, turning the metal over in her hand.

"The annealing process is crucial," Hortensius said, taking the metal from her and handing it to a worker at the furnace. "We heat the brass to make it more malleable, then quench it in water to retain that malleability. It does make the metal harder to handle, but it allows the metal to be formed without significant tearing. Or at least, that was what the original plans indicated. Then we use this machine to draw it into shape."

The metal was put onto a flat stone surface that glowed red from an intense fire behind it. The man then used tongs to carefully pull out another, identical piece that had already been in the furnace and handed it to a man with thick gloves, who took it and placed it over a die that looked like what she imagined the inside of a bullet casing would look like.

He then pulled a long lever that caused the large upper part of the machine, which had the second part of the die, to lower, pushing down on the metal, elongating it and pulling it thin as it went from a flat circle to an elongated metal tube with a circular bottom.

They then took the finished piece and dropped it into a tube of liquid. Hortensius reached in and pulled out one that had already been in there, handing the wet metal to her.

"It's quite remarkable to see in practice."

It was so different from the paper cartridges currently used, holding loose powder and ball, that a soldier would tear open and pour into the end of a rifle. Sophus had explained how these would be used as part of a 'breech-loading' rifle, and while she understood the basic explanation, it was still hard to wrap her mind around it. It felt like they'd only just gotten used to the firearms in general and how rifles worked. So to see a metal casing that would essentially be discarded each time a rifle was fired seemed extravagant in the extreme.

Both Sophus and Ky, however, had been adamant that this type of weaponry would revolutionize how battles would be fought.

Considering what they'd already done, she was not about to doubt them.

"Yes, it is, but it is also not working. It doesn't fail every time, but often when drawing the casing, the brass cracks. If it was large cracks every time, we would, of course, just write that off as losses during the production process and melt them down again. Unfortunately, those cracks are often very small, and only found when the casings are filled with powder. Worse, some are not found even then. Firing off some in testing, we found several that ruptured catastrophically, in such a way that could only be explained by a crack too small for our eyes to see. If those were moved into soldiers' hands, it could be disastrous."

He reached into his pocket and handed her several shell casings, each of which had visible vertical cracks.

"From the description of the process and errors, the most likely cause of this issue is the metal not holding an even temperature throughout the process. It is possible that, if there is a spot that is under temperature, it could be below the point of necessary malleability, and crack as it is

stretched. A multi-stage drawing process with additional stress-relieving annealing between stages should resolve this issue. Additionally, the use of a lubricant during the pressing would further reduce stress on the metal. Singularly, each will reduce the rate of cracking, and collectively, the likelihood of defects should drop to acceptable levels."

Lucilla listened to the voice in her ear, trying not to show any indication that she was listening to anything.

"I believe I may have a solution," she said when Sophus finished. "Have you considered a multi-stage drawing process?"

Hortensius blinked, surprised. "I ... no, Your Majesty, we haven't. We've been following the original plans quite closely."

"Which is understandable, although I will say that Ky's original plans are often not tested in the same conditions as we have available, so there are sometimes discrepancies," Lucilla said, sounding more like the voice in her ear than herself.

She had heard that explanation enough times from Sophus, who was often displeased with the quality of Britannian work compared to whatever its standards were.

"You should consider implementing additional stress-relieving annealing between stages of the drawing process," she continued. "It should prevent the brass from becoming too hard too quickly."

"That ... that could work," he said, nodding slowly. "It would certainly add time to the process, but if it solves our cracking issue ..."

"It would. You could also consider adding lubricant during the pressing stage."

"That's ... actually very clever, Your Majesty. I can't believe we didn't think of that ourselves. I'm certainly glad the Consul included contingency suggestions in his notes to you."

Hortensius had a mischievous look on his face, but Lucilla just ignored the jab.

"I'm happy I could help," she said.

It wasn't critical, but she knew Ky had plans for the weapons that would use these shells and wanted to get everything finished in the next year. As with so many of his inventions, this was just the first step.

But the sooner they could get it in production, the sooner they could get to the next piece.

Chapter 24

Sardinia

The sprawling villa was, at first glance, opulent and over the top in the classic Italian style, which had become something of a melding of older pre-diaspora Roman style and follow-on Carthaginian styles melded together.

The closer Llassar got to the villa, however, the more signs of wear and age he could see. It was the kind of place built when there was great abundance, but was not kept up as the money disappeared. The decline wasn't significant, the kind of thing that happens in bits through bad weather and mishaps.

Llassar wasn't an expert on the upkeep of properties like this, but if he was to put a wager on it, he'd guess the money had run dry five years ago. A very suggestive time for the money to run out, but one that fit with what he'd learned about Nuraian.

If he was willing to sell out his neighbors to work as some kind of middleman for a corrupt Roman, he would definitely be willing to sell them out to the Carthaginians.

There was still enough money for servants, one of whom met Llassar as he arrived at the front gate and led him into a room that was a close approximation of the new Roman-style libraries that had become popular after the sudden introduction of mass-printed books that came with the Consul's printing press and technologies for paper and binding. The name made sense, considering it was essentially a small personal version of the large repositories found in places like Alexandria, although it was a bit egotistical.

Which also made sense, considering it originated with the Romans.

Llassar looked across the books on the shelf closest to him, the majority of which were Britannian, which also made sense. Most books printed came out of Britannia; although the presses had started being sold in other regions, and books in Egyptian and Phoenician, which were still widely spoken and read across the pieces of their former empire, had also begun to pop up.

The man had spent some money on this collection, and based on the condition of the books, it had been fairly recently.

Llassar turned from the books as Nuraian walked in and demanded, "What are you doing here?"

"We haven't spoken for some time, and I was hoping we could continue our discussion on Sardinia's future."

"There's nothing to discuss. My stance hasn't changed. Sardinia doesn't need Britannia or its meddling."

"It's interesting you should say that."

Nuraian clearly did not expect that answer because he paused, as if he was trying to figure out Llassar's game.

"Why is it interesting?"

"I just couldn't help but notice all of the shipments you have been receiving. It's interesting just how many of them come from Britannian merchants, for someone who is so much against Britannian *meddling*. In fact, it's really interesting how many of them come from the same Britannian merchant."

"I'm ... not sure I know what you mean."

"Really? Considering the amount of business you've been doing with Marcellinus, I'm surprised you don't know who he is. I know I'd want to be aware of the name of a man I took shipment after shipment from."

How Nuraian had managed to double deal as long as he had baffled Llassar. The planter's face read like one of the books on the shelves, displaying fear, then worry, then feigned confusion that told Llassar exactly what he needed to know, without the man saying anything.

"I'm afraid I don't follow," Nuraian said. "What exactly are you implying?"

"I'm not implying anything. I'm stating facts. You've been receiving regular shipments from a Britannian merchant named Marcellinus. A man who, by all accounts, shouldn't be doing business with someone so vehemently opposed to Britannian involvement in Sardinian affairs."

"You're mistaken. I've never heard of this Marcellinus. Perhaps you've confused me with someone else?"

"I'm sorry, but I believe I am not the one who is confused. Although I can see it would be difficult to grasp that your deceptions are finally at an end, the records are quite clear. As are the testimonies of your staff."

"My staff? What nonsense is this?"

"Are you telling me you didn't notice several of your servants going missing recently? A curious time for them to up and leave, wouldn't you say?"

"People come and go. It's hardly noteworthy."

"Perhaps," Llassar conceded. "But when those same people somehow found their way onto a Britannian warship in the harbor, under guard, all telling the same story which corroborates those documents, well ... then I would consider it noteworthy."

"You bluff."

"Often ... when I gamble, but not now. Your secrets are out, Nuraian. Marcellinus is in Britannian custody. He's been quite forthcoming about his business partners."

"This ... this is outrageous. You can't just come in here and make these wild accusations!"

"Again, I am not making accusations. I am simply stating facts. It seems your business partner was quite the record keeper. We have shipping manifests, financial records, and eyewitness accounts, all of which tell the same story."

Nuraian's face drained of color. He must have been trying to think of how Llassar knew Marcillanius's name, or how he knew anything about his activities. He also looked like he wanted to bolt. Although, where the man thought he could go on an island that could be made aware of his treachery at any moment, was beyond Llassar.

The Sardinian's composure crumbled as the reality of his situation sank in. Llassar allowed the silence to stretch, giving Nuraian time to fully grasp the precariousness of his position.

"What do you want?" Nuraian finally asked.

"Don't sound so down, Nuraian, I have no desire to see you ruined publicly."

"Why should I believe that?"

"Because if I wanted to destroy you, I wouldn't be here having this conversation," Llassar replied matter-of-factly. "I'd be presenting my evidence to the other landholders and major town leaders and watching your world crumble."

"If you're not looking to destroy me, what are you after?"

"I want to use you. You have quite the reputation, especially in the more rural sections of Sardinia. It's why you were able to do what those paying you wanted so well. I want to use you exactly the same way, except I want my sale to be final."

"And how much will this cost me," Nuraian said, sounding almost disgusted, his 'better than you' attitude returning.

"I think you misunderstand me. I am not asking for a bribe, Nuraian. I'm offering you a chance to do something for your people ... for once. I want your full support behind Sardinia's unification with Britannia. Not just passive acceptance - active, vocal support."

"And how exactly am I supposed to explain my sudden change of heart?"

"I don't care, and honestly, that isn't my problem. But surely someone as skilled in persuasion as yourself can find a way to spin the narrative to your advantage."

"And if I refuse?"

"Then I will ensure that everyone in Sardinia knows about your treachery. Your former friends and allies will turn on you faster than you can blink. Your reputation, your wealth, your influence - all of it will vanish."

Llassar could see Nuraian working the offer over in his head. He also was the type of man who didn't like to give in and cared very much what his public image was.

He was trapped, and he knew it.

"Damn you."

"I take it that means you'll do it."

"Yes," he said sullenly.

"Good. We have a meeting in three days, and I expect you to speak at it. Lay whatever groundwork you need to beforehand, but know this ... there are people watching you. If there is even a whiff of betrayal, you will be exposed."

The man looked as if he wanted to chew nails, but Llassar could see his resignation. He'd do what he was told.

Factorium

Hortensius trudged up the worn stone steps to Sorantius's chemical workshop, trying to suppress his annoyance at being pulled away from his own work. The summons hadn't been urgent, but he knew the chemist had been working on the nitrocellulose for some time and was eager to get the testing over and move on to the next step.

In truth, Hortensius needed this stage done as well, as several of his current projects required the new propellant, especially the metal cartridges he was currently working on. As soon as he finished his testing, that would be the next step.

He found the chemist in the section where they'd been working on the nitrocellulose, talking to several workers.

"Ah, Hortensius!" Sorantius said, seeing him. "Excellent timing. We're just about ready to start the test."

"Good, although I am in a bit of a hurry. I've been elbow-deep in resetting the line process for the new contained metal shell casings. The tolerances are giving me fits. Just when I think I've got the right balance of malleability and tensile strength, another batch comes out warped or ..."

"No, move that over there," Sorantius said, yelling at one of his assistants.

Hortensius frowned, biting back a sharp retort. Sorantius had always been like this - brilliant, but utterly self-absorbed. Hortensius was usually the live-and-let-live type, but at times, it could be very grating. Besides, there was a larger goal they needed to focus on.

"So you think it's ready then?" Hortensius said, bringing the topic back to one Sorantius would care about ... himself.

"Oh, yes. Yes, I believe so. The burn rate is much more consistent now, and the pressure build-up ... well, you'll see for yourself. Come; let me show you to the testing area."

He led Hortensius through a door at the back of the workshop and into a larger chamber. Dominating the center of the room was a massive steel box surrounded by thick cement barriers, clearly designed to contain any potential explosion. A thin cord ran out of the box, dangling in the air outside the metal.

Hortensius stood aside as Sorantius fussed over the final preparations. Finally, he stepped back on the other side of the barricades.

"Everyone ready?" he said, looking around. "Right then. Put in the test strip."

The assistant, moving with exaggerated care, placed a thin strip of a more solid material into the box. The side facing them was open, so they could see what was happening, but other than that, it was closed, to contain the explosion. The barriers they stood behind had a slit to look through, but otherwise left them protected by thick concrete. It seemed a lot of precaution for such a little piece of material, but he knew firsthand how badly tests that failed could go, and didn't fault Sorantius for his caution.

The assistant then lit the fuse sticking out of the rear of the box before hurrying to take cover on the other side of the barrier. The flame traveled up the fuse. It got to within a few finger spans of the test strip before there was a bright flash of light and flame leaped up from the material. Not compressed, there was more of a pop than a boom, but he'd done enough tests with gunpowder to easily see how much more flame and heat was released by this than a similar amount of gunpowder would produce.

Unlike the gunpowder, however, only a small amount of whitish smoke remained, instead of a thick cloud of black smoke.

"Well, that was unexpected," Hortensius said, moving closer to inspect the results.

"Yes, and look at the burn pattern."

Hortensius peered into the box. Where the strip had been was now just a faint, sooty residue.

"Remarkable. The burn rate is much faster than gunpowder. And judging by the color and intensity of that flame, it's burning much hotter, too."

"True, but it's still not meeting the exact specifications the Consul outlined in his instructions."

"Come now, Sorantius. This is already a vast improvement. Faster, hotter, and significantly less smoke? That's revolutionary. Besides, this is much looser than grains would be once you get it to the final form, if I read the instructions correctly."

"I suppose," Sorantius conceded grudgingly.

"What about the pressure? With black powder, it was easy to see the gases produced. But this being what the Consul calls 'smokeless,' though I'd argue that name might be a bit premature, is harder to gauge. Does it generate sufficient pressure?"

"I thought you might ask that. Come, I've prepared another test."

He waved his assistant to bring out another box, this one closed on all sides with a wick out the back and what looked like clay packed into one side, and set it inside the larger box that had held the previous test.

"This setup will give us an idea of the pressure without actually firing a bullet. The clay isn't sealed, so it can be ejected, but it's much safer than a metal bullet, which has to wait for your end before I believe we can test it successfully."

"Clever. Shall we?"

Again, Sorantius nodded to an assistant who lit the wick and ran. The fire traveled up the fuse and into the box. For a moment, nothing happened. Then there was a sharp crack from inside the box, not as loud as when a bullet was fired, but louder than the sound the test strip had made. Almost at the same time, the clay plug shot out, splattering against the wall of the larger box.

"So it is generating pressure then."

"Yes. We won't know how much or what kind of velocity it puts out, at least not until your stage is done."

"Still, I think we can call this complete and move on to whatever else you need to do to make it production-ready," Hortensius said.

"I am not sure. At least not quite yet. There is still work to be done."

"What more could possibly be needed? The burn rate is excellent, the pressure generation is clearly sufficient. What is the holdup?"

"The current state of the nitrocellulose is good, yes, but not perfect. Ideally, I would like to get it perfect before I begin to put it through the final process to stabilize and granulate it."

"I am not sure we have that kind of time. We have a long list of projects waiting on this, and you have additional things the Consul has asked for that you have not even started yet. I believe the Consul would point out that we are at war, and we do not need perfect. We just need good enough to produce. I would say this reaches that level."

"Maybe," Sorantius said, still clearly not convinced.

"What else do you have to do after this point?"

"We still have to stabilize it before we can granulate it. From the instructions, it is an involved process, although it is hard to tell how involved before we actually get into it. But, without it, the compound could degrade over time, and the last thing you want is to fill a bunch of rounds, have them sit in a stockpile, then go to the front lines and not have the punch to shoot the bullet. According to the Consul's notes, stabilization significantly improves shelf life and reduces decomposition."

"If it is necessary, then it is necessary," Hortensius said. "But you should start on that right away."

"I have already prepared the necessary solvents. We can begin the stabilization process immediately. We will still need to conduct a series of fire tests once the stabilization is complete. However, I would like to finish processing the powder first. Then, we can move on to simple pressure tests using your cartridges. Assuming they will be ready at that time."

"They will be ready," Hortensius said. "From there, it is simply a matter of embedding the primer and seating the bullet. Then our new rounds will be complete."

Of course, this was still only one step on the way to having the Consul's new weapons. Still, progress was progress.

Carthage

The beggars' quarter of Carthage, which wasn't its official name but rather what the residents had taken to calling it, was a winding mess of incredibly narrow streets and alleys that crisscrossed and bisected in seemingly random ways.

Had it not been for the pair of praetorians Claudius had helpfully sent to guide her to them, it was doubtful they would have found this one out-of-the-way alley on their own. Even with the guides, they had to double back several times when they made wrong turns.

It occurred to Medb that, should an uprising happen, it would be fairly easy for the locals to block off certain routes and make it very difficult for troops to get in and dig them out. They could turn this quarter into a fortress fairly easily.

She also couldn't see a way to easily fix that problem without razing this quarter of the city to the ground and rebuilding it in a more sensible way. Of course, that would be as likely to cause an uprising as anything else.

The alley, when they made it there, was filled with a handful of praetorians, some holding flickering torches that provided the only light in the small, cramped space.

Claudius stood among them, his face more pensive than usual, which was saying something. They were all gathered around a sheet-covered form lying on the ground at their feet.

"Lady Medb, thank you for coming so quickly," Claudius said when he saw her.

"Your message sounded urgent, although the men you sent were a little opaque on details. What is this about?"

Without a word, Claudius knelt beside the body lying at his feet and pulled back the rough cloth covering it. Had Medb not schooled herself so carefully on controlling her reactions, she would have gasped. Even in the faint torchlight, she recognized the face of Geral, the informant she'd sent into the midst of the instigators of the unrest in Carthage. She stepped closer and knelt next to Claudius, looking at the corpse closely.

The cause of death was immediately apparent - a deep, savage cut across Geral's throat. The wound gaped open, a silent scream frozen on the young man's face. Medb took in every detail. She knew she came across as cold and uncaring to many, but she took her responsibilities to heart. And she'd been responsible for this man.

She'd known the danger she was sending him into, and made him aware of it, but that didn't make her feel the responsibility for his murder any less severely.

Standing, she began to look around the alley where the body lay. The narrow passage was littered with refuse; the stench of rotting vegetation and refuse was overwhelming, and common for this kind of place. Especially in this quarter of the city.

"We saw that too," Claudius said, seeing where her eyes were tracing. "No dried pool of blood and it hasn't rained recently, so nothing to have washed it away. No blood anywhere, in fact, except a little around the head. No sign of struggle or fight. Wherever this happened, it didn't happen here."

Medb nodded as the tribune followed her thoughts. He was actually quite good at this kind of thing. Better than she would have expected.

"How long has the body been here?"

Claudius scrunched up his face, considering. Medb was fairly certain he'd already considered that answer, given how he'd treated everything else. He didn't seem like the sort to shirk from offering his own opinions, but he was young. He also didn't hedge or clam up, only hesitated briefly.

"We found him about an hour ago. But if I had to guess, I'd say he's been dead for at least a day. The body isn't stiff anymore, and ..." He gestured towards the corpse with a grimace. "The maggots have found him."

"Were there any witnesses?" she asked, trying very hard to keep her anger in check.

"No," he said, shaking his head. "This part of town ... well, people keep their heads down. Even with increased patrols, crime's common enough that most folk pretend not to see anything."

Medb's lips thinned. It was the answer she'd expected, but it didn't make it any less frustrating.

"How did they manage to find him? Was there any indication his cover had been compromised?"

"Not that I'm aware of. In fact, during our last few meetings, while you were in Sardinia, Geral seemed to think he was making progress. Said he was close to getting some names that could lead us to whoever's funding this mess."

"But he didn't know who yet?"

"No. Not yet. But he was fairly certain it wasn't someone from Britannia, nor anyone from the far north like Scandia or Germania. He'd said there were comments made that suggested whoever it was has interests in the Middle Sea."

"And nothing else?"

"I'm afraid not. That's all he told me. He said he would keep digging and find what we needed."

Medb frowned, dissatisfied. She'd hoped for more. Geral had been her best shot at uncovering what was happening, and if he'd taken most of his secrets to the grave, it would leave them in a difficult spot.

"When was your last contact with him? I've been signaling him for a meeting ever since I returned from Sardinia, but hadn't gotten a response. Now I know why, but still ..."

"Almost a month ago. Nothing since then."

Medb put the pieces together, trying to work out a timeline. If Geral had gone silent a month ago, it meant he'd either been compromised or had gone to ground long before his death. What they'd done with him in that intermediate time, she did not want to think about. Either way, it didn't bode well for their intelligence-gathering efforts.

"Is it possible they had him for all that time?"

"I ... I assumed he was maintaining a low profile. Given the sensitive nature of his work, I didn't want to risk exposing him by pushing too hard for contact."

"I'm not blaming you, Claudius. These were the very dangers I warned him about when we first started using him. I just want as many facts as I can collect, if we are to figure out a new way to get inside their network."

"But they know we're trying now. That we know an organization exists and that we sent someone in to get information out of it. They will be more cautious in the future, especially of new people."

"True, which might force them to slow down. Even if it doesn't, groups like this have to deal with a constant cycling of new faces, to keep from being easily tracked. It's one of the dangers of what they're doing. But you're right, it won't be easy. Still, I want increased surveillance on all known troublemakers and rabble-rousers in the city. If Geral was close to uncovering something important, his killers might make a move soon if they're worried we've uncovered anything."

"I'm not sure what good that will do. Everything he said, the people we know about are stooges, distractions, and not part of the real plot."

"I know, but there's little else to do at the moment."

"I'll take care of it."

Medb patted him on the shoulder once, and turned, leaving the alley, already thinking through plans and contingencies. Geral's death was a tragedy, but she couldn't afford to dwell on it. There was a bigger game at play here.

She just needed to find out what it was.

Chapter 25

Port Vikhavn

Liu Yi looked over his fleet and was finally satisfied as the dying light of the sun cast everything in a soft orange glow. It had been a hard several weeks to get enough of his damaged vessels back in shape after the mauling they took on the attempts to break into the Westerners' port, but they had finally gotten the job done.

Five of the ships had to be beached and torn down for scraps, but that had given them just enough parts to get the rest of his fleet in sailing shape.

He wasn't happy that he had to give up on this port or that the Westerners had managed to thwart him at every turn. He'd lost countless men to the forts and natives and could not lose any more if he was to make the attack on the Westerners' base of supply with any chance of success.

"I want to position the Celestial Dragon squadron and the Iron Phoenix squadron on either side of the outer island," he said to two of his four remaining squadron commanders. "You'll form a blockade, cutting off the Westerners' escape routes. You are to stay on this side of the island, clear of the enemy forts. Your sole responsibility is to keep their ships hemmed in, unable to sail out or return to their homeland. It will still be weeks before the messenger boat I sent will arrive home, and well into winter before we can expect any reinforcements, so you have to make do with what you have."

Sub-Commanders De and Xin both nodded their understanding. They'd already had discussions about this in private, but he wanted all of his commanders to understand the responsibilities and duties of the other squadrons, which should allow them to adapt as necessary.

The plan was not perfect. It left him only twenty ships for the remainder of his mission, which was not enough. But it was what he was going to have to make do. The last thing he wanted was to assault one of their ports only to find a large fleet sailing up behind him. And if he failed, he wanted at least this port dealt with so the commanders who came after him could continue on without worry.

"Now, I know ..." Liu started to say when a shout from the crow's nest cut him off.

"Enemy sail!"

Liu pushed past the sub-commanders and moved to the railing, his eyes straining against the fading light. It took a moment to pick out the dark shapes against the trees and the shimmer coming off the water, but they were there.

"They move sooner than I expected. That bodes well for us," he said, more to himself than anyone else. "Return to your ships and form lines. I want to catch them head-on as they cross the line of the outer island."

The commanders saluted and hurried to the launches that would take them back to their own flagships. He could guess what the Westerners were doing. It was unclear how much support their vessels had, trapped in the small port, or how many supplies, but they had been bottled up for several months. If they were looking to make a run for it now, it meant they were shorter on supplies than he'd anticipated.

The timing suggested they were making a run for it, and not launching a foolish attack. They'd picked the moment where there was enough light for their pilots to guide them through the channel, which now had the added danger of all the sunken ships, but late enough that it would be dark shortly after they got on the seas, making their escape easier. Especially since this would be another moonless night.

Liu did not plan on giving them that opportunity.

Fleet actions took longer to play out than land battles, which played havoc with a man's nerves, but did allow time for consideration and adjustment.

As his commanders returned to their squadrons and the ships finally began to move, Liu watched the enemy, his curiosity growing. He knew they had some thirty or forty ships of their own all stacked up inside the estuary, and yet they'd chosen only eight ships to send out on this escape attempt.

Perhaps it wasn't an escape attempt. Perhaps they were sending ships to run home and call for support. If that was the case, why would they not send out the smaller ships that made up a third of their remaining fleet? They couldn't take on his ships in battle, but he'd seen how fast they were.

If running was the plan, why take the larger warships instead?

There was a trick here, but he wasn't seeing it. Not that it mattered; he would deal with these ships, leaving the enemy weaker and in the same position as they were before.

The Westerners had clearly seen his fleet, veering to hug the coast as they cleared the protective bubble of their forts, keeping their broadsides pointed at his own ships.

As if in answer to that thought, a flash of light erupted from the lead Western ship, followed by a thunderous boom. Liu barely had time to brace himself before the cannonball whistled overhead, splashing into the water beyond his flagship.

"Return fire!" Liu bellowed.

The air filled with smoke and the deafening roar of cannon fire as both fleets exchanged volleys. The breeze was light, so it was taking extra time for the haze to clear which, coupled with the almost completely faded light, meant he had to strain his vision and wait for an opportunity to see the results of the fire on the enemy.

The Westerners, for their part, showed what made them a dangerous opponent. They may be lesser in number, but they were not without teeth. One of his ships was already listing heavily to port, water pouring in through a gaping hole in its hull. Two others had taken significant damage, their crews scrambling to bail them out as the carpenters tried to repair the holes and keep them afloat.

Liu looked back at the enemy fleet. The smoke had cleared enough for him to make out his own effectiveness, and what he saw shocked him.

The Western fleet appeared largely unscathed.

"Impossible," Liu muttered.

He'd been assured that his weapons were a match for the Westerners. Yes, they seemed to have better training that allowed their gunners to be faster and more accurate, but that was the demon at the heart of the conscription system. There was never enough time to train his men to the level he wanted them.

This, however, was something else. He'd sunk enemy ships in the past, so how was it possible for them to be completely untouched. His men had been improving in their gunnery with every battle and hadn't missed this badly, even in their first skirmish.

Liu called for his looking glass, snatching it from a nearby officer's hands. He trained it on the nearest Western ship, studying it closely as it maneuvered through the chaos of battle, with both fleets still firing. It took a moment, but he found the answer. It was ... ingenious.

"Chains," he breathed, lowering the glass. "They've wrapped their ships in thick chains!"

The clever Westerners had found a way to armor their vessels, causing Liu's cannonballs to bounce harmlessly off their sides. It was so simple, he wondered why no one had ever thought to do that before now.

It did explain why only eight ships. It would have taken nearly all the chain they had in their stores and on the ships to come up with the amount of chain he saw. This was almost certainly all they could muster.

"Order all ships, aim for their masts," he called out to the signalmen. "The chains can't protect them there. If we can't sink them, we can at least cripple them."

"Commander, those shots are going to be ... difficult to make in these conditions," the man said, almost cowering as he did.

"I'm aware of that, you idiot," Liu said sharply. "It's also the only thing we can do. Send an order to the Iron Phoenix squadron; I want them to try to bring the enemy to grapple."

It was a dangerous play. The sun had gone down and nearly all of the light was gone with it. Trying a boarding maneuver against undamaged opponents in the dark was nearly certain death, but he couldn't let them get away. He would waste shell and shot, but if he could take out a few masts, he could cripple enough ships that the remainder would be forced to slow to support them.

Or abandon them, but the Westerners had been slow to do that in the past.

The enemy, however, was having none of his attempts to get in close. It didn't help that the wind was from the northwest, giving them a speed advantage as they curved away from his fleet, tearing into the front of the squadron as they did, able to shoot broadsides down their throats as his ships tried to close.

"Order them to pull back. I want the fleet to sail out southwest, see if we can't force those bastards to sail against the wind and give us a chance to run up on them instead," Liu said.

It would also make them turn enough to disengage their broadsides and give his injured ships a short breather to repair before the firing began again in earnest.

As Liu's fleet maneuvered southwest, Liu continued to watch the enemy, straining to pierce the darkness that had swallowed the sea. Occasionally, one fleet or the other was lit up as they turned just enough to unleash a broadside, the bright red and orange gunpowder illuminating their ships for a moment. Thankfully, in the dark, even the Westerners' accuracy worsened, letting only a few shells find their mark.

Suddenly, a cry from the crow's nest shattered the tense silence.

"More enemy ships to the south!"

Liu whirled around, training his glass in the direction the man was pointing. It was hard to see with only starlight, but finally he could see what his man saw, seeing the faint glimmer of lanterns on the decks. A second Western squadron was emerging from the estuary, making for the far side of the outer island.

"Damn," Liu muttered under his breath as he realized what had happened.

The initial attack had been nothing more than a feint, a distraction to allow the remaining Western fleet to slip away under the cover of night.

It would probably have worked, too, had the captains not lit lanterns to see their way clearly through the inlet and out into the open sea. A necessity, to be sure, but one that had doomed them.

"All ships, change course! Intercept those ships as soon as they cross the outer island!"

Liu considered his options as the fleet curved more south, tacking against the wind. The chain-wrapped boats posed a greater threat, but if he could engage the newly revealed ships in close combat, they would be forced to shoot into their comrades in order to hit his ships, nullifying their advantage.

"I want our ships to close the distance as quickly as possible. We'll force them into close quarters where they can't risk firing without hitting their own vessels."

The signalman relayed the orders to the rest of the fleet using lantern signals.

The enemy saw what he was doing and tried to run, turning further south and slightly west, probably hoping to get out into the open ocean, which would force Liu to choose between chasing the second group of ships and leaving the port unguarded, or letting them go.

Liu was not giving up the chase. This was the entire western fleet, aside from the eight ships following him. He could come back and deal with them at his leisure once these were dealt with.

"Push harder!" Liu shouted to his crew. "We cannot let them escape!"

Not that they could do much to go faster. The wind was the wind. Liu just didn't want them escaping. If they could close the gap before the Westerners reached open water, they stood a chance of crippling this squadron before the armored ships caught up to them.

The chase was on, and they were actually gaining ground. He didn't know if the enemy was panicking or just confused in the dark, but they were sailing more into the wind than they should, sometimes even turning southeast directly into it before veering back south.

He'd almost passed the center of the outer island when a sailor's voice pulled him out of the total focus he had on the enemy ships retreating south.

"Commander! There's something in the water!"

Liu turned, irritated. "Just ignore it."

Still, his men were not complete incompetents. If whatever they saw was concerning enough to bother him with it, then it was worth looking at himself. Liu went to the far rail and peered over the side.

He did not expect to see what he did. Dozens of small native canoes bobbed in the water around his fleet, barely visible in the dim starlight. Even as he watched, one of his ships barreled over a canoe, not seeing it in the dark. Why would the natives have pushed so many of their boats out here, especially empty? He couldn't see a single man in any of them.

"Ignore them," Liu ordered. "Focus on the Western ships. We can't let them—"

He paused mid-sentence, something nagging at the back of his mind. Liu leaned further over the railing, squinting into the darkness. The canoes weren't empty, there was something in them, but it was hard to make out. Some kind of cloth was laid over something in the bottom center of each of the canoes. He looked from boat to boat until he found one where the cloth had blown back, revealing what was underneath, only to get more confused.

Barrels. There were several barrels in each canoe.

It took a moment for his brain to catch up, the sudden, unexpected appearance throwing him as he tried to think not only why there would be boats just floating out here but filled with barrels.

There was one obvious answer, which took much too long for him to arrive at.

Before he could put the thought into words, a flicker of light caught his eye. Off to starboard, a small flame appeared in yet another canoe, this one distant enough that he hadn't seen it until the fire drew his attention. Liu watched, frozen, as twenty flaming arrows arced through the night sky, trailing sparks in their wake.

Time seemed to slow as the arrows descended, their targets all too clear. Liu's mouth opened, a warning forming on his lips, but it was too late.

"Order the fleet ..."

Three of the twenty arrows struck the blanket on a canoe close to the ship opposite him, which must have been covered in some kind of flammable tar or pitch. For a heartbeat, nothing happened. Then the cloth burst into flame.

The barrels caught fire. With a deafening roar, the canoe exploded in a massive fireball, engulfing the front part of the ship, sending flaming boards into the sky. Enough sparks fell to the deck that the barrels of powder on the gun deck of the ship caught on fire and began to explode, reaching the magazine in a heartbeat as the chain reaction ripped the ship to pieces in an even more massive fireball.

The flaming debris rained down, setting off more canoes. More ships. Barrel after barrel detonated, each blast more violent than the last. The sea around Liu's fleet erupted into a maelstrom of fire and destruction.

"Abandon ship! All hands, abandon ..."

His words were cut short as a massive blast tore through his flagship. The deck buckled beneath his feet, throwing him against the railing. As he struggled to regain his footing, Liu caught a final glimpse of his once-proud fleet. Ships were breaking apart, their hulls shattered by the relentless explosions. Men screamed, their cries quickly swallowed by the inferno.

In those last moments, as fire consumed everything around him, Liu understood. The Westerners had outmaneuvered him completely. Their escape had been a ruse, drawing his fleet into a deadly trap.

The realization brought no comfort as a final, thunderous explosion engulfed Liu's ship when the powder magazine below him went up.

Eastern Germania

Ky walked along row after row of dirt mounds, waiting to be wheelbarrowed away to emplacements and protective build-up around gun emplacements, or just taken to the rear and dumped, and looked down the long scar being dug into the ground.

The trenches weren't a solid line, but a series of lines, some forward and some a little further back, the in-between ground filled with pit traps and coils of wire, making them all but impassable without hard work, and vulnerable to flanking fire as they did so, along with some buried surprises.

Even with the temperatures starting to cool, the men in the trenches had their shirts off and were perspiring heavily as they dug, the new style of spades making the work easier, if not easy.

"Shore up those sides! We need this trench to last, not collapse at the first sign of rain," Ky said, pointing at a section.

Some of the men still didn't see the benefit of wooden supports to hold back the hard-packed earth, as if it would stay hard-packed once the first serious rain came through.

The men didn't argue, however. They got the needed supplies and began the work. They were good men, but like soldiers across the centuries, they would take shortcuts if you let them. Thankfully, they didn't need much handholding once they were reminded of their duties. It hadn't taken long for them to learn how to become expert trenchers.

"I have to question the wisdom of this strategy," Bomilcar said, catching up to him and falling in step. "We're sacrificing our greatest advantage. Mobility is what won us the war with Carthage, now we're digging holes in the ground to hide in?"

"This isn't the same war that we fought with Carthage. We'll maintain mobile reserves and cavalry, but we can't afford to keep paying the price we've been paying for our victories. The cost in men has been too high."

"But surely ..." Bomilcar began, only to be cut off by Ky's raised hand.

"We've been over this. We know the enemy has completely reinforced and even managed to add more troops than they had when we first made contact. Meanwhile, we've been struggling to keep up with our losses."

"Not anymore. The last two legions have finished outfitting and integrating the new recruits and should be here in a day or two.

Admittedly, we won't see brand new legions form before the end of winter, but that should at least get us close to their size."

"Even with all that, why would they attack us where we're strong? They could just go around us."

"Not that easily. We're all but backed up into the mountains to the south, and we have enough centuries there with locals who know every goat path and vantage point, we could lock up a much larger force. If they go north, there are rivers that will slow them down. This is the clear shot into Germania, which is why I wanted to keep pushing them back. This is defensible terrain," Ky said and then made a placating motion as he predicted Bomilcar's next response. "Yes, I know they could go further north or south and find other paths. If they do, we'll follow them. But I don't think they will. South is incredibly mountainous, making resupply harder and north has incredibly thick forests, which will inhibit them. This is the best type of ground for them to attack over. But if they move, then we will move with them. If they wait long enough to move, we will have new legions to send out and set up new trenches, blocking them further."

"You turn the continent into a fortress."

"Essentially."

"But then how do we give chase when the enemy is repulsed and flees? There are the rows and rows of this new wire, the furrows dug in the ground, the stakes, and these new boxes filled with gunpowder that explode when stepped on."

"Mines," Ky added.

It was something Ky had given Hortensius the plans for months ago, but it had been put on the backburner allowing the fuses to be developed first. In concept, a box filled with shrapnel and gunpowder with a pin fuse on top that ignited when pressure was applied was a good, although basic, mine. And it was impressive when it worked.

However, it had a bad habit of not going off, only exploding about half the time it was stepped on, especially if it was buried too deeply, which was an easy mistake to make. Ky just hoped that with a fifty-percent success rate, if a sufficient number were seeded, they would still be deadly enough to force the enemy soldiers back.

Bomilcar had been right about there being limited space they would be able to cover with trenches with the number of men they had. Recruits were beginning to pour in and that would change, and the geography of eastern Europe lent itself to this kind of warfare, but there would be gaps, and the mines, hopefully, would serve to fill those gaps.

"Yes. They are impressive, and I can see how burying them along our flanks will help funnel the enemy where we want them, but it further limits the mobility of our men, especially forward. When they run, how are we to give chase?"

"That's not the goal, Bomilcar. This isn't the same kind of war that we've fought before. With the weapons they possess, mobility isn't our primary advantage anymore."

"Then what purpose does it serve?"

"Combined with our new artillery ammunition, even our slower-firing weapons will be devastating. Their artillery will be far less effective, at least until they figure out fuses of their own, and volley fire won't have the same impact. In time, there are solutions around this, but I hope to have new weapon systems in place by then."

"I am also concerned that we are spread too thin along this line to be able to put enough fire down to keep them from overrunning us."

"Possibly. It is a danger of this strategy, until we get more men in the fight, but we're nearing winter and their supply lines are very long, so I hope they slow their advance as the weather changes. But that is why I have Hortensius making all this wire and why we are laying it down so thick. It will slow them as they try to pick their way through it, and we've pre-sighted all of our artillery, which will be firing without line of sight and in a deep arc, since with fused shells plunging fire will be more effective. This will have the added benefit of limiting their ability to conduct counter-battery fire, since they need more of a direct shot, and pushing their barrels high enough will cause most of their solid shot to just bury itself in the ground unless it is a direct hit."

"Maybe. I still think ..." Bomilcar started to say as a mounted rider came tearing toward them.

His lictore were nervous, as they were every time someone came riding hard at their protectee, but Ky held up a hand, holding them in place. He had spotted this man through the drone feed some time ago and watched him come in.

"Sirs," the messenger said, pulling up hard and saluting them. "The optio wanted me to report that a portion of the enemy have broken off and turned north."

Bomilcar gave Ky a 'see' look, but Ky ignored him and said, "The remainder are still coming this way though, yes?"

"Yes, Consul. They had another group join them shortly before I was sent to deliver the report. They had a large number of horses with them and the optio thinks that was what they had stopped to wait for. There were signs of their breaking the camp they've been in and starting their march west, although they hadn't left while I was still there."

"Horses?"

"Yes, sir. They mounted up several groups that had clearly been infantry, maybe seven hundred in total, and rode out with a large part of their cavalry. They also had a large number of horses loaded with supplies but no men, along with three smaller cannons that looked to be light enough for a single horse to pull quickly."

"I see. Thank you. You did well. Go get some food and rest."

"Thank you, Consul."

"Exactly as I said. What do you want to bet the extra horses were for carrying bridging material? Mounting infantry on horses for rapid travel is clever. They will get behind our lines before we can position men to stop them."

"Dragoons," Ky said.

"What?"

"Mounting men for travel but deploying as infantry is called 'dragoons.' It's very concerning."

"Ahh. It's still a concern. They will get around us."

"Not entirely," Ky said.

"I'm not sure I'm sold on the effectiveness of this boat of yours."

"I know, but I need you to trust me. It will stop them. It's also not alone. There is a century of infantry with it."

"Versus seven hundred men, plus cavalry and some cannons. They will not last long."

"Trust me, my friend. This will work," Ky said.

Bomilcar made a non-committal noise but dropped it, walking further down the trench, watching the men work.

Ky could understand his skepticism. They'd all seen what cannons could do to traditional wooden ships. Conceptually, the idea of armoring the ships would make them able to resist that, but knowing it and believing it were two different things. That, combined with the idea of static trench warfare, was a lot to throw at a man, even one as smart as Bomilcar.

Besides, Ky had his own worries.

"How did they arrive at dragoons so quickly? So far, the only advancement outside of the original, primitive cannons they gave to the Carthaginians have been copied from us. From the weapons themselves to the tactics they use with them. How did they make the leap to dragoons? We've never used them, either in this war or the previous, and it took centuries between the first firearm-using infantry and mounting them for transport."

"While that is true, Commander, that time period was also a rapid development of firearms in itself, and the first uses of dragoon tactics corresponded with pure firearm-armed infantry in under a decade. Prior to that, it had been mixed units, mostly pikemen and arquebusiers. The idea most likely originated from Eastern mounted archers, which the Chinese were in contact with in the original histories. It is not out of the realm of possibility that the idea would have been organic, without any additional knowledge."

"Maybe," Ky subvocalized.

But he wasn't sure.

Rome, Italy

Lucilla sat on the dais at the front of the ancient temple of Venus Genetrix, looking out at the faces that packed the forum, from portico to portico. The space was much different than the carvings of her ancestors, with signs of its previous occupiers everywhere. Although structurally the same, much of the finery and detail had been updated along more garish Carthaginian sensibilities, although elements of its Roman originators from centuries past still remained. She had to admit, it made for an interesting space that was quite unique and served well to mirror Italia's complex past.

There was a noticeable feeling of anticipation in the air as nobles and elites from across Italia filled the space, jam-packed in the open courtyard and porticos on either side. Only the steps of the temple itself, which now served Carthaginian gods that were still predominantly worshiped in the region instead of Venus to whom it was built, were clear. Lucilla could feel the expectations and fears of the people gathered there. She didn't blame them. This was a historic moment, and with everything else happening in the world, one that could very well determine the futures of every person watching. She was just one dignitary on the dais, and not the current center of attention, but she knew there were eyes on her and straightened her back, trying to project an air of calm authority.

She was happy that Llassar had a place next to her. Aside from being a comfort, it also served as a reminder that Britannia was not just a new Roman state, but a multicultural society made up of people from across the continent and its islands. Along with them sat an array of dignitaries from Germania, Gaul, and Hispania, along with regional delegates from Italia itself. This was the first time they were all together in a unified whole, and she was proud to see it, knowing the work it took to get all of these different peoples, with their own worries and goals, together.

Only the addition of Egypt made her nervous. She continued to send missives to the Ptolemies asking for them to join the alliance and take part in the fighting, which only seemed fair after her own people freed them and helped put these very people back into power. They continued to dodge, hedge, and all but ignore her. Considering how much closer to the east they were, and that they could become a subject of attack just like the Greeks, she would have thought they would at least see how it was in their own best interest to join, but so far, they refused to even acknowledge the question.

Standing at the center of the dais was Gaian Hasdrubalis, the current mayor of Rome and a leader in Italian politics overall. Even before the fall of Carthage, he had been a notable figure, a merchant known to smooth over problems, a hard negotiator.

His rise to power following the fall of Carthage had been nothing short of astounding. He'd leveraged many of his friendships and contacts across the peninsula to shift himself from only being a businessman to being a power broker. It helped that he had chosen no sides during the preceding years, dealing with both the small rebel movement that formed, as it looked like Italia might be freed, and the Carthaginians themselves.

It still worried Lucilla that he'd been so willing to work with his overlords while professing a desire to see his countrymen free, but she did not get to choose who these people wanted to lead them. He also wasn't all bad. They'd corresponded often, especially over this last year, and she'd come to know him as both crafty and genuine in his desire for his people's welfare and his own wealth.

She'd take one if she could get the other.

Gaian gestured for the crowd to settle down so his words could be heard. The courtyard had been designed to carry sound well, especially down the porticos, which offered shade and better hearing, making them a preferred spot for those who could hold them.

It said something about Gaian's personal connection to his people that they responded so quickly to his request, a hush falling over the crowd.

"People of Italia. Today marks a momentous occasion in our long history. Today, we stand on the threshold of a new era. An era forged from the trials of our past and the hopes for our future. No longer are we separate regions, competing against each other for scraps, but one people. A unified Italia, brought together from the mainland, from Sicilia, and from Sardinia, together as one."

He paused as a smattering of applause rippled through the audience.

"From the ashes of our fallen overlords, we have risen anew. No longer will we be pawns in the games of empires. For too long, we were the servants of other men, who used our lands, our homes, and our people to further their own will. And yet, in spite of that, the spirit of Italia never wavered. Today, we claim our rightful place as a force to be reckoned with in the Middle Sea. Our people are proud, strong, and free. Together, we will build cities that rival the glories of our ancestors. We will create works of art that will be marveled at for generations to come. We will be the bedrock of a new future, for all other people to look to and admire.

Again he paused as the assembled people cheered him. These were the rich and powerful of Italia, and he was throwing them what they wanted: wealth and power.

Lucilla knew what was coming next, however, because it had been part of her agreement with Gaian for her support in making unification happen.

"But make no mistake," he said, his tone growing somber. "This unity comes at a price. Even now, as we celebrate, dark clouds gather on our horizon. Greece falters before the Eastern menace. Armies march through Germania, bringing fire and sword to our very doorstep. And while we have been here, arguing amongst ourselves, trying to come together for this auspicious moment, the blood of others has soaked the land to ensure we had that time. You have all heard the rumors, the stories of what is happening beyond our borders. War has returned. For too long, we have allowed others to bear its burden. While Britannia, Hispania, and Germania bled, we stood idle. I say, no more. That time has passed. The time has come for Italia to take its place alongside those who are already defending us, those who freed us from our Carthaginian overlords. With unification comes a new obligation, which we will take up as we join our allies in the Western Alliance."

There was applause again, but much less than before, interspersed with an equal amount of talk, which showed that, as popular as unification was, joining the alliance was contested.

"I know this is a concern," Gaian said, addressing the talk directly. "I can promise that this is not taken lightly, or on a whim. The enemy is nearly at our gates and has shown they want to install themselves as our new overlords, and *I say **no!*** No longer will we stand aside and serve the whims of others."

The clapping returned. Still not as enthusiastic as earlier, but with less chatter. He wasn't going to turn the crowd so easily, but it showed that the dissatisfaction was not hard set.

"In the coming days, we will call upon the strength of our people. Sons of Italia will take up arms, not for conquest, but for the defense of all we hold dear. This is the cost of our freedom, the price of our unity. But we do not stand alone in this fight. Britannia, Hispania, Gaul, Scandia, and Germania have shown us the meaning of true friendship. To them, we make this solemn vow: as you have stood with us, so shall we stand with you. The might of a unified Italia joins the Western Alliance!"

The cheer this time was much louder, the side-talk almost non-existent. That didn't mean support, but Gaian was a good speaker and good at getting people riled up. Lucilla had always found that the mob was fickle and easily swayed, but also short in its memory.

"Do not hear those promises from me. The Empress of Britannia and the driving force behind the defense of the west, Lucilla Germanicus, was kind enough to travel all the way here to speak with us today. Your Majesty," he said, stepping back and extending his hand in invitation.

Lucilla rose, giving Gaian a smile and slight nod as she passed, taking his place at the center of the dais.

"Thank you, Magistrate Gaius. I cannot tell you how proud I am of the work you and everyone else has done to make this happen. I dream a dream of my ancestors, of a new, stronger Italia. I stand before you not just as the Empress of Britannia, but as a daughter of Rome. To be here, in this sacred place, surrounded by our shared history, fills me with profound emotion. For too long, we have been separated by more than just the sea. Today, we bridge that divide. We are family once again, bound by blood, by culture, and by a common purpose."

That drew applause, as Lucilla knew it would. She had talked to Llassar about her speech beforehand, and that section specifically, knowing that it would be a good line, but concerned about high-lighting the Roman connection, which could be seen as insulting to the other parts of Britannia. He agreed it was worth the trouble the line could cause, to get support from the Italians, and that she could fix it later in the speech.

"The West is a family worth fighting for, united in our resolve to defend our homes, our traditions, and our very way of life against those who would see it destroyed. The invaders from the east threaten not just our lands, but the very essence of who we are. Britannia has already committed its blood and treasure to this cause. Roman, Caledonian, and Ulaid alike have offered up the pride of a generation, their best and brightest, to ensure the West stands. Even now, my husband leads our armies in Germania, holding the line against the Eastern hordes. Every day, brave men and women sacrifice their lives so that we may continue to live in freedom. But this alliance is about more than just war. When the battles are won and peace returns, the bonds we forge today will endure. Together, we will build a future brighter than any of us could achieve alone."

She paused again, letting that settle in. The crowd was strangely silent, maybe finally considering how serious things really were.

"From this day forward, Britannia and Italia stand as one. I give you my solemn vow: Britannia's strength is Italia's strength. Our resources, our knowledge, our determination – all of it stands ready to support you in your time of need, just as we know you will stand with us. The road ahead will not be easy. There will be hardships and sacrifices. But I have faith in the spirit of our people. Of your people. Together, we will not just survive this storm but make a future that belongs to all of us. A future of freedom, prosperity, and peace!"

As Lucilla finished, the forum erupted in applause. The sound was deafening as Gaian joined her, shaking her hand. With it came a lifeline for the West, with a large infusion of manpower going into the next year of fighting.

Chapter 26

Northern Wistla River

A cascade of animals running down the river, away from the alien chugging sound, preceded the sight of the metal behemoth coming around the river bend, smoke puffing away out of its three metal stacks, making so much noise that it would be impossible for the ship to sneak up on anything.

Even with the noise and the fear it caused the local wildlife, Captain Leodgar was happy with his charge. He'd even admit, to himself if not others, that it was an ugly beast. A flat bottom with an elongated triangle jutting out of it, rounding off at the top, a dark brown where the steel had already started to change colors. It was low in the water and dark, but to Leodgar, it still felt sleek and dangerous.

And that was riding inside of it. He couldn't imagine what others would think seeing the row of cannons sticking out the side, waiting for their first target. He'd considered this day for the weeks since he'd been given command of the ship for its terrifying journey along the coast and into the mouth of the Wistla River for its long journey into the continent.

The curiosity and mild confusion had not been the reaction he'd expected, but it was what he was getting.

The enemy force was where the mounted scouts sent from the Consul's army had said they'd be. According to their local guide, this was the first crossable ford north of the Consul's army, at least in the fall. There were apparently other spots in the height of summer when the river dropped to its lowest point, but the enemy missed their moment to have access to those.

Leodgar had been watching the area he'd been told they'd be in through the spyglass, and as his vessel rounded the bend, they came into view. Instead of charging forward or running away, the men had paused, as if confused by what they were seeing and were trying to figure out what to do next.

By the time he'd pulled even with them and slowed the engines, the majority of the men had dismounted and formed into lines, apparently guessing correctly that his boat was a new form of Britannian warfare. Of the roughly seven hundred soldiers coming toward the ford, five hundred were infantry, who'd dismounted and formed tight firing lines before starting forward, along with two small cannons, each being pulled by a single horse, following along either side of the infantry formation. The remaining two hundred cavalry hung back, perhaps letting the infantry spring this trap and save themselves the pain.

If so, they were smarter than their friends on foot.

"Load shells and prepare to fire, but hold. Wait for my command," he called down to the gun deck below, hearing the gunner captain relay his words to the men working the cannon, which were more like the ones on board navy ships than those now being used by the legions.

Leodgar allowed himself a smile. This iron monstrosity wasn't the only thing being tested today. Although the Consul had gotten the first shipment of the new shells, he'd been loaded up with them as well before sailing out of Britannia and, as far as he was aware, the legions had not actually deployed them in combat yet.

Although their inventor, Hortensius, had been kind enough to give Leodgar a demonstration before he sailed, the German still wasn't sold on having stack after stack of powder-filled metal tubes with charges just waiting to go off on his ship. He also wasn't convinced that these things would really do what he was told they would when used in combat and not on a predetermined range.

But they said use them, so he'd use them.

Finally sorting themselves out, the enemy infantry began moving forward. Leodgar watched and waited, listening to the water hitting the metal hull, estimating when they would enter the correct range to begin firing.

And then they crossed the imaginary line, where they were far enough to allow multiple salvos if they decided to come forward, but close enough that they would have to endure several before they could make it out of range.

"Open fire!"

The men had been standing by, constantly watching the range and making adjustments, cannons loaded and fuses at the ready. The order was barely out of his mouth when the first cannon roared. The *Isarna* shuddered as her guns spoke, belching flame and smoke. Leodgar tracked the first shell's arc through his spyglass.

The shell struck dead center in the Easterners' formation. Nothing happened for the briefest of moments, enough for him to think about nothing happening and to wonder what went wrong. Before he completed the thought, however, a follow-on series of tremendous booms sounded, as the place where the shell landed burst into a ball of fire, sending men ... and parts of men, flying in all directions.

And then the next shell went off, and then the next. He had five cannons on each side, and all five on that side fired shells that impacted along the enemy line, only to explode moments later. The orderly Eastern lines dissolved into chaos as men were flung about like rag dolls.

And then his men finished reloading the cannons and fired again, more shells slamming into the tightly massed men. Even away from the explosions, men fell as the shards of metal from the shells became bullets, ripping across the open ground and into unarmored men.

"By the gods," muttered Leodgar, lowering his spyglass.

He'd seen the demonstration, but this ... this was something else entirely. He'd seen rifles fired and marveled at their destructive ability, which had been unheard of ten years ago. This was another whole level of death and destruction.

Leodgar was again surprised by the enemy. Instead of running for the hills, the men who survived closed up their ranks, forming up again over the bodies of their fallen comrades and marching forward.

It was impressive, or it would have been if not for the few who tried to run. Crazed men who threw their weapons on the ground and made for the rear only to be cut down by what Leodgar guessed were officers placed there for just that sort of moment. A brutal system that certainly made for men brave in the face of combat, but would ultimately backfire on them.

"Keep firing!" Leodgar ordered. "Don't let up!"

The gun crews needed no encouragement. Sending more shells toward the enemy lines before his command was even finished.

The enemy must have gotten as close as they needed, because horses carrying the two much smaller cannons came charging up and turned around, they were unhooked quickly, leaving the guns in place to begin firing as the horses were pulled back, out of the danger area. It was a fast movement, and very well timed.

And futile, although the enemy didn't know that. His ship might not be invulnerable, but the enemy cannons were very small caliber pieces, smaller than any of those carried by their own legions and would throw a comparatively small shot. Seeing how quickly they could move and deploy, he could see the value of the cannon, able to keep up with mounted infantry, but he felt relatively safe in his metal box.

He wasn't convinced his ship was invulnerable, and if hit by rounds shot by ship-sized weapons, he worried the metal would not be enough to prevent penetration, but he wasn't facing that here. He, in turn, not having to carry his guns, had large shipboard cannons, allowing him to fire the largest primed shells available.

It was not an even match-up.

A puff of smoke erupted from one of the enemy guns. Moments later, there was a loud clang as the round connected. From this side, he couldn't even see where the round hit.

The infantry must have also finally gotten to range, because they stopped and let loose a volley, creating more pings, although none were enough to really reverberate like the cannon shot did. They, however, had a little more luck. A gunner screamed from below where a shot must have found a lucky opening, allowing a bullet to get through and into one of his men. Leodgar hoped the man was not too badly hit, but he had to trust his subordinates to deal with it. For now, his attention was focused on the cannons, which fired another salvo, again banging off the hull.

"Silence those two guns," he called out.

If the rifles could get a lucky shot, so could the cannon. They may not be able to get through the hull, but they could break something, like one of the smokestacks, which would require the boat to stop and make repairs before continuing its patrol.

His men's training did them well, although it was a lot easier to hit a target with an exploding shell than solid shot, since for these shells close was good enough. After four rounds, they got close enough to the first gun, landing a few steps away, the blast pushing the small cannon on its side and shredding the men working it.

The other cannon fared even worse when a shell hit almost directly on it, setting off the cannon's small supply of powder, making a much larger display as the barrel was flung high into the air, sailing end over end, until it crash-landed right behind the enemy infantry. Close enough to spook several of them, but not close enough to do Leodgar's job for him.

The enemy paused, clearly rethinking things. They looked on the verge of breaking, and Leodgar was about to put them out of their misery, when their cavalry decided they'd seen enough. They were not foolish enough to tackle the ugly thing in the water and were going to try to make a run for it across the ford.

Leodgar knew from having just sailed over it that it had a deep section in the middle that would probably be easily fordable in the summer but would have them up to their necks now.

It had been a tight fit for him, so much so that he heard the protective casing of the propeller scraping against the ground as he'd passed through and knew that, following this engagement, he would have to have the mechanics he brought with him look at it for possible damage.

On horseback, however, they might just make it across.

"Rotate portside! Bring the other broadside to bear and load canister," he ordered.

It seemed unlikely the cavalry knew he could move around so quickly; otherwise, they may not have tried to make the attempt. What they saw was that there was almost no wind, he had no sail, and the ford was far enough that he would not be able to get his guns to that angle from his current position.

They were in a full gallop when the ship began to swing into its spot, pivoting and bringing the full broadside to bear. They were committed, hoping they could get across before his guns opened up.

Their hopes, however, did not come true.

The riverboat's guns roared to life once more, but this time instead of explosive shells, they vomited forth a hail of lead balls and scrap metal. The effect on the tightly packed cavalry was catastrophic.

Horses screamed in terror and agony as the canisters tore through their ranks. Riders were thrown from their mounts, some bisected by the brutal fire. Those who weren't killed outright thrashed in the bloodied waters of the ford, drowning in the water, unable to stand or crushed by the panicking beasts.

The cavalry's charge faltered, and then fell apart completely as a boom of musketry exploded from the tree line. The Britannian infantry who met them at the mouth of the river and floated down the river holding onto the outside of the boat had been dropped off just before they crossed into this stretch of river, hurrying into place while the Isarna opened the engagement.

Leodgar hadn't been sure they would get into place in time, but he was happy to see they had. Even with his salvo, there had still been a chance that some might make it across and into the Britannian rear.

That one volley had ended that chance permanently.

And then a second volley blasted out, hammering into the horses and men. The few dozen survivors still on their horses had had enough. They turned and fled, abandoning their fallen comrades and the infantry still in the field to the mercy of the river and the Britannians. They galloped back towards the distant hills, giving up the fight for good.

Leodgar turned his attention back to the infantry, which had begun to move forward again. To do what, he did not know. They'd seen how quickly his boat could swing around. Did they think he could not reverse course just as quickly? They were almost to the riverbank and were forming a firing line.

They only got a single volley off before his ship traversed again. "Canister!"

His men were good. They had already anticipated him, the first cannon firing almost as soon as he ordered it. It took only one broadside to break them. They had already been decimated by the explosive shells. The canister finished them.

The orderly ranks dissolved into chaos as men began to flee in all directions.

The few officers in their rear ranks, who tried to reestablish control, were literally ripped to pieces by their own men. Some made desperate attempts to reach their horses, left behind when they'd dismounted to form their firing lines. Others simply ran for the hills, throwing aside weapons and equipment in their haste to escape.

"Cease fire," Leodgar ordered, seeing no need to expend more ammunition on a routed enemy.

The death toll was staggering. Nearly two-thirds of the enemy force lay dead or wounded, their bodies scattered across the field and floating in the river.

To say the enemy's flanking attempt was over would be an understatement.

Eastern Germania

Ky, Bomilcar, and a horde of messengers and aides stood in a low concrete bunker far back from the front trenches. Bomilcar strained to see through a looking glass while Ky half-watched directly, his eyes bringing into view the hordes of men well across the open field between his trenches and the far hills, and half through the drone floating above them.

Row after row of the enemy stretched across the open field, accompanied by a fair number of horsemen and dozens of batteries of cannon. It was a formidable force, well outnumbering his own, well-armed and ready army. As he watched, the wall of men began to move forward like some giant carpet being unrolled, steady and straight.

"They're very confident," Ky noted.

"Overconfident. We've beaten them in every stand-up fight, and they must see our defensive works. They can't be so foolish as to think they can just roll right over us."

"I think they think they can do exactly that. Besides, numbers often play out. They're not the Carthaginians, but clearly they think their size can carry them past obstacles. And it might. This is a good design, but until we get our weapons more advanced and increase the rate of fire, it is not the slaughterhouse it will become."

Bomilcar gave him a look, clearly wondering what the hell Ky was talking about, but Ky didn't explain. He'd seen images provided to him by Sophus of the devastation of trench warfare in the early nineteen hundreds, and he hoped to avoid it, but the accuracy and rate of fire for the rifled muskets were too much for tight-packed firing lines to be a workable solution, but their rate of fire and how cumbersome they were precluded some of the more mobile techniques that followed on from them.

So trench warfare it was, even though Ky knew that if this proved to be successful, the enemy would copy the strategy and the war would bog down into static lines coupled with costly attempts to break through them.

"They're in range," Ky said as the enemy appeared on a pre-set line in his drone feed. "Explosive only for the time being. The first ranging."

They had predetermined eight ranges, going so far as to test shots and mark off elevation to ensure the rounds landed exactly where they needed them to.

The artillery emplacements were not far behind the command bunker, and moments later came the distinctive thud of artillery pieces coming to life. It seemed as if the entire Britannian line followed the trajectory of the shells sailing over the trenches and plunging toward the rows of men marching toward them, falling in the distinctive arch that marked the howitzer as something different than the traditional line-of-sight cannon.

The first impact was breathtaking as almost a dozen rounds landed at the same time, resulting in a rippling wave of tremendous explosions, tearing into the enemy's forward ranks. Men were thrown into the air and buried under the mounds of earth ejected from the blasts as blackened craters appeared. For a moment, the advance seemed to waver.

But only for a moment.

Ky cursed under his breath as the enemy reformed, almost instantly marching forward again as if they hadn't just lost dozens, maybe hundreds, of men. The next volley hit with the same force, and the effect was the same. The enemy soldiers kept moving, absorbing the losses, seemingly without question.

The artillery had created gaps in their formations, but those gaps were swiftly closed, new bodies filling the spaces left by the dead.

"They're pushing through," Bomilcar said.

"I can see that. We didn't think this was going to break them."

"I'd hoped it would slow them a bit. They have to know they can't sustain those losses forever."

"They don't need to. They're hoping to close the distance, get close enough where we can't fire into them without risking our own troops. Once they reach our trenches, they'll rely on their numbers to overwhelm us in close combat."

"Their artillery is moving up, shouldn't we ..." Bomilcar said, watching the enemy, only to have his concern manifest before he could finish the sentence.

A line of smoke erupted across from them as the enemy artillery fired, sending a wave of solid shot toward the Britannian line. The effect was impressive, with spots of dirt and debris shooting into the air with each hit, but the actual damage was minimal. The rounds that got close to the trenches skipped off and landed in the rear. One got close enough to embed itself in the rear of a trench, showering men with dirt and splinters, but otherwise leaving them unscathed.

It was possible they would kill some of his men that way, but only with a lucky shot and even then, it would only be a few. Ky was more focused on what his men were doing. The individual officers had been instructed on when to let their men fire and that they were to fire as quickly as they could manage aimed shots. What this meant in practice was that the first round would be a volley, and then the shots would become more and more scattered as they continued to fire, with some reloading faster, some aiming slower and taking longer to fire. This was a target range, not a set-piece battle.

The trenches were set up with interspaced firing ledges where a man would step up, fire, step back, and reload while the next man stepped up and fired. They had enough men to do this four times, which was theoretically long enough for the first man to have finished reloading and to be ready to go again, the ledges were spaced out much further apart than the traditional firing line, essentially giving them one man for every three men the enemy had in a given length. And the enemy had two rows behind that. Ky had wanted to put the ledges closer to allow for higher volumes of fire, but the numbers just didn't work out. There weren't enough legionaries to man the whole length of the line in as tight of a grouping as he would have liked.

Which meant that when the enemy stopped and lifted their muskets, a volley much heavier than anything the Britannians could produce would be let loose. Even with the artillery, there were still a staggering number of men in the field, and the weight of fire was some of the most impressive Ky had ever seen in practice.

It was also completely wasted.

Although a few men were hit, the legionaries had been ready and, for the most part, ducked down as the enemy unloaded their weapons, sending their fire harmlessly ahead or crashing into the wall behind the legionaries. It was completely ineffectual.

Then his men opened fire.

It wasn't as heavy as the enemy's fire, but the enemy soldiers had nowhere to hide. Whereas only one percent of their bullets hit anyone, probably forty percent of his found their target. Men fell in droves, sliced off the land as a farmer scythes wheat.

And then, the next group took their spot on the ledge and fired. And then the next.

It wasn't as thick as the volleys they'd delivered in the last engagements, but it was unanswered by the other side, and they knew it. This, if anything, caused more unease in the enemy ranks than the shells, that were still landing amongst them, did.

Their officers must have seen it too, because after only two volleys, trumpets blared and their ranks started forward at double time, charging toward the trenches.

Had they been able to make a straight run for it, the enemy would have still easily overrun his legionaries in the trenches. The numbers were that far in the enemy's favor, since they had been able to concentrate their force while Ky had to spread his forces out.

They had gotten within a dozen steps of the first line of trench when they ran into Ky's first obstacle. He didn't really know what they thought it was, but they were certainly not ready for their first introduction to barbed wire. Men screamed as the barbs pierced their skin and cut into them. They found their clothes and weapons tangled in the mass of coiled, thin metal pulling at them, the wire wrapping around them.

Attempts to dislodge it or to push the wire out of the way ended in bloodied hands now unable to hold a rifle. While this was happening the men behind them, who were still being shot at and some even hit with shrapnel from the artillery, continued to push them, trying to get out of the line of fire and sending their friends in the front into the twisted metal.

It became a mess of wire and bodies, the entire advance faltering to a halt.

The few that managed to get lucky by scraping and fighting their way through the wire found the third element of Ky's defense, as their feet pushed down on what might have felt like a soft piece of dirt, until they were thrown back as the ground itself exploded.

They had no way of knowing that just beneath the ground, put in a shallow dugout divot, was a wooden box filled with shrapnel and gunpowder and a flimsy thin top with a pin in it. When enough weight was applied, the pin would puncture into a percussion cap, setting off the simple mine. Legs were blown off and men shredded by the small metal bits crammed on top of the gunpowder.

That was enough. Between wire, mine, and rifle, they'd had enough and began to retreat.

Still, it was more orderly than Ky would have wanted. They were beaten, but not broken or routed, and Ky needed them broken.

"Hold fire until we see what they're going to do," Ky ordered.

His cannon could still reach their artillery, but they had pulled their guns back as well, so that now they were at perhaps longish range. The arc of his guns, with a parabolic arc, gave his weapons actually shorter range than their direct-line fire. That would change when he upped the caliber of his weapons and got a better quality gunpowder to fire it, but with black powder, there were limits to what he could do.

He also didn't have unlimited ammo to throw at the enemy. Hortensius had worked wonders to produce an impressive number of the fused shells, but they'd had only a month and a half of production time, and even a miracle worker couldn't make enough.

"Do you think they are considering pulling back and attacking elsewhere?" Bomilcar asked.

"Maybe, but I don't think so. I think they'll try to push through one more time. They took heavy losses, but they still have an overwhelming number of men. I think they'll try and compress their front and force their way through."

"That would be a death sentence."

"Maybe," Ky said again, but he wasn't sure.

If they were going to retreat, it seemed most likely that they would move soon. The longer they stayed, the more the odds were in favor of another attempt.

He was surprised when, instead, the artillery opened fire again.

"What are they doing? They can't seriously think their artillery's going to do any better than the last time."

Ky didn't answer right away, because something was different this time. A lot of the rounds buried themselves in the field well in front of the Britannian trenches, a few impacted the back of the trench, but the majority hit just in front of the trench, among and near the barbed wire.

The more cannon that opened up, the more that impacted the same perhaps two-hundred-meter stretch of trench. The ground erupted as shots ripped through the barbed wire defenses, sending sharp, twisted coils into the air. Worse, a chain reaction began as several of the mines detonated, triggered by the artillery strikes landing near them. Those mines set off other mines in a cascade.

"They aren't trying to hit our men at all," Ky said. "They're clearing a path for another assault."

"Really?" Bomilcar said, staring hard at the area being impacted, which was covered by so much debris and smoke that it was difficult to see what was happening without Ky's advanced skills.

"Yes. And I think it's going to work," Ky said before turning to a messenger. "Signal the reserves. Four centuries forward now. They're to hold in the communication trench."

The messenger sprinted off without a word, leaving Ky and Bomilcar to continue watching the battlefield. The methodical destruction of the barbed wire was relentless. Every few seconds, another mine detonated, taking out another stretch of wire and softening the ground for the next assault.

Ky unsheathed his sword as he headed to the door, only to stop as Bomilcar grabbed his arm.

"We can't afford to lose you, Ky. If you go out there, you're putting the entire command at risk."

"This is the moment, Bomilcar. The battle rests on this. If they break through now, we'll be overrun. We hold them here, or it's over."

The two men looked at each other. Ky could feel his lictore watching him, but he'd made it clear to them that in battle he was a commander, and they could not keep him from danger.

With a nod, Bomilcar released him.

"Direct the artillery," Ky said. "We need to lay down fire right behind this next wave, break up their reinforcements before they reach the trench."

Bomilcar nodded and gave a quick salute that Ky returned, before turning and leaving the bunker for the communication trench.

Ky reached the communication trench as the reserve centurions came running up. The pounding along the front line was loud, forcing Ky to scream as he gathered their officers.

"We hold here for the moment. Stack rifles and pull swords. This will be close-in work," Ky said.

When the enemy made their move, the trenches were going to be packed. Rifles made good melee weapons in a pinch, but with that many people, getting room to swing them when they were shoulder-to-shoulder would be tough.

The gladius, though, was perfect for the situation.

The officers went to get the word passed and the rifles stacked while Ky watched the enemy from the drone feed as they started forward again. The artillery kept up its barrage, even after the wire was all but ripped to shreds, because it kept the men in that section off their ledges, heads down to avoid the waves of death pounding just in front of their lines. His men to either side were still able to fire shots into the infantry, who were moving at double time, but not enough to hurt them seriously.

By the time the enemy artillery was silenced, their infantry was only a few short meters from the trenches. Close enough that when the men in the trenches uncovered themselves and climbed up on their firing ledges, they were met by legs and bayonets, pushing them back as the enemy swarmed into the trench line. As predicted, the amount of people in this section made it all but impossible to swing a rifle. Some men dropped theirs entirely, choosing to grapple, kick, and punch as the fighting became chaotic and brutal.

Ky was watching what was happening behind the advancing line, before he committed his reserves to the field where more enemy were coming up. Bomilcar had done his duty as a hail of death fell upon them. Not just explosive rounds tearing gouges out of the earth and ripping men to pieces, but the timed fuse air-burst rounds, which were even more effective against tight-packed groups, the shrapnel coming down like rain, killing all it touched.

The second wave, who were coming in packed together, aiming for the cleared section of trench line, were a perfect target. The plan might have been good, allowing them to break into the trench, but they wouldn't do it a second time, not having exposed themselves so badly to artillery fire.

"Let's move!" Ky shouted, taking off at an impressive speed, letting the men follow behind him as best they could.

He could hear his lictores shouting, wanting him to slow down, so they could stay with him, but he could see his men fighting and dying, and he wasn't going to let them do it alone.

Ky turned the corner into the main trench line and accelerated, bounding and dodging past men waiting for their turn on the firing line or heading toward the fight in the trenches, as they surged down into the melee.

Ky cleared the top of the trench as he leaped high in the air, coming down in the middle of the fight. The men around him looked shocked at his sudden appearance.

The quarters were tight. Ky couldn't make bigger slashing moves and kept his gladius close to his body, stabbing out with short thrusts. Most of his men were using similar moves, but they were limited in the damage they could do, as it was hard to get enough leverage into the sword with so little room to work.

Ky did not have that problem. His sword punched straight through the astonished man who'd been staring at him, mouth agape, at his sudden appearance.

Ky knew he was in a dangerous position. With men this close in, he wasn't going to be able to block well. The only solution to that was to kill fast enough to clear his own space.

Ky's superior abilities transformed the confined area around him into a charnel house. His gladius moved with precision, each thrust finding a new target and ending another life. Men crumpled before him, most probably not even knowing where the blow that killed them came from before their life was gone.

Ky did not fight with only his sword. He reached out to any enemy that was close enough, striking out hard enough to fracture skulls or crush windpipes, sending them down gurgling, scratching at their throats, trying to get air in their lungs. A few, he even lifted and tossed out of the trench with one arm, sending the men hurtling over the lip of the trench, landing in broken barbed wire, to be trampled underfoot.

Within moments, Ky had carved out a small clearing around himself. The narrow confines of the trench were now strewn with broken bodies. Blood made the ground treacherous, although this was the kind of place Ky was literally bred for, his genes altered to allow him to do what evolution had not.

Behind him, he could hear the shouts of his reserves as they poured into the trench, tearing into the outer wall of fighting, killing their way to him. The advantage in numbers had suddenly shifted, and the enemy knew it. It took only a few minutes for the tide to turn. The initial surge of enemy soldiers had been blunted, and now the weight of the Britannian reinforcements was beginning to tell. They weren't giving up easily, though. They fought and battled with everything they had, but the Britannians had the momentum now.

"They're breaking!" Ky shouted, seeing the first men begin to pull themselves out of the trench and run for their lives. "Push them out!"

What was one or two became a flood as they began to scramble back up the trench wall and run away. Their reinforcements, men who'd just made it through the wall of death created by the artillery, saw their nearly deranged comrades coming towards them, many covered in blood, looking like they had traveled to the depths of the underworld.

Which, in a way, they had.

The enemy reinforcements only needed a push to send them running with their broken comrades.

"Rifles!" Ky bellowed. "Cut them down!"

All along the trench line, Britannian soldiers snatched up their discarded rifles and stepped up to the firing ledges, now backed by their reinforcements. While runners were sent to retrieve stacked rifles, the extra men made themselves busy reloading weapons and doing what they could to increase the volume of fire into the new wave coming toward them.

The enemy fell by the dozens, still being hammered by artillery and now hit by a steady and increasing wave of bullets. They had had enough! Their lines collapsed as they trampled the officers who'd been pushing them forward from the rear, running past their artillery and on into the hills.

Their lines were broken.

Now, all that remained was to clean up the dead.

Chapter 27

Temporary Legion Hospital, Eastern Germania

"And make sure those supplies reach the forward aid stations by tomorrow," Ky heard Lucilla say, her voice reaching him as he prepared to push his way through the tent flap. "I will not accept any delays."

Ky smiled to himself. Although he spoke to her every day, it was different to hear her voice in person and not over the comms. Ky held up a hand, halting his lictore and directing them to wait outside the tent before entering into the darkened interior.

He was not interested in having this reunion in front of spectators.

"Yes, Empress. I'll see to it personally," the man inside said.

Lucilla gave him one of her curt, approving nods and was about to say something else when her eyes fell on Ky, and her brain seemed to short-circuit for a moment.

"Thank you," she said as she seemed to shake herself awake. "You ... you may go."

The man gave Ky a startled look, apparently not realizing he had come into the tent until he turned around, realized who he was, and gave a sort of half-bow, before hurrying out. Ky hadn't meant to startle the man, but he'd wanted to keep from interrupting and knew he could, at times, be very quiet when he moved.

"What are you doing here?" she asked as soon as the man was gone. "Why didn't you tell me you were coming?"

"I wanted it to be a surprise," Ky said, smiling at her.

She crossed the tent in three quick strides and threw her arms around him, burying her face in his chest.

"Well, you certainly succeeded!"

Ky tilted her face up to look at him and bent down, kissing her deeply.

"How long can you stay?" she asked, a little out of breath when he finally pulled away.

"Not long. The front is still in turmoil. How is Titus?"

"He's doing well. I received a telegraph from his tutors just when I arrived here. He's happy and healthy. You know that already because I told you over the comms just three hours ago, at which point you failed to tell me you were on your way here."

"I know, but it's not the same thing as hearing it in person."

Lucilla smiled at him again. While he was enjoying holding her, he couldn't help but think of how he missed their child, and how he knew it would be a long time till he got to see him again. Longer now that the war had entered a new phase.

Lucilla must have seen the look on Ky's face because she asked, "How are things at the front?"

"We're at a stalemate. The enemy brought up the rest of their men and have started digging. I think they've realized they can't push over us, and with their loss on the Wistla we have a solid line all the way to the Carpathians."

"That sounds positive. You stopped their advance into Germania."

"Yes, but in a way that leads to worse outcomes. This is exactly what I was trying to avoid. We're now locked into these positions, and it will take a lot of blood for anything to move. Gone are the days of outmaneuvering the enemy and achieving crushing victories. Now the battles will be like a meat grinder."

Ky had described trench warfare to her, and why he wanted to avoid it, but he knew that, short of experiencing it herself, she could not understand. The lesson the world learned from this was not one her people had learned yet. It was just another tactic and not something to be feared.

"Isn't there some technology that can change this? Break us out of this stalemate?"

"Maybe, but it will take time. Until then, we are in for a long and terrible war."

To Be Continued …

About the author

Travis writes science fiction, fantasy, and thriller novels (and the occasional coming-of-age story), with the hope of transporting and enthralling readers. Publishing novels since 2015, Travis's passion is creating worlds and characters that live and breathe, and experiencing the joy of those stories with his readers.

When not writing, Travis enjoys connecting with readers and other writers, managing the popular Complete Marvel Reading Order website, where he works on his other passion for comics and graphic novels, and spending time with his family.

If you have enjoyed this book, please consider taking a moment to rate or review it wherever you found your copy, as it helps new readers find my works and ensures I can continue writing book into the future.

Find out more at:
amazon.com/TravisStarnes/e/B072YBDC3S/
Or visit
https://tstarnes.com

Signup to get free previews and notifications of upcoming books at
http://tstarnes.com/preview-notification-newsletter/

Also by

John Taylor Stories

Rebirth
False Signs
The Wrong Girl
Burying the Past
Family Ties
Election Day
Danger Close
Extraction
Designated Target
Border Crossed
Desperate Rendition

Country Roads Series

Playing by Ear
Fanfare
Dissonance
Elegy
From the Top
Center Stage

Imperium Series

Volume 1
The Sword of Jupiter
The Trumpets of Mars
The Sands of Saturn
The Depths of Neptune
The Fires of Vulcan
The Triumph of Venus
Volume 2
The Wings of Mercury
The Plains of Pluto

Shattered Lands Series

In the Shadow of Lions
An Ending of Oaths

False Start Series

Second Down

The Veilguard Saga

Threads of Destiny

Stand Alone

Going Home

www.ingramcontent.com/pod-product-compliance
Lightning Source LLC
Chambersburg PA
CBHW072125250626

47159CB00007B/2569